In Velvet

Antlers are in velvet when blood is still flowing through them. That's before the horn growth is completed, usually June and July. During this time, the antlers are covered with what looks like brown fuzz. This fuzz is mostly dead cells called velvet. The velvet is like an outer skin. Underneath, the cell structure is still alive—blood flowing through a network of capillaries, a living nerve system, calcification, and so on.

Apparently, if the blood can be sealed in the velvet antler the aphrodisiac properties improve.

In Velvet

a novel

BURT WEISSBOURD

100
SKY
161
Bozeman Ranger District
Cut-Across Trail
95
99
Blue Grouse Creek
Culvert
X Trap
0.8
Elk Creek
191
TH
Park Boundary
Blackstone
Butte
1.8
GALLATIN
GALL
TH

STONEY RIDGE

RIM

TRAIL

Cave

WF2

Sentry Hot Spring

SKY

RIM

TRAIL

Set in Goudy Old Style
Printed in the United States
Distributed in the U.S. by Publishers Group West

10 9 8 7 6 5 4 3 2 1

Publisher's Cataloging-in-Publication data

Weissbourd, Burt.
  In Velvet / by Burt Weissbourd.
  p. cm.
  ISBN 978-1-940207-10-0

1. Yellowstone National Park–Fiction. 2. Wildlife management–Fiction. 3. Wildlife conservation–Yellowstone National Park–Fiction. 4. Bears–Yellowstone National Park. 5. Animal mutation–Fiction. 6. Mystery and detective stories. I. Title.

PS3623.E4593 I5 2014
813.6–dc23

For Barney, Ben, and Colin Weissbourd

Prologue
Summer 1994

THIS WAS BIG, EASY country, and Rachel moved quickly through a saddle, a shallow depression between two rises. She was watching for bear signs as she climbed toward her trap. At the top of the far rise, she looked back at the Gallatin River, a well-worn seam winding through the sunbathed greens of the valley below. From so high the river cut seemed soft, practically fur-lined. Ahead of her, Elk Creek curved gently through the long leg of an L-shaped meadow before twisting up, then disappearing into the Gallatin Mountains. Rachel stepped into the meadow, pleased to be alone and thinking again like a bear.

Half a mile further, Elk Creek turned east and the Cut-Across Trail veered west toward her trap. At the juncture, she placed her Telonics TR-5 receiver on an open slope. She carefully adjusted the setting to pick up the familiar frequency sent by the radio collar on grizzly bear #146, the bear she called Woolly Bugger. She'd named him thirteen years ago. The memory made her smile. She'd been unsure of what to call him, the first grizzly she'd studied in Yellowstone Park. Since then, he'd turned twenty-two and she'd celebrated her thirty-eighth birthday. The name stuck.

All those years she'd kept an eye on him, ready when Woolly Bugger needed a hand. Usually it was after he got the attention of park officials who then wanted to relocate him. Or worse. It always picked her up to find him. In her study area he'd become a touchstone. Rachel, honest to a fault, knew it was one of her better relationships.

She put the metal box on her left hip and held the antennae out in front of her. No signal. Rotating, she picked up a faint click. Odd. When she rotated further east, toward the Sentry Hot Spring, the pulse grew louder.

To the east, lodgepole pine spread up from the creek creating an island of timber. She went into the trees, climbing northeast, hoping to get above her bear.

Ten minutes later, she'd scrambled onto the near ridge. From the ridge top Rachel could see down over the trees and into the meadow that held the Sentry Hot Spring. In June, this little meadow was speckled with a dizzying mix of wildflowers. She set up her receiver, and the signal was stronger still. The bear was somewhere between her and the meadow below.

She took binoculars out of her pack and focused them on Dr. Moody's lab tent. Moody studied the microbial life, especially the thermophilic organisms, that lived in the hundred-sixty-degree-plus thermal pool. He often stayed at the spring when it was necessary for his research. Today, his tent and the little cabin in the trees behind it were empty. Glassing further east, just beyond his work tent, she saw the remains of a fire. It looked like a lightning strike had ignited a tree at the edge of the meadow. The grizzly's signal seemed to be coming from the forest, somewhere near the fire-blackened patch.

Seconds later, Woolly Bugger lumbered out of the trees. The animal skirted the timber, moving toward Moody's camp. Rachel's heart pounded wildly. It always did. At the edge of the fire-scarred area the bear stopped and turned back toward the forest. He was checking on something. It looked like some kind of mound. Was it a cache? Rachel took out her spotting scope. The mound was covered with pine needles, decaying vegetation, pinecones, branches of dead trees. Yes, it looked like the bear had buried an animal there. An elk or a deer. Maybe he was bedding in the near timber, and now he'd come out to his feeding site.

Something flashed just beyond the mound—sunlight, reflecting off a bright object. She couldn't see what it was.

She made her way northeast along the ridge until she was above the cache. Rachel came carefully down the hillside, stopping when she had a clear view. She set up her scope. She was downwind and far enough away. If the wind shifted, though, the bear would know she was there.

Rachel focused first on the bright object. *Glass?* It was a pair of glasses. Extra thick, gold-framed glasses. She redirected her scope. The bear was pawing at the far edge of the mound, pulling at something. A limb. *Was that a shoe?* And there was Dr. Moody. *Jesus. No...oh no.* Moody's stomach had been opened. His intestines, innards, buttocks, and thighs had been eaten. And now the bear was on Moody's carcass, feeding again. She watched the back of his massive head and neck. After, she had no idea how long, the grizzly stepped back. Through her scope she could see where Woolly Bugger had just torn off the underside of Ray Moody's left thigh. She bit down on her knuckle, her throat bilious. Rachel was making raspy breathing noises, and she could feel the sweat breaking at the small of her back, on her upper lip. She closed her eyes. The image of her bear on Moody's carcass burned like a heart-rending brand into her brain. Woolly Bugger moved away from Dr. Moody's corpse, apparently distracted.

Rachel took slow, deliberate breaths, watching the grizzly. He raised his head, then her bear—plainly the lord of this realm—meandered along the edge of the meadow and disappeared into the trees. She checked the signal on her receiver and it grew fainter. Still, Rachel knew the bear wouldn't stray too far from his cache.

She took another measured breath, then trained her scope on the corpse. *Go slowly,* she reminded herself. *Clear your head. Don't assume anything. Why would Woolly Bugger kill this man?* It didn't make sense. She reset the scope, focused on the arm. It looked like Dr. Moody might have been burned. Not long ago. *What else?* Something else was off. Rachel carefully examined the corpse again, looking this time for what wasn't there. Curiously, she didn't see the usual signs of a mauling or predation. The scalp was not missing. There was no raking of the face. She was looking at Dr. Moody's arm again when she sensed the grizzly. He was checking out his cache now, turning her way. It was time to go.

Rachel packed up quietly, then backed slowly over the ridge top. She made a wide loop west, away from the Sentry Hot Spring, until she crossed Elk Creek. On her way out, Rachel considered what she'd seen. Woolly Bugger was a savvy old bear. He avoided people. Just what had happened up there? She didn't know. Nor did she know yet how to find out.

In her study area, she was usually at ease and decisive. Today, she was in a pea-soup fog, anxious and confused. And she had a report to make. A report that would likely condemn Woolly Bugger to death. It made her heart ache.

Rachel decided on a starting point. Woolly Bugger had eaten Moody—yes—but maybe, just maybe, he hadn't killed him. She could work with that.

At the trailhead she saw it again, a waking dream: Woolly Bugger feeding lazily on Raymond Moody.

Rainey's Miracle
June 1995, One Year Later

I N SPITE OF WHAT happened, and what people said, Rainey secretly suspected that meeting Jen Donahue was a miracle, or close to it. He was up to his thighs in the Gallatin River fishing upstream and across, working his way toward a pair of fallen lodgepole pines.

The Gallatin here is a meandering meadow stream, not yet the rough and tumble river it becomes in the canyon below. Rainey was trying this section of the stream as a place to take his nine-year-old, big-city niece. He was working his way down with the imagined eye of a child—checking out those spots where the wading was easy, the country was welcoming, the play spaces were handy, and the fishing could be fast. It was a perfect day for it, one of those sparkling, sometimes windy, late-June days. The meadows, sprinkled with wildflowers, were still the startling, vivid green of early summer. From the river, a nine-year-old girl could, with her mind's eye, draw a distant, magical line where the meadow simply disappeared into the forested foothills of the Gallatin Mountains.

Rainey was edging around a submerged, washtub-sized boulder when he saw a rise form, a tiny dimple between two fallen limbs. He laid a yellow stimulator just above the expanding circle then watched that fish sip his fly. He lifted his rod just so, setting the hook. And with the hook set, the fish went straight for the open water under both dead pine trees.

Not two minutes later Rainey landed his fish, a strong fourteen-inch rainbow, easing it out from behind a tangle of deadfall. Releasing the fish became, for Rainey, a punctuation mark, a simple period ending an era. That little trout was the last thing he remembered before seeing an unlikely thing—the thing that started it all—floating downriver, right toward him.

Rainey had his fish in the water, reviving it, when the odd-looking suitcase came bobbing around the bend. He felt the fish swim from his hand, then rinsed wet, fishy fingers—all the while watching this curious case make the bend, riding the seam like a giant mutant mayfly. A floating suitcase was odd to begin with. What made this one stranger still was that this suitcase had a life vest, a fancy Stearns model, carefully tied around it. He grabbed a fistful of vest as the case floated by, then towed the buoyant bag to the bank.

With a frown that aged his weathered face, Rainey lifted the heavy case onto the bank. There was something inside. He'd felt it shift. He looked upstream then down, hoping to find the case's owner. No one. Someone wanted this case found, he reasoned. *Why dress it up in a life jacket? What was inside?* The case was big enough to hold a baby—or almost anything else. He'd better find out. Rainey knew it was his nature to ignore certain things—especially when they weren't on his agenda—then pay for it later. Rachel had made that point, unforgettably.

On the bank he tried to open the case. Unable to work the lock, he hauled the thing downstream to his pickup and drove it back to Lloyd's—Lloyd's Cabins and Café—where he was a regular.

The café sat on a bluff overlooking the river. The cabins, barely life-sized, Lincoln Log units, were strung along the river just twelve feet apart. A flickering blue neon sign—with "Lloyd's" written in script—hung just about perpendicular to the café's plate glass window. This window framed an ancient wooden counter with a faded fir-green Formica top. At the café counter, Rainey had learned to pick out the regulars: he'd look for the ones taking Tombstone frozen pizzas over Lloyd's chicken-fried steak.

Lloyd was chopping vegetables for dinner—tonight was Chinese night—when Rainey drove by the café. He took the suitcase into the far cabin where he always stayed. The cabin, a log shoebox, was dark and dank. It boasted a bed, a Coors lamp, and a fourteen-inch television. Fishing paraphernalia hung out of old dry bags and duffels on the floor. Rainey cleared a place on the unmade bed, untied the life vest, and inspected the case.

It was an old-fashioned liver-brown case, the kind that was hard around the edges. And it had a lot of mileage on it, even before it floated the Gallatin. The clasps were brass, and the lock was sturdy. He used a pair of needle-nose fishing pliers to pry open the clasps.

It was hard to tell what might be inside because the suitcase was so big that he didn't know whether it was the case or the contents that gave it weight. Rainey drew back the lid. At that very moment the door burst open. Rainey looked over, then he jumped maybe a foot in the air when the rattlesnake in the case bit him on the arm.

The first words out of Jen Donahue's mouth were, "What in hell is wrong with you, buster?"

Not long ago, Rainey would have taken the bait and taken her head off. The words were already there, on the tip of his tongue. Instead, he ignored her, carefully sidestepping to the corner, one eye on the rattler. It was raising its head up now, out of the suitcase. He stopped moving when she drew a .38 from a holster at the small of her back and blew the snake's head off. One shot.

Rainey checked his forearm. The snake had barely broken the skin—slowed down, he thought, by the rolled-back cuff of his canvas shirt. Relieved, he looked over at her, trying to remember where his first aid kit was. She was brooding over the headless snake—red hair cut short, full breasted yet lean like a runner. She wore blue jeans, a hot pink tank top, and a black satin Chicago Bulls jacket. Rainey pulled the first aid kit out of an old duffel. The lady was sassy, all right, and she could shoot. Take a beat, he decided. Size this thing up.

His lips turned up, just barely. "Snake's dead," he said, correcting her, like she'd been talking to the snake.

"I can see that, you grinning jughead. That dead snake cost me a hundred dollars. Didn't you hear me yelling at you?"

Grinning jughead?

"I was up at the highway, tracking my suitcase," she went on.

"How'd you manage that?"

"Binoculars, of course. When I got down to the river you were gone. Mister, you stole my case."

She was gaining momentum, like a runaway train. Maybe he could still slow her down. "Yelling from the road?" He shook his head. "No way I could hear you."

"You still got one hell of a nerve stealing my case."

"Once it's floating downriver, lady, it's flotsam, jetsam...whatever."

She didn't bother to answer.

He tried another tack. "You put a life vest on a suitcase, then you float it down a river—it's like sending a note in a bottle. A person can't ignore a thing like that."

"What are you missing, mister? You take my case, it's grand theft." And after a beat, "You're just lucky you have that ugly red pickup. Otherwise, I would've lost you completely and who knows what would've happened. The way it is, I guess I saved your life."

She was unstoppable, he decided, as he applied a cloth bandage to his left forearm. He almost asked her if she drove a tow truck, the way she talked to strangers.

Instead, Rainey took a closer look at this startling woman. There she was, standing tall in the foul, musty mess of Lloyd's cabin eight—a .38 Special smoking in her hand and a dead rattler at her feet—smiling that sassy smile. Her face revealed her mind working its way around some idea. Watching her, Rainey realized that he missed the company of bright, brassy city women. "Say you grab that rattler by the tail and I buy you a cup of coffee," he suggested.

———

JEN HAD NOTICED RAINEY at once. She was upstream by the highway, watching the river with high-powered binoculars, and there he was—a big, well-built guy with this little black ponytail—casting a fly like it mattered. He'd ease it down right behind a boulder, run it under an overhanging willow. Jesus, he even floated it between two logs. The guy had this rhythm going, this intensity. She realized he was a predator, a hunter stalking trout. When he hooked the fish, the big fella pretty much crossed the river and coaxed that fish right out between the logs. And that put him downstream of the case, which was floating just about right.

Well, how could she know that here in the middle of this particular stretch of river she'd run into a fisherman who couldn't mind his own business? The kind of guy who couldn't just let a thing go—probably called it in whenever he saw a sign on a bus that asked, "How am I driving?" She decided that this was one of those obvious things that you had to learn the hard way, like to break it off, tout de suite, when a guy said sex wasn't *special* anymore. Anyway, before this thought could go any further, this cowboy just walks her case to the bank—and now she's yelling her head off but he's too far from the road to hear her—and while she's working her way down, the guy takes off in an old red pickup.

A fast runner, Jen got back up to her rented Nissan less than five minutes behind him. Nearly skidding her car down the hillside, she made her way north, away from the park. She'd seen him take off in that direction, and the way she saw it now was that her luck just had to improve. Fair was fair. Jen spotted the red pickup near a cabin in this roadside overnight setup. It was not the kind of place they featured in *Sunset*, but the price was probably right—and she could imagine guys in checkered shirts with buttoned pockets, drinking coffee and talking about cows at the washed-out café counter. As she pulled her Nissan next to the pickup, she wondered if the big guy was married. How this idea got going, she wasn't sure. God knows the last thing on her mind was a new man. She knew Ellen, her on-again-off-again therapist, would have asked about the snake. No kidding. She imagined that her answer to that obligatory question would have made El frown to keep from laughing while the tops of her ears turned bright red like a boiled lobster.

Crashing through the door, Jen realized that she was maybe ten seconds too late. The cabin was fishy and dark, but she could see where the snake was out and the damage was done. She had no choice but to blow away her investment.

What she couldn't believe was that this guy just went about his business, like a rattlesnake bite was no big deal. He even made conversation. As the daughter of a Jewish mother (a feisty working girl turned rep in the meat packers' union) and an incorrigible Irish police detective, she decided that under the circumstances—particularly when your snake did the biting—offense was easier than defense.

So she came on strong—maybe a little over the top with *grinning jughead*—but that was okay. As a rule, she was at her best when she cranked it up a notch or two. It interested her that he didn't rise to her tone. He thought of it, though, a couple times. She could see that shadow cross his face. She had to admit, he made her feel kind of silly when he acted like she must be talking to the snake. It also pleased her that he didn't push the obvious question: *What, Sweet Jesus, was that snake doing in a suitcase floating down the river?* The fisherman assumed that she had her reasons—which she did—and didn't make a big thing about it. When he asked her for a cup of coffee, she picked up the rattler and followed him to Lloyd's Café.

———

RAINEY HELPED HER LAY the snake on the floor near the kitchen. The café was small: five tables, a concession area showing off canned goods, sundries, a local pork rind, beef and game jerkies, and the long washed-out green counter that butted into the kitchen wall. On the counter, where it met the kitchen wall, sat an ancient cash register. Lloyd Taylor, owner, cook, and café-counter raconteur, liked to tell how his daddy won it in a poker game. Or how his granddad *stole* it from the Wells Fargo Bank.

Behind the counter, there was a calendar photo of a little girl, her bare bottom and back squeezed between adult cowboy boots and an oversized cowboy hat. This was flanked by a rack of elk antlers and an ancient six-pound rainbow trout. Near the door, the old pie case was covered with prized pieces from Lloyds rock collection. The place was empty except for a bald, wiry local in the corner, drinking coffee and reading a gun magazine.

Lloyd, doing dishes in back, leaned out the little window where his wife Ruth gave her orders to the kitchen. "Two bucks credit for those rattles, ma'am."

Jen nodded. Lloyd touched the brim of his cap. A thank you.

"You snakebit?" He pointed at Rainey's forearm.

"Nothing much," Rainey said. "Shirt must've took the venom."

There was more to it than that. Still, Jen was relieved.

Lloyd wandered out of the kitchen. He didn't look to Jen like the cowboy on his faded Lloyd's Café cap—even taking into account his silver rodeo buckle, shiny shirt buttons, and the toothpick between his lips. Lloyd poured out two cups of coffee. "This Chicago Bulls gal shoot the head off that snake?"

"One shot," Rainey explained. "Cabin eight."

Lloyd pursed his lips. Jen stuck out her hand. Rainey took the hint. "Lloyd, this is...I'm sorry—"

"Jen...Jen Donahue."

"Hi there, Jen. Lloyd." They shook hands. Lloyd picked the snake up by the tail, turned to the kitchen.

Jen glanced at Rainey. "And you?"

He was inspecting one of Lloyd's carefully tied mayflies, picked from a plastic box on the counter. "Rainey."

"Just Rainey?"

Rainey looked her way. Before he could elaborate, Lloyd made an abrupt turn at the kitchen door, causing the snake to swing around behind him in a semicircle. When he had everyone's attention, he said, solemnly, "I tell ya what...it's worse than that." He dropped the snake, showed a leathery palm. "Truthfully, the man's proper name is a story and a half. Ma'am, I can only tell you what's known. But you say the word, I'll give you the true, known facts."

"Uh—" True known facts? This was going to be good. "Sure."

Hand raised high, stone-faced, Lloyd started right in, "Here's how she went. As a baby, little Rainey here was left crying in the dead of night on the stoop of Clem's Double Dice. Well, one of the regulars, ol' bug-eyed Tiny Quinn, hears this crying sound. Tiny, he staggers out the door, sees this little bundle an' yells, 'Clem, what's this?'" Lloyd lowered his voice, confiding, "Now Clem's a big Polish fella lost his farm in North Dakota. This man's about as smart as a tree trunk, and, well, he decides Tiny's whining about the water pours through the gutter when it rains. So Clem, he yells, 'It's raining, ya dumb shit...'" Lloyd let this hang. When he went on, he had a real twinkle in his eye. Jen was sure of it. "Tiny, he puts the bundle on the bar. Right about here, Clem turns on him. 'Whose damn baby is this?' Tiny, he pokes two fingers into Clem's chest. 'Don't lie to me. Not a gaggle'—and I swear to God, Tiny said gaggle. I was there. Anyway, Tiny roars, 'Not a gaggle a North Dakota Polish in the whole damn state...Name like Rainey Yadumbshit—this babe's related to you.'" Lloyd laughed out loud—a singular, satisfied cackle. Jen held her lips between her teeth, wanting to burst out laughing, not wanting to offend Rainey. But dear God. The guy made up cowboy Polish jokes. Really worked on them. Ripley, believe it or not. She watched Rainey gently place the mayfly back in its box.

Rainey turned to his friend. "I hear that lie again—ever—I'll tell how I found you superglued to the old blue toilet seat in cabin seven—" The wiry old man snickered. "The cabin seven crapper...huh." Lloyd ignored Rainey and the old man. He dragged the snake through the kitchen door. It occurred to Jen that Lloyd was, in fact, a cowboy: he was the unlikely cook driving the chuck wagon, the feisty one with wispy gray hair and whiskey breath that gave you a start the first time he smiled wide. The old-timer laid a dollar on the counter. At the door he pointed at Rainey, summoning him with a simple movement of his outstretched finger.

———

RAINEY FOLLOWED THE MAN outside. Jen came behind him. When they reached the parking lot, the old man was already at the back of an '86 brown Chevy pickup, pulling a fish wrapped in newspaper out of his dented green metal cooler. He unwrapped a fat brown trout. "Lookit this," he snapped. It could have been painted by a colorist: deep, rich yellows and browns, fiery red and jet black spots, bright orange at the dorsal fin. It had an unusually large kype, or hook, to its lower jaw.

"When did you catch it?" Rainey asked.

"Couple hours, give or take."

"That can't be. This brown's in full spawning colors."

"Sonny, I can see that. That's how come I asked Lloyd for the expert." He spit—an involuntary response, Jen thought, to the word expert. "So, can I eat it?"

"I don't know what to tell you. This trout is supposed to spawn in the fall." Rainey touched the trout's jaw. "And this kype is huge, even for a large male spawner." He poked at it, puzzled. "Where'd you catch it?"

"That's none a your damn business."

"Right."

"Some kinda freak?" the wiry man asked.

"Could be hormones," Rainey offered. "But I don't know."

The man set the fish back in the cooler. "Freak a nature," he muttered. "Well, fisherman, can we eat him?"

"Truthfully, I don't really know."

"Maybe Lloyd was right about your name." The man snorted. He turned as he opened the truck door. "Hell, I'll mount it and sell it to one a those catch-and-release fly fishermen." And then he was in the cab and off.

"What was that?" Jen asked.

"I'm not sure." Rainey turned toward her and the café. "Weird day. Unnatural brown trout. Snakes in suitcases floating the river. Sassy, redheaded city women..."

A change in his expression caught her eye—something about his glance, the tilt of his head—was he hitting on her? She saw Rainey's shoulders inch up, his brow rise.

"That was a funky trout," he mused.

Jesus, he was thinking about the fish. Jen held back a smile.

She followed him in and sat down at the counter beside him, thinking she liked Rainey. Jen watched him more carefully now. He was sturdy, about six foot three, two hundred thirty pounds, forty-one, maybe forty-two. Without his cap and ponytail, his black hair was a little too long, and it showed flecks of gray. Rainey had nice, sea-blue eyes under unruly black eyebrows. His lips were thin, his features etched, then worn by sun, wind, and rain. Like her dad, he'd been a boxer. She could see where his nose had been broken and the faint scars on his brow. Still, it was a good-looking face, open and responsive. When he'd frowned she'd seen how his face was crisscrossed with lines, and how it hardened.

She touched his scarred knuckle, a *knuckle pad*. "When did you fight?"

"College."

"Any good?"

"Had my moments," he said, then shrugged.

"My dad did a little boxing."

"I gave it up," was all he said.

She leaned in, wanting to start again. "Listen, you're probably wondering just what's going on here."

"I am."

As Jen watched, curiosity and concern gently rearranged all the hard-set lines on his face. Jen leaned in further still, aware now that he made her feel like talking. "As you probably noticed, when I'm agitated, I come on strong. And I forget my topic sentences...

15

but you can believe this—at my age, you don't get this far into a thing without an awfully good reason."

"I understand. I've reached that age myself."

She turned away, revolving slowly on her counter stool. Turning back, Jen smiled her little smile, then she took her first sip of Lloyd's coffee. She made a sour face, pushing her cup away. Then she was looking at him again. "Give me a minute."

Jen opened the door and stepped outside, where she chose her spot purposefully. At the riverbank she sat on a log, watching the river wind its way along the Gallatin Mountains.

———

RACHEL WAS IN THOSE mountains, three miles up the Elk Creek drainage, thinking about Woolly Bugger. Since discovering him on Dr. Moody's carcass almost a year ago—that unforgettable moment still came to her often, especially in dreams—she thought of him whenever she was in her old study area.

She came over the crest into the L-shaped meadow. It was alive with wildflowers, as if a fine, fanciful painter had touched this vast green canvas with every color that tweaked some painterly nerve.

Ahead of her, Elk Creek wound through the meadow, eventually disappearing into a stand of timber. At the distant tree line a movement caught her eye. She focused her binoculars on a small bear cub, about thirty pounds. It was a black bear, less than six months old, moving along the edge of the timber. *Odd,* she thought. Where the ears should be, the bear's head was covered with skin and fur. She'd never seen anything like that, never even heard of it, she was thinking, when the earless bear cub disappeared into the trees.

A deformed bear cub. It was like being in her own unsettling dream.

———

RAINEY WATCHED JEN RISE, then turn away from the steep cliff face that fronted the river. She came back into the café and sat at the counter, pensive, rubbing her thumb on the countertop. He went to the loud, old GE refrigerator, took out two Millers, and set one in front of her. She looked his way. Jen's eyes were pale green and lively. Then, just like that, they locked on—intense, almost intimate—and, Rainey realized, she had him. He cared how he measured up in those eyes. "Okay." She hesitated. "My ex-husband—we split up almost five years ago—he's after me for money...always calling and making up stories...and he's run off with our ten-year-old son." Jen stopped, letting it sink in. "Now that sounds worse than it is. I mean he's done this twice already, and both times, I worked it out. You see, I'm a cop." She raised her hand, nodding yes, it's true. "In Chicago, where we live, I'm on leave for I don't know how long. Until I work this out, at least. Anyway, Cockeye—that's my ex—he won't leave me alone." Jen looked away. "Excuse me, but lately whenever I start talking about Cockeye, I get scattered and upset. He's gotten pretty crazy. Like trips to Vegas to win a fortune and 'win me back.' Thank God he ran out of money." Jen smiled faintly at the small favor. "Two years ago a police shrink said he might be—what's that word?—bipolar. Yeah, put him on meds. That same year, Internal Affairs tied Cockeye to one of his brother's shady deals and made him resign. Anyway, now he's always got a scam or some weird deal going, and he's always wanting me back. So this time I want to back him off once and for all." She lowered her head, off somewhere.

Rainey waited, thinking she was an uncommon woman. It was the way she held your eyes and got close to you when she was talking, that brash, confident edge—she even dressed like she didn't give a fuck what she was supposed to wear. And she knew she looked good. Jen's fingertips on his forearm brought him back.

"To be specific, he wants me to put money in that suitcase, then float it down the river to a small bridge. He calls it a *drop*. Cockeye loves weird deals like that—don't ask me why. Anyway, after he counts the money, he'll leave my son. Now, the one thing he's afraid of is snakes. He's got like this nightmare phobia—I've seen him run from a garden snake, hives all over his face. Cockeye sees that rattler, he's gone, out of the picture." She edged closer. "So you know, I stopped off at this vet in Bozeman. He put that rattler in a snake jar, then showed me how to drip in a sedative. That snake wasn't supposed to wake up for another hour. And he promised me he cleaned out the poison."

"So—"

"Don't start," Jen interrupted. "You can't be sure I didn't save your life, and I don't want to talk about it anyway." Jen tapped the countertop. Rainey waited. "Look, I just want my boy back," she finally said, weary. "And I know what you're thinking. But Cockeye was a cop. If I send him to prison the way he is, he won't last a week."

"I didn't think of that," Rainey admitted, guessing a fair amount of reason, and reasonable plans gone sour, had preceded this plan. He glanced into the kitchen—where Lloyd was deftly chopping up little brook trout for his chop suey. A fair amount of pain, too, was surely part of it. "Is this in the planning stage? You've got...well, it's a bold idea. Still, there's quite a bit of room for the, uh, unexpected in a deal like this." As soon as he said it, her eyes got smaller, and Rainey knew he'd screwed up.

"What do you think I was doing when you fished my property out of the river? I was planning. But now I don't have a snake. Do I? And I don't have the money either."

Rainey knew he could make people mad. Sometimes, it was because he went too slowly. Other times, it was because he offered his opinion too quickly or came on too strong. When he was younger, he had a hair trigger, which made that even worse. Lately, he couldn't strike a good balance. He tried again. "Lloyd can get you another snake," Rainey offered. "And he'll juice it himself."

"Juice it?"

"Remove the venom sacks," Lloyd explained, looking out the opening from the kitchen to the café. "You bet. Now who's Cockeye?"

Jen shifted to face him. "Earl James Donahue. I married him the day I turned twenty-three. Back then he was the smartest, best-looking Irishman you ever saw." She turned back to Rainey, clearly feeling better. "He was a forensic investigator. A science nut. My dad always said the guy was off. And yes, Earl could be, I dunno, one of a kind." Her tone was fond, though, Rainey noticed. "Some of the things he wanted me to do." She laughed, then confided, "Lucky I was half Jewish. That's the only thing that saved me."

Rainey hesitated, squinting, then he raised his eyebrows, showed his palms. Who could argue with that?

The Hunt for Bear #146

THE DAY AFTER RACHEL found Dr. Moody's body, last June, they'd closed the area from Lava Butte to the northern boundary of the park. Mitchell Picker, an assistant superintendent, took the lead, and predictably, the small area in the northwest corner of the park was closed for bear management. That same day park officials helicoptered in to pick up Dr. Moody's remains. When they landed at the Sentry Hot Spring, all they found were bone fragments in scat piles, hair, some skeletal remains, and a piece of a toe. The autopsy was necessarily inconclusive. Nevertheless, the park officials decided to kill the bear.

Rachel fought for his life. She'd seen the charred body, and she knew this bear. She did not believe that Woolly Bugger had killed the scientist.

The day after the autopsy, Mitchell agreed to see her privately. Mitchell, she knew, liked bullet points—at least when others were talking. So she hit the important ones precisely, she thought. "The body showed none of the usual signs of a mauling or predation," Rachel explained at the end, laying the groundwork for her conclusion. "There were no puncture wounds in the back of the neck or the skull. There was no clawing along the rib cage or raking of the face."

"I see," Mitchell said, his way of interrupting. She watched him tap his wire-rimmed glasses impatiently on his desk. "The bear had him cached. You saw him feeding on the carcass."

"Yes, but remember, Moody was badly burned. You could see it on his arm." Mitchell was tapping again, but she pressed on. "What if he died in the lightning-strike spot fire near his campsite? Say the grizzly found the dead body, dragged it to a cache, then—okay—he fed on it for several days. That doesn't mean he killed him."

"Interesting, but unconvincing. And we have no evidence. Literally. A prominent scientist died. The public is demanding that we eliminate this bear. They're not going to believe that Dr. Moody was struck by lightning or caught in some lightning-strike spot fire. You know that." Mitchell put his glasses on. The meeting was over. "Rachel," he gently added. "Find the bear, then put this tragedy behind you."

The next day Rachel was sent to trap Woolly Bugger. By late July she'd failed to catch him, and teams of predator trappers from the U.S. Fish and Wildlife Service were sent in. These predator control agents were full-time troubleshooters. Real hard cases, Rachel thought. They set snares throughout Woolly Bugger's home range, even helicoptered in four culvert traps. In October they trapped a bear and killed him.

Rachel was flown in to confirm the identity of the dead grizzly. When she arrived, heartsick, several predator control agents were still hanging around, talking about their kill. The bear lay on the ground. She took a look at the dead animal, checked his toes. Rachel had to bite her lip to keep from crying. She was that relieved.

When she could, Rachel turned to the trappers. "You killed the wrong bear," she said, matter-of-fact, though her face was sad. "You hot shots killed an innocent bear."

"How can you know that?" the trapper team leader asked.

"This bear's coloring is not as dark, and he has less grizzling than the bear you're looking for. This bear has all his toes. The grizzly you're after lost a toe, long ago."

"A toe? That's it?" The agent wasn't convinced.

Rachel wanted to scream at him. Instead, she motioned him over. "I know the bear you shot. He's the sub-alpha in my bear Woolly Bugger's home range." She saw that he wasn't with her and realized she was mad. She rarely called her bear Woolly Bugger with these guys, or on any park business. She was past caring. "He's Woolly Bugger's shadow. He gets a piece of the action when Woolly Bugger's done."

"Anything you don't know?" He was smiling now at the woman they called the Bear Lady.

20

"Don't be a jerk. I want to show you something." She lifted the dead bear's cheek. "Check out the inside of his upper jowl. You'll find a lip tattoo. It's number seventy." He knelt beside the bear. "Woolly Bugger, as you know, is number one-forty-six." That wiped the smile off his face.

He stood, whistled to his men. "Wrong animal," he told them. He twirled a finger in the air. Time to roll.

Within the week, they were gone.

Throughout that summer and fall she'd been directed to help these trappers. And by the book, she had. Rachel pinpointed Woolly Bugger's general location several times. She even set her own traps. She did this, however, with the belief that they'd never catch him. If he was avoiding her traps, he'd avoid theirs. What she'd figured out, and never said, was that the last time she'd trapped him, after an incident with an outfitter the prior fall, he'd been mishandled by an inexperienced field crew. They'd used rubber bullets on him. Adverse conditioning, they called it. After reading their report, she suspected they inadvertently exposed his eyes to sunlight and used too much tranquillizer for a bear of his weight. Since then, he'd become one of those bears that avoided traps. Over time, he'd figured out that you just don't come into these areas where there are the smells and the patterns of trapping—humans with guns, vehicle fumes, anything metal. In other words, he had become untrappable. At least by the predator control agents. Even when they boiled their snares, or put them in burlap bags and buried them so they smelled earthy. They just didn't get that he was on to them. Thank God. When asked to explain it, she'd say: "Big old male bears avoid people. That's how they got to be big old bears."

After the predator control agents left, the situation changed. Without saying it, Mitchell communicated to her that maybe this thing would die down. "Keep me in the loop. I'd like to help," he said. All winter she kept track of Woolly Bugger. When she'd last trapped him, she'd put on a collar that sent out both a radio signal and a Global Positioning Satellite signal. She'd followed his movements on her laptop. Oddly, he'd stayed active through the winter. In February, she'd gotten confirmation, an active signal on an overflight. What bothered her was that as long as she'd known Woolly Bugger—at least for five of the six years he'd worn a collar—

this bear had slept in his den for more than five months every winter. What was wrong? In March, she'd filed a bear observation form describing his unseasonal behavior. Though the area had reopened on December 1st, the northwest corner was closed again April 1st, just weeks after she filed her report. Why? By May, Mitchell had informally suspended the search for Woolly Bugger. Still, the area was never reopened. When she pressed him for an explanation, Mitchell replied: "Don't draw attention to the closure. If you do, you'll only draw attention to this bear." He might as well have put an ice pick to her eardrum.

So she kept her mouth shut, and they let Woolly Bugger live a while longer. Still, when officially asked about the closure, Mitchell attributed it to the "dangerous, rogue bear." Now it was June again. Woolly Bugger had been active all winter. Not an hour ago she'd seen a deformed bear cub—likely, a mutation—in the same closed area. And now she was four miles up Elk Creek, and still no sign of her bear. Something was wrong. Until recently her efforts to find him had been halfhearted. Today, she was determined. She needed to see Woolly Bugger. She knew it in the way a salmon knows where it's born. And she was worried about—she wasn't sure what.

———

LLOYD KNEW THAT LATELY, it was not uncommon for Rainey to simply get up and walk away in the middle of a conversation. This curious behavior went back to his forty-first birthday, when Rainey announced that he'd made a resolution to walk away from any conversation that might provoke him. Lloyd believed that an unexpected side effect of this attempt at self-improvement was that Rainey found that he liked walking away from conversations. In fact, in the past year, Lloyd noticed that he'd started excusing himself from any conversation that didn't particularly interest him. These days, it was unusual for anyone to hold the guy's interest unless they were talking fishing.

That Rainey was still sitting at the counter listening to Jen was, to a seasoned observer like Lloyd, nothing short of amazing—the quiet fisherman had been at it for a damn hour and a half. When he got up, Lloyd assumed that he was leaving. When he got two more beers, Lloyd mumbled something about testosterone, and turned away, bored, until the fella looked like a movie tough guy walked in.

As soon as Lloyd saw the man's glass eye, he knew why Jen called him Cockeye. The eye was a dandy, a perfect match, but the true ink-black eye always seemed to be wandering because the glass eye stayed fixed. Tall, muscular, with carrot-colored hair, and a world-weary, leading-man's face, Cockeye did not seem the type of man who would respond well to denial, deception, or a rattlesnake bite.

"Honey, thank God I found you. I've got news." He tossed his cigarette in Rainey's water glass, and put his arm around Jen. She slid over to another stool.

"You stay away from me. I've got a court order, and you know it."

"C'mon honey, listen to me. I just want to talk."

"You get Jimmy and I'll talk to you."

"Honey, I can't get Jimmy. That's my point. He needs an expensive operation. I need five thousand dollars, right away."

"You're making things up," she said, plainly used to this. "Our deal was two thousand. Okay. I'll give you twenty-two-fifty for my boy—that's M-Y. I should call the judge."

"That's cold, babe."

She locked onto his good eye. "Take it or leave it."

"Deal." Cockeye pointed toward Rainey. "Who's the stud?"

Rainey walked toward the kitchen.

"Hey, doofus," Cockeye called.

Rainey turned, a rolling pin in his hand.

Jen stepped between the two men. "Outta here, Cockeye. I don't want trouble. I mean it." She took his elbow, stern-faced, and eased him toward the door. "You want your money, you be by that bridge at ten tomorrow morning. When I see that Jimmy's fine, I'll send the old brown suitcase floating down with the money in it. Just like you said." At the door, he hesitated. "You don't leave right now," she warned. "I'll pitch a fit and kick your ass myself."

Cockeye winked over his glass eye, then he was gone.

Lloyd liked that wink all right, but it didn't change anything. He could see how Rainey was getting sucked into a bad deal, again.

JEN STOOD AT THE door to the café, watching as Cockeye drove off in his black Cadillac. Rainey could see the sadness settling in and around her eyes, in the turn of her lips.

"Cockeye's all but forgotten his old self," she murmured.

"Sorry, how—"

And interrupting, "Truthfully, he...well he sort of stopped trying." Jen was making little circles on the doorframe with her forefinger. "The way I like to think of it—when I'm feeling kind that is—he just got lost." She hesitated. "It's like he's twisting and turning in his own sad country and western song."

"I'm not sure I follow."

Something about the six-pound trout on the wall had caught her attention. Rainey supposed it was the slight grin Lloyd had added with a magic marker. "Rainey, I tell you what. I'm not sure I follow either."

When Jen turned back, her pale green eyes were resolute—she'd made up her mind about something. She sat beside him at the counter. "I was wondering whether you might help me?"

The way she asked, like it was no big deal, had to be a policewoman thing. But it was a big deal. He knew it. She knew it. "Oh?"

"Look, I'll pay you. Like a private detective."

"I *was* a private detective." He shrugged. "It didn't work out."

"No, c'mon." And when he didn't respond, "What happened?"

"I had a bad time with the county sheriff." Rainey tensed. Just thinking about the sheriff still got him going. "My license was revoked last summer."

She waited. When Rainey didn't elaborate, she asked, "You do anything else?"

"I used to guide. Mostly fishing, some bird hunting." And seeing her look, "Even tried my own fly shop." Which hadn't worked out either, though he didn't say that.

"What do you do now?"

"Odds and ends for the park service. I still guide when I have to, sell some flies."

"You some kind of burnout?"

Zap. The hook set. "You could say that."

"From what?"

"I taught English literature at a community college."

"Huh," she said. "Not what I would of guessed, no." Jen paused. "Will you help me?"

"Let's talk about it. But not for money."

"Then why?"

He weighed that. "How often do you meet a beautiful woman who's put a snake in her suitcase and floated it down the Gallatin?" Rainey moved closer, liking that she didn't move away. "One time. One time, only...so you mustn't let a thing like that pass you by." He nodded, thinking about what had just happened.

"Well...thank you." She nodded back. "Where's the ladies?"

He pointed her to a door with a collection of old calendars on it.

Lloyd stuck his head out from the kitchen. "She doesn't look like a cop, does she?"

"Uh, Lloyd, what does a cop look like?"

"I swear to God, you must have been the worst fuckin' detective that ever lived." Lloyd disappeared, once more, into the kitchen.

Rainey pressed a napkin to a line cut, bleeding again, on his left forefinger. His hands were covered with the calluses, cuts, and abrasions that came with regular fishing. He wondered if women found his touch too coarse. Rainey sighed. Women were still a mystery to him. Lately he couldn't make relationships with women last—his recent love affairs had been intense and steamy, and quickly over. And the women were getting younger. His most recent—two months ago, for three weeks—said she was twenty-six. He worried she was maybe twenty-three.

Rachel—the last woman his age he'd loved, and listened to—said he went too slow. She knew he'd been in trouble, often, and she understood he was trying to be more careful. Still, Rachel believed Rainey had become overly cautious. He'd been living with her for fourteen months. It was early November—they were talking about his fortieth birthday, a month away—when, out of the blue, she said: "Rainey, you're thirty-nine, I'm thirty-six. If we want children, we have to have them now. There is no *good* time. I don't want to think about it. I don't want to give it time. I want to have babies."

Rainey thought about it a while. "Let's discuss this again," he suggested. "After I turn forty."

"I'm going up near Big Horn Peak," she said. "There's a bear I want to check on. When I come back—two, maybe three days—I expect you to be gone."

And that was that.

Now here was Jen, and watching Lloyd carefully slice a wild mushroom for his chop suey, Rainey wondered if he was on his way to another broken heart.

———

SHERIFF JESSE STINSON WAITED at the Elk Creek Trailhead. The area was closed for so-called bear management, so it was a safe place to meet and a good place for his man to hunt. In the back of his truck he had the mother of all racks. The poacher had sawed it off an elk he'd killed earlier that afternoon. He'd sawed off the cape and the skull with the horns still attached. The blood was still dripping from the velvet-covered antlers.

He was startled to see the black Caddy parked beside him. One minute he was alone, then there was Cockeye peering in the back of his pickup, poking at the bloody rack. How in the hell did Cockeye do that? The crazy sonofabitch must have glided in with his engine off, or something else just as fucked-up. Just to give him a jolt. The guy was one of a kind, a classic, he had to say.

Cockeye leaned in Jesse's open window. "Hunting season a year around deal for you, sheriff?" he asked.

"Arrest me, asshole," Jesse said as he handed him two stacks of one hundred dollar bills. Twenty-five bills, each. "One more thing," he added, handing Cockeye a picture of Rainey.

Cockeye looked at the photo. "Is there any asshole you don't know?" he asked, squinting at the photo.

"You know this guy?"

"This dickhead's hanging out with my wife."

"Perfect." Jesse smiled meanly. "His name's Rainey Jackson. I'd like to send him a message...there's this beekeeper owes me a favor. You want to earn another K?"

———

RACHEL HAD COME SIX miles up the Elk Creek drainage, and now she was off-trail, climbing an open slope. She stopped to point the antennae toward Stoney Ridge, and there it was, the distinctive ploik that meant she'd located her bear. She could feel goose bumps on her arms. With binoculars, Rachel scanned the side of the ridge in front of her. The ridge articulated the head of the drainage, forming the top of an inverted U. In the valley below, meadows spread in and around large patches of spruce and fir. Where the streambed came out of the snowfield, a bear could eat the cow parsnip, the green sedge and the succulent grasses. As the meadows stretched up the slope, they gave way to rock, loose rock, or scree, and patches of snow. Fingers of subalpine fir reached up, somehow finding purchase in the steep slope. Higher still, there were isolated clumps of whitebark pine. Above and between the stringers of fir, she could see where the snow had avalanched, carving out chutes in the steep hillside. Even in June, there were still large patches of snow.

The tracks were in a snow patch at the upper end of an avalanche chute. The chute descended from a clump of whitebark pine. At the edge of the whitebark pine there was a mound of dirt, as if a bear had been digging. The signal was still steady. This had to be him. But what was he doing up here in June? He should be down near the Taylor's Fork preying on the elk calves. It made her worry, again, that he'd been active all winter. Rachel took the spotting scope from her daypack. She set it up, then foraged through her pack until she found her thermos. Tense and hopeful, she settled in to wait on Woolly Bugger.

It had been a year.

He was a wily old bear. At twenty-three, he'd done just about everything. To live this long, he'd had to fight and lick every adult male grizzly in the region. And in the last year he'd gotten good at avoiding people, an adaptation, she believed, that had saved his life. After all these years, she still privately hoped he'd become tolerant of her scent, though now it seemed less likely.

With her spotting scope, Rachel tried to find the familiar identifying mark, a missing toe, on one of the tracks. He'd had a paw disfigured—in a mating battle, she supposed. She tried to picture the six-hundred-pound animal bringing his paw down with the force of a pile driver. He must have been a young bear then. She suspected he'd gotten the best of an older bear, but not before the more experienced animal grabbed the offending paw in his mouth.

Rachel was pouring a cup of coffee when she saw an animal step out of the fir stringer that wound up toward the avalanche chute. He seemed to be grazing his way up the chute. She could feel her body tighten. She'd once bugled in a bull elk, got it in to about eight steps. When the animal finally bolted, she was sure it was because he had heard her pounding heart. Her heart was going like that now. She focused the scope. "What?" she muttered. It was a black bear, not her grizzly. A mature adult male, maybe three hundred pounds.

The black bear climbed higher. He was in the chute, below the patch of snow, grazing. He wouldn't be so relaxed, she knew, if he thought a grizzly was nearby.

She went back to her scope and slowly tilted it above the black bear. Beside the clump of whitebark pine, like a king considering a poacher on crown lands, Woolly Bugger was staring down at the black. Because the wind was blowing up and over the black bear's back, the smaller animal had no way of knowing that the grizzly was near. Woolly, all six hundred pounds of him, was less than fifty yards above the smaller bear. Rachel could hear her heart again, pulsing now in her ears. She wondered how long he'd been watching.

She saw the grizzly's ears go back, and she imagined hearing the huffing sound, like a locomotive, that preceded a charge. Then her bear went tearing down the slope at thirty miles an hour, actually leaping into the air before blindsiding the black bear. Woolly struck the black's head with a right front paw as he landed on his back. The blow would have snapped a man's neck. The black rolled over the top of the grizzly, careening down the steep slope. The grizzly grabbed onto the scree, regaining his balance.

The black only stopped when he banged into a large fir, butt first. In a panic, he scurried up the tree.

The fir sat at the edge of a steep drop. Graceful as a gazelle, the grizzly bore down on the fir. Woolly crashed into the tree, snapping the trunk like a matchstick. The black fell—a great, fat acorn—and then bounced off the cliff face. He was limping when he ran, full-out, into the forest.

Woolly Bugger put his nose to the ground, an unlikely quarter-ton pointer, and made his way around the steep cliff, following the black's scent into the forest.

Rachel felt her legs shaking. She sat on the ground, worried that even now her heart might somehow overheat, like her car engine. A wave of relief broke inside her, washing away a host of unspoken worries. It was, she decided, about the best thing she'd ever seen. Rachel poured another cup of coffee from her reliable Stanley thermos. It was a gift from Rainey. She rarely thought about him anymore, she realized, and saw him hardly at all. She went back to studying the mound of dirt at the edge of the whitebark pine.

What was Woolly digging? At first she thought he might be caching a carcass. Up here it could be a mountain sheep or even an elk, but he wouldn't have gone after the black bear and stayed away so long if he had a carcass hidden in the pines. Maybe he was digging in the root structure, looking for marmots? Or maybe it was just a day bed?

Well, she had to find out. She took out her receiver. He'd been gone for over an hour. The bear's signal was very faint. She glassed the tree line, then started hiking into the valley. She came at the avalanche chute from the west, carefully avoiding the spot where the bears had entered the forest.

She stopped, focusing her binoculars on the dirt mound. From this angle she could see that there was more dirt than she'd seen before. *An excavation of some kind? And was that a shadow?* It was a hole, right at the base of the pine, at a V formed by two dominant roots.

The excavation made her nervous. Rachel turned to scan the valley below. Her adrenaline kicked in when she saw the grizzly, still a dot, coming out of the timber. She was downwind, so he couldn't smell her yet. She backed away slowly, staying upwind as she hiked to the trail.

A half hour later, Rachel was still going over what she'd seen. The fresh dirt, the hole beneath the pine roots, the location. She knew what it was supposed to mean. Rachel tried to explain it some other way. She couldn't. She felt suddenly very anxious. Things she relied on were coming undone. It didn't make sense, but there it was—bear #146 had apparently dug a den. In June.

———

RAINEY WAS SECOND-GUESSING HIS decision. Soon after Jen left, his doubts began. Now, it surprised and in some measure worried him that he had actually agreed to help her.

Since the day his license was revoked, almost a year ago, Rainey had tried to avoid thinking about himself as a detective.

The problems started, Rainey knew, with Sheriff Jesse Stinson. Lloyd's singing—no, it was a rap, actually, something about brook trout—distracted him. Rainey tossed a spoon at Lloyd, rather than rehash, again, his problems with Jesse. If he let those memories come, they'd wash away the good feeling Jen had left behind. The point, though, the shouldn't-be-necessary reminder, was that taking on cops, even retired cops, was a bad idea. He was asking for trouble. He'd learned that much. And to do that in Jesse's jurisdiction was throwing dice with the Devil. Period.

Rainey fingered a battered knuckle. As a student he was suspended from college after a fistfight with his boxing coach. As an assistant professor, he led a strike that shut down his community college. Twice, he was arrested. In his first year of guiding, he left three Texans stranded in Eastern Montana when they insisted on killing hen pheasants. He waded his clients aggressively and famously clashed with inhospitable property owners over the high water mark. He'd finally sued the fly shop owner that scheduled his services—the guy was fraudulently double-booking expenses and underpaying all of the guides. And then, of course, there was Jesse. With hindsight he could see that he was quick to anger, unlikely to back off, and not sufficiently afraid of bad consequences. In the past year he'd worked to become more deliberate, and stay out of trouble.

Why, then, had he agreed to help? Some macho idea of himself? Lust? Boredom? Maybe he wasn't built to tiptoe around? Whatever. He'd call it off in the morning.

AFTER FILING HER BEAR observation form, Rachel fed her infant daughter, Molly, then fell asleep, fully clothed, beside her baby. Rachel slept fitfully. She was dreaming, her neck flushed, her face strained. In her dream, Woolly Bugger was on Dr. Moody's carcass.

When the grizzly raised his head, she saw Ray Moody's torn flesh in his teeth, hanging from his open mouth. When Woolly Bugger turned her way, Rachel startled. The top of the great bear's head was fur-covered. He had no ears, no eyes. She woke up, fearful. It was just a dream, she reminded herself, a nightmare. She looked over at Molly, sleeping peacefully beside her. Rachel sat up in bed, and without knowing why, she began to cry.

RAINEY WAS DRINKING COFFEE at Lloyd's counter when he saw Cockeye's black Caddy cruise by. It was 7:15 A.M. He was meeting Jen at 8:00, when he'd back out of this. What was Cockeye doing? Where was he going this early? It occurred to Rainey that if he followed Cockeye, he might locate Jimmy. Come up with an easy way out. He hurried to his truck. Rainey was surprised when the Caddy turned up the dirt road near Jack Loomis's place, then pulled off at a small grass-covered parking area for a campground nestled in a patch of cottonwoods.

The dirt road to the Loomis's angled off the highway toward the mountains. Before reaching the cottonwoods Rainey pulled the pickup off the road and made his way on foot. He saw Jack Loomis on his porch, watching. Rainey waved. Jack ignored him. He could see Cockeye, sitting in his car, smoking a cigarette. Rainey was circling behind the trees when a thunder-like noise rocked the cottonwoods. He turned into a wave of heat. A fireball rose from the Caddy. Shattered glass rained down onto the clearing. Then he saw Cockeye. He was twisted forward through the blown-out windshield. His head lay on the hood. The Caddy was blazing, and Cockeye was dead.

The car was too hot to get close to, and the wind was pushing the smoke his way. Edging between the trees and the fire, Rainey heard a sound among the leaves. Someone hiding in the cottonwoods. Rainey lay in the grass behind a boulder. He heard it again. A rustling. Rainey saw a man step out of the trees. The man carried a metal box. He set his cargo on the ground and tried to get close to the car. It was still too hot. Seeing him near the car, Rainey realized that the man was a child.

The boy was sitting now with his arms around his knees. He was hugging his legs and slowly rocking back and forth. Rainey guessed he was crying. Rainey circled through the woods and came out behind the child. "Don't be afraid," he said as gently as he could. And when the boy looked up at him, fearful, Rainey put it together. "Jimmy," he said, "I'm a friend of your mother's. I won't hurt you."

Jimmy was a gangly, fine-boned boy with dark curly hair. "Did you hurt my dad?" he asked, barely a whisper.

———

JEN WAS ON HER way to check out the bridge before meeting Rainey. She'd spent a restless night at a motel near Bozeman, worried about her son. As she drove, Jen was working to keep her spirits up, watching the river and humming "More Than a Woman," her favorite song from *Saturday Night Fever.*

As she entered the canyon, the road edged right beside the river and the light changed. In many places the early-morning sun was shut out by the steep canyon walls, and the river looked black. Jen wondered how fish could live in this dark, fast water, then she forced herself to focus on the morning's business.

She went over their plan one more time. Rainey had been right to talk her out of the snake. Okay. Jimmy would walk onto the bridge. Rainey would be hiding in this crawl space, underneath...

Smoke was coming from a patch of trees several hundred yards off the road. As she got closer, Jen saw Rainey's red pickup.

She arrived at the trees in a cloud of dust, and there was Cockeye's black Cadillac, looking like it had been firebombed. Under one tree she saw Jimmy, sitting next to a metal case. Rainey was checking out the case. She ran to her son.

"Are you hurt?"

Jimmy shook his head—no—then he started crying, soft hard sobs, burying his face in her chest.

"Am I glad to see you," she whispered, kneeling beside him, holding him close. She turned to Rainey. "Where's Cockeye?"

"In the car. I'm sorry." Rainey waited, watching her put it together. "The car blew up."

She rose, still holding Jimmy, and stared at the Caddy. It was still burning. She pressed Jimmy's head to her shoulder and looked through the melted remains of the rear window. The backseat had bubbled like a blistered hot dog. In front, Rainey had covered the charred body with an old army blanket. *Dear, God. What a sad, awful way to die.* She backed away, arms still around her son. "It's over," she said. "At least it's over, honey. We can be thankful for that." Then she sat in the grass with her son and cried. Jimmy cried, too, arms around his mother, as she gently rocked him back and forth.

When they were finished crying, Jimmy stood.

He led her toward the trees, away from Rainey. At the trees he whispered, "Dad woke me before he left. He told me to *guard our loot.*" He touched the metal box. "I went back to sleep." Jimmy pointed at a campsite beyond the trees, then looked up at his mom. "He's dead, isn't he?"

Jen held him tight. "Yes."

After a while Jimmy took a step back, toed the dirt. When she tried to touch him, he pushed her back. "I'm okay, mom."

She settled Jimmy in the front seat of the Nissan and sat with him, her arm around his shoulder. Jen wondered why some kids had to carry so much. When Jimmy drifted into sleep, she went over to Rainey, who was looking inside the car.

She looked in the car. "At least he's out of his misery," Jen said, matter-of-factly and mostly to herself.

"I'd better call the sheriff," he said.

Rainey took a last look at the remains of the burnt-out car. He brought over the metal container, opened it, then showed her one of the petri dishes in the smaller thermos-like containers inside. The concave glass dish was about two inches wide. Under the glass cover she could see several tiny mole-like clusters in some kind of auger, a firm, jelly-like substance.

"What's going on here?" Jen eventually asked.

"Was Cockeye doing scientific research?"

"Who knows? He used to be a pretty good forensic scientist. But lately?" She winced. "A month ago he told me that he wouldn't let his lady friends use a diaphragm anymore because he didn't believe a chemical could kill his sperm." She stared at Cockeye's body. "I'm not kidding."

Something in the metal container caught his eye. It was a photo, wedged between a container and the side of the box. He eased it out. *His picture*...on the back were directions to his house. He showed the picture to Jen, turned it over. "Directions to my house," he said.

Her face clouded over, saddening. "Earl..." she whispered.

"Let's get out of here," Rainey said.

Irish Elk

R ACHEL STANLEY HAD A happy, comfortably demanding daughter now. No thanks to Rainey. She'd married Leon, a popular summer manager at a dude ranch. Her marriage was doomed when Leon left seven months into her pregnancy to fish—oh, three, four weeks—in Patagonia. When he called to say he'd stay there awhile—*fishing is great*—she told him he didn't have to come back. He didn't—come back, that is—and now her seven-month-old daughter, Molly, was the solid center of a loosely structured, often chaotic life.

At the moment Rachel was worrying about getting out of a meeting early enough to freshen the bait in her trap, check out whatever wildlife she could find in the closed area, and still get the babysitter home on time. Good sitters were hard to come by, and this one's mom handled her gifted daughter like a teamster's rep—late meant golden time. Normally, Rachel hated meetings. She liked being with animals that couldn't argue, or with her own child, who had no use for sequential logic. Well, this time she was stuck. After thirteen years in the park, this was the first time a meeting had been called because of one of her reports.

Yesterday evening she'd filed her bear observation form, explaining that bear #146 seemed to be denning in June. Less than sixteen hours later, here she was, at the North Yellowstone Ranger Station, part of a group that included: Mitchell Picker, the assistant superintendent behind the bear management closure; Gummer Mosk, an enforcement ranger for the North Yellowstone subdistrict; Phillipe Renard, Dr. Moody's former assistant; her friend Danny Briley, a government Grant Administrative Officer; an elk biologist; and two park researchers, now part of the National Biological Service.

Meetings like this were generally called to pool information and resources so that problems could be identified and managed optimally. But why, Rachel wondered, were they moving so fast? Why hadn't they given her more time to sort this out? Yes, her bear was four or five months out-of-sync, but Woolly Bugger was just going back to sleep.

And then the elk biologist started detailing the unseasonal behavior she'd observed in a band of six bachelor elk. She described how an antler hunter found a rack of gargantuan brown antlers. "They were discovered outside the northwest corner, just past Blackstone Butte," she explained. "Well, the usual gossip started about crossbreeding moose and elk. I decided to check it out. I had collars on a couple of bulls, and five weeks ago I started following a group of six. That's when it got a little strange. So far I've seen four up close, and one, maybe two, have this incredible antler growth—I'm talking palmated, like the Irish Elk."

Gummer, the lean-faced enforcement ranger, interrupted, "Did you say Irish Elk?"

"No, I said like the Irish Elk. Irish Elk is an ice age species. They're extinct."

"I've seen pictures showing Irish Elk with bigger racks than your Boone and Crockett world records. These babies in that league?"

"Yes."

"You sure?"

She turned to the others. "What confused me, to tell the truth, was that two of these elk were in fall pelage, and bugling—typical fall rutting behavior—in June."

Out-of-sync elk? And what about that deformed bear cub? Rachel couldn't explain that. *Agh.* What had gone wrong in the closed area? This was not the kind of thing she could think through at a meeting. Especially a meeting with Mitchell. She had to get back up there, take another look.

"Maybe someone's growing dope in there. That'd make 'em bugle," Gummer said. No one laughed. "Yo, that was a joke."

Rachel knew Gummer wasn't the least bit bothered by the awkward silence. That's how he was. She volunteered a conclusion, hoping to buy herself some time. "The bear and the elk are probably suffering from some kind of hormonal disorder. Gummer, you can relate to this. It's the kind of thing you hope for when one of your girlfriends is late." She touched his arm, heading off his protests. "Something is causing a misreading of the photo period. I have no idea what it is. Could be anything out there—weather, a virus, a change in the ozone, or in the case of the bear, an out-of-whack endocrine system—who knows?"

"Could be nothing at all," Dr. Moody's French assistant, Phillipe, said. "All we have is two times, the out-of-sync behavior." He waved a hand. "No big deal. My question is why is this area closed? Why am I not allowed to visit the Sentry Hot Spring?"

Mitchell shot him a look. They'd been over this. He tapped his glasses on the table, all the answer Phillipe would get. Rachel thought it was a good question.

The other scientists agreed that two instances of unseasonal animal behavior were not so unusual. Rachel, though she didn't say it, disagreed. There were too many unlikely events in the same area, starting with Ray Moody's death. And why was Woolly Bugger so quickly blamed for that? Now this unseasonal animal behavior was in the northwest corner, too. On top of that, the prolonged bear management closure didn't pass her "smell test." And why was Mitchell all over this? She wasn't surprised when he suggested that they meet again in a week.

At the door her friend Danny Briley, the Grant Administrative Officer, asked her for coffee. He was bearded and scruffy looking, wearing blue jeans with a hole in the knee. Rachel noticed for the first time that the faded picture on the front of his old sweatshirt was of Richard Nixon with his dog, Checkers. It made her smile. Rachel said she had traps to check, but she'd call him on the weekend. It picked her up. She could talk to Danny—really talk—about the troubling circumstances in her former study area.

As she turned to leave, he asked, "What does your gut tell you about your bear?"

"I'm mostly confused...really hoping that it's no big deal."

"Are you worried? Mitchell says he's dangerous."

Rachel took off her thick glasses. Looking right at Danny, she repeated his statement. "Mitchell says he's dangerous," and then she said it again, slowly. Apparently satisfied, she offered, "Okay, suppose you coat Mitchell's privates with honey and dangle them in that bear's face. I think Mitchell wants a guarantee the bear's going to bow at the waist then lick that honey off." Rachel's full lips turned up in her saucy smile.

Danny laughed out loud, squeezing her shoulder as she turned. Rachel raced from the meeting to the entry hall. She waited at a pay phone. Beside her a tourist grabbed Gummer the ranger's arm. The visitor wanted to feed the bears. As she dialed, the guy insisted, "In Florida, we got gators eat a bass right out of your hand."

"I'm running late, hon, I'm sorry...your mother's there? Uh, hello Mrs. Lane...I understand about the overtime...I'm sorry about my tone, Mrs. Lane...I'm at a pay phone, and someone's waiting...I need her until seven. Of course I'm glad you're interested in my work...baiting bear traps...grizzly bears, yes...they're big traps, Mrs. Lane...it's not dangerous...I know I'm a single parent...suppose I bring chocolates?"

———

RAINEY, JEN, AND JIMMY stopped at Lloyd's to call the sheriff. Rainey went straight to the outdoor phone. Jen led Jimmy down to the river. "Did you talk to your dad at all?" she asked.

"Yeah," he said, barely audible.

"What did you talk about?"

"Being men." Jimmy skipped a stone on the river.

"Oh." She smiled. "What did he say about that?"

"He said it was hard. That you've got to be on your guard. For a while he sounded crazy. Then he was nice." Jimmy was curling a lock of dark hair around his forefinger, looking out at the river.

She tried to skip a stone. It sank.

Jimmy showed her how he did it. "It's the flat side has to hit the water, mom," he explained.

"Oh," Jen said. "The flat side." She held back her smile.

Jimmy skipped another stone. "Did you hate him?"

"I hated when he did crazy things—like taking you without asking. Right now, though, I'm remembering how funny he could

40

be, how much he loved his son—and I don't hate him." And she didn't, now that it was over.

"Well, I hate him. But sometimes I don't. He was my dad you know."

He picked up another stone, a bigger one, and looked over at her. She drew him close.

Jimmy stepped away, threw the stone at their car. It put a dent in the driver's side door.

Jen's stone dinged the rear window.

———

FOLLOW THE GALLATIN RIVER ten to twenty meandering miles after it leaves the northwest corner of Yellowstone Park and it winds behind the Frontier Mall in North Yellowstone. "North," as the locals call it, is larger than Gardiner, smaller than West Yellowstone, and more beautiful than either. What all three towns have in common are motels, souvenir shops, outdoor clothing emporiums, fly-fishing experts, fast-food restaurants, bars named Mint, Stockade, and Silver Dollar, and hordes of tourists every summer. North, however, is distinguished in one special way: Sheriff Jesse Stinson, a man who, as he liked to put it, "knows right from wrong, how to protect wildlife and wild country, and how to attract the tourist dollar." If he were talking off the record, as he often did, he'd add that he hadn't met a tourist yet who "knew how to close a ranch gate or why the cowboy was helping the sheep over the fence." Then he'd laugh his hearty laugh.

North, the county seat and hub of Clearwater County, had been his town for the past fourteen years. His supporters swore by him, called him *Our Jesse*. They pointed out, for example, how Jesse had made the town a great place to do business, welcoming and safe. How he spoke out to preserve the Western feel of the town. And yes, he was always there, with his own money when wildlife in the county needed help.

When Rainey had called earlier, Jesse insisted he *come on over* to the office. As he and Jen drove toward town (they'd left a quiet Jimmy fishing reluctantly with Lloyd), Rainey wondered how he might step lightly around his past with the sheriff.

Jen punched him softly on the arm. "Try a baby step."

"Got me." His laugh was tinny. "Suppose I tell you about my past with Sheriff Jesse Stinson?"

"Okay."

"My problems with the sheriff go back to a horn poaching deal."

"Excuse me?"

"We got people here that steal antlers and sell 'em to the Asians—Koreans mostly—for aphrodisiacs."

She scrunched up her eyebrows, skeptical.

Rainey nodded. It was true. "On the deal where I met Jesse, the poachers were working the Tom Miner basin and their buyers were Asian aphrodisiac producers. The Tom Miner Basin is just over those mountains." He pointed east toward the Gallatin Range. "A rancher in the basin got tired of finding dead elk on his ranch, dead elk with their antlers cut off." Rainey tapped a meaty hand on the seatback. "This rancher was no fool. He knew about the illegal antler trade, so he hired me to poke around. Well, first thing I did—this crackerjack detective—I asked Jesse for his help. It never occurred to me that our sheriff was behind the poaching operation himself."

"Let me get this straight. They were killing these elk for the antlers so they could sell them to the Koreans for some kind of love medicine?"

"That's it. Velvet antlers from this area can go for maybe seventy-five dollars a pound. If a rack weighs twenty pounds, that's fifteen hundred dollars a rack."

"Velvet antlers?"

"They're in velvet when the blood's still flowing through them. That's before the horn growth is completed, say June and July."

"Just try and bear with me here. What's 'in velvet'?"

"It's the period of time when the antlers are covered with what looks like brown fuzz. That fuzz is mostly dead cells. It's called velvet. The velvet is like an outer skin. Underneath, the cell structure is still alive—blood flowing through a network of capillaries, a living nerve system, calcification and so on. Apparently, if the blood can be sealed in the velvet antler, the aphrodisiacal properties improve. When the velvet comes off, the blood vessels have gone dry, and the antlers are a shiny brown. The price goes way down."

"Are you telling me that grown men eat antlers to get hard?"

"More or less. I don't know much about Asian pharmacology, but many people believe that processed velvet antler is an aphrodisiac and will, among other things, protect against impotency. And since natural products are often preferred to pills—"

"Then there's real money in this."

"The big money's in processing. The processing plants, though, are all in Asia. That's where they grind the rough antlers to powder. To process antlers, you have to have a processing secret. That's a secret recipe for a love potion made with the fine velvet powder. It fluctuates, but processed velvet antler can go for two hundred dollars a pound."

"Two hundred? That's four grand for a twenty pound set. People do really stupid things for less." Jen ran a hand through her hair. "You ever try it?" She raised her palm. "Never mind," she said. "Don't answer that."

———

RACHEL WAS IN A bad mood. The meeting had been unsettling. And this on top of a short, troubling night—that awful nightmare, then waking up twice with her baby. Damn. She was too tired to check bear traps. So the hike in seemed harder, steeper than it normally did, and she wasn't sure she could handle even one more instance of unseasonal animal behavior. She suspected that if she didn't figure out what was going on soon, she'd get so antsy and preoccupied that she'd be unfit company, period—which was bad, since at her best she had the social skills of a bottom fish.

Her culvert trap was a little more than three miles from the trailhead, hidden in the forest that came down the backside of Blackstone Butte then swept north toward the Cut-Across Trail. Her trap had to be checked, and the bait freshened. There were two young female bears she hoped to collar. A breeze was blowing, and the sky was layered with ashen, lazy-looking clouds. They dulled the greens of the meadow, coloring them deceptively gray until the sun broke through to reveal a startling bright patch of green. She picked a stalk of fescue, put one end in her mouth and lengthened her stride.

43

The smoke took her by surprise. It was a wavy white line, working its way toward the clouds. It was coming, she guessed, from the patrol cabin beyond a ridge to the northeast. But why? The area was closed.

Twenty minutes later she was on the ridge with a view down to the cabin. She glassed the little clearing. Gear was spread out near the steps. There were two packs, supplies, and three metal containers. The American Science Foundation scientists. Had to be. The foundation had funded some of Dr. Moody's work, and after he died, they'd sent in two East Coast microbiologists to finish up. They had permission to be at the Sentry off and on, but she'd been told they weren't up here often. Two men came out of the cabin. Each of them picked up a metal container and carried it back inside.

Rachel had met these men once with her friend Danny, the grant administrative officer. He said they didn't like it here. They worried about bears, wolves, moose, you name it.

They must be bringing out their samples. Yeah, okay. The large metal containers held petri dishes. A ranger probably left their supplies here, at the cabin, then packed their samples back to town. Maybe they were finally finished. Well, she'd ask Danny. In the past year she and Danny had become friends. A little more than friends, actually, for just a moment. It was a night that she didn't regret but didn't want to repeat. She couldn't say just why. Something too casual about it, she guessed. Rachel made a wry face—men were a sore subject. She pushed on.

JEN PICTURED HERSELF STRUTTING into Johnny "The Bug" Delvechio's pawnshop with this big rack of velvet antlers in tow, telling him how they were worth maybe two grand. The Bug would get a hoot out of that one.

Rainey pointed out a billboard. The sign said: Entering North Yellowstone. It featured a landscape with mountains, a river, and a grizzly bear catching a trout. On the bottom it said: Clearwater County. Underneath, in script: Reelect Sheriff Jesse Stinson.

"He just leaves it there," Rainey explained.

"Suppose you tell me about you and the sheriff?"

He took the truck down a dirt road, stopping beside the river. "I more or less got off on the wrong foot with Jesse on this horn-poaching business."

"Uh-huh," she replied, wondering if he thought this was news.

"Jesse suspected I was withholding evidence—which I was. He ordered me off the case. When I refused, he kept me in jail overnight, cuffed to a bunk. That night I was beaten by my so-called cell mates." Rainey shifted to look at her. "I couldn't let that go. So I locked a skunk in Jesse's house along with his hunting dogs."

He was serious. For the second time in twenty-four hours, Jen had to bite down on her lip to keep from laughing. "How'd he take it?"

"He couldn't prove anything, but he came straight to my front door and accused me of fouling his nest. He said he was going to school me. I swear. Not two hours later my pickup was impounded, a tax assessor showed up to revisit my assessment, and a building inspector came by to recheck my brand-new drain field. This cowboy had a backhoe. He ripped up my yard, my garden, my drain field." He tapped his thumb on the seatback. "I'd spent a lot of time on that garden."

Jen sensed Rainey's anger. He kept a lid on it, though.

Rainey described Jesse's political savvy and his vengefulness. His enemies all told the same story: cross him, and he was relentless. When he was able to get his pickup, the engine blew on the way home—someone had put sugar in the gas tank. When he finally arrived home, the building inspector was back. He had eight issues, none of them easy or cheap.

Yes, he told her, a sensible person would have backed off. But he'd learned that Jesse had figured a way to sell confiscated whiskey to his own saloons. And he'd found Jesse's whiskey cache. So Rainey had set fire to Jesse's whiskey shed with one hundred and twenty-six cases of whiskey still in it.

Whoa, where did that come from? Jen pursed her lips and blew—more whoosh than whistle—unsure what to think.

RACHEL SET A STRONG, steady pace. Walking made her feel better, especially in her former study area. She was angling up along Elk Creek where it twisted around a large patch of timber. To save time she pushed through the trees.

A change in the light marked the meandering line where the forest ended and the meadow began. She knew that if you came out of these woods at exactly the right place, Elk Creek was suddenly, magically, at your feet, winding off like a fine, fat caterpillar creeping through an oval-shaped meadow. She found her spot, and there it was.

Rainey, she remembered, had taken his little niece to fish in this stream almost three years ago. She'd just turned six. How funny he'd been, worrying that he couldn't show her a good time, that she wouldn't like fishing. What, thought Rachel, could be more fun for a child than fishing with Rainey? And for the rest of her trip, Emily, of course, had talked nonstop about their "fish fish" day.

For a quarter mile she walked along the creek, then stepping on a large stone, Rachel waded across the creek and angled west behind Blackstone Butte. A half mile later she reached a familiar rise. It was a good place to wait for an elk or a deer. She set up her scope.

Ten minutes later Rachel was on the rise, stewing, when she spotted a mule deer working his rack against a pine sapling. From above she could see that he was rubbing the velvet off his antlers. Here it was mid-June and the antlers should be much smaller, in velvet and still growing. The blood should be pumping through these antlers. Instead, these antlers were fully-grown, and they'd soon be shiny brown. And then this out-of-sync buck raised its head, and Rachel saw that instead of points, the tines were starting to form clubs and moose-like palms. She'd never seen that. Never heard of it. What were these animals responding to? Some change in the food supply? The water? Her anxiety was back.

She caught herself. There had to be a perfectly reasonable explanation. So why was she so jumpy? Because something was haywire, that's why.

Stay focused, she told herself. *Slow down. Make lists.* Okay. This afternoon she'd freshen the bait in her traps, replace her bear lure. Yes, she had her own formula of cantaloupe extract, bear urine, and citronella. After piercing a pin hole in the rubber bottle top, she'd put the lure in a burlap bait bag along with some deer-meat scraps and an open can of blueberries. She'd rigged a tree branch so she could hang the bag just over the trap. In the old, cylindrical culvert trap, the bait, part of a roadkill elk, was attached to a cable. The cable was set on a vice grip trigger and held the steel-barred door. When the bear yanked on the bait, the trigger released the heavy door.

She startled at a noise. The wind, she realized, rustling the leaves. Jesus, why was Woolly Bugger digging a den?

———

WHEN RAINEY DIGRESSED AGAIN—to explain how Jesse was an alcoholic, how he couldn't sleep since giving up alcohol—Jen realized he was afraid she'd disapprove of what he'd done to the sheriff. Here, he'd been bitten by her rattlesnake, and he was worried what she'd think. Kind of sweet.

So she told a story about how she'd backed her squad car into a corrupt police sergeant's new Lincoln Continental, and a few minutes later Rainey was back on track.

He told her how, on nothing more than a hunch, Jesse had charged him with arson. When he made bail, Jesse took him aside to explain that if he didn't confess, he'd "be unwelcome in this county."

Rainey explained that it had been a confusing time for him, how not long after meeting Jesse, he'd been thrown out by a woman he really cared for.

Jen wondered why he told her, and why a woman he really cared for would do that.

Rainey pointed out several small trout rising to hatching mayflies. Then he came back to Jesse. "I saw only two ways to go: leave the county or get something on him. The reasonable course of action was to walk away, cut my losses, but you can see how—I mean this is my home."

She understood that.

"I hired a lawyer to stall Jesse—tell him I was moving, whatever—and I spent the next seven weeks digging around in his past. Jesse grew up in Las Vegas. I found his one-time Vegas girlfriend, Mary, now a retired madame living in Miami. It took six of those seven weeks to find her. She had a new identity, a new life." His mood, Jen noticed, had changed. He'd liked finding Mary. "Mary and I came to an understanding: I wouldn't tell her new husband she had another name, another life. She'd give me a deposition detailing how Jesse, a corrupt cop, had extorted payoffs from Las Vegas call girl operations. Mary swore that after one of the girls, Sally, went to the cops, Jesse disfigured her with sulfuric acid. He scarred her beautiful face and blinded her in one eye. Jesse told Mary that he only blinded the one eye so that Sally could see her ruined face in the mirror."

"Bastard." She watched him check out the rising fish, and slowed down.

Rainey turned back. "Eleven months ago I put that deposition on Jesse's desk. For an instant the man looked like that witch in *The Wizard of Oz* just when she realizes she's about to melt. We cut a deal: he'd back off, but my detective days were over. Since then he leaves me alone. The statute of limitations has run out on what I've got, but it would finish him politically if I gave the deposition to the *Chronicle*."

"A wounded sheriff fighting for his political life, he's a dangerous enemy." And Rainey, it seemed, was too.

"Yeah...It's been a fragile stalemate." Rainey kept his eyes on her.

"What have I gotten you into?" she asked.

"I was already in it."

With another man, she'd call it off. For him. For her. This one could decide for himself. So could she. She took his arm.

———

THE CULVERT TRAP WAS in a forested draw on the northern edge of a stand of fir that came down the backside of Blackstone Butte. It was almost a mile north of the rise, a straight shot if you knew the way. Rachel followed a game trail into the forest. At this altitude, almost sixty-five hundred feet, the trees looked to be lodgepole pine, but in fact the forest was in transition, the lodgepole pine was actually an overstory—something like a canopy—covering the alpine fir and spruce that would take over as the pine began to fall from beetle kill.

The trail came out on a crest above the draw where Rachel stopped to sit and glass the valley to the west and the trees beyond. She took her time, looking for she wasn't sure what. Some minutes later she saw movement in the forest. A large animal. It didn't move like an elk or a deer. She waited, focusing on the slow, stalking movements. The animal was on its hind legs. What? Was that a man walking among the trees? What was he hunting here?

It was difficult to see him because he was bent over and the cover was thick. He might be the same man she'd seen eight or nine days ago. She'd spotted him tracking an animal on the cliffs below Stoney Ridge. A poacher, she'd thought at the time. His face, she remembered, had been badly scarred. When she'd tried to follow him, he'd lost himself in the forest. Whoever he was, the man knew his way around these woods.

She shouted across the valley. He looked up. Through her glasses she could see his ravaged face, then the barrel of a .30-06 pointed at her head. She hid behind a tree. When she looked again, he was gone. She was scared now and felt pasty, like overcooked spaghetti. Damn. A poacher working in and around the closed area. What was he tracking? An elk, perhaps, with oversized antlers?

And what about Jesse? This poacher was outside the park, in his jurisdiction. "Slow down," she counseled herself. "Try and think practically, for a change. And honey, no one cares that it doesn't come naturally." She needed to sort this out, she knew that much. Until she did, could she hide the poacher from Mitchell? She had to. Otherwise, the assistant superintendent would have to bring in Jesse. Mitchell and Jesse—the spin doctors. The mind reels.

Okay, she'd keep this to herself. Today or tomorrow, latest, she'd get close to one of these out-of-sync animals. Take blood. Tissue samples. Figure this out. In the meantime suppose she told Gummer, the enforcement ranger, that she'd seen a poacher working just outside the park near Blue Grouse Creek. He'd leak it to Jesse, his law enforcement colleague. Okay sheriff. Spin that, you sonofabitch.

Rainey's Nemesis

J ESSE WAS FIVE FEET four inches tall, too short for a lawman, particularly a Western lawman. He was built like a fireplug, with strong simian arms and an unexpectedly soft, soothing voice.

The sheriff had shrewd, raisin-colored eyes, a carefully groomed black mustache, and pitch-black hair, which he combed straight back. He always wore a colorful, monogrammed neckerchief to hide a scar that ran from his ear to his collarbone. Today he'd chosen little black diamonds on a powder-blue background. Women, apparently, found him attractive. Men couldn't understand why. Today, he sat behind his mahogany desk as Rainey and Jen sank into the deep burgundy leather chairs facing him. Rainey guessed he had a platform back there to give him an extra couple of inches. Jesse was cleaning a short-barreled twelve gauge while he listened to their story.

"Rainey Jackson," he said when they were finished. "You are luckless."

"How's that, Jesse?" While the sheriff busied himself with his gun, Rainey guessed Jen's skewed little smile was about his name, Lloyd's unbelievable story...his best friend, the idiot savant of ornate lies.

Jesse closed the breech, a sharp metallic crack. "Sorry fella like you meets a fine-looking woman like this and before a day goes by you're sinking in—pardon me, ma'am—cow pie. Up to your neck in it." Jesse pursed his lips. His expression went from stern to pitying. "You just can't stop yourself, can you, sport?"

"I don't see that," Rainey said, wanting to ask him if he was part dwarf, watch his face then.

"Apply yourself, boy. I got a witness puts you at the scene of the fire. S'cuse my candor, ma'am, but a man gets firebombed—" he showed his hands. "And the sport here with a history of arson." Jesse let that hang out there. "Say you polish a bad apple—it's still rotten. Albeit shiny."

Rainey exhaled. "You're smarter than that," he finally said. "And smart as you are, why are you always saying *albeit?*"

Jesse ignored him. "Ms. Donahue, I see you're a twice-decorated, albeit former police officer. You'll understand when I say the man's unemployed, unstable—"

Jen interrupted, "Let's start again."

"Cap Conte was right. You do have a mouth."

"Captain Nathan Conte? From Chicago?"

"Nice fella, Jen. Says you made police work a little less—how did he put it? Foreseeable. Cockeye, he said, was slipping, but you—he said he'd take you back." He snapped his fingers. "Like that."

Jen eyed him carefully, a bug in her spaghetti sauce.

"Did you know Cockeye?" Rainey asked. When Jesse ignored him, Rainey edged closer. "Your kind of guy. Man-oh-man. You two? Peas in a pod." Rainey watched Jesse's face tighten up, like a prune. It was a guilty pleasure. He should have kept his mouth shut.

Jesse spread his arms. "Son, you ever seen a dog on a porcupine? Nine a ten times that dog has these nasty barbed quills hooked into his snout, his gums, even his tongue. That dog is howling, suffering a world of hurt—because he didn't know when to back off."

Rainey knew what he had to do. "Look, I'm helping you on this one. I'm here. I'm telling you what I know. How would you like to proceed?"

Jesse stood, his mood apparently shifting again. "I appreciate your coming forward. I'll look into this matter immediately. And be where I can find you, boy." He turned to Jen. "The American West is an unpredictable, lawless sort of place. Out here, a big silver buckle and fancy leather boots can hide a lot of nasty things." His raisin eyes turned beady. "Watch yourself, ma'am."

The audience was over. Jesse punched a speakerphone. "Stacy, hon, show these nice people out, then find Mitchell, our park's dandy assistant superintendent." He winked at Jen, then Jesse cocked a thumb and forefinger at Rainey. "Professor, Mary sends her best."

Rainey turned and left, swallowing the bile rising in his throat. Jen followed. She pulled a pink satin hat from the pocket of her Chicago Bulls jacket. On the front, it said Montana, in black script, and there was a drawing of the head of a growling grizzly. Rainey watched, and whistled, as she put it on and checked herself out in a window. Apparently satisfied, she took his arm and announced, "Yuck, I need a shower then a stiff drink." And after a beat, "I'm sure he knew Cockeye."

Rainey nodded. "I'm guessing he gave Cockeye my picture, sent him to my house on some creepy mission."

"I'd bet on that."

"He must be close to finding Mary. She moved again after I found her. Still, Jesse's resourceful."

"I'm sorry, but yeah, that makes sense." She squeezed his arm. "Peas in a pod? Jesus, Rainey."

"Okay. Cheap shot," he admitted. He was glad, though, he'd taken it.

"Cockeye used to talk about a cop that had it made in Montana," she offered. "He even did some kind of work for him. I should have put it together. The way he responded, he had to know."

"I'm sure he did. Jesse's got a hand in every weird deal in the county."

He started the pickup.

"Let me guess...the people around him get rich, and he's sheriff for life."

"That's pretty much how it works, yeah. Jesse's actually a popular sheriff. *Our Jesse.* In Clearwater County they call him that. He keeps bringing home the bacon, sliced extra thick. And what's even better, to hear him tell it, he's never bloodied his hands on a pig." Rainey's face hardened. "He's fooled 'em. The man's some sort of genius at presenting himself as he wants to be seen. The lying's pathological. He couldn't stop if he wanted to."

"Weird cops creep me out." Jen said, and after a moment, "Some girls love guys like Jesse."

Rainey nodded, somehow pleased that she got that about Jesse, unsure just how she got it.

Before he could ask, she leaned in, "Some gals are just drawn to dangerous cops—smart, manipulative guys with power who seem to have the world by the tail. If the guy's got a sensitive side, well...for some women it's the first relationship they've ever had where they feel like anything they do is okay. It's like being with an outlaw—only it's legal. Lots of cops take advantage of that."

"There are young women in town who pine over him."

"That's too bad." Jen opened her window, breathing in the June air, plainly done with this, then turned back to him. "In this motel I stayed in, there was this picture of two sheep, the tan ones with the curled horns..."

"Bighorn sheep. Rams."

"Right. These rams, they're knocking their horns together. You ever see that?" she asked.

"Once. Why?"

"Listening to you and Jesse, there's some of that."

For a time they drove on in silence. "I like you," Jen said. "Took me by surprise, too."

———

ON THE GATE AT the entrance to the Bear Tooth Ranch sat two black bear skulls that came from bears that Jesse had somehow acquired in 1986, the year he bought his ranch. Jesse's ranch was only four hundred and eighty acres, a hobby ranch as opposed to a working ranch. Still, he liked the idea of owning a ranch, especially as a place to do business or to entertain the celebrities that came to recreate or just to fish in Yellowstone country. (Though why anyone wanted to fish was a mystery to him. Privately, Jesse likened fishing to herding sheep or goats, only even more boring.) If asked about his ranch, Jesse would put on a deep-thinking face and explain, "Some of our town's fancy financiers, and even your out-of-state notables—well—I've seen those rich boys get all red and itchy waiting in a sheriff's office."

The main building, known as the lodge, was a log structure featuring a great room with a twenty-six foot ceiling. In the center of the great room, there was a stone fireplace that opened on two sides. From the covered porch you could look across the valley to the mountains or shoot ground squirrels, commonly called gophers. The last bit of driveway, as it wound its way up to the porch steps, was rightly called Gopher Gulch.

Jesse liked to listen to country music when he shot gophers. He could pick a favorite song and calibrate the volume from a panel on his front porch rail. Today he was listening to Willie Nelson's "Red Headed Stranger" when he dropped a fat male. Satisfied, Jesse lowered his gopher gun—a classic 1858 Remington Old Silver .44 revolver with an ivory grip—and sat down to unwind.

Jesse leaned back on his porch swing, spreading his simian arms on the seat back. He was thinking Abe Lincoln was right—you couldn't fool all of the people all of the time. Where he disagreed with Abe, though, was that he figured you could fool most of the people all of the time, and the others, you could back off—unless they had something on you, like Rainey. And why was it that when he tried to relax—thinking about Abe Lincoln for christsake—his mind invariably turned to that imperious prick? How had that agitator, that insufferable meddler, found Mary anyway? Well his man would find her any day now. Too bad Cockeye got roasted before he could leave his surprise. He was gonna hide a couple beehives in Rainey's basement. Wear a bee suit and set 'em free. Push the jerk off's macho button. Put him on notice, period. Jesse looked away, rueful. Just the idea of it was sweet.

Now, he had another idea, even better. Whatever. He'd take the guy down the minute Mary recanted. And she would recant. Damn...the high and mighty sonofabitch was like an irritating, maddening itch in his inner ear that he couldn't quite get at. Well, that was about to change, he thought, seeing Gummer driving his Jeep Cherokee up the winding driveway.

Jesse took a deep breath, trying to get in his Gummer frame of mind. By God, after all these years it still took a deep breath to get in the right mood for Gummer.

He'd first met Gummer at one of the get-togethers in the park hosted by Mitchell, the assistant superintendent. Jesse had perceived that the long-legged enforcement ranger was one of God's quirkier creations. At the time he imagined that the man simply marched to his own kind of pokey drummer. Little by little, though, Gummer's persistent interest in business got his attention.

Jesse had come to see that young Gummer the ranger was good with animals; surprisingly able, in a meandering, dopey sort of way; dead serious about making money; and, more to the point, ideally positioned to help Jesse make money. The problem was that Gummer knew how to peg his value in a transaction the way a fish knew how to swim. Hell, the man was like a goddamn Japanese—always bowing, letting you know what a doofus he was, then getting the best of you. Lately, Jesse had started wondering if maybe he'd underestimated his hard-to-read, often-goofy associate.

Gummer was early, a good sign. Jesse considered raising his gopher gun, putting a round through the Jeep's back tire. Instead, he steadied his porch swing as, unexpectedly, he flashed on Rainey saying "peas in a pod."

———

GUMMER LIKED COMING TO Jesse's ranch, especially since he'd taught himself to smile at the sheriff's occasional potshots at his tires. Today, he parked the Cherokee, took off his park service hat, and wisely sat his long, lean frame below the sheriff on the porch steps. His black hair was cut short, army style. His soft gray eyes invited candor, though they didn't give away much. "I came early," he announced, "because I heard something going to interest you."

"How do you know what interests me?"

"This is going to interest you or I'm Granny Goose."

"Get it out, son. Don't just sit there like some Zen Buddhist big thinker contemplating your uncircumcised—albeit horse-sized—pride and joy."

Gummer nodded, earnest, guessing Jesse must be worrying again about his own short-guy package. He had to be feeling low. When he felt good, Jesse routinely put himself with Paul Bunyan or Goliath. "Well, sir. The Blackstone Butte area's got some more freak elk in it—racks the size of your Irish Elk, yes siree bob." He grinned, a classic shit eater. "Boone and Crockett records, no problem. And there's more than one."

Jesse made an impatient, hurry-up gesture with his fingers. "We know that, Gummer. Bodine was up Elk Creek, and he got one."

Just hearing the scar-faced poacher's name made Gummer edgy. He and Darrell Bodine had damn near killed each other over a grizzly cub Bodine had trapped in the park. One of them would be dead today if Jesse hadn't sprayed the both of them with #8 birdshot. "That loopy poacher sonofa—"

"Easy, son. Forget Bodine. What I want to know is why you're coming here early with nothing but yesterday's news?"

"The big bulls, they're collared, sir."

"Collared? Collared?" Jesse was up now, pacing.

"That's right. And I got a receiver—the one that picks up the federal frequencies." Gummer let this hang, pleased. He liked it when Jesse focused. It was a sign of good things to come.

Jesse drummed his fingers against a post. He stopped drumming, then he turned both palms up. "And, Gummer? And?"

"Oh. I got two of the frequencies. It'll be like shooting fish in a barrel."

"That a boy, Gumby." Jesse snapped his fingers. "There we go, there we go. Trophy hunts...Bodine can take 'em in. Let's up your cut to fifteen K a kill." He changed the subject before Gummer could respond. "When did you give the petri dishes to Cockeye?"

"Petri dishes? Jeez, that was yesterday morning. Yes, sir."

"And what were his plans?"

"Said he was on his way back to Chicago today. His lab guy was waiting. Said he had everything set up, no sweat. Musta said three times how his guy knew Moody's work."

"You gave him all the dishes?"

"You bet. A metal container packed just so." Gummer didn't like where this was going. Here he was really up, the messenger with the good news, and now Jesse was doing some kind of a number on him.

"He's dead. Burned up. Roasted in that Caddy like one a those Conoco take-out chickens. No sign of the doodahs you brought out."

"Jeez, I'll be." Gummer ran a hand over his crew-cut hair, troubled. Not even a screwball like Cockeye deserved that. "Well, like I said, there were five petri dishes packed up just so in one of their metal boxes."

"Well, they're gone and so's Cockeye." Jesse stood, preoccupied. "Fucking Cockeye. He was perfect for this."

Gummer waited, thinking Jesse had a knack for finding these outcasts, then getting them to do the work he couldn't touch. And Cockeye was smart. As Jesse put it, "The guy invented 'thinking outside the box.'" The problem was that lately Cockeye couldn't think inside the box. Gummer had to smile. Jesse didn't care. He just made a bigger box.

The phone rang inside. "Wait here," the sheriff snapped, going up the stairs. "Fucking Cockeye," he muttered.

"Yeah. Sure." Gummer called to his back, wondering why Jesse was so worked up about the darn petri dishes.

——————

LLOYD'S WAS IN THE Gallatin canyon, a fast, rough, boulder-strewn section of the river. At North, the river was not so boisterous—the canyon had opened up, giving way to a more pastoral, inviting landscape. Driving upstream, The Taylor Fork enters the river from the west, and above this junction, the Gallatin becomes an even gentler meadow stream. Rainey and Jen passed Blue Grouse Creek and then a little brown sign, the only indication they'd entered Yellowstone Park.

"My first time in Yellowstone," she said, smiling wide.

Rainey stopped at a pullout. "Take a look. This is a good spot for that."

Jen stepped out and onto a small boulder beside the road. From her perch she had a splendid view of the multi-colored meadow that carpeted this portion of the Gallatin Valley. The sun was articulating the detail of the meadow in a fine warm light. A lone bison grazed near the tree line and wildflowers showed colors she'd never seen before. The valley was narrow here, an easy walk from the foothills of the Madison range to the foothills of the Gallatin Mountains. Looking up the valley, Rainey pointed out the tree-lined paths of the smaller streams winding down from the mountains to feed the meandering river.

"I love it," she exclaimed. "Especially the scale of things. I mean I've been in nature—you know—The Grand Canyon, Niagara Falls, but this is life-sized and—I dunno—welcoming."

Rainey thought she had it just right. He helped her off the boulder and back into the pickup. They took the winding road south into the park.

"Who's this woman we're going to see?" Jen eventually asked.

"Rachel? She's a bear biologist," Rainey said.

"This woman likes bears?"

"She does."

"I'm afraid of bears. I'm not kidding." Her face was set, she was sure on this. "Will she know what's in the Petri things?"

"How to find out anyway."

Jen squinted. "Was she the girlfriend?" she asked, out of the blue.

"Uh—"

"A guess. It was—I dunno—"

"She was. We lived together for fourteen months. It ended just before I turned forty. That's—what?" He did the math and looked surprised. "Only nineteen months back." Rainey tried to remember how it had been. His time with Rachel, once vivid, was now dull, shrouded in fog. "Honestly," he said, "it feels like much longer."

———

RACHEL'S MOOD HAD GONE from uneasy to surly. The buck had worried her, more than she cared to admit. She'd lost her glasses somewhere between the Cut-Across Trail and the trap, and she'd had to backtrack at least a quarter of a mile before finding them. Then, at the culvert trap, her vial of lure had broken while she was rearranging the bait. Some of the mixture had spilled on her leg, an unbelievable smell, so all the way down to the trailhead she had to watch carefully for bears. Because she was, literally, bear bait, she didn't dare stop for the blood and tissue samples she needed. And now she was running late.

She hurried to her office, aware that she still smelled like bear lure and looked like she'd spent the night in a boxcar. She'd decided to call her friend Danny, talk with him about the deformed bear cub, the poacher, the buck, all of it. He'd help. After, she'd clean up. She opened her office door. There was Rainey—dammit—sitting on the edge of her desk, accompanied by a striking woman.

She watched them grimace, an involuntary reaction to the awful smell.

"It's just like you to show up, uninvited, when I reek of bear bait." She opened a window. "I'm late to pick up the sitter, I have problems to deal with, I—"

"It's important. And it won't take long. First, I want you to meet Jen Donahue."

Jen stuck out her hand. Rachel took it. "I'm Rachel Stanley. I apologize for the way I must look and smell, but I've been baiting bear traps."

"We're the ones who should be apologizing," Jen said. "We barged in uninvited."

"Well, pleased to meet you."

"Likewise." Jen tried to connect Rachel with the cluttered office. The walls were covered with tattered, marked-up maps. Behind the desk books were falling out of three improvised bookshelves. Hanging above the top shelf were an MS from the Berkeley Forestry School, a PhD from the University of Alaska, and a certificate from the Interagency Grizzly Bear Study Team. There were pictures of Rachel's infant daughter between books, on the maps, everywhere. Jen had half-expected to meet Smokey the Bear. Instead, here was a beautiful woman who looked like she belonged in one of those old paintings where the women's cheeks are always red and their breasts are round as cantaloupes. Ripe was the word she wanted— full bust and hips, an oval face with luminous, hazel-brown eyes, tall and strong but definitely oh-so feminine. Her brown hair was packed in a ball on top of her head, her jeans and sweatshirt were dirty and torn, and she wore awful glasses. Jen liked her right away.

"Is he the type who just turns up when you don't need him?" Jen asked, genuinely curious.

"Always. And when you do need him he's off fishing. I remember one time—"

"I called," Rainey explained. "You weren't here, and you rarely call anyone back."

"You're not exactly easy to reach." She turned to Jen. "I once tried him at his house eleven days in a row. No answer, no machine, nothing."

"I bought a machine. Nevermind. You're right. I'm hard to reach. Look, we need help. I didn't know who else to ask."

Rachel raised her hands, an I-give-up gesture.

He produced the container of petri dishes. "We found these near a car that had caught fire—a bomb, I think—with a man in it. The man was Jen's ex-husband."

Rachel's face fell. She turned to Jen. "I'm sorry."

"He had it coming," Jen said, matter-of-fact.

"A bomb?" Rachel was frowning. "Is Jesse in it?"

"We told him what happened. We didn't tell him about these."

She opened the insulated metal case, checked out the thermos-like containers inside. "Standard issue," she told them. "For packing out certain kinds of samples." There were five or six numbers on each label, no special markings. She shook her head—they meant nothing to her. "Jesse finds out, he's gonna nail you." She held up her hand to stop Rainey from speaking. "I know, okay, I know. He doesn't need to find out. And I suppose you want me to find out what's in these dishes and what it does, etcetera, etcetera."

"Thank you," Rainey said. "It may be nothing, but still..."

Listening to these two, watching them, Jen's Jewish mother was already worrying; this was going to get complicated, had to. Her Irish dad prevailed. The train's left the station. Buckle up for a fast furious ride. Devil take the hindmost.

Rachel took off her oversized tortoise shell glasses and looked straight at Rainey. "Why are you doing this? Why?" she asked. "Haven't you had enough trouble with Jesse?"

"I'm not doing anything yet. The dead man was a corrupt Chicago cop who knew Jesse. This man, he had a picture of me with directions to my house." Rainey let this sink in. "So Jesse's got to be in it, somehow. I'm a witness, which makes me, in Jesse's eyes, a suspect. Jen's son was there, too."

"Oh, God." She slowed. "What does the boy say?"

"Not much," Rainey replied. "But he's pretty upset, he only talks to his mom."

"So why don't you just back off?" Rachel asked.

"Back off? My *picture* was in the metal container with the petri dishes. So Jesse isn't afraid of me. And Jen needs to know what happened. Besides, it's already too late. I was on the scene. Jesse's gonna frame me, one way or another. I need a place to start, something to trade."

"I can't believe this. A crooked cop dies in an explosion, his son refuses to talk with anyone except mom, so—of course—you and Jesse reopen old wounds."

"Lady, it's been a long day," Jen said. "We'll just leave."

Rachel looked at her. "How long have you known this guy? Twenty-five minutes? Do you have any idea what you're asking him to do? Are you aware that Jesse's like a crazed pit bull just looking for a way—any way—to sink his teeth into Rainey? Your ex-husband's dead. There's nothing you can do for him. It's not a job for an out-of-luck detective who's drawn to a lost cause like a moth to a flame."

Jen's eyes widened. "Maybe you're used to talking to animals that can't talk back—"

"Rachel," Rainey broke in. "Don't start. You don't have to help, but I'm in this now. We both know Jesse. Just seeing me—"

"You interrupted me. I can finish my own sentences." Jen said to Rainey, her face flushed. She turned to Rachel, eyes blazing. "And I won't have you presuming anything about me or my family."

"I'm not presuming anything. You've fired up Sir Lancelot here, and you should at least be aware of the consequences of what you're doing."

"Consequences for whom?" She stepped closer, wondering if this bear woman had any idea how it would be if she lost it.

Rachel eyed her, not giving an inch.

Rainey held up his hands. "I'm sorry, both of you, but this is already out of our hands. And I know the consequences of that." He hesitated. He was holding back; Jen could see it in his face. "I wouldn't be asking if I didn't have a bad feeling. I need to know what this is about if he comes at us. Rachel, you understand that."

Rachel picked up the phone, punched in a number. "It's Rachel... suppose we agree on occasionally late...the reason I pay the overtime is because sometimes I have to be late...what tone of voice? Sorry...I understand...no, the bear wasn't in the trap...I'm sure...your garbage? Maybe it was a coyote...I'll check...thank you, Mrs. Lane."

Rachel hung up. "It's been a weird day. Look, I'll see what I can find out about your petri dishes. In the meantime, Jen, please consider what I've said. I'm probably overprotective in a way I have no right to be. But, hell, I worry about him."

"I'm over my head here, and a little testy," Jen admitted, wondering if bear woman had any idea just how close she'd come to getting toasted. "I'll remember what you said."

"Thanks." Rachel followed them down the hall. "It's been a lousy day all around," she reflected. "There's something weird going on in the closed area. I think that's why I'm so edgy." Rachel pursed her lips. "Then again, it could be the blueberry flavored bear urine on my pants."

Before Jen could ask, Rainey said, "I'll explain in the car." In the parking lot he said to Rachel, "I'm at Lloyd's. And thank you."

Rachel nodded, then she turned to Jen, cool. "Luck," she said. Unexpectedly, her expression changed, softening. "Look, I have a child of my own, and her dad's long gone. I appreciate what you're up against." She turned and went to her car, an '87 Volvo sedan. Before they reached the pickup Rachel was gone.

Gummer, The Richest Enforcement Ranger in U.S. History

GUMMER SAT ON THE porch steps, waiting on Jesse. He liked the waiting times. It was like Jesse was making money for him while he was on a break. And lately his breaks had become a time to think, figure the big picture.

At the moment he was looking back. Something—it could have been a dead gopher on the grass—had brought to mind the prophetic advice his father, Gummert "Gummer" Moskovic, Sr., had given him in 1977 before he was mauled by a circus lion in front of 1,894 people. "It's the big cheese that always gets shot first. The dumb fella, the one looks after the general, if he's crafty, if he can get a feel for the politics of a thing, he makes out like a bandit."

Still, it took him eleven years to capitalize on his father's legacy. He was twenty-seven before he realized that the fire in his belly could not be extinguished by sex with teenage girls. Hoping money could quench those flames, he'd finally found his general. And seven years later he was on his way to being, say, about the richest enforcement ranger in U. S. history.

Gummer caught himself starting to worry. He was at the edge of something big, a sea change. He could feel it. The best thing now was to relax, wait and see.

Gummer started thinking about his girlfriend Darcie, the eighteen-year-old Dairy Queen girl. He stopped himself. This line of thought could arouse him, and Jesse would rag him without mercy. Besides, it was time for business; he was due for a raise; and here came the sheriff, who, by the look on his face, was working the dickens out of some idea.

Jesse came down to the porch rail. His face was twisted up in that strained expression he got when he was forcing himself to go slow. "Gummer, you're a fellow likes to think things through. Am I right?"

"Right as rain."

"Rain...uh-huh." Jesse squeezed Gummer's shoulder, a warning signal. "Okay. Now what do you think those scientists are up to, hiding out at that hot spring, playing with that invisible seaweed?"

"According to Danny, they're finishing Dr. Moody's work, writing some report, something about those thermophiles live in the hot spring."

"That's their story, yeah. Now listen carefully. I believe that those scientists at the Sentry are doing more than finishing up. They're working on something. I want to know just what it is...the whole program. I'd like you to find out. Go back up there. Use the back door. Whatever it takes." Jesse paused, letting this sink in. "You see where this is going?"

Gummer nodded. He saw quite clearly that whenever Jesse was this careful, this focused, he—Gummer Mosk—was about to make real money. It confirmed the essential fairness of his relationship with Jesse. He'd provide the inside information, do the *backdoor* work, sit attentively at Jesse's feet, and Jesse would make him rich. And being Jesse's straight man came easily to a boy who'd grown up in a circus troop, straight man for his parents, the Hungarian clowns. Feigning surprise, interest, understanding, these were the first things he learned in life. "Yes, I see it, Jesse, clear as day."

———

RACHEL DROVE NORTH THROUGH the park toward Bozeman. She loved this stretch of highway. The river turned away from the road here, as the valley widened and the trees gave way to flat meadows. It was as if the parallel mountain ranges had been forced apart, expanding to accommodate some huge ice sheet that had melted, or just downsized, before moving on.

As she wound her way out of the park she was thinking about Rainey, a thing she hadn't done in a long time. She didn't understand her reaction to him, or to the girlfriend. Where did he find her? She was pretty damned sure of herself. And she dressed like a Laker Girl. Rachel caught herself. Was she jealous? She didn't think so. No, she was angry. Angry that Rainey and Jesse were facing off again. That she couldn't say no to him. That he couldn't walk away from the sheriff. That he didn't get it. For christsake, a bear could change: adapt to a shift in his environment or learn from a mistake. Woolly Bugger had learned to avoid traps. She'd hoped Rainey would change. Rachel looked out the window, melancholy.

———

JESSE WAS PACING CIRCLES in the meadow, talking on his portable phone, something about poker machines. Gummer sighed. It was damn-near impossible to keep up with the hyper sheriff (Gummer wasn't sure whether he was hyper-active, hyper-thyroid or what). Anyway, the guy hardly ever slept—two, maybe three hours a night. Gummer secretly believed that if Jesse had slept more as a kid, he'd be able to see over the top of his police car today.

Gummer stretched his arms, relaxing on the porch steps, and there it was again, the idea that he was on the edge of something big, some kind of sea change. He could feel big changes coming on the way some people felt weather changes—in his bones. And a front was coming in. A real humdinger.

He wondered then, if he would actually miss explaining to mom and dad why Junior couldn't ride a bison. Or what about the husband who wanted a shot of his young wife sitting in the front seat next to Yogi Bear. He probably would miss those things.

Into it now, Gummer began replaying the turning points in his career, a trick he'd learned from Mr. Memory at the circus. How he met Mitchell in D.C. back when Mitchell was with Interior, running purchasing for the Park Service. How it was as a lowly Park Service purchasing agent. How he made his big decision to go to the police academy, become an enforcement ranger. And there he was twiddling his thumbs at Craters of the Moon Monument in Idaho, when Mitchell shows up again, suggesting he apply to Yellowstone—all this by the time he's twenty-six. He made a note on a scrap of paper to come up with a good story for Mitchell about why he was leaving. He was putting the note in the wallet he kept chained to his belt loop when Jesse finished his call.

"I've been thinking over this Sentry business," Gummer said, focused now, like a laser, when Jesse pocketed his phone. "I'm thinking I could maybe steal some of Dr. Moody's notes, if that would help."

"That's a start. You bet."

"Now I'm thinking twenty thousand dollars is my fair share for the elk hunt," he went on, seemingly oblivious to his non sequitur.

"You come on Uncle Buster, the bumbling rodeo cowboy, while you're homing in like a spawning damn salmon. I say to myself, it's instinct. You're unaware. Twenty K? Unlikely."

They heard a car then, an '84 black Ford pickup with a homemade shell turned up Gopher Gulch. "Bodine." Jesse grinned.

Even at a distance Gummer could see the scars covering one side of Darrell Bodine's face. The poacher approached the porch taking long, slow strides. No one knew why, but he didn't answer to the name Darrell. If he responded at all, it was to Bodine. Bodine. That meant the trophy hunts were already on. Jesse worked like a lightning strike.

Gummer swallowed the bad taste in his mouth. No one could get under his skin like Bodine. And the guy worked at it, like a hobby. Gummer didn't see how Jesse could do business with the jackass poacher.

Gummer never could find out how it happened, but Bodine had been Jesse's man—off the record—for years. Bodine guided for Trophy Outfitting. The boss at Trophy did what he was told, Gummer knew that much. Today Bodine wore dirty Carhart coveralls, old logger boots, and a greasy cap that said Clark Ropes.

"How's business?" Jesse asked.

Bodine put up two fingers, then he spit.

"No one up there. Like taking candy from a baby, huh?" Gummer said.

Bodine ignored him. "Brown fucking antlers on one," he told Jesse.

"It happens," Jesse answered, reassuring. "Got some new business. Trophies. Collared trophies."

"Hmm." Bodine packed a pinch of chaw under his lip. "Saw a monster bull in there—eleven points. Some kind a freak. Bigger even than what I killed. And a baby bear with no ears. A devil sign—"

"Eleven points," Jesse interrupted. "Damn."

Something was bothering Bodine, Gummer thought. This was the longest speech he'd ever heard him make. And what was a devil sign? It couldn't be good.

"Let's have your boss make some calls," Jesse went on. "He's got high rollers chompin' at the bit for trophy mounts. He can line 'em up. But we gotta get our story straight, scatter these trophies around some. Don't want to raise any eyebrows."

Gummer noticed a very slight twitch under Jesse's left eye—proof positive that something, or someone, had him on the ropes. Before this thought could go any further, Bodine lofted a wad of chaw through the open window of Gummer's Jeep Cherokee then followed Jesse into the house.

———

WHEN RAINEY AND JEN got back to the café at about seven, Lloyd's wife, Ruth, told them that Jimmy and Lloyd were still on the river.

Rainey stopped at cabin eight. Jen thought about following him in, then she pictured the fishy cabin, the snake. Uh-huh.

When he came out, his face was clean, and he was wearing a black-and-yellow checkered flannel shirt tucked into a fresh, worn pair of jeans. His wet hair stuck out under a washed-out purple Lloyd's Café cap. He looked so good she considered kissing him then and there. But she knew where that would go. To her cabin, for sure. And she couldn't make Jimmy wait anymore. No, she wouldn't do that.

Jen reminded herself that with good-looking guys she'd never made a mistake by going too slow.

———

GUMMER GOT TO THE Dairy Queen five minutes before Darcie finished her shift. He liked to be early so he could watch her work the grill in her DQ uniform. He especially liked the short white pleated skirt, and the tight royal blue panties that flashed when she leaned over to turn the burgers.

Not half an hour later they were parked near Jack Creek, and her royal blues were beside him on the backseat of the Jeep. Gummer was leaning back, his hands on her bottom while she straddled him, her short white pleated skirt rising and falling as he guided her movements. When his grip tightened, she opened her eyes, watching him. Early on she'd told him, in her matter-of-fact way, that she liked watching because when he came, his gray eyes got bright and all the acting was over.

A few moments later Gummer eased her onto the seat beside him and orally brought her to climax. Pleasing his young lover, the apple of his eye, was, for Gummer, a serious matter, and he took pride in doing it properly. It was one of the courtesies that set him apart from the swarms of adolescent boys who lusted after her.

Gummer buttoned his pants and stepped out into the night air. Some men relaxed and enjoyed a post-coital cigarette. Gummer preferred to solve business problems after sex. For nearly half an hour his mind was as clear as a cloudless sky, and it was easy to concentrate. Tonight he was figuring trophy hunts on a straight percentage when Darcie rolled down her window. "Baby G," she called, her mouth turned down in just a little pout.

"Huh?" She only used his favorite nickname when she was especially pleased with the sex.

"I'm at Amy's tonight."

"Jeez, why didn't you tell me?"

"I'm telling you now, dummy." It was her eyes, true green and missing nothing, that suggested that there might be a good deal more at work here than the firm breasts pressed against the window.

"Can you get away?"

"Maybe, yes...maybe, no." She flashed the smile of a born horse trader.

He leaned in and kissed her open mouth, then took a step back, wondering just what she was angling for. "Maybe, yes. Now hop up front and let me get you home. I got to work." Gummer went to the driver's side. He watched his young lover, climbing over into the front seat. He had to say, she had the cutest backside he'd ever seen.

As soon as she sat down, Darcie asked, "This work you got to do. It have anything to do with the sheriff?" She fished a pack of Marlboros from her rawhide purse and pulled out a joint.

"Yes it does, darling, I got to see Jesse after I finish my other business."

"Well, seeing as you're seeing him, there's one little thing you can help out with. Denny Smith—he used to be a big-shot MSU football player—he got caught robbing the Nugget over on Third. Can you fix that?"

"The Gold Nugget?"

"Yeah, that's it." She lit the joint, took a drag, passed it to Gummer.

He took a hit on the joint, set it down in the ashtray. "Jesse owns that bar, honey. There's nothing I can do to help anyone fool enough to rob one of Jesse's liquor set ups."

"Denny's my cousin. And I don't want you getting jealous here or anything, but he was, well, a kissin' cousin. Anyway, you know how I feel about family."

"This is a hard one, Darce. You know how much I want to help, but this is complex."

"You could do it." Darcie had that look—I may be only eighteen, but I know what I know.

Gummer's eyes softened. "I'll work on it honey, if it's important to you."

"Baby G, people think I love you for...you know...and I have to say, I do love that. But I love your—I dunno—it's the way you think or something. I love that even more. I swear, you can work out anything."

Gummer kissed her again. "Honey, you and me together, we could work out all the problems in—oh, say Russia." He nodded. "Now let's get you home before your daddy asks why it took so long at the DQ."

AFTER DROPPING DARCIE, GUMMER turned toward Dr. Moody's lab. He was whistling "Looking for Love," marveling how she was only eighteen. Thinking about that, he realized that it was ten months now he'd been marveling how she was only eighteen. Huh. That made her almost nineteen. He hoped he'd have more than the one year to look forward to. Experience had taught Gummer that when a woman neared twenty, things could get complicated and confusing. Maybe Darcie would be different. Hell, she already was different. The girl had the touch of a ward politician. A natural. And lately he sensed how she was starting to think long range, see the big picture. When she got that down—he tried out a sharp, two-tone whistle—stand back.

At the turnoff for Dr. Moody's lab, Gummer pulled over. Finding Moody's notebooks should be easy enough. He laid his ranger jacket in the back seat, put on a white lab coat, then drove in.

Quite a few cars were still in the lot. University types, he reminded himself, worked odd hours, and they slept during the day. Maybe it was getting the simple things backwards that made them come on so puffed up.

Gummer took the back steps up to the lab. At the second floor directory he found the name he was looking for: Phillipe Renard, 233. Dr. Moody's assistant.

He turned down the hallway, following the numbers on the half-glass doors. The hallway smelled like a hospital.

At Renard's door he heard a man's raised voice.

Gummer peaked through the tinted glass. All he could see was shapes—yes, two people leaning over something. A microscope? Maybe. A man was explaining, making gestures. Then louder, "Espece de merde...mais oui...absolument. It is my work, my work they are stealing."

Something broke. More swearing.

"This foucking Mitchell. He said they are closing Dr. Moody's program. They finish and...*poof*...he promised me this. The area, it is closed. So I am waiting. Waiting, while his scientists, they are working. Eleven months. This is not possible. This is merde."

"I've seen 'em." A woman's voice. Soft, hard to hear.

The guy lit a cigarette. Gummer put his ear to the door. "Why do they keep me from the pool? They tell me there is a dangerous bear. I am not afraid of this foucking bear. This closure, she is a trick, a lie."

Gummer went back to the Jeep and settled in to wait. He knew some university types who liked to argue. Especially with women. Five minutes later the short, sinewy Frenchman came out of the building, carrying a case that he put in the front passenger seat. He muttered something in French and fishtailed out of the parking lot.

One down.

A few minutes later the woman came out. Gummer recognized her immediately. *Rachel!* What was she doing here, anyway? She'd done something to piss off the little Frenchman, and Lord knows, if anyone could piss a man off, it was Rachel. Especially a short guy. He watched her drive away.

Gummer warned himself about being careless. He should have spotted Rachel's ratty old Volvo in the parking lot. Rachel. He sighed. Maybe he wasn't meant to have an easy life.

He lightened up—maybe he was being too hard on himself. After all, not even Mr. Memory could keep track of all the ratty old Volvos in the university parking lot.

He went back into the building and listened at Phillipe's lab door. Nothing. Using a lock pick, he was inside the door in less than two minutes. Three minutes later he had Dr. Moody's notebooks, six of them.

Dr. Moody's Homemade DNA

AT LLOYD'S, JEN GRILLED burgers beside a rough, boulder-strewn stretch of river. Rainey, Jimmy, Ruth and Lloyd sat on logs around the fire eating and drinking heartily, trying to forget the horrors of the day.

The June sun sets late, and it was the hour before dusk becomes true night. They were sitting quietly by the fire now—Jimmy had just fallen asleep with his head on Jen's lap—when Rachel's Volvo came to an abrupt stop in front of the café. Rainey was up and on his way to the car before she was out the door.

Rachel saw him coming, vaguely backlit by the fire, and she picked up her pace. They met beside the café.

"We've got to talk," was all Rachel said, buttoning her sweater bottom button to second buttonhole. The ball of hair on top of her head had somehow come undone and she had to keep pulling her hair back and out of her face. She pulled a corner of her blouse out from under her sweater and cleaned her thick glasses. She turned away from Rainey squinting now, trying to make out the faces around the fire. "Jen should hear this," Rachel said. "No one else."

Sizing up the situation, Ruth crisply instructed Lloyd to carry Jimmy to cabin six and leave these people in peace.

As soon as she was settled on a log, Rachel started in. "I dropped off the petri dishes at Phillipe's. That's Phillipe Renard, the graduate student who helped Dr. Moody—"

Rainey interrupted, kindly, "Who's Dr. Moody?"

"Sorry. He's the professor who died at the Sentry pool, the one they blamed on the grizzly, Woolly Bugger."

"Okay."

"Here's the thing: Dr. Moody was doing research on thermophilic organisms. They're single-cell heat-loving bacteria, also called thermophiles, that live in the hot springs. They colonize in bacterial mats." Rachel raised her hands. "I know. I know. I'm getting off the track. I have good reason, though." She shifted to face them. "That's the culture that was in your petri dishes—the little thing in each dish, looks like a mole, it's millions of thermophilic organisms loosely clustered in a mat. The thermophilic organisms in each hot spring are unique. Phillipe recognized the stuff as soon as he put it under the microscope. He takes one look and he goes crazy. I mean, off the wall—"

"Why?"

Rachel hesitated, looking at the hair in her hand again, her mind actually registering for the first time that her hair had come undone. "He's been told the Sentry was shut down. Closed. But your thermophiles have been superheated, which means they're doing experiments." She tied her hair back in a ponytail.

"I don't understand."

"He's been following up Dr. Moody's work. To hear him tell it, it's his work. The point is, he's dying to get back up to the Sentry. But every time he asks, they tell him it's closed. There's no way he can go up there. No way. Mitchell, an assistant superintendent, told him that the American Science Foundation biologists were just going to make a report, tie up loose ends and leave. Formalities." She sighed. "Well, here I show up with superheated thermophile mats from the Sentry. Then I tell him that scientists have been working in there for months. I had to tell him I saw them packing out samples yesterday."

"And he started screaming?"

"He hit the ceiling. Scared the bejesus out of me." She hesitated. "Phillipe's brilliant, but he's—I dunno—what you'd call a prima donna. I remember the time he phoned Jonas Salk and got pissed off when the guy didn't call him back. He thinks he's going to win the Nobel Prize for finishing Dr. Moody's work. The idea of those scientists, the idea he'd been lied to—he just came unglued."

Rainey knew better than to guess at how serious this was. He'd seen Rachel walk out of a raging forest fire, no problem. He'd also seen her come undone when she called home and her babysitter didn't answer the phone. "There's more, isn't there?" "I'm at the worst part. The yelling was bad. But then he explained that now, tonight, he was going to tell the press how the park service has been lying about the bear management closure, that they closed down a section of the park to do secret experiments. He says the thermophile samples prove this. When I tried to argue, he stormed out with the petri dishes. When Jesse reads that story in the paper—hell, it's just what I was afraid of. I give you two days, max, before he ties you to the dishes." She massaged the bridge of her nose. "I'm sorry. I get on your case about being careful, then turn around and screw up the whole deal."

"You also found out exactly what he wanted to know," Jen noted.

"You don't get it," Rachel said, terse. "If you fall in a well, you can't help but find out how deep it is."

"You'd be surprised," Jen shot back, a cop on a hard case again.

Rainey looked downriver. He considered backing Rachel off. Not yet. So far Jen didn't need anyone's help. Rainey warmed his hands over the fire. "Can you tell us more about Phillipe?" he asked Rachel.

"Phillipe? He's about as French as fancy champagne. And vain. Vain as a peacock. A few years ago he student-taught a course I gave at MSU. He was the best I've ever seen. I went to him tonight because if you're willing to polish that ego, he's always been smart and reliable. When Phillipe asked what was going on at the Sentry, I didn't know why—I just told him what I'd seen, what little I'd picked up...am I rambling?"

"No," Rainey answered.

"Well, it's been an awful day. Truthfully, even on good days I lose track of what I'm saying." Rachel tried a smile. Her eyes, though, were tearing.

———

AFTER LINING UP THE first trophy hunt, Jesse took a break to visit the widow, Terry Hadley. She was the one woman he slept with on a semi-regular basis. Today their lovemaking had ended prematurely. Jesse took it personally, and he snuck out while Terry was in the bathroom. At the car he started thinking—again—about Rainey, and he couldn't shake the bad feeling. It was happening more often. Like a mind tic.

Soon after Jesse got back to the ranch, Gummer arrived with Moody's notebooks. They were a meticulous record of Moody's work, and the sheriff started reading, working on a notion. Everything was coming together when his mind shifted back to his meeting with Rainey—the guy was like a hemorrhoid, an irritating, maddening itch that you couldn't scratch—and Jesse started in on himself, revisiting his mistakes, lingering on shameful moments. Before long he was thinking about what he must have done to cause his dad to abandon him, nine years old, at the Las Vegas Downtowner Motel. He felt a little twitch under his left eye.

Jesse knew from experience what was coming. From here on, at unexpected times—especially when he felt good—he'd worry about Rainey. His weak spot. His Achilles' heel. How Rainey had beat him, tied his hands. How the man could humiliate him, undermine his authority. Anytime. And, inexplicably, any good feeling would give way to depression. And then he'd go to work on himself, finding fault. Painful, little things. And his twitching cheek would get worse until his eye blinked like a souped-up turn signal.

Why, once it started, did he always end up wallowing in this stew of self-pity and gloom? He didn't know. All he knew for sure was that once he got going, he came down on himself like a pile driver. He'd read enough psychology to guess it had something to do with his dad. When he figured that out, he let it drop.

He'd learned this the hard way: there was no way to stop it—no fucking way—unless he started drinking...or, and this had to be done just right, *unless he paid the sonofabitch back.* And he couldn't drink. That was rule number one. Okay. Fine. Jesse touched his twitching cheek. He'd have to wear sunglasses inside...he hated that...Jesse flashed on a Bombay Blue Sapphire gin martini, extra dry...no...he had to turn the screws on Rainey. Carefully. Just enough to get his macho deal going. Lean on him, maybe he'd make a mistake. His Florida detective had a line on Mary, the bitch who ratted him out to Rainey. Any day now his detective would brace her. And, one way or another, he'd bring back a new deposition. And then his own hands would be free. And then—payback—he felt better.

He went back to Moody's notebooks. RNA, DNA. The stuff was like a fingerprint, only better. It was a tiny little blueprint of a person, or an animal. Jesse's tic stilled.

———

THE NIGHT HAD GROWN darker, and the air, crisp. They sat beside their fire, thinking private thoughts. "Just what was Moody doing up there?" Rainey eventually asked.

Rachel was brooding. Upset about the mess she'd made, and then she was remembering Rainey during his problems with Jesse, which, in turn, led her to depressing self-recriminations. It took her a moment to realize that he was asking her a question.

She glanced at him—he was frowning now, puzzling over something—and Rachel took some measure of comfort from knowing that he was so very able. Maybe when you were in trouble often, you learned how to unscramble it, how to read the twisted-up tea leaves. The least she could do was teach him the science, get him going. "Give me a second, I'll walk you through it."

Rachel set her wine glass down on a rock. "You have to understand that Ray Moody had carved out a niche for himself. His area was microbial life in extreme environments, and he'd become the expert on certain thermophilic organisms. At the Sentry he was studying unknown microbial properties found in some of these unusual thermophiles. According to Phillipe, he was onto something big. He was superheating the Sentry thermophiles, causing them to reproduce at a phenomenal rate. He found significant quantities of new, unusually stable proteins among the superheated thermophiles. These are super-stable proteins we've never seen before. You with me?"

"Back up a little."

She understood what he was asking. "Here's the guts of it. DNA makes RNA. RNA is the template for protein. These new proteins last longer, are more efficient, and survive at higher temperatures than normal proteins. Moody's goal was to find the new DNA that encodes the genes for these unusually stable proteins and clone them."

"To any particular end?"

"They have all kinds of applications—genetic, industrial, medical, and, of course, in biotechnology. We've already seen how the biotech revolution benefitted from the discovery of heat-resistant enzymes. These enzymes are built from super-stable proteins."

"Sorry, but how, specifically, have we seen that?"

She almost smiled—his questions, the way he thought, brought back so many memories. "Okay. You've probably never heard of the heat-resistant enzymes produced by the hot springs bacterium, Thermus aquaticus. But one of them, a DNA polymerase called Taq, is now used in medical diagnosis and forensics, especially DNA fingerprinting. And it's a three-hundred-million-dollar industry. I'm not kidding. New super-stable proteins are being tested for cleaning up oil spills, treating HIV, improving foods, even recreating enzymes to do the work within a cell more efficiently. The potential is virtually unlimited."

Rainey was throwing pebbles into the fire. He looked over at Rachel. "How do you superheat thermophiles?"

"Superheating is the process of quickly raising temperatures artificially. In the lab, it can be done many ways, such as in an oil bath, or through chemical reaction."

"And what happens then?"

She wrapped her sweater more tightly around her. "You have to remember that thermophilic organisms are a life-form unique to the thermal pools. They thrive in harsh conditions—not only are the temperatures often over a hundred and fifty degrees, but the pH is frequently very low, so these pools can be very acidic."

"Like the Alien, they can live in boiling acid?" Jen asked, skeptical.

Rachel softened; at least Jen wasn't shy. "That's closer than you'd think. They have cell structures that won't denature— that means the basic properties of the cells don't change except at extremely high temperatures." Rachel fell into a teacher's easy cadence. "And the Sentry thermophiles are unlike any other. At a hundred and sixty to a hundred seventy-five degrees the Sentry thermophiles live in a steady, dormant state. There's very little reproduction. Normally, the pool never gets much hotter than that. Most hot springs are self-contained ecosystems. They vent—go off—

in the molten layer of the earth's crust. In a pool like the Sentry they've probably been in this steady, dormant state for hundreds, possibly thousands, of years. By superheating the thermophiles as high as a hundred and ninety-five degrees, Moody was using heat to activate the cells and induce reproduction. In as many as five percent of these new thermophiles, he found these new super-stable proteins. I read his first three articles. They set the stage. He was on his way to publishing a fourth, then a fifth, conclusive article when he died. Phillipe's been putting together the pieces from his notes and now he's so into it, he thinks they're his ideas."

Preoccupied and frowning like a troll, Rainey looked up from the fire. "Jesse knew Cockeye," he said. "Cockeye had the petri dishes. But why was Jesse interested in Dr. Moody's work?"

"I don't know." Rachel sighed. She pointed out a great gray owl perched in a tree behind cabin six, aware she was angry—with Jen, with herself. Between them, they'd drawn Rainey back into his ever-escalating troubles with the sheriff.

Jen watched Rachel. "Let's find this Phillipe," she suggested.

"He'll be at Lester's...don't you think?" Rachel asked. Anticipating Jen's next question, she volunteered, "Lester's a friend of Rainey's, writes for the *Chronicle*."

Rainey was already at the payphone.

JESSE HAD THAT LOOK—the one Gummer called his *if-there's-a-God,-he's-in-my-pocket* special. The sheriff was on the phone with the boss at Trophy Outfitting, telling him if he didn't like Bodine, maybe he'd like facing a jury on his hunting accident. Moody's notebooks were open on his desk.

The sheriff had called, worked up about something. So Gummer came back and waited, he knew better than to rush Jesse. "Did I hear sixty thousand dollars?" Gummer asked when Jesse hung up.

"Listen, Gummer. The world's full a rich people got no more sense than a wood tick."

"I'm with you there."

The sheriff joined Gummer at his sunken bar. "Now, my boy, listen carefully—all this money coming in starts a man percolating.

Gets him itching to fish the big pond, so to speak." Jesse wore the expectant smile of a faith healer, watching his shill hobble painfully to the stage. "Gummer, take this leap with me. Suppose, just suppose, that we could put the profits from the trophy hunts into our own horn processing plant—you heard me right—the first horn processing plant in this entire country?"

Impossible.

"I know what you're thinking," Jesse said. "Now, suppose I could get a processing secret? Say, a hundred K, and a piece of the action, for the genuine, unobtainable article."

"No way—"

"Suppose, just suppose, that Mr. Lew Chan would be our partner?"

Gummer didn't respond. Chan was one of the biggest buyers in the Rocky Mountain West. Why would he want a partner?

"The man's in some kind of trouble. What I did, Gumby, I told him we could supply five thousand pounds of velvet antler a year. To start."

Gummer swallowed hard. Last year, Jesse's *guides* had poached maybe twenty velvet racks. Say twenty pounds a rack. That was four hundred pounds, max.

"You're confused. How can we possibly supply five thousand pounds, you rightly ask? And if we can't—why should you and I make this very substantial investment?" Jesse raised a hand. "I want you to try and wrap your young, double-jointed mind around a concept here. You remember that movie where they found this old DNA, used it to make dinosaurs?"

Gummer nodded.

"Okay, I've been doing some reading. DNA—that's what Doc Moody was cooking up, son, new kinds of DNA." He paused. "Now here's the point—it's your DNA writes the book of life. These DNA determine everything from the color of your eyes to the hang of your ass. Everything, Gummer. We together here?"

"Yes, sir." Gummer sat up straight, focused. "If—"

"Easy there, son. I want you to chew on this: whatever Moody cooked up in that Sentry pool, I've got a hunch—a hunch, mind you—that whatever else they do, these superheated thermoditties might just be some sort of high octane fertilizer for elk antlers." He lowered his voice. "Think about it. Something's causing those elk to grow huge racks at the wrong time of year. We know that near the Sentry, the velvet came early. We're sure of three super elk in that little bitty area. And it's only June...and Gummer, we haven't even started looking. That corner of the park is closed. There's nothing else going on up there. We still together, son?"

Gummer could feel himself heating up. He wouldn't have thought of this in a million years.

"Okay...say I'm right. You lace Moody's overcooked invisible seaweed in the food trough, your bulls are gonna need neck braces to walk around. These North-quad bulls have fifty-pound racks. Processed, that could be ten thousand dollars per rack." Jesse gave Gummer time to run the numbers, then went on, "What if we were to farm these king-sized moose-elk?"

Try taking slow breaths, Gummer thought. It was hard; his mind was racing like a slot machine.

"Say we run a couple hundred on our own elk farm. I have my eye on a place in Idaho. That's right. Picture two hundred of those fifty-pound racks at ten grand per set. That's two million dollars... and it's just the beginning. Hell, son, why poach 'em when we can grow 'em and process 'em ourselves—bigger, better, and one hundred percent legal?"

Gummer could hear his own heart. That's why the petri dishes were so darned important. Jesse'd been working this from the get go.

The sheriff climbed out of his sunken bar area. "At this moment my theory isn't worth the spittle dripping down your greedy chin—I'm just cutting loose with a vision of riches." He picked up one of Moody's notebooks. "That's why you need to go back up to the Sentry Pool—so we can find out exactly what's going on up there."

"Antler fertilizer...those scientists, I don't think they're even interested in antlers."

"Good thinking. I doubt the National Park Service would shutdown a large area of a national park to develop product for the aphrodisiac market. And I guarantee you they're not shutdown so some hunter with the brains God gave a halibut can pay through the nose for a crack at an illegal trophy mount. We got a right to know what those East Coast hotshots are cooking up in our own backyard. I ask the park people, I get nowhere. Cockeye's biologist is waiting. So let's see what's in those petri dishes."

"I'm on it...like glue."

"Glue...yeah." Jesse squeezed Gummer's arm. "Our new business. It depends on you." He showed him to the door.

Super elk. A processing secret. This is why he'd chosen Jesse. Dinosaurs? He had to smile.

The Frame

JEN LIKED LESTER'S CABIN right away. It was a small outbuilding on an old ranch with two rooms: a large living room/kitchen and a tiny bedroom. Newspapers were stacked in piles. The only furniture was an antique pine table, four pine chairs, a well-worn sofa, and a large English leather chair with an ottoman. The English chair sat in front of the fireplace. On the old pine table was an ashtray full of cigarette butts and the metal petri dish container.

Lester's sweater-vest and baggy Dockers couldn't hide the pear-shaped body of a former pastry chef. He bowed with surprising grace. "Rachel, as lovely as ever." And turning to Jen, "My dear, I'm easily smitten by the Irish. Forewarned is forearmed." Jen nodded, thinking it possible that Lester was one of those rare Irishmen whose sexual bravado was just plain winning. Lester showed them in.

Phillipe was hunched over the pine table, smoking a Camel, drinking whiskey, and reading *The New York Times*. He was a slight, handsome man with a neatly trimmed mustache. The Frenchman didn't look up when they came in.

"I asked you to wait just days," Rachel said, glaring at him. "I explained that my friends needed time. But no, you just had to tell the *Chronicle*. Couldn't you consider how it might hurt other people? As you get older, you get even more selfish, self-centered and insufferable...if that's possible." Jen noticed that when Rachel got angry, the volume came down, and she chose her words more carefully. By "self-centered," she'd hit her stride.

Phillipe brushed her off with a wave of his hand. "Poof. For your friends'...*inconvenience*...I am sorry. But this, as you say, is not my problem. If I wait—if I do nothing—for me, the consequence, it is grave." He winked at Jen, who looked confused. "King-sized," he offered.

"Knock it off," Rachel said.

He put down the paper. "Rachel, you are forever missing the point. This work is my life. To let them steal it...agh..."

"It's Dr. Moody's work," Rachel pointed out. "He won't care if you wait a week. For you to make these accusations now is reckless, unbecoming conceit."

Phillipe blew a perfect smoke ring. "I will speak frankly. In the work I did with Dr. Moody, I was the engine—the driving force, if you will. Dr. Moody, he was, more or less, a nice old man who owned the ignition keys."

Rachel picked up his drink and pitched it in his lap. Rainey placed a hand on the Frenchman's shoulder; Phillipe was locked down.

Jen nodded approvingly, liking how Rachel could fight. She knew how to fight, too, though when she got angry, she was ruder, stormier, and less articulate than Rachel.

Rachel's glare was still menacing. "The Sentry's dormant, right?"

"As even you must know, she vents underground," Phillipe snapped, after catching a towel from Lester. "This has been true for two hundred years, minimum."

"So you were taking samples from the pool, then heating these Sentry thermophiles on site?"

"Évidemment. Of course."

"How hot?"

"We go to one ninety-five. Two hundred, a few times. I would have gone higher, but Doctor Moody, he saw that the thermophiles, they become unreliable over one ninety-five, and, as such—"

"Unreliable?"

"Yes, yes. You see, some, they make the tiny explosion and they die."

"What?" Rachel asked.

"I explain this, then you go. Merde." He raised a hand, not another word.

"Okay. Some of these Sentry thermophiles, they have the super-stable proteins. When they are superheated, the normal proteins, they denature." He turned to Jen, who was confused. "They come unglued, the protein unfolds and their amino acid chain turns into the one long piece of spaghetti. Yes?" He nodded, mostly to himself. "But these super-stable proteins, they have the high-energy bonds. Instead of denaturing like normal proteins, when they are heated past their capacities, these bonds, they are ripped apart, releasing energy. In other words—" He spread raised fingers. "Poof." Phillipe stood, finished.

"Are you kidding?" Jen asked.

"Poof," Phillipe repeated scornfully, fingers raised. "We knew this before this miserable bear, she kills Dr. Moody."

"She?" Jen asked Rachel.

"He." Rachel confirmed, plainly annoying Phillipe.

"Imbeciles. He? She? Does this matter? Mon Dieu, I am not *foucking* this bear."

"Good point," Rachel acknowledged.

"Took a man to say it," Jen added.

From the kitchen Lester shot Rainey a look—who is this woman? Rainey was working on keeping a straight face when Lester tilted his head toward the door. Rainey followed him outside.

"You in trouble?" Lester asked.

"I think Jesse's going to frame me. Even without your story he's got enough to take one of his potshots. With your story he'll have me for taking the petri dishes—withholding evidence, obstruction..." Rainey saw at a glance that Lester understood. "I need three or four days."

"To delay a story, I need a good reason—besides friendship."

"I'll go up to the Sentry. Everything leads to that pool. I'll give you whatever I find. I'd like three days."

"Forty-eight hours."

Rainey considered several ploys, but found them all quixotic; once decided Lester was like a rock. He nodded agreement.

"One thing laddie. Could you see your way to fixin' me up with the Irish beauty in your absence?"

"Not likely."

"Ah hah. I see." Lester stepped back, appraising his friend. "It's not my business, but if Rachel would have me, I'd wait on her night and day...tend to her every need." Rainey didn't respond, thinking Lester's rich, pleasing voice—a gift from his Irish grandfather, a local saloonkeeper—resonated like a fine cello. He touched his friend's back, trying to remember if Lester's paternalistic interest in his love life had been so keen before Les lost his wife, then they were inside, where Rachel was inches from Phillipe's face.

"This is not about American women, Phillipe," she was saying. "Just answer the question."

"The American woman—" He held his ground, glowering. "She is loud, bovine, unfit to drive the motor vehicle, and unpleasantly odorless—oui, absolument sans odeur." The Frenchman lit another Camel, which he plainly intended to extinguish on Rachel's body. "I tell the *Chronicle* everything—the park cover-up, the bear closure lie, the secret experiments—everything. Then we see."

Rainey took her arm before Rachel could set Phillipe on fire. "We're late. I'll fill you in as we go." He led her to the door.

At the door, Jen turned. "Uh buddy, I think you want to keep that unpleasantly odorless stuff to yourself." She made a sour face. "No kidding."

———

JESSE WAS DRIVING HIS Range Rover. They were ten minutes from the ranch—maybe less if he pushed it a little—on their way back from a preliminary meeting with Chan on the deal for the processing secret. It had gone well. Chan was in trouble and in a hurry. Gummer had read this early on, and he talked him down on price then skillfully positioned him for closing.

Jesse looked over at the savvier-than-he-seemed enforcement ranger, who was carefully trimming his nails with a clipper he kept on the key ring that was attached to his belt loop with a chain. Jesse wondered if he was thinking about money. He had that singularly blank, kind of dopey expression that Jesse couldn't ever read. He could be working out his share of the deal to four decimal places or worrying about burying a dead gopher. Jesse sighed. Little by little he was seeing why he'd underestimated young Gummer. Suppose, just suppose, Gummer was that rare fox who looked in the mirror and actually thought he saw a dumbass sheep. That would be the best camouflage of all.

Gummer answered the car phone. "Gummer Mosk," he said. He handed the phone to Jesse who sat on a special leather seat that gave him an extra four inches. "Stacy's got your Miami snooper."

"Detective," Jesse corrected. "Put him on, Stace." Jesse replaced the phone and turned on the speaker.

"I found your gal, Jesse. In the Atlantic City slammer, like you said. It's her. I ran the prints."

Jesse grinned, ear to ear. One of the Vegas girls had seen Mary in Atlantic City, two months ago, and she wanted the reward. It had come to him two days ago, walking circles around the bar, that they hadn't checked the prisons. "I'll be right back at ya, Maury." Jesse pushed a button and disconnected. He gleefully banged his fist on the dash.

Jesse couldn't remember the last time he was this happy. Maybe 1978 when he framed, then personally arrested, his dad, Big Jesse. On the day he turned thirty, Little J decided it was time to repay his dad for abandoning him, nine years old, at the Las Vegas Downtowner. It took three years to find the slick bastard then lure him into fronting a real-estate scam. It was strike three. Big Jesse was still doing time. Every year on his birthday, Little Jesse sent his dad a card.

And now this was going to be even better. Jesse adjusted his neckerchief, the orange one with little black stars. He was going seventy-five miles per hour on this winding two-lane highway.

The sheriff swerved abruptly, barely missing a stray dog. Gummer looked up in time to see that Jesse had swerved to the shoulder trying to *hit* the damn dog.

"I like dogs," Gummer muttered, frowning.

"Say what?"

"You're a good driver."

Jesse was mumbling to himself. It sounded like "right as rain."

As THEY DROVE TOWARD Lloyd's, Rainey explained the deal he'd struck with Lester. At the end, he asked Rachel when she was going back in.

"Tomorrow morning," she replied, still irritable.

"Can I tag along?" he asked.

"I'd like to come, too," Jen said.

Rachel stiffened. "I'll be looking for animals, taking samples, then checking on my bear. It's seven, eight miles uphill." What was bothering her? Phillipe? Or maybe she didn't want Jen falling behind, or asking all those questions, or making her worry in bear country.

"Ruth will be happy to take Molly," Rainey said. "Jimmy, too."

"I don't mean to be unkind," Rachel persisted, "but we have precious little time. I think it would be easier if Jen stayed behind."

Jen shot her a hard-ass look she'd picked up at Cook County Jail. "Think again. I'm coming."

"If you come, you keep up or you turn back."

"Do you make all the rules on this deal?"

"If I was making the rules, you'd be staying at the motel," Rachel shot back.

"Lady, unpack the old-boyfriend baggage on someone else."

"And I need your two-bit pop psychology like a hole in the head. And my name isn't *Lady*..." Rachel held up her hands, to stop them both. "We'll start up Elk Creek at first light."

Rainey looked at Rachel. "Suppose you ease up a little—"

"Let it go," Rachel interrupted. "Please."

"Then back off."

"Okay. Fine." The guy was blind, smitten.

Rainey watched the two women, staring out their respective windows. "What exactly are we looking for?" he asked.

"Whatever's causing the unseasonal animal behavior. If it's connected to whatever they're doing at the Sentry."

"Is it?"

"Jesus, how do I know?" Rachel paused. She used to like that he was always so far ahead. Now it irritated her. Maybe that's what Jen was getting at with the old boyfriend crack. Rachel worked to focus. "Okay, I've thought about it. The animals would have to ingest the superheated thermophiles. But how—where—would they do that? They can't possibly drink from a hundred-and-sixty-degree-plus thermal pool." She caught herself unbuttoning and re-buttoning the mismatched button on her sweater. "I need to be up there. I need to know if they're using the bear closure to keep people out...

there's something wrong, and honestly, I'm worried...and I don't know what to do about Phillipe."

"What'd you call him? A reeking cabbage head?" Jen smiled.

"The guy's awful. And my babysitter's mother is going to kill me." And why do I feel frumpy and fat around this woman?

———

RAINEY PARKED THE PICKUP under Lloyd's neon sign. Rachel was in her Volvo and gone before he and Jen reached the path to the cabins.

"You can still change your mind about going," Rainey said.

Jen touched his arm. When he turned, she kissed him. Their kiss lasted longer than she'd intended. "I need a minute alone. Say I meet you in a little bit."

In their cabin, she checked on Jimmy; he was sleeping soundly. She hadn't had enough time with him, and Jen felt guilty. She sat on the bed next to her son—even in sleep, his face was tense—then took a slow breath, hoping to get her bearings.

Okay. Jimmy. Suppose they drove to Chicago, just the two of them? Why not leave tomorrow? Jimmy needed his mom. And she didn't need to go with bear woman into the wilderness. Eight miles uphill? So why was she doing that? Her mind wandered down a sweet winding back road. She caught herself, then focused on the larger question that she hadn't yet answered and had to answer fully: why was she still here?

She was here for Rainey, no doubt. In part, because he was in trouble. Bigger trouble than he'd admit. And he was in trouble, at least in part, because he'd tried to help her. Beyond that—who was she kidding? This was a man she could talk to. This man actually enjoyed who he was. And he didn't seem to be in a hurry. And he wasn't always drawing attention to himself.

Okay, yes, she wanted him, too. And she hadn't felt this way about a man in a long time. She wondered if it was infatuation, fueled, perhaps, by loneliness. She hoped it was something more.

Something else, a totally unexpected feeling, was affecting her. Cockeye, she realized, was part of it. She'd been angry with him, but that was over. And now, she was sadly aware that outside of this tiny cabin, there was no one else in the world that cared why he died. His life would just disappear here, if she let it. And no, that wouldn't do. This was the end of a long story, a story that had once been wildly passionate and deeply felt. As it stood, the ending was part of the last, bad years, disconnected from the rest.

It occurred to her, then, that perhaps most of all she was here for Jimmy. In his short life, there was already a backlog of unfinished business. Left unresolved, the death of his father would go bad, fester. But if they did sort it out, if they insisted that this awful wound heal properly, it was not impossible that Cockeye's death could be the occasion for a new beginning, a starting place that wasn't cluttered with all kinds of junk from Jimmy's confusing past. She stretched out beside him, fingers intertwined beneath her head, realizing that as much as Jimmy needed her now, he needed answers—resolution—even more. Her son deserved a clean slate. That would be worth working for. That would be a lasting gift from father to son.

———

RAINEY PUT HIS GEAR together, then went down to stoke the dying fire. When Jen didn't come out, he knocked softly on the door to her cabin. No answer. Through the tiny window he saw her, fully clothed, sleeping on top of the bed next to Jimmy. It was odd seeing her so still. Awake, she was always moving, animated. And you could pretty much see her mind working—quick, insistent, putting together the complete puzzle from scattered pieces. She turned from her side to her stomach, her arm going over her son's back. He enjoyed just watching her sleep.

That, he knew, was what made Rachel edgy. The way he looked at Jen was, for Rachel, like chalk scraping along a blackboard. Why? It wasn't rational or, he realized, even conscious. Rachel, he reminded himself, relied on her instincts, often unaware of the crosscurrents and complexities underlying her reactions. It helped her think like an animal in the wild, though it made it harder to reason with her when her behavior was inappropriate. In this instance she was out of line. Jen deserved better.

―――――

JESSE'S CHESSBOARD SAT ON the bar. Gummer was working at losing. He likened beating Jesse at chess to taunting a grizzly bear. Their game was interrupted by a chime. Jesse opened the door for old Judge Dirkey.

Dirkey's leathery face could no longer hide a life of excess. Light from Jesse's skylight sparkled off the engraved stallion on the gold buckle that held in the judge's paunch. His maroon suspenders had gold clips. Gummer thought little Judge Dirkeys would make fine hood ornaments.

"Thank you for stopping by, Judge." Jesse waited for the judge to sit at the bar, then he got to the point, "You remember the incident we discussed? Former Chicago police officer got himself burned-up over by the Loomis place?"

Judge Dirkey grunted. Gummer watched. When he was with the judge, he sometimes worried that great wealth would make him fat.

"Jack Loomis saw it all. The car—a black Cadillac, no fooling—leaves the campground, maybe six forty-five. Half-hour later it comes back—no one in it but the ex-policeman, Earl Donahue. Then Jack sees Rainey Jackson, coming up on Earl. Next thing Jack sees, the Caddy's in flames, firebombed."

"Jack swears he saw Rainey there?" Dirkey asked.

"Deputy Hanson got it in writing." Jesse passed the deposition to the judge. Gummer hadn't been told about this. Still, he should have known. Jesse hated that guy, hated him like a vampire hates daylight. He was gonna frame the guy, sure as sunrise.

"Jack Loomis is a respected man," Dirkey said, after reading the deposition. "He says the man was there, that's a start."

"A start?"

Judge Dirkey scowled. "Jack didn't see the man commit a crime."

Jesse skewered an olive, dipped it in a tumbler of Bombay Blue Sapphire gin, then sucked the olive like a lollipop. It was as close as he came to drinking. "Gummer," he said, looking straight at the judge. "Gummer, if I say a mosquito can pull a plow, what do you do?"

"Well, I hitch it up...that's what I do."

———

AT 4:45 A.M. RAINEY knocked on Jen's door. "What time is it?" she called out.

"Quarter to five."

"Shit. Double shit. I'm not ready." She opened the door, sleepy. "I set up a pack for you last night."

"Thanks. I'll wake Jimmy. Give us five minutes."

"Lloyd offered to take Jimmy fishing. Keep him away from Jesse." She resolved something in her mind. "I'll need to talk with him." And after a moment, "Listen, I'm sorry about last night. I just crashed."

He put his hand on the small of her back and lightly kissed her neck, her face, and finally, her lips.

"We're going to be great," she whispered before he turned back to the café.

Five minutes later a barely mobile Jimmy came into the café with his mom. Ruth was behind the counter, coffee was brewing, and pancakes were cooking on Lloyd's griddle. "Jimmy, how'd you like to go into the backcountry with Lloyd—fishing, camping, the works?" she asked.

Jimmy looked at his mother, worried. She took him aside. "You don't have to," she whispered. "We talked about this. We'll get you on a plane and you can stay with my sister. It's up to you."

Jimmy tugged at her sleeve. She knelt. "Can you come for part of the time?"

"I'll try, honey. I'm going to find out what happened to your dad. I think you and I need to know that. It won't be too long, and yes, I'll see you as soon and as often as I can. After we find out what happened to your dad, we'll take as much time together as we want. Which is a ton."

Lloyd set a platter of pancakes in front of Jimmy. Jimmy took it to a table in the corner. Jen sat with him. "I hear he's a great fisherman."

Jimmy didn't respond.

"I'd rather be with you, too, but for now this is the best we can do. It's hard, but I have to do this—for us and for your dad. Honey, my sister would love to have you stay with her. And I know you like her."

Jimmy toed the floor, glanced at Lloyd, then softly said, "I'll fish."

"You okay with Lloyd?"

Jimmy nodded, sullen. As Jen stood, he grabbed her hand. It made her teary. Jen squeezed his hand, kissed the top of his head.

———

MOLLY SLEPT PEACEFULLY IN the backseat of Rachel's Volvo. Her mouth was open, and Rachel could hear her breathing. Molly was a seasoned traveler, at home in the backcountry or in the car seat.

Rachel was always uneasy leaving her daughter. Her lips tightened into a line. This morning, her uneasiness had morphed into acute anxiety. This morning, she woke up wanting Rainey.

Rachel knew that in her life things generally overtook her. It was not her nature to step back and think something over. Rachel lived with it—unaware, often overwhelmed—until she knew just what she'd do. Her best decisions were, as she put it, *the ones that snuck up on her.* For well over a year she'd been able to keep Rainey out of her life, and her thoughts. Until this morning.

If Rainey were a grizzly bear, she'd know just what to do. He'd mate with this female, but to stay too long with one mate is not the way of an old bear. He would seek her out, if she made herself available. The trick, Rachel knew, was to keep him away from other females. Not easy. Still, life would be simpler if Rainey were a bear.

Her face scrunched into a pout. Since she wasn't any good at all at scheming, manipulation or deception, and she didn't have the kind of mind that conceptualized, then solved, difficult problems—such as stealing other women's men; she would have to go about this in her own way. What that would be, she had to say, was, at best, vague.

She marveled at her knack for creating awkward situations. Here she was, taking him into the backcountry with a woman he liked. Even worse, Jen got it. About him. About her. She felt herself growing panicky. When it came to people, she was often at her worst. Men were as mysterious to her as the mountains on the moon. Rachel swerved to avoid a coyote, spilling her coffee on the front seat.

She felt sad, and a little angry with herself. Molly started crying as she turned into Lloyd's parking area. Rachel pulled over. Damn. Jesse was with one of his deputies, poking around cabin eight. She backed up and parked near the kitchen door, out of sight. Ruth came out to take her daughter. Molly stopped crying when she was safely in Ruth's arms. "They've got some kinda warrant for Rainey," Ruth said. "Lloyd snuck 'em down the river trail."

"A warrant? For what?"

"Accessory to I don't know what...he says dizzy old Jack Loomis was watching the road. Hell, nevermind what he says."

"What do I do?"

"They'll cross over at the Willow Park. You know it?"

Rachel nodded.

"You can pick them up where the trail comes to that clearing near the road—in the forest, maybe a hundred yards past the mile marker. I'll take care of Molly, honey. I'll spoil her. You just take care of these people. They need you, more than you know. Now go."

As she drove the river road, Rachel worried about Jesse. In the months after she threw him out, Rainey talked with her regularly about his problems with the sheriff. That is until he told her he was going to burn down Jesse's whiskey cache. What had she said? "That's so crazy. That's macho self-destructive bullshit." And when he did it anyway, they just stopped talking for several months. Still, since the night Rainey was beaten in his cell, she'd loathed Jesse Stinson.

It made her crazy that such a man could be sheriff in a county that bordered Yellowstone Park. It frightened her. Most of all, it made her angry, a rage that washed over her now. She could feel the heat, the redness spreading across her cheeks, down her neck to her chest. He'd hurt Rainey, really hurt him, if he possibly could. She knew she'd do anything she could, even things that scared her, to keep that from happening.

Nature Gone Awry

"YOU RUN INTO JESSE?" Rainey asked Rachel. The sun was throwing pink lines into the dark sky above the Willow Park. He let Lloyd, Jimmy and Jen walk ahead so he could talk to her.

"I got away before he saw me. Ruth filled me in. What's he up to?"

"He's throwing out the biggest net he can. And, as you'd say, pushing my buttons."

A gust of cold wind sent her arms across her chest.

"You remember Mary, the ex-madame from Vegas who told me about Jesse?"

"I do."

"Six weeks ago she called, really scared. She said Jesse was looking for her. Mary's moved, but Jesse found a friend of hers. I can't reach her. If he got to her..."

Rachel knew the whole story. Mary's deposition was the only thing holding Jesse back. "We gotta figure this, get ahead of him."

"Can you get us to the Sentry without anyone knowing we're up there?" He noticed Jen stepping off the trail ahead of them.

Rainey moved up to help Jen readjust her pack. Rachel watched him whisper something in Jen's ear.

"I'll try," she replied, into the chilling wind.

———

AN HOUR LATER THEY were at the trailhead. The sun was up now, slowly warming the sage-scented air, and it was easy walking through the open, U-shaped valley. The trail more or less followed Elk Creek, starting at sixty-seven hundred feet, then winding up into the rising mountains. Rachel set a brisk pace, trying to put them as far as possible from the highway. The grass was still damp and the scent of sage hung in the cool morning air. When the clouds covered the sun, the greens of the meadows were almost gray.

About half a mile in, the top of Blackstone Butte was suddenly visible—its stand of Douglas fir sticking straight up from its flat top, like a punk haircut. As they hiked further, the butte showed itself, little by little, beyond the hills. Its top had not suggested the bulk of this fat, worn-down mountain. On the south and east faces game trails zigzagged up the treeless, eroded hillsides. In front of them the Gallatin Mountains nearly touched the clouds, a no-nonsense reminder of the climb ahead.

Two hundred yards further the creek veered to the left, and Rachel, hearing something, signaled a stop. She led them to cover then worked her way forward. From behind a tree she saw three men. One of them had what looked like a small motel refrigerator on his back. It was connected by a cord to a rod he was sticking in the creek. Another man was barking orders. She recognized that gruff, irritated voice: it went with Rob Bolton of the U.S. Fish and Wildlife Service. These men were shocking then counting the stunned fish that rose to the surface of Elk Creek. Rob, a stocky one-armed man, ran the crew. Rachel worked her way up and around the men. When she was well above them, she started back down the trail. "'Lo Rob."

He scratched his head. "Where there's a berserk bear—"

"Right," she interrupted, offering a smile. Rachel liked Rob. He was outspoken and proudly all-Montana. "How'd you get in here anyway?"

"They said we could count rainbows up to a mile in. That is until maybe an hour ago when that assistant superintendent, Mitchell, sent some guy to tell us to be out by nine."

"Did he say why?"

"The usual—that's the way it is. But I tell you this: something's not right up here. First off, and this is last night, you got these East Coast scientists helicoptered out. They said there was a grizz started a fire at the patrol cabin." He frowned. "Now chew on this—down below, today, we counted three brownies in full spawning colors, a thing I've never seen in June. Try to make sense out of that."

Rachel rubbed the back of her neck, where the tension was settling into little knots. A feeling was coming on, one she'd felt here, in her study area, only once before. It was the day she'd seen Woolly Bugger on Dr. Moody's carcass. Today, like that day, she felt dread. She changed the subject. "You think a grizzly started the fire?"

"Those cheechakos? My guess, it was a black bear that scared 'em."

She hoped so.

"And you know what? I bet the rude gangly one comes from New Jersey." He cracked the knuckles of his good hand with his thumb. "I'd bet a six-pack on that."

Rachel smiled, then checked her watch. "It's eight thirty already. I'm out of here."

"Yeah, we better shake it." Rob hailed his shocker.

Rachel waved and walked down the trail, glad that people like Rob counted, and cared about, fish.

They had to hide for ten minutes before Rob and his crew walked past them, on their way out. Then, keeping a steady pace, they continued up the grade. Somewhere in the second mile they curved behind Blackstone Butte. Jen said the stand of fir on the butte's top looked like a recent scab covering an ancient, badly-healed wound. Rachel explained that the layers of scar tissue were actually volcanic ash that had fused together over two million years ago.

They followed the creek into an open meadow. Elk tracks and elk droppings were everywhere. The creek was high but clear, good trout water. Rainey told Rachel about the spawning brown he'd seen.

"Rob's seen three spawning browns," she added, preoccupied.

"Three? Three's too many."

"Yeah. Something's triggering those hormones early. Same deal as the bear." Rachel picked up the pace, plainly troubled.

"I don't know the first thing about animals," Jen offered, keeping up easily. "What I know about hormones, though, is that they're pretty much unstoppable. An angry transvestite explained that to me."

Rainey's expression brought back Rachel's buried memories of uninhibited lovemaking. She wondered if—no, *when*—Jen would enjoy that. Agh. She was losing it, like a jealous teenager. What was wrong with her? Whatever. At the right time, she'd talk to Rainey. In the meantime, she'd try not to pick a fight with this unreasonably upbeat woman.

She turned to Jen, making an effort. "It's the same sort of thing for a fish. Your hormones say spawn, you're on your way—even if the stream's frozen." But why would that happen? She slowed. "Maybe there's an easy explanation for these hormonal abnormalities." Rachel willed herself not to start obsessing about the alternatives.

Ten minutes later, on the north side of the creek, they moved into the fingers of timber coming down off the backside of Blackstone Butte. At this altitude the soil held water and trees could grow. They stopped to rest at a shaded bend. Rainey helped Jen off with her pack. When they sat on a boulder, Jen leaned against his shoulder.

The dam holding back Rachel's memories of lovemaking with Rainey burst without warning. She remembered a fervent moment, not far from this shady bend.

———

BEYOND THE BUTTE THE creek wound up through a low-lying stretch of meadow. The trail angled toward the creek, and coming onto high ground, Rachel could see where a dead pine had fallen into the water creating a small logjam. Something caught her eye. The hind leg of an animal was sticking out of the jam. She signaled the others to wait.

Rachel waded into the stream. She grabbed the protruding hind leg and pulled slowly. Another limb came into view. An elk calf. She backed onto the bank, dragging the dead calf through the stream.

The calf was less than a month old, she judged, looking at its waterlogged body curled up on the bank.

She walked slowly around the sour-smelling carcass. Instead of front legs, there were two nubs. Coyote could have bitten them off, she supposed. She ran her hand over one of the nubs. Odd. There was skin and hair all the way across.

Rachel took a Buck knife from her pack and cut a flap horizontally across the chest of the calf. With the ease of a surgeon, she started pulling the chest skin towards the nubs looking for wounds, bruises on the muscles, any evidence at all of animal predation. Finding none, she pulled the skin over the nub where shoulder and front leg normally connect. The bone was smooth. Where the front leg should be, there was no bone growth at all.

She examined the other nub, certain now that this was some sort of mutagenic birth defect. She'd seen aborted fetuses but never anything like this. Inbreeding is very uncommon in elk, she reasoned, so it pretty much had to be something else. Her anxiety came on again, wave after wave.

Rachel took a garbage bag and a rope out of her pack. Rainey and Jen joined her. Together, they put the carcass in the bag, bound the hind legs, then tied off the bag. Rachel explained what she'd found, then she told them about the deformed bear cub.

"This stuff happened at Hiroshima," Jen muttered. "Or—I dunno—Chernobyl."

"It scares me," Rachel admitted, grim-faced, then she explained how they'd hang the calf, take it out with them tomorrow. Rainey, following her instructions, climbed a tree with the rope and threw it over a large, high branch. Rachel pulled, lifting the carcass into the air. When it was about twenty feet up, she secured the rope to a branch. When she was done, she led them toward the Sentry, aware now that here, in this place that she studied and loved, nature had quite possibly gone awry. Wildlife—her charge—were confusing the seasons, their young inexplicably deformed.

———

GUMMER LOVED MORNINGS. HE thought it was because, at the circus, he used to spend mornings with his dad. They'd get up early and prowl around. Sometimes he'd have ice cream for breakfast.

Since those days, he made an effort to accomplish something, first thing. This morning, he'd gone to his Jeep, looking for a contour map of the Elk Creek drainage. What he saw, it darn near broke his heart. The windshield was in tiny pieces all over the dash, and that jackass Bodine had planted three nasty wads of chaw on the front seat. Just to let him know who did it.

The Jeep dealer met Gummer at ten thirty to set him up with a loaner. Gummer chose a new blue Cherokee, though he had a hard time paying attention. He was mulling over going up to Bodine's hiding place, the cache where he kept his poaching gear. Say he left a little something for him. Payback. That would slow him down. He drove to the North Yellowstone ranger station, his plans for the day shot.

———

RAINEY TOOK THE LEAD, hoping the women would talk. Unlikely. Still, he needed time alone, time to batten down for the storm that was raging around him, time to understand the unexpected feelings fomenting inside.

As he'd grown older, Rainey had come to believe that real change was earned. And mysterious. He tried to make good, thoughtful decisions, but he was wary when it came to predicting the impact of those decisions. So he was pleased when sometime later, bits and pieces would come into focus. Two years ago, before Jesse, he saw how he was coming to identify and sort out day-to-day problems with quiet confidence, how life choices were less convoluted, not so abstract or angry. At thirty-nine he was a pretty good detective, and he was getting better with Rachel. Then came Jesse, and he wasn't ready to give Rachel what she wanted. So she threw him out, and he went to war with the sheriff. Over many months he fought Jesse to a slippery stalemate. When he could finally go back to his life, he didn't know what he wanted anymore.

And now, once again, Jesse had him in his crosshairs. This time a draw with Jesse wouldn't do. He knew that much. Rainey stepped off the trail, waited for Jen. He took her hand, warmed by her smile.

The Secret of the Sentry Hot Spring

RACHEL, RAINEY—AND THEN Jen—worked their way into a stand of spruce and subalpine fir. They'd come almost four miles, and now they were moving more quickly, beginning to find a rhythm.

They crossed Elk Creek and turned west. At this altitude there were trees on both sides of the drainage. They could see where the creek twisted north toward the rim and narrowed to a sliver in the mountainside. Rachel led them around a bend and then she climbed a gentle rise.

Ten minutes later they passed a tributary of the larger mountain stream. Rachel took out her binoculars and trained them on a cliff beyond the little creek. In the volcanic rock on the cliff face she easily found the flattened depression where golden eagles had nested. She told them how she'd been watching these eagles since early May and had been pleased to see a newborn eaglet several weeks ago. The cliff face was an ideal nesting spot, large enough and well protected from predators. Rachel focused on the huge nest, over four feet in diameter. There was something inside—maybe a marmot or a ground squirrel for the young bird.

Without a word she was off, reaching the base of the cliff then scrambling up the cliff face. She carefully approached the nest. At the nest Rachel gently lifted the animal and wrapped it in her neckerchief.

When she came off the cliff face, they were waiting for her. "The nest is abandoned," Rachel said, then she unwrapped the neckerchief.

"Oh God," Jen said. "What is that?"

It looked like a fat, wrinkled, brown sausage with a beak.

"This is the eaglet I was telling you about. As best I can tell, it was born with no wing structure whatsoever."

"What does it mean?" Jen asked.

"I'm not sure. If these mutated babies are more than a strange fluke, we could have a horrific problem." She shook her head. "Suppose unseasonal behavior is just part of it. Suppose the next generation has birth defects, and they're dying...I need to walk."

———

THEY MADE THEIR WAY northeast, toward Elk Creek and the Sentry Hot Spring. The sun had broken through the clouds. Nevertheless, part of their hike was through trees so dense that the light barely shone through. Rachel signaled a stop when they reached a wide, flat wooded area. It was a timbered park. The trees spread out to the east, an oval sea of green held back by a ridge on the far side of the creek. To the north the mountains were steep, stark and intimidating. By contrast, the pine forest beside them was open and airy. There was little vegetation on the ground, so walking was easy, and long shafts of light broke through the treetops in ethereal, crisscrossing columns.

"Kind of place you might see—I dunno—elves or fairies sprinkling fairy dust," Jen pointed toward a cylindrical beam of sunlight coming through the pine boughs. "Riding down one of those shafts of light."

Rachel watched Rainey check out a sunbeam and muttered, "smitten."

They walked on, silenced by the quiet of the forest.

Rachel selected a game trail that wound into the timber. In ten minutes they were on the ridge.

Rainey was pointing at something Jen couldn't see.

"There's a fire at the patrol cabin," Rachel explained.

Jen tensed up, every muscle. "This forest is on fire and I don't know it?" Her question rang through the trees. "A forest fire? Perfect."

"You're well clear of it," Rachel said, barely polite. Jen heard her Gentile grandmother scolding her, saying worrying was a "deep-dyed waste of time."

She turned to the billowing smoke. The fight coming with Rachel, it was no big thing. It might even help. This fire, though, scared her almost as much as facing a bear.

———

THE SENTRY HOT SPRING was between their perch on the ridge and the distant fire, so they made their way southeast. Coming off the ridge, Rachel showed them a small red opening set in the hill. She directed her flashlight at a carving on the cave wall, an elk with an exaggerated rack of palmated antlers. "This petroglyph was done thousands of years ago," she explained. "People theorize that these elk were worshipped. They were thought to be sentries for the spring, guarding it for the spirits. Thus, the name."

"The Sentry Spring," Jen said, plainly pleased.

Rachel watched her—so animated and happy—and out of the blue, she was envious. She pushed on, "Dr. Moody found a partial palm from an antler imbedded in a bank near the spring. He had it dated and that moose-like palm was over three thousand years old. It had been decorated. He believed the Native Americans carved them then used them ceremonially."

When they reached the path to the Sentry Spring, their pace slowed, as if by unspoken agreement that from this point on they wouldn't miss anything. The forest was open here, and appealing, though as of yet there was no sign of the spring. Near the meadow, however, the sulphur smell was unmistakable.

The clearing was a surprise. One moment the forest was everywhere, then the trees simply disappeared, revealing a hidden meadow, several hundred yards across. And then, just as quickly, the forest took over again. The meadow was sprinkled with wildflowers, and so well-hidden by the trees that it suggested a secret clearing in Sherwood Forest. At the far edge of the meadow there was a large framed canvas cook tent. Beyond the tent, partially hidden in the woods, was a small cabin.

The only sign of the spring was steam. Wisps drifted skyward in no discernable pattern. As they got closer, the soil underfoot turned light gray. Then, suddenly, they were on top of the Sentry. The area containing the spring was a crater, almost thirty yards in diameter. At the edge of the crater the meadow stopped, giving way to a descending geyserite surface of white calcified rock. At the center of the crater was the pool, perhaps twenty yards across. The three of them looked into the deep pool. Steam rose from the surface, forming little clouds that seemed to hover over the stark white rock surrounding it. The pool was clear and blue, calm as the meadow in the timbered park.

"If one of those top-heavy elk comes thundering out of the trees, I'd swear we were in some kind of freaked-out beer commercial," Jen mused. When she turned, her companions were gone.

Jen spotted them entering the walled tent. They were inside by the time she caught up with them. The tent was clearly a laboratory. There were portable tables with Bunsen burners; racks of test tubes and vials—most of them marked with varying strengths of a solution, something called exothermic nitrogenous compound or ENT; microscopes; notebooks, discs, and computers; several heavy metal containers; smaller thermos-like containers that held petri dishes; and at least sixty petri dishes, neatly ordered and labeled. A memo was tacked to the tent pole. Rachel recognized the signature of her friend Danny Briley, the grant administrator. Below Danny's memo was a chart with dates, temperatures, pH levels and specified amounts of ENT. Rachel didn't know what to make of it.

Each thermos-like container had a label with five or six numbers on it. Rachel checked out the numbers: ten numbered 604207, fourteen at 524205.

Jen volunteered, "six-zero-four-two-zero-seven...uh...June fourth, two hundred seven degrees?"

"I think so," Rachel said. "And it means they're superheating these thermophiles at astonishing temperatures. Even in his lab Dr. Moody never brought the Sentry thermophiles above one ninety-five."

Rachel led them toward the little cabin. It sat in the woods northeast of the lab tent, just past the line where the trees stopped and the meadow began. Inside, they found one large room with two bunk beds, a wood stove, a table and an improvised wooden sink. A window over the sink provided a view of the meadow. Rachel glanced out the window, then leaned over the sink to look again. Suddenly she was out the door, down the steps and running to the pool. Rainey and Jen followed, confused.

They found her staring into the water. "What's up?" Jen asked.

"Look at the pool."

"It's bubbling," Jen volunteered.

Rachel didn't respond.

"Is hot water coming in?" Rainey asked.

"Yes. See how the water's risen right to the lip of the pool?" Jen leaned in. "Yeah. So?"

This time she answered Jen's question eagerly. "The Sentry's been dormant for over two hundred years. Phillipe said it won't go off for another century. We know it won't erupt within my lifetime." Rachel stepped back. "Here's the thing—it's going off within the hour."

Two-Faced Bastards

THE TREES SURROUNDING THE Sentry meadow were dwarfed by soaring water and steam spouting high into the sky. Towering white pillars of boiling water burst into a fine spray that rained back down over the meadow. When an eruption was over, the pool became a hissing cauldron. Then it would explode again, drawing from inside the earth, spewing great steaming shafts of water above the pines. At first Rachel merely stared, as if she were seeing a cure at Lourdes. Then she whooped and hollered. Now she was talking to herself, muttering something about acts of God. "Do you know what you're seeing?" she asked them.

"A geyser," Jen answered.

Rachel's pained expression made Jen shoot her a black look.

"Let's start over. This geyser should not be erupting. Not now. Not in the foreseeable future. I promise you, this is not something we're supposed to see in our lifetimes. It's—I dunno—crazy. Unnatural."

A gust of wind blew spray within inches of Rachel's feet. She followed the runoff into the meadow, then knelt beside the little stream of water. After a minute she called them over. "It's weird. This gully should be covered with vegetation. It's not. There's no vegetation at all."

"Looks like it's flushed out," Rainey said.

Rachel paced a circle in the meadow. Then she was back down on her knees, inspecting a second gully, then a third. "I think all the gullies are flushed out." She paused. "I think that means...Jesus, it has to mean…the Sentry's been erupting for quite some time." She watched the geyser spray the sky. Everything about this picture was wrong. "A geyser going off a hundred years early is a big thing. An event…damn," she muttered to herself. And again, "Damn." She turned to them, her face sober. "The scientists working up here, and the people they answer to, they know about this. They have to know. No one's said anything. Not one word. That's Mitchell… and that's Danny…and that miscreant Phillipe was right: they're covering it up." She stopped, alarmed by her own words. Then, still disbelieving, "They know this geyser is active, and they're deliberately misleading us. No, they're flat-out lying…the bear management closure—it's a scam." Little patches of red had broken out on her drawn face. "It's a miserable, unforgivable scam!"

Danny. Her friend, Danny. He had to know, and—on top of everything else—that made her a colossal chump.

Rachel wandered off along a gully, her head throbbing. She'd been shamelessly used, and she felt angry and betrayed. When Rachel came back, her face was still red. She had to talk about this. "When I decided to work in the park," Rachel said to their backs. They turned, something in her tone. "It was in part because this was supposed to be a place where this kind of double-dealing, duplicitous…whatever…didn't happen. I mean, I reported unseasonal animal behavior—right here, in my old study area. We met. Mitchell set up a group to figure it out." Rachel gestured toward the Sentry. "Mitchell's an assistant superintendent. He's the park person overseeing this grant. He knew the geyser was active. Danny's with the American Science Foundation. They made the grant. They brought in these scientists to finish Dr. Moody's work. They're paying for whatever the hell these guys are doing. So Danny had to know, too, but no one said a word. Not one word. Why? Why? And what in hell are they doing? The bear management closure, it's a ruse, a mare's nest." Then, almost a whisper, "two-faced bastards."

––––––

RAINEY CIRCLED THE POOL, his third time around. Rachel listened to Jen, who was detailing the lying machinations of men she'd worked with. Jen meant well, okay, but it wasn't making her feel any better.

"It may be right here in front of us," Rainey said when he reached the women. "Plain as the nose on my face."

"That helps," Rachel muttered.

He ignored her, pointing at a gully. "Don't these gullies drain into the ditches we saw on our way in? And don't they in turn drain into Elk Creek? Bear with me here. Just suppose the scientists are somehow superheating the pool itself—"

"Okay," she interrupted. "Yes, that could explain why the Sentry's erupting. And it would explain that weird chart—they're dumping their souped-up nitrogenous compound right into the pool. Those assholes—"

"Still," he broke in, unfinished. "There's the problem you raised. How can the animals possibly ingest the superheated thermophiles?" He had her full attention. "The animals can't drink from a boiling hot thermal pool. There's no way. But what if the overcooked thermophiles are flowing into the water supply? From the geyser, to the gullies, to the creek." Rachel lowered her head, considering this. "What if the animals are ingesting the Sentry thermophiles right out of the stream, in their drinking water?" He showed his big palms.

Rachel raised her head, smiling now. "The best detective ever." And then her face fell as the horrific possibilities exploded onto her radar screen. Rachel's mind raced with questions: *Do the superheated thermophiles from the Sentry pool affect hormonal activity? How? How long does it take? Is it cumulative? Is it causing the mutations? Why are they heating the pool?* "If they get it hot enough, often enough, that could cause the eruptions," she said, thinking out loud. "And if the pool's been active for most of the eleven months Danny's scientists have been working up here, that's more than enough time to produce the unseasonal behavior we're seeing. I mean it's possible. Suppose that somehow hormonal activity is distorted by the superheated Sentry thermophiles—" She stopped, beginning to see how bad this could get. "If that's true, and if they'd been drinking them out of the stream for some time, the problems are just starting."

"For christsake, this is Yellowstone Park," Jen muttered. "Animals are supposed to be safe here."

Rainey didn't respond. He was walking, again, around the geyser.

Rachel turned, a grim picture coming together in her mind. "Whoever's behind this, they don't seem to care—hell, I bet they don't even notice—how it affects wildlife. If we're right, and the superheated thermophiles do affect hormone production, or—God forbid—cause mutations, we're just at the beginning. The tip of a giant iceberg." Her face was flushed again. "How could they allow a thing like this? Why would they?"

When no one spoke, Rachel took a test tube from her pocket, lowered it into a gully to catch some water, then corked it. She turned purposefully toward the tent, though she was feeling lost.

"What do you have in mind?" Rainey asked.

"I don't know. Let's just take whatever discs, notes, and petri dishes we need."

"Don't give Mitchell an excuse to throw you out of here."

"Okay. Yeah. I'm just so angry, no, appalled—I dunno." She tried to slow down. "Suppose I copy the files onto a new disc, read the notes, take some photos?"

Rainey waited.

"Maybe take one of those ENT vials. And just lift a few petri dishes. One or two notebooks."

"For Lester, huh?"

She laid her hand on his forearm, glad he was here. "That's what I was thinking, too."

Phillipe's Exploding Spaghetti

DANNY WAS SITTING ON a deck chair, feet propped up on the porch rail of his cabin. On his lap he had a memo from the senior scientist at the Sentry. The man was smart—ill-mannered, but smart. Still, his memo was a damned feeble explanation for all the delays. For christsake, who cared about bears or eruptions? And the fire was a mile away. His phone rang. "Lester, hey, good to hear your voice. Are we fishing Sunday? Great, a favor? Just tell me what you need...uh-huh...Les, are you sure those petri dishes are from the Sentry Hot Spring?"

———

MITCHELL WAS REVIEWING PARK concession agreements when the buzzer on his phone rang. "You can always put Danny through, my dear," he said.

"Mitchell, I don't care who you're meeting with...I got a call from Lester...yes, the Lester who writes for the *Chronicle*...I do fish with Lester, yes." Danny's voice had an edge now. "He has four of my petri dishes...he knows they're from the Sentry...Moody's assistant looked at them, that's why...you heard me...what isn't park business? It's been going off in your park for eleven months...yes, do make it your business...just listen...Lester said your sheriff is trying to frame some friend of his, something about the petri dishes. He wanted to know about the Sentry. Get this sheriff to your office right away...because Lester's a newspaperman, goddamnit." Danny hung up on Mitchell, his eyes cold as a stone.

AT LAST, THE SENTRY stopped spraying the sky. Rachel announced that they had almost four miles to climb with the steepest, most difficult part ahead of them. She had what she needed from this disturbing place, she explained. They were going on to Stoney Ridge, where she hoped to find Woolly Bugger.

She led them along the trail as it angled back and forth up the mountainside. The erupting geyser, the wingless eaglet, the deformed elk calf, and their subsequent discussion had unnerved all of them. No one felt like talking. In less than an hour they reached a long open subalpine meadow. At this altitude the trees dotting the meadow were whitebark pine. Rachel pointed out the spot on the ridge where she'd seen Woolly Bugger. Behind them Yellowstone Park was a medley of greens—from the deep, dark greens of the trees to the lighter verdant shades of the rolling hills and meadows.

The ridge was over nine thousand feet high, and as they climbed, the forest thinned out, then opened up into parklands—grass meadows set between little clumps of forest. Irregular patches of snow spotted the ridge. They could see the Tom Miner Basin on one side of the ridge, the Elk Creek drainage on the other. On the Elk Creek side stark cliff faces, spires, and snow-capped peaks glistened in the fading sun. The hills on the Tom Miner side were smaller, rolling gently down to the Yellowstone River in the Paradise Valley.

Rachel stopped at a spring near a cluster of whitebark pine. "We're here," she said, dropping her pack with a sigh.

Rainey stretched, tired. Jen walked to the highest point, seeming pleased to be on top of this ridge, proud of herself.

"Is that the fire?" she asked, pointing at the small plumes of smoke rising on the Elk Creek side.

Rachel nodded, distracted. She was sitting against a pine, pouring over the Sentry scientists' notes. Rainey offered to cook dinner, but she didn't respond. Rachel didn't understand what she was reading. These scientists were not finishing Moody's work. No way. And yes, they were superheating the pool itself, which was unquestionably prohibited in the park. The notes actually specified the amounts and strengths of their exothermic nitrogenous compound required to reach specific temperature levels. ENT was, apparently, an intense heat-producing agent they'd developed for this purpose. Relatively small quantities raised the temperature in the pool very quickly. But what were they doing? And why? She read on. Sometime later Rachel smelled the campfire and saw that they'd set up a tent. Still brooding, she set aside the notebooks and began unpacking gear.

"Can you make any sense of the notes?" Rainey asked when she approached the fire.

She frowned. "It doesn't make sense. I don't see any connection to Dr. Moody's work. It's something else entirely." Something sinister. Rachel poked at the fire with a stick, weighing dark thoughts.

———

OVER DINNER, THEIR CONVERSATION invariably came back to the experiments at the Sentry. It was so compelling a mystery that the tensions between them had receded. Rainey eventually encouraged Rachel to take her best guess—what were these guys doing?

"I'm not at all sure," she replied, grim. "But, okay, here's what I'm thinking. They were heating the pool above two hundred degrees, periodically as high as two ten. Though it's hard to know what causes changes in hot springs, daily heating of the pool and the explosive properties of the thermophiles could explain why it's erupting. Apparently, the American Science Foundation biologists didn't care. They wanted the pool at these extreme temperatures."

"Which means they weren't finishing Dr. Moody's experiments," Rainey said.

"Absolutely not. I think they're interested in the properties of the Sentry thermophiles in a much higher temperature range—when they become more volatile, that is to say, explosive. This is another phase entirely, where the proteins in the Sentry thermophiles begin to denature and the thermophiles become unstable. Moody and Phillipe described this but never pursued it. In this phase the high energy bonds of the super-stable proteins can break apart, releasing the energy that was in those bonds as an explosion. Only a very small percentage of the thermophiles explode. Still, that's all they focus on in their notebooks."

"I'm not getting this," Jen said.

Rachel didn't seem to mind. "Here's the biology. A protein is made of a long chain of amino acids folded into a distinct shape. It's the bonds between these amino acids that hold the protein together. At high temperatures a normal protein denatures. That is to say, the bonds are easily broken, and it simply unfolds."

"The spaghetti?" Jen asked.

"Phillipe's spaghetti. Right." Rachel set down her plate, continuing, "But some of these Sentry proteins have unusually strong bonds. And these super-stable proteins don't denature gracefully. Just think of dynamite. The energy of dynamite is in stable high-energy chemical bonds. Activating energy—in this case a blasting cap—pushes it over the edge, and it cascades, breaks all its bonds, in an explosive reaction."

"Okay."

"I'm pretty sure that's what they're studying. Besides the notebooks, there's Dr. Moody's early journal piece, *Volatile Properties of Novel Super-Stable Proteins from Thermophilic Bacteria in a Natural Hot Springs Environment*. He stumbled on these volatile characteristics when he inadvertently overheated the thermophiles. This is new." Rachel was emphatic now, talking with her hands, her eyes. "We've never seen this in nature. Dr. Moody never pursued it. He wasn't interested in the explosive thermophiles. His brief article, however, is referenced on their computer files, again and again. Then there's the amount of this exothermic nitrogenous compound around. And remember those heavy metal-insulated containers. They're used to transport radioactive substances, HIV viruses, hazardous waste...or highly volatile materials."

Rainey watched her, head down, sinking into a funk. "Who could have an interest in the explosive properties of microscopic thermophiles?" he asked. He considered possibilities—The American Science Foundation could be fronting for God-only-knows-what.

Rachel looked up from her notebook. "I have no idea. Whoever they are, they were sending these cultures out of here in those protective containers, packed with specified amounts of ENT. The way I put it together, they'd take a thermophile sample at a given temperature, pack it in a petri dish or culture with enough of the nitrogenous compound to keep it in an acceptable temperature range, then ship it out to some other lab where, presumably, they'd continue their experiments. They've clearly spent a lot of time determining exactly how much of their high-octane nitrogenous compound to pack it in. There're pages of notes on acceptable temperature ranges for thermophilic organisms heated over two hundred degrees, but why are they heating the pool itself? And where are they sending it? And what are they doing when it gets there?"

It was quiet. Jen took Raincy's arm. Rachel didn't even stiffen.

"Why would they need to keep them so hot?" Jen asked.

"I have some ideas about that," Rachel offered. "Moody learned how to keep superheated Sentry thermophiles alive and relatively stable for his experimental purposes. He was packing them out at one seventy to one seventy-five degrees, in their dormant, steady state, then reheating them at his lab. However, once they're superheated over one ninety-five, they become unstable. According to these notes, you have to keep the unstable Sentry thermophiles within a higher, very narrow temperature range. If they cool down, they can lose their volatile properties. If they get too hot, they either denature or explode."

Rachel checked a notebook. "Moody says the thermophiles are in a steady state between one sixty and one seventy-five degrees. The American Science Foundation guys never packed them out below one eighty-five. I suspect that once they've become unstable, if you pack them out in the same temperature range as Dr. Moody did, they fall back into the steady state and somehow lose the explosive properties they're studying."

It was quiet. Rachel closed her eyes.

Rainey was sure she was seeing the mutated eaglet, the legless elk calf, the unnamed horrors to come. It was, for her, a violation: the natural world she counted on had been upended.

"You see what Lester can find out," she eventually said. "I'll lean on Danny. He played me like a mark. Behind his friendly, hippie persona, he's lying every minute." She stood. "I've been a perfect fool," she said, then Rachel walked toward the low evening sun. They heard her moments later. Somewhere on this pristine ridge, Rachel was throwing stones.

Spawn 'Til You Die

THE SILVER DOLLAR WAS Jesse's first saloon. During his reign as sheriff, it had grown from a seedy watering hole to a full-fledged tourist attraction. Today, it had a family style restaurant beside a sprawling, multi-level gift shop where you could watch five species of live trout in tiny little tanks or choose from three thousand trinkets made in countries without a minimum wage. A spacious, carpeted pit for poker machines was centered on the lower level. And, off to the side, was the main event, the delightfully western, big as a barn, Silver Dollar Bar. At the bar there were ten thousand silver dollars—count 'em—individually displayed in wood mountings climbing two stories up the pine walls.

At six, Gummer walked in. Ten minutes later a ripple of noise went through the restaurant, then rolled into the bar, a sure sign that Jesse had arrived. As Jesse glad-handed his way to the office beyond the bar, Gummer could see he was in a foul mood. When Gummer had talked with him earlier, Jesse was sulking, ticked off about missing that Rainey guy at the motel. Since then he'd gotten worse. His oversized sunglasses gave him away.

Part of his job, Gummer believed, was to help Jesse with his bad moods so they didn't get in the way of business. But lately he wasn't very good at it. He rose from his barstool. Gummer turned left at the rack where Jesse sold shot glasses from all fifty states. To reach the office, he worked his way through Western jewelry, Yellowstone knickknacks, and pastoral Native American scenes hand-painted on saw blades. He stopped to marvel at Jesse's new Woodland Babies series—little squirrels with big eyes, rabbits snuggling, even a mother gopher, sleeping with her three little ones—when it came to tourist art, Jesse's fine eye had made the Silver Dollar, well, Mecca.

Gummer had to smile, remembering how this fancy New York City gallery guy, Antonio Corelli, wanted to do a show of *classic western folk art* from the Silver Dollar at his big time Chelsea gallery. Chelsea Corelli strolled into the Silver Dollar wearing a black silk suit, diamond cufflinks, and a pair of three-thousand-dollar cream-colored alligator boots. Jesse took one look at the guy and said he wanted three letters of reference from people whose last names didn't end with a vowel. That was that.

Tentatively, Gummer opened the office door. Jesse was sitting at his desk and staring out the window, moping. When Jesse took his sunglasses off, Gummer could see how his cheek was twitching pretty good. Jeez. The last time he got like this, Gummer had to pay off a sassy waitress with a fork wound in her thigh.

The phone rang. Jesse punched on the speaker. "Talk to me, Stacy."

"Mitchell called. All worked up. Wants you to come meet with some federal big shot right away. Tonight. Jesse, he said ASAP."

"Tell him you can't find me."

"I did."

"Good." Jesse punched off.

Gummer stepped forward. "About the meeting—"

Jesse swiveled his chair. "Remind me to talk with you about topic sentences."

"We've talked about that, sir. That's why I said about—"

"Fine, Gummer, fine." Jesse punched a number into the phone. "Post a reward for Rainey...and Stace, meet the detective at the airport."

Why was it, Gummer wondered, that when things were going really good, the sheriff got so distracted with that fella Rainey? Didn't they have enough to do? The buzzer rang, the signal that Mr. Chan had arrived. A half hour later Gummer had Mr. Chan's share down to twenty percent, and Jesse—who was almost back to his old self—had a fourteen-day option to buy a processing secret for one hundred thousand dollars down.

RACHEL WAS SITTING BESIDE the spring, watching the wind push doughy clouds toward West Yellowstone. The rain would pass to the south, she guessed. That good fortune, however, did nothing to improve her mood.

Time to get back to the world—try to get a general location on Woolly Bugger before it got too dark. She walked over to Rainey and Jen, who were sitting by the fire.

"You okay?" Rainey asked.

Rachel didn't know where to start. She ignored his question. "I need to check on my bear again."

"Why do you have to find him?" Jen asked.

Jen was likely a very good cop. It didn't make her questions any less irritating. Rachel made an effort and explained, "He's digging what must be a trial den in June. That could be the beginning of who knows what. He may need my help." And almost an afterthought, "I've known him, kept my eye on him, for thirteen years."

"You find that bear, you let me know right away, okay?" Jen asked.

"You bet. I'll be gone for at least an hour." Rachel looked at the two of them, seated side by side, and turned away.

THE ONLY THING JESSE hated more than losing—if being short was an insult from God, losing was the devil rubbing salt in the wound—was waiting. And after a two-hour-plus drive, Mitchell had kept him in the waiting area for twenty-six minutes. The sheriff was considering setting up a roadblock at the Gardiner entrance to the park and rerouting all the cars a hundred fifty-plus miles to West Yellowstone when Mitchell came out of his office looking peeved. "Sheriff, good of you to come on such short notice."

Jesse followed the tall, genteel assistant superintendent into his office. Mitchell had chosen Early American furniture. Oil paintings—scenes from the Yellowstone countryside—hung on the walls. At the cherry plank table, Danny—wearing torn blue jeans and his Spawn 'Til You Die T-shirt—was sipping some kind of fruit juice. Jesse wondered if the guy ate garden burgers. He stood up when Mitchell said, "Danny Briley, meet Jesse Stinson, our local sheriff. Jesse, Danny's a grant administrator. He's our liaison on some important federal projects."

"Feds know you dress like that, son?"

Danny grinned. "It's the beard they rag me about back east."

Jesse sat. "What's the problem?"

"Danny got a curious call from Lester McDougall," Mitchell said. "You know, the fellow who writes for the *Chronicle*."

"I know Lester." Jesse nodded. "You bet I do."

"Yes. Apparently, Lester's worried about his friend Rainey. As he so succinctly put it, he believes you and Judge Dirkey framed him. Moreover, he intends to make a public issue of it." Mitchell looked up with an aging politician's practiced smile. "That, however, is not our concern." Mitchell pushed his wire-rimmed half glasses up on the bridge of his nose, then looked down at Jesse. "An ancillary purpose of his call was to question Danny regarding the Sentry Hot Spring. He suggested that you and Rainey shared an interest in some petri dishes from the Sentry. Can you explain what he meant by that?"

Not yet, you sanctimonious sack of—Jesse reined himself in. "Hell, Mitch, just because you talk like some kind of royalty doesn't mean everyone else is dumb as a fencepost. Any fool can see the northwest corner's not closed because of some rogue bear. You bet I'm interested in whatever hanky-panky you're cooking up in my county."

"Your county, yes. But as you know, not your jurisdiction." Mitchell steepled his fingers. "Please answer my question."

Jesse snorted. "For a year now I've been trying to get some kind of straight answer out of *you*. Every time *I* ask a question, you start dancing around like some tree hugger caught with an eagle on the barbeque. The truth is, my deep well of patience has run dry, bone-dry. If you don't level with me now, I'm forced to work with Lester 'til he gets the whole story—the secret experiments, the out-of-town scientists, the park cover-up, the whole sorry deal."

Mitchell's smile faltered.

Danny cleared his throat. "Sheriff, I'm going to say this once. The work being done at the Sentry's classified. If you so much as breathe a word about it, to anyone, I'll see to it personally that you're prosecuted to the full extent of the law. And I'm not talking your turn-the-other-cheek poaching-style law enforcement. There's mountains of federal law to work with here. The only reason you're in the loop at all is because Mitchell would prefer to handle it locally. And believe me, I have absolutely no time to listen to half-assed threats."

Jesse leaned forward. "Whatever you are son, it's best not to talk to me like that in the state of Montana. That's friendly advice."

"No. That's a half-assed threat."

Jesse shot Mitchell his "is-this-guy-mental?" look, waiting on Danny, giving him rope. Mitchell was squirming in his chair. He's afraid of this D.C. hippie, Jesse realized. Why in hell is that?

———

"You ALWAYS DRINK COFFEE this late?" Jen asked. She was standing behind Rainey as he poured the water he'd carried from the spring into their coffee pot.

He set the pot on the fire. "I'm heating the water so you can wash later."

"Oh," she said. "You wanna walk?"

"Sure."

They went west. Though the sun had dropped behind the mountains, they could still make out the lines and shapes of the ridges, the draws and the meadows below them. The sky was gray except where the setting sun had left a streamy pink wake. In spite of Jesse, in spite of the inexplicable machinations in the park, Rainey felt good, unmistakably happy to be in this wild place with this demanding woman. There was a very pleasing urgency about Jen. She was always right there, touching, asking questions, present. "I'm very glad you came," he said, taking her hand.

"Me, too. Even with all of this weirdness." She leaned against a pine tree. "I've never been in a place like this. Ever. I mean, I've driven through pretty country. But up here, it's got to be like it was a thousand years ago."

"Actually, it's pretty much unchanged since the ice age ended, and that's—oh, seven to ten thousand years." Rainey watched her eyes, little pastel emeralds. She put her hand behind his neck. Their kiss was tender. They lingered in each other's arms.

Rainey sat on a boulder and looked down the Elk Creek drainage. He pointed out several bighorn sheep climbing toward the ridge top. Jen, he could see, was distracted.

"What are you thinking?"

"Rachel's sense of what goes on up here, it's unusual, isn't it?"

"Yes. It's a gift. She's able to get inside an animal's skin, feel what it's feeling."

"What happened between you? Do you mind if I ask?"

There it was. "If I were you, I'd ask. What I think now—I couldn't keep up with her. That's the gist of it."

"I doubt that."

He stood, looking out at the pink and gray, in places candy-striped sky. "I'd been out here five years, and, I don't know. I just didn't get it. I'd lived around universities since I was a kid, and here I was trying to make a life in a place that didn't work anything like the places I knew."

Rainey shrugged. It was what it was. Then he grinned, remembering something.

"I'll tell you a story. One night Lester and Lloyd decided it was time I learned to hunt turtles. They showed me how you hit the water with a shovel, and then, when the turtles stick their heads up to see what's going on, you drop 'em with a .22. Well, I beat that shovel on this pond, and I shot the pond full of holes. It was half an hour before I realized I'd been had. I was shooting at every weed and stick in the pond." He chuckled. "You had to see me—doing everything just so. The thing is, I was just starting to make a life as a detective, a life with Rachel. I was trying to get along. Avoid trouble. So I sat down on the hair trigger. I became careful, maybe even plodding, but it was a good life. Just before I turned forty the business with Jesse started. And when Rachel was ready for more, I was feeling cautious. She knew just what she wanted. She's always been good at that. It's like she had this gut sense it was time for her to have kids. She was right in seeing I wasn't the man to have children with her."

Jen looked at him. "If I was her, I would have waited."

———

"SHERIFF, YOU'RE OUT OF your little duck pond now," Danny was standing, palms planted on the table, inches now from Jesse's face. The way he was glaring, Jesse thought this raggedy-ass hippie might bite his nose off. Jesse sat back in his chair. "You're swimming in the deep blue sea," Danny went on, leaning in even closer. "If I don't like you, North will be crawling with federal agents tomorrow morning, and you'll be shredding files—on your knees—praying for a judge you can buy."

Jesse wet a forefinger on his tongue then ran it along the side of his carefully-groomed black mustache, reconsidering the garden burger idea. "I believe this man's ignoring my advice...right here in my county."

For just an instant Mitchell's practiced smile gave way to an expression of need—a plea, actually—help me out. I'll owe you one. Why you gasbag, Jesse thought. I'll take that IOU. Still, he let it dangle.

"Mitch," he finally said, aware the guy went by Mitchell. "I'm wondering if maybe I'm missing something here?"

Mitchell put a hand on Jesse's shoulder. "Allow me, please, to clear up any confusion. Gentlemen, no one wants public attention brought to bear on the research at the Sentry. And if we can contain it locally, well, we all agree that would be best."

Danny grunted, then he sat down.

Mitchell went on, "Now Jesse—"

"Just what does this Lester know?" Jesse interrupted.

"He has a container of petri dishes with thermophile samples from the Sentry," Mitchell replied.

Lester has Cockeye's petri dishes. Rainey was there when Cockeye died. Jesse liked the feel of it. Take it easy, he warned himself. Set this up just so. "Slow down. What's thermophile?"

"They're finishing up some research." Mitchell tapped his glasses on the table. "I can't say any more than that."

"Can't say any more than that? Don't tool me—"

"Okay sheriff, let's start over. I'm not at my best today." Danny's tone was conciliatory.

"I can appreciate that. I mean, even the pope gets a hair up his ass...eh, buddy?" Jesse adjusted his neckerchief.

"Look, there's been one screw up after another in the last twenty-four hours. The scientists working up there have fallen behind schedule, then last night they had to come out because of a fire. Now, there's a newspaperman with stolen petri dishes. Frankly, I'd appreciate your help."

"Fair enough," Jesse said. "What can I do for you?"

"Do you have any idea how Lester got those petri dishes?"

Jesse squared his shoulders—this was the pitch he'd been waiting for. "I'm afraid it was a fella calls himself Rainey. He's a known felon. I've had trouble with him before."

"Where is he?" Danny asked.

"On the run. You see, I'm on him for worse than algae theft. He took off, and—my guess—he left the dishes with Lester. Told him there was a story there. Lester calls you hoping to sort out what they mean and maybe help his friend." Jesse almost snapped his fingers, this was coming together so nice. "Suppose we do this. I'll issue an all points on Rainey. Then, say I drop in on Lester." Jesse flashed a smile at Danny—before this was over, he'd leave this hippie buck-naked in the Gallatin National Forest. Let him spawn 'til he died in the Spanish Peaks. "Young fella, I do believe I can help you out with this. I'll be in touch."

In his car Jesse slapped the dashboard with glee. Rainey had withheld evidence, he'd bet on that. He had him just where he wanted. And once Mary was out of the picture, he had him whenever—hell, however—he wanted. He decided to call Nellie, a higher-up in the CIA. He'd got her out of a tight spot in the Las Vegas days. She could get a rundown on his new friend, Danny. Federal liaison, what the fuck was that?

————

In Mitchell's office, Danny was up, pacing. "The man's out of control."

"Hardly. Don't let our sheriff fool you. He's about the quickest study I ever met." Mitchell pointed his wire-rimmed glasses at Danny. "And the best back-shooter I've seen since D.C. As good as the Nixon guys. One way or another, he'll manage to contain this."

"I can rely on that?"

"Don't underestimate him. He's counting on that."

"This sheriff gets cute, I'll make an example of you." Danny spit into Mitchell's wastebasket."You won't care for that."

Woolly Bugger

A SOUTHWEST WIND COOLED the ridge. The temperature had dropped ten degrees, Rachel thought. She listened to the wind, wondering whether Molly was asleep. Rachel wished she could be with her now. She turned her thoughts to Woolly Bugger and decided to start looking for him at the clump of whitebark pine where she'd last seen him digging.

Rachel went west, along the ridge. Leaving camp, she recognized the familiar early signs of depression. Mostly, it was this sense of helplessness—an inability to focus, come up with a plan, and tension in her neck and lower back. And, a bad sign, she was anxious about becoming an old maid. Looking out toward the Paradise Valley, she gave herself a little pep talk. Her pep talks rarely worked. This one—the gist of which was fighting depression tooth and nail—actually backed off the gloom a little. What surprised her even more was her startlingly lucid, no-nonsense delivery. "That a girl," she whispered to the evening wind.

Rachel walked almost a mile on the ridge then looked down—a quarter of a mile—at the clump of whitebark pine where she'd seen the signs of Woolly Bugger's excavation. A few minutes later, she carefully placed the receiver on the open slope. No signal. Rotating she picked up nothing whatsoever.

Slowly, she sidestepped down the avalanche chute toward the mound. It was fresh dirt, and, looking in, there was far more than she'd seen before from the hillside below.

The mound of dirt was at the base of one of the pines. Rachel set her daypack by a tree and took out her flashlight. Shining it in the hole, she realized that this was not the rough digging of a trial den. No, she was standing on the front porch of a more substantial enterprise. She leaned in. The entrance was about two feet across by two feet up and down. Rachel considered crawling in. She knew better, but...extraordinary times. She put on her game face and then she was inside.

Rachel guessed the hallway was three feet by two feet, leading to a chamber under the root structure. Peering in, she put the chamber at six by four by six. It was complete with subalpine fir boughs.

Rachel climbed out carefully, then she hurried out of the pines. She checked again for his signal. Nothing. Rachel climbed back to the ridge, wondering why Woolly Bugger was denning this summer.

———

HALF AN HOUR LATER, Rachel was still looking for her bear. She'd hiked back along the ridge, working her way beyond their campsite. Every quarter of a mile, or thereabouts, she'd choose a spot where she'd check for Wooly Bugger's signal. Nothing, so far.

She chose her next spot for its view of the evening sky. The sun had dropped behind the Taylor-Hilgards, leaving wavy streaks of pink. As dusk crept toward night, the pale-pink brushstrokes got smaller, their edges fading to gray. She guessed she was almost a mile beyond their camp when she set up her receiver again. In less than an hour she'd lose the light.

She was surprised to hear a faint click from the receiver. She was picking up something. Rachel rotated slowly to the north, and the signal got louder. Could the bear be on the Tom Miner side? It was possible. As she continued to turn, the signal got louder still. When she faced their camp, the pulse was even stronger.

She secured the can of bear mace on her belt and started walking toward camp. "Okay, Mr. Bear. I'm coming your way. Nothing to worry about. I'd bet you're somewhere between me and my friends. That makes us pretty close. You probably can hear my voice. Are you maybe side-hilling below me? We'll find out, won't we? Right. Say I sing you a song." She hoped Rainey and Jen hadn't wandered off anywhere. At least they'd made a fire. They'd be okay, she reassured herself, so long as they stayed in camp.

Rachel approached the campsite from the east. It looked deserted. The fire, untended, was barely burning. Running now, Rachel fought back panic. She called out. No answer. If they'd gone for a walk, it had to be west. She'd go after them. She hurried past the dying fire toward the two gray dome tents. Rachel reached into the near tent for her pack, looking for another can of Counter Assault, the bear mace she carried. Her pack was empty. She'd put the mace in Rainey's pack, she remembered, and hurried to the far tent. His pack was standing behind the entry flap. She sensed them before actually seeing them. And when it hit her, Rachel just turned and stared at the intertwined bodies, taking a moment to ride out the wave of feelings that crested over her. "Sorry," she muttered, when they noticed her and stopped their lovemaking.

Jen sat up, naked. Her face was flushed.

Rachel stood, holding open their tent flap. The wave of feelings broke inside of her. She wanted to scream at them.

"You can go now," Jen snapped, when Rachel didn't move.

Rachel didn't seem to hear her. She was picturing Woolly Bugger, out there somewhere, and then she saw the grizzly on Dr. Moody's carcass—the back of his massive head and neck swaying slowly, his jaw working on Moody's flesh.

Rainey was sitting now, his nakedness partially covered by a sleeping bag. "Hey, how about some privacy?"

"Sorry," Rachel murmured again.

When she didn't move, he asked, "Where's the bear?"

Just like that her paralysis was over, as if that breaking wave had washed away the confusion growing within her since she'd first seen them together. She loved this man, and she'd do what she had to do to have him back. And just as suddenly she was thinking like a bear again, wanting to keep them safe. "He's close. On the edge of camp. Get on some clothes and come out, make as much noise as you can. Outside, no fast movements."

"Make as much noise as you can?" Jen asked, groping in the dark for her clothes. "I can't believe this."

Rachel hurried toward the campfire, uneasy. The night sky was clouding over. She threw on three more logs, turned on her flashlight, then collected everything edible in a duffle. It always made her nervous to be with others in a bear situation. Just keep busy. Stay focused.

"Yo, bear. Yo, bear," she said in a soothing voice. "I know you're checking out our camp." She looked around the perimeter of the campsite for a good place to hang their food.

Rainey and Jen came out of their tent. Rainey turned on a flashlight.

"What's happening?" Jen called out.

"We've got to hang the food." Rachel pointed her flashlight at a stand of whitebark pine, perhaps sixty yards southwest of their campfire, and handed Rainey the extra can of bear mace. It was in a holster that he fastened to his belt. "Grab that rope and stay close," she told Jen, pointing the flashlight at a coil of rope on a log. "And keep making noise."

Rachel noticed the .38 Special at the small of Jen's back. "Why are you wearing the gun?"

"You guys may want to wait until that bear's in your face then spray it with mace," Jen said. "But before he takes a bite out of me, I'm going to shoot him."

"Put the gun away. I hope to keep you out of trouble. I can only do that if you do exactly as I say. To begin with, guns are illegal in the park. But in this case, that's incidental. So you know, the only gun that will stop a charging bear is a shotgun, firing slugs. Even then, you've got to hit the bear in the chest or head, which is no mean feat when he's coming at you thirty, thirty-five miles an hour. Your .38 will simply irritate him and could turn a bluff charge into an attack. Clear?"

"Bear attack? Oh my God."

Rachel turned on her receiver. The bear was nearby. She took Jen's arm. "Now stay close, and sing, holler, whatever."

They were almost shoulder-to-shoulder. Rainey and Rachel shone their flashlights ahead of them. Jen walked in the middle. They sang "(I Can't Get No) Satisfaction" as they approached the stand of trees, eerily illuminated by the in-and-out moonlight and the intersecting flashlight beams.

"Where's this bear likely to be?" Jen asked.

"If he's interested in our camp, he probably circled into the wind. That's so he can smell what's going on. If he approaches us, it'll be from downwind, the northeast. I'd keep my eye on that forest canopy just ahead. My guess is that Woolly Bugger's in there now, checking us out."

"This is too goddamn scary."

"You know how to climb a tree?"

"Only if the branches are set up like a stepladder."

"Okay, we'll climb the trees. Take this." She handed Jen her can of mace. "You climb the far one," she said to Rainey, pointing. "Jen, keep making noise while we hang the food." Rachel cupped a hand to her mouth, "Hola...hola, Mr. Bear," she whooped.

"How do I work this?" Jen held up the can.

"Take the red safety clip off the trigger. Now, if you press down this black tab, it'll fire. The bear will be coming into the wind. It should work up to ten yards."

"This bear's coming at me at thirty miles an hour and this spray is supposed to stop him when he's less than ten yards away?"

"About eighty percent of a bear's sensory equipment is in his nose. To a bear, a noseful of this spray is like a person getting his eyes gouged out. He'll stop on a dime or be so disoriented he'll ignore you completely."

Rachel held one end of the rope and scurried up the near tree like a ten-year-old shinnying up the backyard elm. Rainey was already in the adjacent pine, about twenty feet up, with the other end of the rope. Rachel tied off her end and took the duffle off her shoulder. She used a second rope to hang the duffle over the rope that was now stretched tightly between the two trees. Jen sang down below. "My Girl."

Rachel was halfway down the tree when Jen reached the chorus. Jen looked up at the duffle swinging above her, then back at their camp. A half moon was out and their fire was burning brightly, a safe harbor in this unexpected storm. She slowly played her flashlight along the edge of the forest. The tree trunks looked like pilings under a dock or caissons supporting a highway ramp. They cast long, black shadows. The forest seemed strangely still compared to the raucous sounds of her singing. Jen's eyes went back over the sweep she'd just made south to north, this time, without the light. Still quiet. Nothing. Jen kept up her singing, feeling slightly foolish at having been so frightened. Rachel was tying off the duffle rope to a third tree, while Rainey adjusted the bag from above, when Jen thought she saw two tiny red embers suspended in the air at the edge of the forest canopy.

She blinked to clear her vision. It had to be a trick of the night. The two red dots were too far apart for eyes. Then she turned her flashlight toward the embers and saw the huge black silhouette: the bear was no more than forty yards away, and he was looking at her.

From his perch in the tree, Rainey heard her gasp.

"Back away slowly," Rachel said, moving toward Jen, careful not to make any jerky motions. "Hey, bear. Hey, bear," she said softly. "We don't mean any harm."

Jen stood transfixed. "Turn your head to the side," Rachel said. Jen did as she was told. The bear, however, had already lowered his head. He growled, a harrowing sound. Then he made a blowing noise out of his mouth, a loud sort of huffing.

"Whoa, Woolly," Rachel said calmly, inching her way toward Jen, who had dropped the flashlight and was holding her can of Counter Assault with both hands. Rachel was careful to keep her eyes away from the bear, though she feared the damage had already been done. The bear huffed and clacked his teeth.

"Jen, the mace," Rachel whispered.

The knuckles of both Jen's hands were white around the mace can, as if she were trying to strangle it.

"We're going to move away slowly, Mr. Bear," Rachel said. "We know this is your house. Yes, we do."

"Here," Rainey called softly from the tree.

He pitched his can of mace. Rachel caught it and turned back to see the bear's ears flattening. The hairs on the upper part of the bear's body were bristling now as he huffed and blew. His lower lip curled back to reveal his huge lower canines at the back of his salivating mouth, his head was down and rolling, and his canines were clacking as he made one more blowing sound.

Then he charged. Head low to the ground, mouth open, the grizzly's massive, muscled body flew toward Jen with the grace and speed of a jaguar.

Rachel slid in front of Jen with her mace in front of her. At twelve yards, she fired the first burst. At six yards, the great bear hit the spray like a wall, swatting his nose and face, sneezing, and making a strange woofing sound. And then he turned, graceful even in his agony, and ran off into the forest.

Jen sank to the ground, wide-eyed. The evening wind had picked up, and it was drizzling. For a moment no one moved. Then Rainey came down out of the tree. He put an arm around Jen, helping her up. Jen shook her head, side to side. Tears were running down her cheeks. "Is it over?"

"Yes," Rainey softly replied.

Night sounds filled the silence. "What? What did I—" Jen started crying again before she could finish her question.

"You looked him in the face," Rachel said, sorrowful. "He's the king up here. That was a challenge."

Jen wiped her tears with the sleeve of her Bull's jacket. "I didn't know."

"No one told you otherwise," Rainey said, gently.

"I didn't want to mace that bear," Rachel said to herself, utterly defeated by this day.

"I'm going to be sick." Jen sank back down to her knees and vomited on the grass. "My God," she said, after a while. "*Oh my god.* I've never been so scared in my life."

Rachel held her hand straight out. It was trembling. "Let's get back. It's going to be a long night."

Rainey helped Jen back to camp.

Rachel walked ahead. Inside her tent, she pictured Woolly Bugger thrashing through the forest—his eyes, nose, throat, even the inside of his head, on fire. She pulled her sleeping bag over her head, and then Rachel was crying, too. Crying for all the things that had gone wrong on this, about the worst day of her life.

The Stinson/Mosk Elk Farm

I N THE TALL GRASS behind the Hidden Ridge Trailer Park, Gummer was making love to Darcie. This more hurried union—a *quickie*, she called it—was at their secret turnoff near the trailer park where she lived with her dad.

Gummer was trying to hold on—thinking about dead gophers, fault lines, thermophiles. Hell, anything. It was hopeless. Darcie, he knew, could hold off forever just to see how he'd please her later. Besides, when she said *quickie*, she meant him. She did something special with her pelvis and he lost his will. Afterward, he gently coaxed her to orgasm. He didn't stop until his sweetie was sated.

After sex with Darcie, Gummer's mind was clear and anything was possible. At the moment, he was working on the elk farm and the antler processing plant. He'd run some numbers. The way he saw it, having access to a processing secret increased their net on any antler by two hundred percent, minimum. Once the word got out to other sellers, the processing alone could be a pretty darn good business. They could buy up antlers from all over the Rocky Mountain West.

The elk farm was another matter. The start-up costs were significant, then you had to get your elk. Once you had 'em, a farmed herd could be infected with any number of diseases. He'd read where a farmed herd had recently been ravaged by tuberculosis, so you had to know what you were doing. A little mistake could be bad. Unless—and here's where Jesse's mind never ceased to amaze him—unless they could increase the size of the antler mass by some kind of thermophile treatment. If, in fact, they could routinely produce forty to fifty pound racks, one hundred bulls should produce almost one million dollars of velvet powder, no problem. And they could easily handle two hundred bulls in the first year. Still, they'd need to become good elk farmers, or hire good ones. I could be a good elk farmer, he thought, and that brought him to the heart of the matter. Jesse was only offering him thirty percent of the farm. It was time to take the next step. This was not going to be the Jesse Stinson Elk Farm. No, it should be the Stinson/Mosk Elk Farm. Well, maybe it was too soon for that. But, by God, he was going to be a full partner—fifty-fifty. The idea of it made him feel older, in a good way.

Darcie sat up and pulled down her sweater. "G, you got something goin' later on?"

"Got some work, Darce."

"It's nighttime, baby."

"Sorry, sweetie, but I got to work."

"Yeah, I guess." She looked up at the stars. "I want to go to Reno. I have ID and everything. Will you take me to Reno?"

"Tonight?"

"No, dummy. On the weekend." She eased her panties on under her DQ skirt. "You know why I want to go to Reno?" She walked toward his borrowed blue Jeep.

Gummer saw her touch the roof and shoot him a sexy look, glad he'd picked her favorite color. "Well, I know you're a gambling fool." It was true, and he never tired of watching her at the tables. The last time Darcie was up all night playing blackjack, counting cards. And she made money, too.

"That's only part of it." Darcie took his hand. "Baby, if I win in Reno, you know what I'm gonna do?"

"What's that? Buy the DQ?"

"Don't be a geek."

"Well, hey, how should I know?"

"I'm going to invest it with you, G. Whatever you say."

"Sweetie, I may have found just the thing."

LESTER WAS INTERVIEWING AN apoplectic Phillipe for the second time in two days when he heard a car coming up his neglected road. He was unable to hide his surprise at seeing the svelte, stubby sheriff smirking at his doorstep. Phillipe seemed eager to meet him. The Frenchman stood. "Sheriff, allow me to present myself. I am Dr. Phillipe Renard." He stuck out his hand. Jesse ignored his outstretched palm. Phillipe went on, oblivious. "And if I may say so, it is my honor to meet you. As a student of the cinema American, of the classic westerns, I comprend—how do you say? Oui, I *get* the importance of the sheriff in the great American West." Phillipe bowed. "We met once, on the unhappy occasion of the death of Dr. Moody, my mentor. I am completing his work—"

"Whoa there, bud." Jesse raised a hand. Phillipe had his attention now. Worked with Moody, huh. And Wild West-loving Frenchies were a specialty. He'd sold a big piece of the Hebgen Lake property to some French condo outfit that was starting a Wild West club. And he'd seen how they ate up the down-home cowboy drivel he could dish up blindfolded. On a bet with Sandy, his barber, he got 'em to pay off his zoning guy with cash stuffed into saddlebags. They had some other *deep* ideas, like every Indian being a noble warrior. Well, this guy looked to be cut from the same sort of know-it-all, intestine-eating cloth.

When the sheriff took in the petri dishes sitting on the table, he slapped Phillipe on the back and said, "Pierre, I'm gonna want you to wait outside a minute. Just remember this: we're riding to the same water hole. We're just coming at 'er on different trails. Okay, buddy?"

"Pierre?" Phillipe scowled, then his face softened. "The same water hole—yes, I see this."

Jesse pointed at the door.

When Phillipe stepped out the door, the sheriff cocked his raised thumb and forefinger at Lester. "You're under arrest."

———

GUMMER—LOOKING LIKE A million bucks—turned into the Bear Tooth Ranch at 10:58 P.M. Perfect.

He was surprised to see a black Turbo Saab in Jesse's driveway and waited to be buzzed in. He moved right to the sunken bar, where

Jesse was with the French guy he'd stolen the notebooks from. And the notebooks were right there on the bar, all six of them. And yes, next to them was the case of missing petri dishes. Damn.

"Welcome, Gummer," Jesse said. "Let me present Phillipe Renard, the eminent French microbiologist."

"Good evening," Phillipe shook Gummer's outstretched hand. He was about an inch shorter than Jesse, which, Gummer was pleased to see, brought a smile to the sheriff's face.

"Same here."

"Gummer, I stopped off at Lester's, picked up our petri dishes, and had the good fortune to meet Dr. Renard." Jesse adopted his best, sincere tone. "Phillipe and I, we've come to a meeting of the minds. We've scoped out the lay of the land."

Cha-ching. The cash register opened and closed in Gummer's head. He was reminded of a thing his mother used to say. Some business about turning sow's ears to silk purses. Well, Jesse had the knack for it.

"What I propose is that Dr. Renard work with us on our—" Jesse searched for the word he wanted. "Product development. As an expert on these particular thermophilic organisms." He touched the metal case. "He can help us perfect our program. In turn, we are going to help him finish up his experiments at the Sentry. As you can see, I've already recovered his notebooks."

"Never, ever, have I seen such police work," Phillipe said. "Three short phone calls and bof, voila...the stolen notebooks, they are in my hands. Can you imagine, three phone calls?"

"That many?" just popped out. Gummer bit his tongue.

Jesse shot him a look, a real chiller. "As it happens, my friend Gummer here, he's an enforcement ranger in the North Yellowstone subdistrict. What I'm thinking, Phil, is that Ranger Gummer's overdue to hike up to the Sentry. So, tomorrow, say you work on our project, figure out just what we need from that hot spring. Then the next day, suppose he takes you up there with him. That work for you, buddy?"

"Formidable."

"That a yes?"

Phillipe raised his glass of champagne. "Fantastic," he said, exaggerating the first two syllables.

Gummer grinned, wondering if this Frenchie would eat buffalo chips if he told him he'd prepared them the Indian way.

AT THEIR FIRE, JEN sat by Rainey, watching the immense night sky. She wondered why she was still so shaky, why the charging bear was so much harder to get over than any of the other frightening things she'd had to manage. She was utterly undone, spent. Right now, all she wanted was her own bed. Jen closed her eyes, let her mind drift. She drifted right back to the giant grizzly. She could see his massive head, his powerful shoulders, his curled lips, and even now she got so scared it made her dizzy. Rainey put his arm around her, and she began shivering.

When she was finally still, Jen opened her eyes, listened for the bear. The night was so strangely quiet. All she could hear was the wind rustling the leaves. No city noises, none at all. How had she ever ended up in this place? Perhaps Rachel was right. She should have stayed behind.

Rachel, she guessed, wanted to be alone. Since the bear attack she hadn't come out of her tent. If she were alone, Jen was sure she'd still be shaking and, from time to time, yelling incoherently at the bear, or something else just as useless. She was that fucked-up.

"Do you miss police work?" Rainey eventually asked.

"Not yet." He was trying to take her mind off the bear. Sweet. Unlikely, though.

"You're good, aren't you?"

"Yeah, pretty good." She snuggled up against him, making an effort, pushing herself to talk. "I grew up around cops. My dad, the uncles, my grandpa..." She caught herself drifting, refocused. "My mom was always trying—how did she put it?—to expand my horizons. Yeah. When I was five, she made me take piano. There were eleven cops at my first piano recital."

Rainey pulled her closer.

"I'm not kidding."

It was quiet. Jen stared out at the tree line, the spot where the grizzly bear had first appeared. She saw him again—rolling his head, making that woofing sound, and then he was charging her, unstoppable. She lowered her head, queasy. "Rainey, I'm still so scared. I've never been so scared in my life."

Rainey covered her hands with his large palm.

WHEN THE FRENCHMAN LEFT, Gummer had steered the sheriff back to the subject of the elk farm, even got him pumped up with his numbers. But then Jesse had dialed his Miami detective and walked out. Gummer fixed a Diet Coke, adding a cherry. Okay, the guy could keep six balls in the air at once. And, he reminded himself, the elk farm was Jesse's idea. He had to admit: Jesse saw the connections in things, even when they weren't connected. Like the thermophiles causing the elk to grow huge antlers. Even the park people hadn't figured that out yet.

Still, he was concerned.

Gummer stepped out onto the porch. Earlier he'd had a startling glimpse—something like a vision, he believed—of the future. He could see himself, the Lord of the Manor, or whatever you called an elk farm and an antler processing plant. He wandered down Gopher Gulch, trying to see it in his mind.

Gummer could pretty much picture the setup. The property would be wooded and isolated. He imagined a view of Raynolds Pass. The plant would be at the edge of a stand of trees, out of sight from the road. There would be a Quonset hut, a workshop, barns, and chutes where they'd immobilize the elk, anesthetize them, then cut off the antlers. He could even see himself coming in, say, twice a week, sitting in an office above the workshop, overseeing the operation, handling the finances.

He pinched the back of his neck, double-checking that this wasn't a dream.

———

RACHEL CAME OUT OF her tent and slowly walked to where Rainey and Jen were sitting on a fireside log. She said she'd take the first watch. When Rainey asked her how she was doing, she shook her head and told them to get some sleep. Her eyes were red and there were lines where she'd wiped the tears from her cheeks.

"I'm sorry I screwed up," Jen offered.

Rachel turned. "Why wouldn't you stay behind?"

"You're upset," Rainey cautioned, recognizing her tone. "Let this wait. Don't—"

"Upset? Upset?" Rachel faced him. "You have no idea how I feel. None whatsoever! She undid thirteen years of work with that bear."

"For christsake," Rainey rose from the log, angry now. "That's out of line."

Rachel waved the back of her hand through the air, dismissive. "What are you doing, anyway?" she asked. "Jesse wants to put you in jail, hurt you, maybe even kill you. The risks, the consequences for you, they don't even seem to matter. You could have given Jesse the petri dishes, and you'd be out of it. But no, you had to come to her rescue. And now Jesse's going to hurt you, and likely, she will, too."

"That's it, lady. That's enough!" Jen was up now too, in Rachel's face. "What's wrong with you, anyway?" And breathing fire, "I'm tired of watching you pout. And snipe at me. And snidely run him down because you can't say how you feel."

"Haven't you done enough damage for one day?" Rachel interrupted, holding Jen's blazing eyes. "Just leave me alone. Please," she raised her hands. "Just leave me the fuck alone." Rachel stormed off. Beyond their fire she sat against a rock, her back to them.

Jen sat beside Rainey looking, at least, a little less afraid. "That didn't work."

"Nope." Rainey hesitated, wondering how this day could be undone. He held Jen close, watched the fire. When he eventually turned to her, still at a loss, Jen's eyes were closed. Rainey helped her to her feet, hoping for clarity in the morning.

In their tent Rainey sat beside Jen. When he judged she was sleeping, Rainey touched his palm to her cheek, then he dozed off, too. Sometime later Rainey opened the tent flap. He could see Rachel leaning against the large rock. Her breathing was irregular, though her eyes were closed. He walked toward her, remembering the way her face turned childlike in sleep.

She was sleeping fitfully, her expressive face strained. Rainey wondered if she was having a bad dream. He guessed that the thing that had scared him the most, the bear, had been the easiest for her. Rachel wouldn't be afraid of that. That's how she was. When she was frightened, it usually came on unexpectedly, and at those times, she felt overwhelmed and helpless.

When they'd lived together, occasionally he'd wake up at night to see her sitting in bed, crying. When he asked her about it, she often didn't know why.

Rachel stirred in her sleep. He touched her shoulder. She looked up, startled, and took his offered hand. She stood, all but asleep, and went to her tent.

Rainey sat on a rock and lit his one cigarette of the day, a thing he'd gone back to after Rachel. He was changing, an unexpected change, and he wasn't at all sure what to make of it. At first, he'd thought it was nothing more than the startling events of the past two days. But no, there was more to it. Something about the way he was with Jen. And the way he was thinking about Jesse. It had caught him off guard.

He inhaled, thinking that in his life, change was rarely linear or logical. It was about focus, shifting landscapes and instinct. Much of the time he was reactive, unsure where he was going, relying on his gut in the face of uncertainty. His greatest liability, and what he liked best, was that he wasn't afraid of conflict. And if the number of salmon returning to the river measures the well-being of the watershed, the measure of his own well-being was how he managed this special attribute.

He remembered his move to Montana. He'd come in 1990. He'd settled in—guiding, writing articles, fishing a lot, spending most of his spare time alone. Still, he was fighting with streamside property owners, clients, even his boss. After several years of that, he found he was still unsure where he was going, only it didn't seem to matter so much. In his fourth year, when he met Rachel, he was walking away from conflict.

And then Rachel threw him out. He lost his bearings, and he went to war with Jesse.

And now, because of Jen, he could feel bits and pieces coming into focus again.

———

IN HER TENT, RACHEL kept her eyes open, unnerved by her own disturbing dreams.

Outside, she heard Rainey stoking their fire. Rachel raised her tent flap. She watched his silhouette, the red glow of his cigarette.

The Devil Bear

RAINEY HAD COFFEE GOING when Rachel came out of her tent. It was 6:30 A.M., and the rising, apricot-colored sun played through wisps of smoke spiraling lazily skyward from their fire. Rachel ran a comb through her long brown hair. During the night she'd made up her mind to talk with him. Tell him how she felt. That decision had changed her attitude, her mood, everything. She had this unexpected sense of well-being. She even felt attractive. For many months she'd been denying herself this feeling. Hiding it behind thick glasses, old clothes, her apparent indifference. This morning, backlit on the ridge by the rising sun, she felt alluring, and sexy.

"Even lovelier than I remember." Rainey poured out two cups of coffee. "Still take sugar?"

"Uh-huh." She grinned at him, kind of saucy. Well at least he'd noticed. Rachel watched his large hands carefully setting the coffeepot near the fire. Jen was still sleeping. Good. God, she hoped Jen was just a fling. Even last night, at her worst, she had to admit that Jen and Rainey had something together. Still, Rainey was a slow, tenacious wader through complexity and Jen, the hare, was going too fast for him. Sooner or later she'd turn in a direction that he'd turn away from. Hard to know when...not a thing to count on, certainly. Agh. She imagined funny little chicken noises in her head—accusing clucks—you'll be an old maid, and a damn fool besides, if you wait on something like that.

"I'm sorry about last night," Rachel began, sincere. "You were right. I was out of line."

From his seat on the log, Rainey touched her arm. "It was a lousy day. And the bear, well, no one was any good after that." He sipped his coffee. "I'm sorry, too. And I know Jen would like to put it behind us."

"I want to apologize to her. But first I'd like to talk with you." She sat beside him at the fire. "What are you thinking?"

"Is it too early for a personal question?" Rainey asked.

"Not at all."

"Is there a new man in your life?"

Rachel averted her eyes. "No."

"I was hoping you'd met someone," he offered.

To his surprise, she ran to her tent.

Jen poked her head out. "Coffee, please. Is there any coffee?" She crawled from the tent.

Rainey poured Jen's coffee in a large green plastic cup. "What'd you do?" she asked. "It looked like Rachel was about to cry again."

"I'm not sure."

"Well, what were you talking about?"

"She apologized. I did too. Then I said she looked great. I told her I was hoping she'd found a new man."

Jen set down her coffee. "Sensitive. Like a tree stump."

"I beg your pardon?"

"For christsake, Rainey. The woman still loves you."

"Whatever we had, it ended long ago."

"So? You don't get it, do you?" she asked.

"No. Not really."

"I'm pretty sure Rachel's about to change that."

They turned when Rachel came out of her tent. She muttered something about checking on the bear, then hurried away.

Jen watched Rainey's face work itself into a tangle of lines. She reached for him.

Sometime later he opened his eyes to see her little suggestion of a smile turn to something inexplicably grand.

———

BODINE WAS IN A good mood, a thing that he figured happened once a week, for maybe half an hour, except when he was alone in the woods.

Given that he'd spent the morning with a fancy excuse for a hunter who treated him like a pack horse, only one thing could have made him feel so good—taking a trophy animal. And, by God, they'd killed an elk with the biggest rack he'd ever seen.

They'd started up the Blue Grouse Creek trail at 4:45 A.M., then cut behind Blackstone Butte. By 5:30 they had the receiver doing their work for them. It took an hour and a half to locate the bull. An hour later the guy had his shot, a shot that Bodine could have made when he was six. It took the high-and-mighty trophy hunter three bullets to bring down the bull. Even with a rifle that cost more than a Cadillac. The asshole was so excited he almost fell into Elk Creek as they waded across to claim their trophy. By 9:00 A.M. Bodine had the cape off. Ten minutes later they were on their way out with the cape and the skull, the horns still attached. And by god, it took both of them to carry that monster rack. Eleven—count 'em—eleven points on each antler. At 10:00 A.M. the guy, grinning like a great white hunter, was sitting near the trail, guarding his trophy, and here Bodine was, going back in to quarter the beautiful bastard. Feeling good.

Bodine crossed the creek, heading for a stand of fir. He thought how he might lead the hunter over one of the steel-jaw, spring traps he'd set. The guy wouldn't be so bossy with only one foot. Of course Jesse would be unhappy, and that wouldn't do, no sir. Jesse was the only man in the world that he wouldn't cross. Jesse was not a God-fearing person. No, he was the type of man who'd bite your nose off then smile—like the smart fella with the plastic mask in that movie with the weird title. *Silence of the Lambs*—what the fuck did that mean? And why didn't the nose-biter eat that bitch at the end? Anyway, Jesse was as wild as that guy. Yeah, he'd seen Jesse poke a man's eye out once for killing a bear caught in one of their traps. The thing was that the poacher had only the one eye to begin with.

At the edge of the trees Bodine heard a sound he didn't like. He focused his binoculars on the elk carcass. A grizzly bear had torn into the belly, and its muzzle was buried in the elk's innards. Bodine raised his shotgun. He was downwind, and the bear couldn't smell him yet. Okay. He was going to take a grizzly and a trophy elk, all in the same day. Besides, this looked like the devil bear—the crazy one that didn't sleep in the winter. The same bear he'd seen digging in that bowl near Stoney Ridge, higher up than a bear should be in June. Any grizzly bear that didn't behave like a grizzly bear should was capable of surprising him one day—like Satan's sow, the devil bitch that raked his face back when he was seven. (His grandma used to say he was the good-looking Bodine before he snuck up on that hoodoo bear's cubs of the year. His mixblood gramma called it a hoodoo bear, and the name stuck.)

Bodine stepped out into the meadow. The bear turned. He could see where the grizzly had blood on its muzzle, then he could hear the huffing. Something about this bear—maybe it was the way he kept shaking his nose, side to side, then swatting it—was unnatural. It hit him then—a bloodcurdling revelation—this bear was the son of Satan's sow, had to be. Bodine took slow breaths as he watched the bear's ears go down, then the grizzly lowered his head, roared, and charged. Bodine fired a slug, hitting the animal in the shoulder. The bear tumbled, causing the second shot to miss, and then it ran into the woods, bawling. Bodine swore—a cacophonous burst of abuse—enraged. Now he had to get out of here—lickety-split—and keep an eye out for a wounded bear. There was no surprise worse than a wounded bear surprise, a wounded hoodoo bear surprise.

WHEN THE PHONE RANG, Jesse was pacing circles around his bar, thinking about the trophy hunter. The guy had arrived in a camouflage Jeep. Jesse knew Bodine wanted to set the guy's jeep on fire.

"Talk to me Stacy."

"We're past the assistant. Your CIA dragon lady's on the line."

"Nellie herself, huh." This is serious, Jesse was thinking. "Put her on, Stace." He waited. "Nellie, how you doing?"

"I can't talk long. The matter you're looking into. Be careful. All I have to do is ask about this Danny Briley, I get the deep freeze. Chilled out. The guy scares people, Jesse."

"So? Life is no fucking beach."

"Right. Still cocky. Never mind. For you, I woke people, and I called in a favor. He's running some top secret program. A so-called R&D operation for the Defense Department."

"Shit."

"He's a black ops manager. Bet on it."

"In English?"

"You illiterate smartass. Okay, I'll speak slowly. They're the no-title guys handle the it-never-happened work...they do the heavy lifting no one—and I mean no one—can touch. Capiche?"

"That's nasty."

"Jesse, I know you don't listen. So print this in big letters, then put it where you can see it. *Guys like this can write off Montana.*"

———

THEY'D BROKEN CAMP BY 8:00 A.M. and started down the mountain. Rachel had willed herself to stop obsessing about the wildlife. What she would do now is gather samples. Get them to the lab. Find Phillipe. Corner Danny.

Fine. Except she was back on Rainey. Obsessing about him. Jesus. Last night was a disaster. And this morning had been awful, too. Since then she'd been all nerves, and floundering. She'd managed an apology to Jen, who was gracious about it, but it didn't make her feel any better. In fact, she felt inept. She was walking down this mountain hoping against hope that a sensible way to reach him would somehow grow in the darker recesses of her mind—spontaneous generation, mice from cheese. Her muscles were tightening up, even her stomach was tight. Talk to him, dammit. If she could just let him know where she stood, at least...at least something.

She picked up the pace, pulling well ahead of them, then stopped where a game trail wound off toward the Sentry. She heard first one shot—a shotgun blast, she thought—then another, and Rachel was off, a mother hearing her child's distinctive cry among scores of children playing in the school yard.

Rachel arrived above the Cut-Across Trail in time to see a man turning off toward Blue Grouse Creek. He stopped and looked in her direction—apparently having heard something—and for an odd moment, they each raised their binoculars, one looking for the other. Rachel, behind a tree, was sure he wouldn't spot her. She, however, had no trouble recognizing him, the same disfigured man she'd seen before.

What, she wondered, would scare a man like this? Had he surprised her recently-maced grizzly bear? She watched him hurry down the trail then took the receiver from her pack.

There was no signal. She turned toward the Blue Grouse Creek trail. Nothing. Rotating away from the poacher she picked up a fuzzy, crackling sound. She followed it, crossing the creek and entering the timber. Rainey and Jen were behind her now, and she motioned for them to stay close. Jen, she could see, was frightened. In the forest the signal was stronger. Something was wrong—the signal was a low, dull throb. Woolly Bugger wasn't moving at all. Rachel's gut began working on broken glass.

The throb grew louder as they pushed through the trees. Twenty yards to her right Rainey had his binoculars out, glassing the line where the trees gave way to the meadow. He stopped on a flash of red, passed her the glasses. She could make out something buried in the brush beneath a tree. Focusing on it, she was sure it was fluorescent red... And then there was yellow. And then red again. Rainey was already at the tree line, where he pulled a multicolored band out of the brush. A radio collar.

Rachel hurried to the tree line and checked it. She let out a measured breath. This wasn't Woolly Bugger's collar. She was sure of it. A wave of relief washed over her. Palpable.

Jen came up to them.

"Tilt collar," Rachel explained. "These are motion sensor collars. When the animal dies, it lays on its side, sending the collar into mortality or 'tilt' mode. Whoever threw the collar in the brush didn't destroy the acrylic packaging. It was sending the signal it's supposed to send when the animal dies."

"Where's the bear?" Jen asked.

"This collar was never on a bear." Rachel said, grim. "It was on an elk."

"And the elk?" Jen asked, still visibly worried.

"Dead, I'd guess." Rachel's lips made a tight thin line, holding back she wasn't sure what. "Let's find the carcass. It can't be far."

———

"I want Major Ramsey...The Ram, yeah." Danny said into the phone. He was talking with a colonel, his Defense Department liaison and one of a few men in the world he listened to. Danny was sitting in the chair on the back porch of his cabin, looking out over the Gallatin River. "That's why I need him...you know how you get a feel for a job. Well this one's got too many rough edges. I mean, hell, there's the fire, the sheriff, the weird animal shit. And the righteous attitude on some of these gung-ho park types? I swear to God they stay up at night worrying about wildlife. Some bear misses her period, it's a damn meeting...I'm not kidding...we need to upend that shit...remember Haiti? And that Afghan deal...sir, I want a guy eats his young."

———

THE ELK'S NECK HAD been sawed through. Innards hung out of a gaping hole where an animal had torn open its stomach. Rachel took a camera out of her pack and shot pictures of the mutilated carcass. She saw where the elk had been shot by a high-powered rifle and dug out the bullet with her knife. When Rachel turned, her jaw was set. "They're tracking these animals by their collars... it's unbelievable," she muttered, trying to hide how upset she was. "The one with the scarred face—he's a poacher. I've seen him up here before."

"The scar-faced poacher's named Darrell Bodine." Rainey frowned. "At seven he was mauled by a sow grizzly. At twelve he started setting forest fires. He's been in and out of state institutions ever since. I had him picked up for selling animal parts during my poaching investigation."

"Is Jesse in this?" Jen asked.

"There's big money in trophies." Rainey hesitated. "Suppose that's Jesse's interest in the thermophiles. It's not explosives. It's these oversized racks."

Rachel was working the back of her neck again. "I can't think about this now," she confessed, her head ready to burst, and led them out of the trees.

Forty yards beyond the carcass, Rachel saw blood in the meadow. She studied the matted grass, recognizing the sign of a wounded bear. Her senses went to heightened awareness, she could feel the adrenalin start pumping, and her movements became slow, deliberate. There was blood and hair where the bear had fallen, and she could see how he'd pulled himself up and run into the woods. It looked to her as if he'd run off on three legs. Yes, he'd dragged his left front paw. In the woods she saw bloodstains. She guessed he'd been hit in the left shoulder or leg. She examined a right front paw print, the third toe was missing. Woolly Bugger. She hoped he was safe now, dug in, nursing his wound. She hoped the slug had passed through. Rachel turned back to see Rainey and Jen—in the distance, they blurred into one fuzzy spot. She sat down against a tree, her throbbing head in her hands. Her world was spinning, topsy-turvy. She closed her eyes then, to ease an uneasy heart, wondering if her fate and Woolly Bugger's were irrevocably intertwined.

———

GUMMER HAD CHECKED THE trailheads, just to be sure no one was poking around, before his walk up the Blue Grouse Creek Trail. He had his snake sack in the Jeep, and the tripe from Edwin the butcher were in his pack. The way he was feeling, that walk would be good.

An hour later he knew Bodine had moved his cache of poaching gear. The shifty lowlife probably moved his cache every other week. He'd pretty much given up on finding it when he saw a bull elk at the edge of the trees. It was too far away to see just how many points, so he doubled back through the forest. This might be a chance to see a super elk. His first. Gummer made a wide loop, hoping to get above the bull, downwind. In the forest he noticed a dead-animal smell. He crept toward the unmistakable odor of rotting meat. Not even a half mile from the trail, right there in front of him was a cubby set—a bear trap. Bodine's work, he could tell. The cubby set was about four feet high, positioned against a tree and covered with brush. The back end of its A-frame tunnel sat against the tree. The front end was open. Bait hung in the tunnel, wired into the back of the cubby over a snare that was set on a spring. The bait was half a deer. The cable snare was attached to the tree. When the bear went for the deer, the snare would close on its foot. Bodine would kill the bear then cut out the gall bladder. He'd take the claws, the hide, and the skull as well.

Gummer wondered if Jesse knew about this. Probably not. Bodine probably gave him the parts to sell to Chan, without telling how or where he got them. Gummer could look the other way if the poacher killed an elk. There were too many of them to begin with. Bears were another thing. Gummer sprung the trap with a stick. Beyond the trap he noticed that the area around the base of a good-sized pine had been trampled. He approached it carefully. Looking up, he saw Bodine's cache, a duffle suspended on a cable hanging between two pines. A rifle rolled in canvas was strapped to the duffle.

He used Bodine's pulley system to lower the duffle. There was another hook, for his pack maybe. It was a good system. In the duffle there was a crosscut saw to cut logs for the cubby and a box of deer slugs for bear protection. Further in he found a CO_2 gun that could discharge a dart, and a handgun with a silencer. At the bottom of the duffle was an old fishing bag. In the bag, he found M99, a drug that could kill large mammals; Telazol, used to tranquilize bears; a skinning knife; rope; tools; and all kinds of trapping paraphernalia. In the pouch on the side of the duffle he found two books wrapped in butcher paper. Books? Bodine didn't carry the Audubon field guide. Gummer unwrapped them. Weird. One was a dog-eared Bible. The other was something about hoodoo conjuring. Leafing through it, Gummer could see protective spells. And there were markings. Underlining. Stars, circles. Just touching this book gave him the willies.

He took the rifle out of the canvas wrapping. Yes, there was an elaborate cross, carved on one side of the casing. Gummer checked the deer slugs and saw the cross, carefully cut into the nose of every thumb-sized bullet. Bodine had worked hard on this. The guy was really gone. Worse than Gummer had imagined. All the more reason to slow him down.

He replaced everything exactly as he'd found it, then Gummer emptied his snake sack into the duffle. When the snakes had settled down, he added the tripe. Let the poacher sonofabitch chew on this.

RACHEL TOOK HAIR AND blood samples from the meadow. When she was finished, they turned down again, descending in single file through the trees toward Elk Creek. Rachel pointed out unseasonal behavior in migratory birds, deer, even small mammals. The wildlife in this drainage, she said, were teetering on the lip of a black hole. So, Jen thought, was Rachel.

Plumes of smoke rose above the near ridge. Jen knew they had to check on the fire and asked to stay behind. When Rainey offered to stay with her, she shot him a look that sent him on his way.

Clouds were starting to move in from the southwest. Jen sat back against a large pine. Things were going so fast. Here she was back in the same sort of thorny mess she'd been in so often as a cop. Only she wasn't a cop now. And the clues were incomprehensible if you didn't understand wildlife. And she was falling for the guy who was going to get blamed for murdering her ex-husband. A guy whose old girlfriend wanted him back. Nice. She turned off her brain but couldn't sleep. She tried counting sheep. The sheep turned into headless elk.

———

THE FIRE HAD HARDLY moved. Rainey and Rachel saw no flames to speak of, though there were smoldering embers and the smoke still billowed. "Firefighters say on a windless night, a fire goes to sleep," Rachel explained, buying time.

"Do we need to go down there, check it out?" Rainey asked.

"No, it's not going anywhere," she said and sat down in the grass on the ridge. Secret experiments, mutations, a wounded bear, out-of-sync animals, poachers hunting the freak elk. Horrible things to worry about, and she worried about Rainey—how to tell him, how to get it right. So be it. "You remember that time you took me fishing and we got lost?"

"That was embarrassing. I'd marked the way to the lake, and I just missed it."

"By a mile."

"Never did see that lake, did we?"

"Un-unh, but I loved the campsite."

"Yeah, I finally admitted I was lost and we followed this little stream down to a meadow."

"We never even pitched our tent. We built a fire streamside and slept under the stars." She closed her eyes, opened them. "It was my fault, too," just came out of her mouth.

Rainey turned, unsure what she meant.

"I mean, I could have waited."

Rainey didn't respond.

"I know now that I handled it badly."

He hesitated, his face drawn. "How's that?"

"I miss you, Rainey." Rachel touched his arm. "Don't answer. Just let me talk for a minute." She took a slow breath. "Look, here's the deal. Every time I see you touch Jen, it makes me edgy. I can't help it. For some time now, I've worked hard to ignore that kind of feeling." She threw up her hands. "Hell, I have no idea how to work up to this, so I'll just say it...I love you. I do. There it is. It's out." Rachel sat back, relieved, almost light-headed. She had that look—I get this, and it's out of my hands. "I love you. I want to be with you." And after a beat, "That's how I feel. Please think about it...I'm hoping you'll give us another chance." She waited, watching his puzzled expression. "Think about it...then please talk to me." Rachel kissed him lightly on the lips, then she was up and running down the hill.

Rainey sat there. Confused. Annoyed. What was she thinking? Why was this happening? Was it just a reaction to seeing him with another woman? He hoped so. He and Rachel were friends. Finally. And nothing more.

He stood. It was just like her to wait until it was finished, dead and buried. Then dig it up again.

———

THREE HOURS LATER—CARRYING a foul-smelling, mutated, baby elk carcass in a plastic garbage bag, a dead wingless eaglet, a piece of the shoulder of a huge headless elk, various blood, bone and tissue samples, insects, animal droppings, petri dishes, and dozens of test tubes—they were back at the car.

Jen watched them both, perplexed. If emotional stuff had gone down, no one was owning up to it.

Rachel suggested they set up a base in an old park service cabin she occasionally used up Little Bear Creek. It was between the park and North, and only two miles off the road. Jen didn't have the nerve to ask if it had a toilet.

———

BODINE WAS PISSED OFF, confused and scared at the same time. The Seagram's and the uppers he stashed in the truck hadn't helped. And now he couldn't get his mind back where he could tell it what to do. It was spinning out there like one of those upside down roller coasters. He was thinking about killing the trophy hunter, cutting his head off and mounting it like a trophy elk. No, Jesse would get mad. Jesse the heathen.

He'd done his job—the trick had bagged his fuckin' trophy. Only that wasn't enough for Jesse. No. Bodine had to take him back in day after tomorrow. Go back in where the hoodoo bear was waiting for him. Waiting with a slug in his shoulder and a mad-on that wouldn't stop. So he tried to explain the situation. But when he told Jesse how the bear was the devil's own instrument, Jesse cracked wise, telling him how the Almighty would be his guide. He called God a pointing dog. He said that.

Bodine had known then that he couldn't tell Jesse about the sign. About the entrails, the bloody snakes in his bag. A warning. He'd gone to get more twelve-gauge slugs, and Satan's snakes had exploded all over him. He couldn't get it out of his head—the bloody, gut-drenched snakes on his face, his neck, everywhere.

He'd tried reading his Bible, but he couldn't concentrate. The words, even the ones he'd underlined, didn't fit together right. He kept seeing the bear. And the bloody writhing snakes. And the trophy hunter, treating him like a porter on a train, or a waitress. And Gummer's fancy Jeep Cherokee. And Jesse, with red eyes. Yeah. He thought of setting the Silver Dollar on fire. But then he pictured Jesse, setting him on fire. Smiling while he burnt up. A mean, little payback smile.

So he'd gone cruising, looking for a way to stop his mind. At the ranger station he saw a brand-spanking-new blue Jeep. How could that pussy Gummer have a new one already? Just seeing it made the inside of his head start burning. The smart-mouthed ranger didn't deserve that fancy new car, or that Dairy Queen girl.

He could picture Gummer fucking his girl in that new Jeep, while the snakes exploded all over him.

When he passed by the Dairy Queen, he got his idea. A good one. Gummer's whore, she worked there. He'd followed them, watched them do it in the skinny shitbag's fancy Cherokee. Well, he needed some of that. Uh-huh. Right now. That would settle him down, cool him out.

Pleased now, his mind coming back on line, Bodine drove to the trailer court. She'd be coming out sooner or later, walking back into North.

There she was. He got excited just watching her walk the highway in those jeans and that tight little T-shirt. He started following her in his pickup. He pulled over maybe fifteen yards ahead of her, turning the truck so it was at an angle to the road. When she reached the truck, he swung the door wide open, right in front of her. She turned, startled, and he pulled her in. Easy as pie. She yelled once, but that stopped when he punched her face. She looked at him then, kind of strange. Like she was excited. There was blood on her upper lip.

Bodine couldn't believe it when she put her hand between his legs.

She was quiet until he turned off at the big boulder. The same place she went with Gummer.

"You been watching me?" she asked.

How did she know? Shit. She was smart. He turned toward her, pulled her hair back. When she cried out, his face got hot and his eyes got tiny. He eased up when she ran her tongue along her bloody upper lip. "I like that you been watching me," she said. "I like it. You wanna get high first?" Her hand was rubbing his bone now, and the bitch was breathing fast, into it. "I got some weed," she whispered. "I got a J."

He nodded, pulling her T-shirt up. She was evil, had to be, the way she wanted it. He'd kill her, after. Bodine could feel his mind take a nice easy plunge, find a groove.

Her right hand pulled a joint out of a pack of Marlboros in her purse. "Please, baby, go slow," she said. "I'm better when I'm high."

Bodine squeezed her breast, hard enough to hurt. She was crying now. Good. His mind was grooving, working up a vision: he saw the forest on fire, with Satan's stoned slut burning up in it.

"Baby, be nice," she pleaded. "Lemme get high." Darcie reached into her purse for a matchbook.

Bodine had his head between her breasts, and he was pulling her jeans down with both hands, when she leaned over to light the match and planted the Buck knife in his back. It went in a good three inches, into his shoulder, just above his heart. She twisted the blade as hard as she could before she rolled out of the pickup door. When he came staggering out, his face a blotchy red mask of rage, Darcie smashed a good-sized rock into his nose.

Bodine grunted. Blood gushed down over his mouth and chin. She ran down the road toward the trailer park. He pulled the knife blade out of his shoulder. Then he curled up in a ball in the tall grass. He'd get the lying hoodoo whore, he thought, feeling his blood pumping, surging, washing the evil from his body.

Phillipe's Viruses

ON THE SECOND THURSDAY of each month, from May through October, Jesse hosted a barbeque at his Bear Tooth Ranch. The cooking was done on polished spits and massive cast-iron grills set up especially for the occasion. Jesse's barbeques always featured one or two wild game entrées—deer, elk, antelope, waterfowl or upland birds—and, of course, buffalo or beef. Weather permitting, the lavish buffet was served outside on the covered porch. Today, Jesse was offering elk or buffalo burgers to about one hundred and twenty folks. He said it was his way of giving back something to the community that had been so good to him.

While people filled their plates and listened to a country and western singer, Jesse leaned over the railing at the far corner of the side porch pretending to listen to Danny Briley.

Jesse was feigning listening to Danny's plans for containing the five-acre fire while he worried about Bodine. The man had come back cursing and grousing about some crazy wounded bear. Satan's own grizzly, he'd called him. Jesse had told Bodine to use a silver bullet on this evil sonofabitch if it bothered him so damn much. And maybe get some help from the Almighty, he'd added. When he got into the specifics on that, Bodine shot him a bone-chilling look and Jesse let it go.

Jesse turned back to Danny—living proof, by god, that the federal government had even fewer scruples than he did. Look at him. The guy was wearing patched blue jeans and a Yellowstone T-shirt that said Bear Whiz Beer. The shirt had a picture of a bear relieving himself in a bottle. What kind of federal creep would wear shit like that to his ranch?

"Danny boy," he said, soft and silky, when Danny finished. "I do believe I have favorable news for you."

"How's that, Jesse?"

"Well, I located those missing petri dishes. Yes, I did."

"And?"

"Behind those clothes—I mean, Jesus, you show up at my barbeque looking like some kind of hippie been in a coma for twenty-five years—behind those clothes, I say you're a smart fella."

Danny scratched his beard. "You are a man of unique talents. Tell me, just what are you wanting here?"

"You know the big picture—that fella Rainey stole the petri dishes, killed a man his way out. Left the dishes with Lester. Now that's how she happened. Sure as death and taxes. But—" He put a hand on Danny's shoulder, confiding, "But Danny, those of us who are elected, we need—no, we require—your slam-dunk type of proof. And I don't have that just yet. So, what I'm needing here is some federal help. Think of it like when your federal banks step in to help out your little local banks. Anyway, suppose you were to work out—I dunno—some kind of federal warrant. You see we hold him on that type of deal 'til I get my ducks in a row."

"Do I look like one of your ranch hands?"

"Well, no, dressed like you are, you look more like a goat herder." Jesse ran thumb and forefinger down his mustache. "Besides, I don't guess you ride well enough to be a ranch hand."

Danny's eyes went cold. "I understand that you only declared seventy thousand dollars in income last year. The same year you received significant undisclosed cash payments from local condominium developers, from dummy corporation land sales, from selling whiskey confiscated from unlicensed sellers back to your own saloons. Should I go on? I know of—lemme see—five, yes, five counts of tax fraud, so far. That, Slick, is federal help."

Jesse was sure his privates had just shriveled up to pinworm size. He reached under his neckerchief and fingered his scar.

———

154

GUMMER, WATCHING FROM THE steps, recognized Jesse's scar-touching as a sure sign that the sheriff was getting upset. He was relieved when Jesse went into the house.

Gummer hung back where the porch turned the corner, ready to intercept any unwanted visitors. He picked Phillipe out of the crowd. He didn't trust that guy. The Frenchman acted like a know-it-all, especially when it came to Native Americans, sex, or fast food. Gummer knew enough about two of those three things to smell a rat.

The call came at 5:24 P.M. Gummer would always remember the exact time. No one had ever called him before at one of Jesse's barbeques, so it took him by surprise. One of the cowgirls handed him the portable phone. He put it to his ear and listened for about fifteen seconds. All he said was: "Wait at the trailer. I'm on my way."

———

DARCIE WAS WRAPPED IN a blanket, shaking. Her daddy's twelve-gauge was still in her lap, even though Gummer was sitting beside her on the green, plastic-covered couch.

"He was filthy dirty, G. He knew about our special place."

Gummer put his long arms around her. "Shh, shh. You're safe now. I'm here, baby. I'm right beside you now."

"You got to understand. When he punched me, I knew he would hurt me. Hurt me bad. That's what he liked. I could see that in those sick, mean eyes." She pulled her arms tightly against her chest.

"Easy, hon. Easy. I do understand." He felt nauseous. "It's all over now. I promise you that."

"I had to pretend with him baby. I made him think I liked it." She laid her head on his shoulder and cried. "That was the worst thing."

"It's okay, baby." He hugged her close. "It's okay. You did the right thing. You did good. Really good. You thought way ahead like you have to do when there's danger. And you sized it up right. He likes to hurt women."

"He was evil. I should've killed him."

"You may have."

"You go up there, G. You see if the pickup's there. I betcha it's gone."

"If he's not dead, I'm gonna kill him," Gummer said. A matter of fact.

"You better," she whispered.

They drove back to their special place together. Darcie didn't want to be left alone. She started shaking when they saw smoke coming from the hillside beyond their spot. Gummer stopped the jeep on the near side of their boulder. The pickup was gone. Darcie clicked off the safety on the twelve gauge. Gummer took his service revolver out and stepped down from the Jeep. He checked out both sides of the boulder then positioned her with her back to the boulder, facing the trees and the road. "Stay here, sweetie."

Gummer searched the clearing. There was a patch of blood not far from where the pickup had been parked. He could see where Bodine had turned the Ford around.

"He's gone."

"You sure?"

"Uh-huh. We better check the fire."

They drove up a logging road for almost a mile, then they took the fork to Rattlesnake Ridge. At the edge of the ridge they could look down into a ravine. There were three or four old wrecks in the ravine. Kids used to push old cars off this ridge until a boy suffered multiple snake bites. The ravine was overgrown now. The fire was in the ravine, a larger fire than it had seemed from below.

"He set it," Darcie said. "I know he did."

"Good place for it. No one's gonna notice right away." Gummer took her hand. "Let's go call it in."

"What now?" Darcie asked when they were back in the trailer.

"Report the fire, then make sure you're safe. You call in sick to the DQ?"

"Yeah."

"I got some business. You wanna stick with me?"

"Is he gonna come back for me, G?"

"I don't think so. But he's so crazy, I can't say for sure. Can you stay with a friend?"

"Patsy's mom won't mind. I'll stay with her." Darcie took his hand. "What are you gonna do, hon? You gonna look for him?"

"No. He'll hide in the woods somewhere. When he shows, I'm gonna be ready."

She put a palm on his chest. "You be careful, G. Be real careful."

———

"Don't be an ass," Rachel said. Phillipe had insisted the Sentry could not be erupting. "I saw it erupt. I took pictures of it erupting."

Phillipe paced around well-ordered cardboard boxes in his small, smoke-filled living room. Lab equipment sat on the coffee table. Rachel thought she recognized the metal container with the petri dishes. She sunk into a cheap armchair, trying to keep her temper in check.

"Ma cherie, for perhaps two hundred and seventy years, she does not erupt. How could it be that now, out of the blue, as you say, this is happening?"

Rachel shifted her weight, uncomfortable. "Let me put it to you this way. That pool is so damn hot, I'd bet your thermophiles are melting as we speak."

"Unthinkable."

"Right." She almost threw a Bunsen burner at him. "I've read their notes. The Sentry pool is regularly heated over two hundred degrees. They have their own very powerful heating agent—an exothermic nitrogenous compound they call ENT—and they're dumping it in the pool regularly. It's far stronger than the nitric acid you and Moody used to pack out thermophile mats. Apparently, small amounts raise the temperature in the pool very quickly. They bring it as high as two ten."

"This is not possible. Allow the deterioration of the pool?"

"Phillipe, listen carefully. The whole drainage is out of whack. All kinds of unseasonal animal behavior—elk, fish, bears, birds, you name it. And the young have birth defects. I know of elk calves and golden eaglets that have died from them. It's like a lousy science fiction movie up there." She paused. "The animals are drinking the thermophiles right out of the creek."

"What you are saying—"

"The superheated thermophilic organisms are draining into the creek after the Sentry erupts. The animals are ingesting them in their drinking water. That's right—their drinking water. I think they're screwing up both the timing and the amount of hormone production. And eventually, causing deformities in the young. Look at this—" She took a box from her jacket pocket and removed the mutated eaglet.

"Merde!" He turned away.

"You know more about these Sentry thermophiles than anyone. Is what I'm suggesting possible?"

Phillipe took a notebook from one of the boxes, muttering something about the foucking smart-as-hell sheriff. "It is possible, yes. Before I explain, however, you must agree to tell me everything— everything that is happening at the Sentry. I will also want to see notes, samples, whatever you have taken out."

Sweet. What sort of deal, she wondered, did Fleming have to make for penicillin? She sighed. "Is what you have worth it? Gimme a taste."

"The normal high temperatures in the Sentry pool recreate some ideal steady state—before the ice age—when the thermophiles, they flourished. Allow me to say that I know how the viruses hosted by the Sentry thermophiles behave in the unsteady state."

"Viruses? What viruses?"

"Rachel, you may not like me today. But believe me, I studied this. There are viruses in these Sentry thermophiles. The viral DNA, she is my project. No one knows this. I was studying the viruses when the area, it is closed. I think I can explain what is happening to your animals, and no one else can. And yes indeed, it is worth it."

She waited, because she knew it irritated him. "Okay. Let's have it."

"Here is what I am thinking. We assume, first, that the pool is in the temperature range you suggest. Above a hundred and ninety-five degrees the Sentry thermophiles, they become agitated and unstable. The viruses, however, they cannot replicate without the happy, functioning host. Once these thermophiles become unstable, the virus, she recognizes this, and hoping to survive, the viral DNA within these thermophiles reproduces quickly—very quickly—forming more and more viruses. These viruses, they are like the rats on the sinking ship—looking for a way out—trying to escape the distressed, often dying, and, in some cases, potentially explosive host. I've seen this. Suppose the thermophiles are then transported, by the untimely eruption of this hot spring, into the cold water in Elk Creek? At this lower temperature, the Sentry thermophiles, they will eventually die, unless—" He paused, dramatically. "Unless they are ingested by an animal. If that happens, they will, I think, hone in on the animal's hypothalamus—hone in on a stable place where they can recover in the warm, protected environment."

"I don't understand."

"The hypothalamus, it is a warm, steady state area. And it is in the brain, so it is relatively safe. You see, the immune response in the brain is not nearly as strong, as potent—yes? As in the arm, or the kidney. The hypothalamus is, as you say, an 'immune privileged' environment. For the unstable thermophiles it's a 'home' to recover from the cooler, deadly environment in the creek. They are simply saving themselves."

"Can you walk me through this?"

He snorted, a haughty Gallic snort. "Cherie, I can waltz you through it. I discovered it. You see, in my lab, I—we...agh." He waved his hand. "Here are your mechanics. Once ingested by an animal, the infected Sentry thermophiles go to the hypothalamus, where the virus infects the cells that regulate hormone production. The virus, it then—how do you say? Co-opts—yes, it co-opts the cellular machinery to make more of itself." He lit a cigarette off his first, then flicked the butt into the sink. "It is likely that because of this, it is no longer possible for these cells in the animal's hypothalamus to regulate the timing of hormone production—thus, your unseasonal behavior. Or the amounts of hormone production—thus, your oversized antlers." Phillipe raised a palm. "Too fast for you, honey?" He winked at her nasty look.

It was as bad as it could be, Rachel thought. "So you're telling me that once ingested by an animal, these viruses can pretty much turn off the genes that regulate photo period or hormone cycles?"

"Absolutely."

"And hormone production...even during pregnancy?"

"I'm afraid so. And, I fear, it's cumulative."

"Which means more and even deadlier mutations?"

"Probably, yes."

There was a knock on the door, it swung open, and there was Gummer—uniform freshly pressed, hat in hand, all smiles. "Well hey there, Rachel. Where you been, hon?"

159

"She's been—"

"Shut up, Phillipe, and don't 'hon' me Gummer," Rachel snapped. And why was this altogether-too-folksy ranger here at all?

"Excuse me. Didn't mean to offend. It's just that, well, we've had an outbreak of foolishness—"

"Foolishness is right," Phillipe interrupted, poking his cigarette at Gummer. "What you and your sheriff friend neglected to tell me is that the Sentry, she is erupting. My experiments, they are at risk."

Gummer frowned. "I'm confused here. What's this about the Sentry erupting?"

"You, you don't know this?"

"Well, I'm not up there often. It's a closed area."

"Well she says this." The cigarette shifted to Rachel. "She says they are heating my pool. She says—"

Gummer cut him off. "S'cuse me Pierre—" And to Rachel: "You were up there? Rachel?"

"And just what's your interest in this? Oversized racks? Trophy hunts?" Rachel asked, hoping to get under his thick skin.

"Trophy hunts?" he asked, looking like a confused Eagle Scout. "What are—"

Phillipe stepped in front of Gummer before he could finish. "And I'm foucking tired of being interrupted by crackers." He exhaled a lungful of smoke at Gummer. "You, uh, get it?"

"Whoa..." Gummer took a step back. "You folks smokin' dope, or what?"

"Get out of my house, now." Phillipe pushed Gummer to the door. "I'll talk with you later," he murmured, then closed the door.

Rachel waited, patient. There was still work to be done before her next stop, Danny Briley. "Sit down, Phillipe," she said, readying herself for more bad news. "Let's talk about the volatile properties of superheated Sentry thermophiles."

———

GUMMER STOOD A MINUTE, listening through the door. Maybe he was dreaming. He knew he was still reeling from Bodine. How did Rachel know about the trophy hunts? And why was the Sentry erupting? He had to ask Phillipe about that. One thing was sure as sunrise—for the French guy, lying and talking was the same thing.

―――――――

BODINE DROVE THROUGH THE grass parking area. He went around the barriers at the trailhead and gunned the truck up the Blue Grouse Creek Trail. The first mile would be easy going, then he'd hide the truck and disappear into the forest. His forest. He'd be okay there. He still had some of the Seagram's left, and he used it to wash down an upper. His shoulder was hurting, even after the painkillers. Well, he was going to set fire to the lying whore. It made him feel better, thinking how he'd send her on her way to burn in hell forever. But first he had his job to do, his mission. It had come to him when he was curled up in the grass, bleeding from his back and his nose.

Maybe it took the pain and blood to be a channel. Blood coursing through his veins, emptying into the earth. Because lying there, he'd felt the blood washing out the forces of evil. He felt that. Later—he couldn't tell how long—he felt clean, on the inside. And just like that, he'd seen what needed to be done. And he knew he'd been chosen to do it. Then, like a sign, he could stand up. So he set the rattlesnakes in the ravine on fire—a warning—then drove to North. At the drugstore he made the guy bandage his shoulder, then give him the painkillers and some uppers. When the guy cracked wise—something about downers—he shot the smartass pharmacist and set his damn drugstore on fire. It hadn't been in the vision, but it was right. He didn't have to take sass. Not anymore. He was no man's hired hand. He'd seen what he was. Since then his head had been clear, and his mind had stayed on line.

Fire had been the first sign. In the vision he'd seen the forest burning up. It had to be the fire those so-called scientists set at the patrol cabin. That fire had burned up his best trap. He should of seen right then that Satan had chosen Elk Creek. Well, he knew now—for sure. Satan lived in the fire. And he lived in the son of Satan's sow, the hoodoo bear. In his blood. And he was in the elk that the trophy hunter had shot. That's why he'd been punished. For taking the bloody head of his evil elk. The devil had entered him when he cut off the head. Marked him with his snakes at the cache. Then he'd led him to his lying she-bitch. His hoodoo whore. And Satan's slut tempted him, tricked him and tried to kill him. It was the blood—*his blood*—that washed the evil out. His blood saved him. Cleansed him. Made him an instrument of God. Sworn enemy of Satan. And now it was his turn.

———

JEN WAS MISSING JIMMY again when they arrived at the Little Bear Creek cabin. It was set in a grove of firs, spitting distance from the creek. The cabin looked tiny and old, and it was padlocked. Rainey had to break in through a boarded-up front window.

"Cabin" seemed to Jen a misnomer. Inside, it was more like a one-room shack. Rainey explained that whatever water they needed had to be brought up from the creek and boiled. Jen decided to brighten it up with flowers, which Rainey picked then handed in to her. She'd call out colors, and he'd do his best to oblige. When she was satisfied, Jen went outside to wash up in the creek.

She stood beside the creek, watching the water spill over a rock the size of a pumpkin, feeling low. She felt one of Rainey's big hands on her hip, and Jen turned, responding eagerly. Something about their lovemaking was different. It was not that it was hurried, even needy, though it was both of those things. No, there was, she decided, a certain unmistakable sweetness.

Afterwards, she lay on the grass by the creek. Her head was on Rainey's thigh. Jen stared at the sky and thought about Jimmy, again.

"Is something wrong?" Rainey asked.

His hand, pressing on her stomach, was somehow reassuring. "Jimmy. I'm worrying about Jimmy."

"He's a tough little guy. He'll be okay," Rainey said, then added, an afterthought, "I like him."

"How can you like him or not like him? He never says a word you can hear."

"That's why I like him. Your boy's got the good sense to keep his mouth shut until opening it will do him some good."

She took his hand, pleased Rainey understood the usefulness of silence to a boy with a father like Cockeye. "I want to see him, tomorrow."

"I'll try."

Jen nodded, keenly aware how at ease she felt with this man. And how easily he'd brought her to such a hard-to-reach comfort level. Rainey moved more slowly than she did, but somehow, he'd taken them further and faster than she ever could have. How had he done that? Most people, she decided, zigzagged, finding their way by searching out known or recognizable footing. In other words, they crossed the creek by stepping on the stones they could see. Rainey didn't do that; he charted his course by some inner compass. He didn't even know he was on it. Yet he trusted his direction and followed that path purposefully, tenaciously, wherever it took him. She wondered where that path went. Jen looked up at him. "Was I right about Rachel?"

"What do you mean?"

Her head cocked up so she could look him straight in the eye. "You know exactly what I mean."

"You were right." His eyes held hers.

"And?"

"Whenever I try and figure out why Rachel is doing this, I end up thinking about you."

That had to be good.

Undectable Thermophile Bombs

I T WAS AFTER 7:00 when Rachel drove up to Danny's. He was sitting in the old, overstuffed porch chair reading this fat memo. He waved her inside when she opened the Volvo door.

"What a nice surprise," he said, waiting at the door. "Drink?"

She walked up to him, stopping inches from his face. "You're a goddamn liar. I've been to the Sentry. I want to know exactly what you're doing. You tell me now or I'll go straight to the superintendent."

"Rachel—"

"Don't patronize me," she cut him off, seeing how easy it was to be fooled by this expert liar. "The Sentry's erupting. You're superheating the pool. Why?"

"Hey, there's no mystery." He led her inside. "Dr. Moody was onto something. We're following through." Danny's jaw muscles were working. "We needed more samples. What's the big deal?"

"Are you kidding? You can't heat a Yellowstone hot spring pool."

"An exception has been made."

"An exception? Jesus, for what?" And when he didn't answer, "You're lying. You're not finishing his work at all."

"I don't understand what you're talking about. Would you like to see our reports?"

"The Sentry's going off," she persisted, growing ever angrier at his patronizing lies. "Animals are drinking the superheated thermophiles from Elk Creek. It's fouling up their hormone production. Their babies are mutating and dying. You've been lying all along, covering up whatever you're doing. I'm going to the superintendent, the papers, all the way to D.C. if I have to."

He showed his palms. "You're in over your head here. Now, I'm going to ask you—please—take it easy, let this go."

"What an incredible creep. There's nothing you could say that would make me *let this go*."

"Then you leave me no choice. The work at the Sentry is classified. If you say word one, to anyone, you go to jail. Classified," he repeated. "Think about that."

"Classified? Research in Yellowstone Park is classified?" Danny nodded, ice-cold. He was an alien. "Fuck you."

Danny took her left wrist, twisted it behind her back. His thumb on some pressure point, he forced her to her knees.

"Let me go. You're hurting me."

He forced her wrist up behind her back. He kept raising her wrist until she cried out in pain. Her eyes were tearing when he slowly whispered in her ear, "You don't get it. This isn't the park service you're dealing with. I don't have to go to meetings. When I say let this go, you let it go, nicely."

"Okay. Please. Okay." When he released her Rachel got up slowly, head down, ever-so-fucking tired of being used, lied to, and now, viciously bullied. She pulled the safety off a canister of bear mace in her jacket pocket, raised her head and fired a burst at his neck.

Danny fought for breath, choking and coughing between great heaving gasps. His eyes were tearing.

"Do exactly as I say or I'll spray your face." She pointed the canister at his mouth. "Grab that post." She nodded toward a post that supported the cabin's loft. "Both hands. Just do it!" She wasn't sure where that came from, but man-oh-man, she felt better.

Danny did as he was told. He set his head against the post, too, unable to stop wheezing and coughing. His eyes watered. He fought for each breath.

"Don't think about moving." Rachel kept the canister on his face as she tore a drawcord from the blinds. With her free hand, she looped the cord around one wrist, then the other. She fired another short burst at his neck, then Rachel pulled the cord tight. She set down the mace. While Danny struggled to breathe, Rachel tied his hands tightly together around the post.

"You're crazy," he gasped. "I'm burning up." His eyes were wild, furtive, and his lips were pinched.

"Stay still," she ordered, mace raised again. "You don't know the half of just how crazy I am. So far, you just itch and burn. This bear mace in your face will make you wish you were dead. Tell me all of it, now." She fired a short burst on her fingers, near his face. The fumes made him gag.

"Untie me. Please, god."

She touched the orange residue on her fingers to his mustache. He cried out, then coughed, breathing through his mouth. Tears flowed from his eyes. He cried out again. She held the can of Counter Assault three inches from his nose. "One...two..."

"Okay," he gasped. "It's research. It's classified. Moody didn't know what he had. I couldn't tell you anything. Untie me, please. I'm burning up."

"What research? What are you doing? What?"

"I can't say." He shook his head, breathing fast.

"You can't, but you will." She fired a burst at his shirt. He fell to his knees, wailing now. "Tell me now or I'll spray you again."

"Defense Department..." He gasped. "Explosives..."

Jesus. "More."

A long hollow sound came from his throat as he fought for a breath.

"More," she repeated. She sprayed his shirt again.

He blinked repeatedly to slow the horrible itching in his eyes. She knew the inside of his nose was on fire. Tears trickled down his cheeks. She fired a short burst at the floor beside his knees. He turned his head away, defeated. "Bombs," he whispered. "Little, undetectable bombs...powerful..."

Oh shit. "How?"

"Superheated thermophiles...some other chemical." He stopped to swallow, his voice a gravelly rasp. "Extremely high energy bonds... biomolecular explosions." He rested his head against the post. "They test back East. That's all I know. I swear. I'm not a scientist."

There was sweat on his brow now, his cheeks were wet, and he was still gasping for breath. "I swear."

"Why heat the pool? Why can't you heat them at a lab?"

"We tried." He worked for air. "Problems..." He let it trail off. She stepped closer; it was enough. "Poor outcomes," he managed.

"Why?"

His head was against the post again. Tears were running down his cheeks. "We don't know why."

He was telling the truth, she decided. It was too awful to make up. "Take slow breaths. I'll get some water." She made sure that his hands were still securely tied, then Rachel stepped into the bathroom. She went over what he'd told her, unable to fathom this shocking news. When she came out, he was sitting on the floor, hands around the post. She cleaned his upper lip, face, and eyes with a washcloth. "That should help."

He stood up slowly. She watched him for a minute. Danny, once considered a friend, now made her physically uncomfortable. He began to breathe more regularly. "You were my friend. I trusted you, and you used me. Why?"

"I like you. I like you a lot. We were friends. We can still be friends," Danny suggested in a raspy voice. "Untie me now, please."

"Friends? How many times did I tell you I didn't understand the bear management closure? How many? And you lied, every time. You convinced me I was better off with the closure, that my bear was better off. And that phony meeting—you just wanted to know what you had to cover up. Lies on top of lies." She lowered her head. "I hate it when men lie to me. And I hate being so gullible." She raised her head just enough to look at him. "And, god, how I hate that I slept with you."

Danny wasn't listening. "Untie me. Now." His bloodshot eyes had glazed over. She thought they looked weird, dead. Unfriendly alien eyes.

"No chance."

Danny's face was expressionless, a lifeless mask. He looked fifteen years older, a person she didn't know. "Untie me now, or I'll kill you." This was, apparently, a statement of fact.

Rachel just looked at him.

"You want to die, Rachel?" he asked, as if asking a slow child. "Just do as I say. Now," he calmly commanded.

"You come here under false pretenses, you lie to everyone, you kill wildlife without a thought. I find you out, and then you order me around. Just who do you think you are?"

"You stupid bitch! You do exactly—"

She stepped to his side, then fired a burst of bear mace in front of his face.

She left, her own eyes watering now, as Danny dropped to the floor, gasping obscenities.

———

GUMMER WAS AT HIS apartment, running numbers for the elk farm. Mostly, he was working to keep his mind off Bodine. He was regretting the snakes. Thinking he'd used bad judgment. On the way home he'd blown Jesse's damn elk burger out the Jeep window. At least now, when he thought of what happened to Darcie, his stomach didn't hurt. He just got crazy mad. Which was okay, except he had to be rock steady when he told Jesse about it, because there was no way of knowing just what Jesse would do with something like this. The guy could get really weird, he was thinking, when the phone rang.

"Rachel? Do you a favor? Do myself a favor? Make up your mind, sweetie...what word? Sweetie? Jeez, Rachel, so a guy's old-fashioned. It's not like I'm stoned or anything...time is of the what? Sorry...Danny? Danny Briley? He's what? No...no way...bear mace? Where? Why you devil...I know it's just minutes from here...now you're doing me a favor? Well, I tell ya what, I'm doing Danny a favor...take it easy sweetie, I'm on it."

When Gummer opened Danny's front door, the smell, even the burning taste, of bear mace was still in the air. He covered his nose and mouth with his handkerchief as he stepped back outside. On the porch he coughed, and his eyes started to water.

Danny came out the back door, stepped onto the porch. "What are you doing here?" He was still wet from the shower. He wore a robe. His face was puffy, his eyes were swollen and red, and he had a gun.

"What the heck happened? Rachel Stanley called. She said something about macing you. She said you were a liar, that you were with the army or something. Jeez, I never heard her so mad. Anyway, she said you might need some help."

"Get out of here before I shoot you."

Gummer had never seen Danny act this way. He let it go. Gummer figured the guy was spooked, and embarrassed, big time.

Gummer drove straight to Patsy's. Before anything else, he wanted to see Darcie. Right there, in the kitchen, he told her about the snakes, and the tripe.

She started crying again.

"Hon, I made a mistake. And I'm sorry. What that crazy animal Bodine did, I take part of the blame. I'm just sorry. That's all I can say."

"It's not your fault, G, if the man has no heart and an ugly, vile nature. You didn't make him like that."

He wiped her tears. "You're a good person, Darce. Don't think I don't know that."

On his way to find Jesse, Gummer decided that Darcie was one in a million.

———

THE PHARMACY FIRE WAS under control by the time Jesse arrived. As luck would have it, the pharmacy was in his own Old West Mini Mall, so the sprinklers and the alarm had worked, and the firefighters had responded with demonstrable vigor. Jesse was in such a bad mood, however, that he didn't even care that his fancy old stagecoach—the one he'd wrangled, on loan, from the Cody museum—was mostly ashes.

He sat on the tailgate of a fire truck, feeling edgy and low. When they pulled the pharmacist out, gutshot, Jesse had this sinking feeling—this was gonna turn out bad for him, really bad. When they told him it was arson, it got worse, sort of a bone-scraping worry. When someone said they'd seen an old Ford pickup with a homemade shell parked behind the drugstore, Jesse just said, "Aw shit."

———

GUMMER FOUND JESSE LEANING against the PayLess hitching rail, staring across the street at the smoldering remains of Brad's Frontier Pharmacy. When he told the sheriff how Bodine had attacked

Darcie and tried to rape her, Jesse just cocked his head. "What did she do?" he eventually asked.

"She stuck a knife in his back."

The sheriff shook his head, sadly. "Okay. Bodine starts slow. Then he takes some twists and turns the Lord never intended. We know that. But now son, because of your nubile DQ sweetie, our one-and-only guide's frothing at the mouth. Do you have any idea how much money we're losing here?"

"This isn't about money. He could have killed her," Gummer explained, startled by his own forcefulness.

The sheriff sat down on the wooden entry steps.

Gummer wondered why the sheriff was in such a mean funk. He didn't care. "If you don't lock him up, I'm gonna put him to sleep, like a rabid dog."

"Easy, killer. You got enough blood for your dick and your brain. After what he did to our pharmacist, I'm gonna have to put him away." His left cheek twitched once, just barely. "What a goddamn waste." Jesse put on his sunglasses, and listlessly, he trod toward the Gold Nugget, his bar.

Gummer suppressed his rising anger. Jesse had to be cheered up—he knew that much—before he did something stupid. Besides, he hoped to raise his elk farm proposition tonight. Okay. Yes. He had an idea.

———

SAVE THE BATTERIES, RACHEL decided, looking up at a nearly perfect three-quarter moon floating in a calm sea of stars. She switched off her flashlight and picked up her pace.

She'd talked with the chief of research. After thirty-two years of service in the park, he couldn't fathom how this had happened. Why hadn't he been told? The integrity and the mission of the park were at risk. The very idea that Defense Department scientists could be superheating a hot spring pool to research explosives in a national park—and doing it without the knowledge of the park's biologists, or senior park administrators—well, it was insane. And now wildlife was at risk, and as far as he was concerned, they had to protect it. Well, with the chief helping, Rachel felt slightly hopeful.

She was aware that she had sidestepped the part about Danny. Yes, she'd explained that Danny was in charge of this military research. But she'd slid right by her revenge. Maybe it was because she was keeping it to herself, kind of savoring it. He'd try to get her back. That much was written in some book of things men like Danny do. She knew she should be afraid of him—he was twisted and dangerous—but so far, she wasn't.

Rachel wondered how Rainey would react to her new attitude. And in that instant—she would always remember stepping over a big dark rock on the trail—she pictured Rainey, and she crashed. She was adrift. Waiting on him. And she had no idea, no idea at all, what to do.

———

"GO THROUGH THE WHOLE deal again," Jesse exclaimed, darn near gleeful, after he heard Gummer's story about Danny. He was standing on a box, belly up to the Gold Nugget's old marble bar, feeling like a new man. There was sawdust on the floor, a mounted grizzly rearing up on his hind legs in the corner, and poker machines dinging away in the background. This was the best news. This just about made up for that butt-ugly cretin Bodine.

Until this news he'd been on the decline. This particular downhill slide had started when Danny—who, Jesse decided, had the demeanor, and was likely the seed of, a great white shark—had detailed just how the IRS attack dogs were about to look into his tax returns. Did that on his own front porch, at his own barbeque. Well, Jesse had laughed it off, as he tumbled toward his own private slough of despond.

Then the fire, and that retard Bodine.

And now—poof—out of nowhere, Danny gets his. Bear mace? Who would have thought Rachel had it in her to do something like that? He was going to thank her personally. He knew that it took a kind of artistic mind to come up with just the right kind of payback.

Jesse slapped Gummer on the back. He made him tell the story again, then they were back on super elk. Running numbers, really into it. Jesse even had a gleam in his eye. "Gumby—"

Jesse took Gummer's arm then he signaled the bartender for a phone and punched in a number. "Hey, Phil. Just Jesse to you, buddy." Jesse winked at Gummer, who looked confused. "We're having sort of an impromptu meeting. Running some numbers, talking product development...right here at the Gold Nugget...I own that wretched saloon.Wretched *rocks*...I never heard of Beavis and Butthead...never mind...right away." He put the phone down, winked at Gummer again. "You see where this is goin' son?"

Gummer shook his head, no.

"Suppose we have our French biologist harvest these thermophiles, create our own private stock? Do it before that asshole Danny blows up the hot spring." Jesse paused, pensive.

When he got it, Gummer tapped his forehead with his palm.

"Harvest the thermophiles..." Jesse waited until this came together just so. "Harvest the thermophiles...then Bodine can set undercover Danny on fire."

Gummer whistled, a two-toned beauty.

———

THE CREEK GOT WIDER above the cabin. Rainey watched a medium-sized pool, an oval-shaped patch of gentler water below a fallen tree limb. Where the faster water came around the limb, the difference in current speeds created a seam. Trout rose regularly along the seam.

Caddis flies were hatching, though it was almost impossible to see them actually fly from the water. The mature pupae were swimming to the surface film where they emerged into the adult stage. Rainey knew that most of the swirls he was seeing were the fish eating the ascending caddis pupae. Gulping them as they swam to reach the surface, spread their wings.

He was distracted by a particularly splashy rise, a big rainbow. He wished he had time to fish.

Not tonight. No. Not for a while. The last time he'd squared off with Jesse, he'd missed the salmon fly hatch on the Gallatin. He'd been in Vegas, then Miami, looking for something on the sadistic sheriff. Lloyd still talked about it, the best salmon fly hatch ever. The last time, though, it had been all about stopping Jesse. It was easy enough to disappear, take whatever time he needed. And Lloyd had lied about the salmon fly hatch anyway.

This time stopping Jesse was just a piece of a larger puzzle. And there was no time. How did you measure the value of wildlife? He was thinking about Yellowstone. How it had sustained him in all kinds of ways, large and small, since he moved here. The park was an extraordinary world unto itself, a world that depended on caretakers like Rachel to protect the delicate balance that gave wildlife a chance to succeed. Rainey lit a cigarette. Considered options. He tossed a large grasshopper onto the seam below the fallen tree limb. Rainey watched it twitch, helpless in the current, until a little rainbow rose—almost slow motion—to inhale it, effortlessly.

————

TWO DOUBLE-BLADED CAMO CHOPPERS came in over Stoney Ridge, white searchlights sweeping across the meadow. Major Ramsey, aka the Ram, barked orders as five soldiers ran from one helicopter, securing the perimeter of the meadow. Six civilians followed when the Ram gave the high sign. They carried gear. Two of them seemed to know the setup. They led the others to the lab, then claimed their cabin. Danny came last. Major Ramsey listened attentively to his instructions.

A half hour later five tents had risen in the meadow, including a framed cook tent lit from the inside by Coleman lanterns. A string of lights went from tent to tent, winding their way to a large generator. The camp was set up to house and feed the six civilian scientists and their armed guard.

"No one gets close without my direct okay," Danny said to Major Ramsey. "That means you have to speak to me personally." The Ram barely nodded. He knew the drill. "Good to have you here," Danny said.

One of the helicopters took off about ten minutes later with Danny aboard. He watched as the lights from the Sentry camp turned to little dots. He fired up a Kool Filter King. The heavy work was about to start. His Defense Department liaison had told him how the higher ups had passed this one up the chain like a hot potato. This one had gone as high as it gets. The answer came back like a missile. Get it done.

Payback

PHILLIPE WAS OUT OF breath. He'd run from the Gold Nugget's parking lot, then climbed the stairs two at a time. He took a big breath, pushed open both swinging doors, and made his entrance.

Inside, Phillipe wished he had an inhaler. This was no Bellagio. No, the Nugget was a dank, grubby barn full of sawdust, with eighty gambling machines—a quick study, Phillipe did the math in his head—four pool tables, and a gaudy old marble bar. As he approached the bar, he was sure he could smell the grizzly bear standing in the corner. He sneezed and started worrying about allergies.

Phillipe blew his nose into a gray silk handkerchief and saw Roy, the cook at the truck stop, playing one of the poker machines. The Nugget was the only place in North that catered to the local service people, and, as such, Phillipe had to admit that it was, at least, authentically wretched.

Since his conversation with Rachel, he'd been evaluating options, and by the time Jesse's call came, he'd worked out a way the sheriff could help him. His plan was loosely based on Dashiell Hammet's *Red Harvest*, where the protagonist double-crosses everyone he meets, usually more than once. It was further informed by his insight that a corrupt sheriff was as fine an ally as you could have in the great American West.

Phillipe sort of jumped up onto the barstool next to Jesse. He smiled at the foucking-smart-as-hell sheriff and his sidekick,

Gummer, a strange, stringy version of Marshal Dillon. "Gentlemen," he said, then listened to Jesse's idea.

When Jesse was finished, Phillipe proposed that he move several mats of thermophile out of the Sentry pool to another compatible hot spring—he had just the place. Phillipe wanted to move these mats tout de suite or ASAP, as he put it, hammering every letter when Gummer looked confused. The Frenchman explained how it would provide the sheriff with his private supply of superheated Sentry thermophiles and allow him to go on with his research. He even drew a map on a Gold Nugget napkin. The fly in the ointment, Phillipe knew, was the mutations. There was plenty of time for the sheriff to learn about that little wrinkle after the mats were moved.

———

JESSE SEEMED TO LIKE it pretty well.

Gummer watched it all, curious. On a normal day—by now—Jesse would have thrown at least one good scare into this guy. Not today. And earlier, when Gummer had tiptoed into his elk farm proposition, Jesse had actually seemed pleased to make Gummer his partner. Really. The man was in such a rare, fine mood it made Gummer worry. It had to be the phone call from Stacy, he was thinking, when Stacy herself appeared at the far end of the bar, pointing toward the back office. Jesse put a hand on Phillipe's arm. "Wait here."

Gummer watched him go. He was whistling some show tune. There was even a bounce to his step. Jeez, he wouldn't wanna be that Rainey guy. Un-unh. The guy was a goner, toast. Nothing else could explain it.

———

IN THE OFFICE, STACY handed Jesse a document. She explained that it was a signed deposition from his ex-girlfriend, Mary, properly witnessed in Atlantic City, where his man finally found her.

He read it carefully. In her new deposition Mary swore she'd lied to Rainey. Lied because he'd threatened her. Jesse, she swore, had never extorted money from anyone she knew. And she'd made

175

up the story about Jesse splashing acid on that girl's face just to get Rainey off her back. In fact, that nasty stunt had been Rainey's idea and, honest to God, that girl didn't even exist. That, she swore, was the truth of the matter.

He smiled at Stacy. They'd had a one-night stand in Vegas more than twenty years ago, and, after trying everything they could think of, they'd sadly concluded that there was no way they could both be in charge. They were both relieved when they finally gave up, exhausted. Since then, Stacy had been his assistant—second-in-command was more like it—full-time. And she was getting a raise tonight.

Jesse picked up the document, read it again. When he looked up, cat on a canary, Stacy said, "Your detective gave her twenty grand. She took off. South America somewhere."

Jesse laughed out loud. It was that good. And riding that wave of good feeling, it came to him just how Bodine could help.

———

A FLASHLIGHT BEAM SPLASHED across the clearing where Rainey and Jen were sitting beside their fire. A moment later Rachel approached the cabin and tried the cabin door.

"Why'd you lock it?" she asked them.

"It was padlocked," Jen said. "We hoped you'd have the key."

"Oh." Rachel walked to an old fir. She leaned under a large branch and came out with a key ring. "Sorry." Before Jen could say anything, Rachel was inside unloading her pack.

The women sat at the table, watching Rainey prepare some sort of soup, while Rachel explained what she'd learned from Phillipe and from Danny. "How many animals are affected?" Rainey asked when she was finished.

"We don't know, and we have no idea whether the problems will spread outside the drainage. For example, if the thermophilic elk don't maintain their fidelity to their range, if they wander, interbreeding with other herds, it could infect elk throughout the West." Rachel's right leg was moving nervously under the table.

"Could the thermophiles spread through feces, like Giardia?" Rainey asked.

"It's possible. I don't know." Rachel shook her head, her leg still working. "And what if the next generation is dying?"

It was quiet. Though Rachel was working hard to stay on task, Jen sensed she was ready to go off.

After an uneasy silence Rachel went on, explaining what Danny had told her about the bombs. Telling them about it made her even more antsy.

Bombs? "Just how powerful could they be?" Jen asked, simply unable to get her arms around this. Undetectable thermophile bombs?

"I'm still not sure. I suppose they could pack billions of specially selected Sentry thermophiles into a pill the size of an aspirin. Phillipe thought that with enough rapidly superheated explosive thermophiles, the millions, even billions, of high-energy bonds being ripped apart could create a powerful explosion. Concentrated and cooked up with whatever chemical the off-site military scientists are adding, who knows how powerful they might be? Imagine tiny mega explosives and God only knows what else. The key, I think, is that they're virtually undetectable." Rachel stood, walked to the window. "The chief of research in the park is going to follow up with Phillipe," she went on, leaning back against the sill. "Phillipe needs him to finish up his work. And there'll be an emergency meeting tomorrow morning—without Danny Briley. The superintendent won't stand for this. He'll be as angry and upset as I am. With a little luck, these experiments will be over by midday."

Rainey looked up from his cooking. "Do I have this right—you could fill a fountain pen full of this superheated thermophile mix, add a specified dose of ENT, put it in a seatback pocket, and blow up a seven-forty-seven?"

Rachel looked out the window. "I think so. Yeah."

Not even Jen knew what to say.

———

It was after 11:00 p.m. before they'd wound down. While Jen organized mattresses and sleeping bags, Rainey led Rachel toward the fire. He explained that Jen wanted to see Jimmy. Rachel said she'd talk to Ruth, set a time and place for tomorrow.

"Thanks. I don't know where we'd be without you."

"Fuck you," Rachel said, really pissed all of a sudden. Feeling okay about it, too.

"What'd I do?"

"What'd I do?" she repeated. "Jesus, it's what you didn't do. C'mon, Rainey. What about this afternoon?"

"You want to talk about that now?"

"Yeah, I do."

Jen came out of the cabin. One look at Rachel—feet planted, hands on her hips, chin out—and she said, "G'night," and went inside.

Rachel's eyes never left Rainey.

"Look, I'm sorry." His voice was steady, clear. "You know me. You know I'd like to think about it for a while—"

"Couple a months?"

He shot her a dark look. "I've had about enough."

"Fine. What I said, what I told you, Rainey."

"I heard what you said. Right now, tonight, when I think about us, I feel sad, and inept. I can't get past that."

"Try. You know there's more than that. Try, Rainey. Please?" How could she get him to engage this? Even consider it?

"Okay. Tell me this, though—with all we have to do in the next twenty-four hours, why have you chosen tonight to reinvent the wheel?"

"I didn't choose," Rachel replied. She regrouped and tried again. "Look. I'm way late, but tonight I see what I'm asking, and why. I understand it. All I want is that you begin to talk with me about it." Rachel looked away, reached somewhere inside herself. "What happened...it wasn't your fault. I needed to have a child, and I knew you wouldn't do that. We were at an impasse. That's no one's fault. This is another time, and you're the love of my life. Period. I want to be with you. I want another chance. Just tell me where you are, what you think. Please."

His sea-blue eyes had lost their luster. "If that's what you want." Rainey paused, choosing his words. "I think we had our time. I can't make myself feel something. It's over. I'm sorry."

"Jen?"

"In part."

A tear started down her cheek. Her head was throbbing again.

"We can't resurrect what we had. At least I can't. What you see now, what's left, is—I dunno—a shadow."

"A shadow?" Rachel repeated the word, examining that idea. She hoped—really wanted—to stay reasonable, even poised. "Rainey, you can be a damn fool. Such a damn fool!"

He watched her storm into the woods.

———

JESSE TOOK THE RANGE Rover. He'd left Stacy, chatting it up with the too-smart-by-half Frog. He was going to look for Rainey. He didn't have a plan. He didn't even think he'd find him. But since Stacy's return all the sheriff could think of was payback.

He drove by Lloyd's, thinking he'd like to have one of his inspectors take a good look at his kitchen. He knew it was his mood talking. There'd been days when he'd counted a couple of hundred thousand acres sipping coffee at Lloyd's counter. The last thing he needed now was to take away their coffee counter. Still, it was just like Rainey to befriend some crazy old goat who'd likely taken a head shot from a lightning bolt.

He drove north toward Bozeman, turning off at an unmarked road.

Jesse bore right, then continued on about four miles until the bumpy old road disappeared into a stand of lodgepole pine. There was a place to leave his car, and he followed a path that wove through the trees before it came out in a meadow. In the moonlight he could see the outlines of a log house—Rainey's house—sitting on a little rise above the meadow. Behind the house there was a steep timbered hillside. In front of the house was a vegetable garden. It was almost two hundred yards through the meadow to reach the garden.

The door to the house was easily jimmied. Jesse flicked a light switch then stepped into the living room. It looked like some kind of library. There were two overstuffed chairs facing an imperfect river-rock fireplace. Every inch of available wall space had built-in bookcases, floor to ceiling, and they were overflowing. There must be over a thousand books in here, Jesse thought. It reminded him how much he hated Rainey. Though he often started a book, Jesse rarely finished one. It annoyed him to think that Rainey had read all these books and might know something he didn't. It was guys like Rainey that made him hate fly-fishing—guys who read too much, and couldn't do anything, and thought it was some kind of big high-falutin' deal to fool a stinky fucking animal with a brain the size of his fingernail.

The kitchen was on the far side of the living room. It had a large butcher-block island in the center. In the corner was a pantry. Jesse opened the pantry door. He pulled a string that turned on the overhead light and found himself staring at eight bottles of Wild Turkey and ten bottles of Dewar's Scotch. *His* whiskey. Had to be.

Jesse emptied the semiautomatic he carried on his belt, blasting away at his damn whiskey bottles. Then he went out into the kitchen and, after a reflective stroll around the island, fired up a pilot light on the gas stove. He lit one end of a roll of paper towels and lobbed the torch into the pantry.

From the pines he could see the cabin burning. Kind of pretty, he thought. Bodine deserved the credit, and the blame, for this. He stayed until the roof caught fire. In the darkness, driving down the dirt road, the sheriff wished he could be there when Rainey came home.

Deadly Mutations

ACHEL, GUMMER, THE CHIEF of research, and the superintendent with the rugged cowboy's face were all fixed on Mitchell, not missing a word. "I talked with the undersecretary's people at Interior," Mitchell explained. "Please call this gentleman." Mitchell passed the superintendent a name and number. "He's authorized to explain my position, and the situation."

"I understand the situation, Mitchell," the superintendent replied. "That's why I called the Secretary of the Interior himself. And when he calls me back, I intend to put an end to these experiments, then have you removed."

Mitchell made them wait while he lit his pipe. He calmly took in the angry faces staring at him around the conference table at park headquarters in Mammoth. "Frankly, sir, we have no choice. Facts of life, and so on. The Defense Department has priority on this one."

"Priority?" Rachel was up. "What the hell does that mean? Do they know you're superheating the hot spring pool? I checked out that nitrogenous compound you're using—'ENT'. It's the most intense heat-producing agent I've ever seen. What do you think it's doing to that pool?" And when Mitchell didn't answer, "Do they know what their experiments are doing to our wildlife? Do they know about the mutations?"

"Mutations?" It was Gummer, busy taking notes.

Mitchell ignored him. "They know everything, and it doesn't concern them. How did he put it? Yes. He said, 'the costs are acceptable.'"

Rachel turned her back on Mitchell. Gummer, at least, was listening to what she said. "Gummer, the young of the animals that ingest the thermophiles are mutating and dying. We know of deformed elk calves, an eaglet born without wings, a bear cub with no ears, and more."

"Elk?" Gummer was visibly upset.

"Yes. I think the whole herd's been hit hard. They're concentrated in the drainage, and they all drink from Elk Creek. If they keep drinking the Sentry thermophiles in the water, it's just a matter of time before they're all infected by the virus that lives in these thermophiles. I'm afraid that will cause mutations in their young."

"No. No way."

Rachel nodded. "Deadly mutations. And it could spread outside the drainage. Any number of ways. Entire species could be at risk."

Gummer groaned.

She had the superintendent's full attention now, too. "We don't know anything about how this works, how many animals are affected, if the infected animals will migrate, how else it might spread, how long it takes. We simply don't know."

The superintendent shook his head, speechless.

"Mitchell, what have you done?" Rachel eventually asked, barely audible. "You're responsible for contracts, concessions, development. We're not talking about negotiations with the American Science Foundation." She raised her hands, ready to garrote him: "We're talking about wildlife. Our responsibility."

Mitchell studied an Ansel Adams photograph on the far wall. "Until today, I had no idea that there was any threat at all to the wildlife you study." He pivoted in his chair, a patronizing expression on his thin face. "But that's finally beside the point. Talk to the man at Interior."

"Is it possible that you don't understand what we're saying?" the superintendent asked. "Put simply—we won't allow it. Ever. They have to make their damn bombs somewhere else."

"There is nowhere else," Mitchell replied softly.

The buzzer on the phone sounded. In the awkward silence it was as loud as a foghorn. The phone sat on the conference table.

The superintendent picked it up. "It's your guy," he mouthed to Mitchell.

Mitchell steepled his fingers.

The charismatic superintendent's face turned ashen as he listened to whatever the undersecretary's spokesman was saying. "That's wrong," he said. "You can't be serious. Then I insist on speaking to the secretary. I understand the president has final authority. Then have the president call me." He slammed down the phone.

"Sounds like the Joint Chiefs took on our boss at Interior, and they won." His voice had a sharp, controlled edge to it. "I intend to find out. For the moment we have absolutely no authority to interfere with this research in any way." The superintendent looked at Rachel. "The guy in charge at this end—and I mean calling all the shots—it's Danny Briley."

"That can't be," Rachel exclaimed, suppressing an expletive.

The foghorn sounded again. The superintendent picked it up. "Who, coincidently, happens to be outside, hoping to join our meeting." He spoke into the phone, "Ask him to wait... What do you mean—?"

Danny walked in. The beard and the mustache were gone. He wore an expensive dark blue suit and a conservative tie. Behind him were two athletic looking men—one tall, the other short—in less-expensive suits. They had their badges out. Side by side they made Rachel think of a fire hydrant near a lamppost.

"The situation has changed," Danny said.

Rachel laughed out loud. She didn't know what else to do.

The tall man was instantly behind her, hands on her upper arms. She stopped laughing, frightened.

Gummer stood. "Let her go," he warned the guy, then Gummer looked at Danny. "That's not okay. No sir."

The short man walked toward Gummer. He unholstered his weapon.

Rachel motioned Gummer to sit down, really scared now.

"Sit down," Danny quietly said, meaning it.

Gummer looked at Rachel again, who nodded, then he sat, reluctantly.

At Danny's signal, both his men stepped back.

Danny went on, "The experiments at the Sentry Spring have been classified Top Secret-eyes only." He paused. "Anyone who releases any information about these experiments that they may have obtained before they were aware of the classification will be prosecuted. Any person, including park personnel, moving within the closed area of the park will be prosecuted."

It was silent. "Questions?"

The chief of research's face was red. "What is this? Who in hell do you—?"

"Any other questions?"

Gummer nodded. "Well, first off, Danny, I want to say how you look better all dressed up like a lawyer."

"Others may put up with your cretinous idiocy, but from here on in, you never—ever—address me directly."

"Cretinous? If I were you, hoss, I wouldn't be bringing up hormone problems. Not today. No sir."

Danny put a hand up, restraining his man. "I'll only warn you once." He took a document from his briefcase.

In the silence that followed, Gummer took out a red-and-blue-checkered handkerchief, then blew his nose—first one nostril, then, the other, an elaborate affair. He turned to the superintendent. "Now, are you saying I can't patrol my own sub area?"

"You'll have to clear it through me," Mitchell snapped. "And that will only happen if Mr. Briley approves."

"What gives you this authority?" The superintendent asked Danny.

"You have no need to know. But try me, and you'll see if I've got it."

"We're getting off on the wrong foot here, young man." It was the superintendent, at his diplomatic best. "Let's start over."

"Any other questions?" He went right on, "Mitchell will be my contact with the park service. Any and all requests must come through him." Danny's ice pick eyes found Rachel. She could see that they were still slightly bloodshot. "You and I have unfinished business," he told her, then he stood, set a memorandum in front of the superintendent and left.

Rachel rubbed the back of her neck, remembering what she'd done to this guy, the human ice pick.

The memo detailed the penalties for violating the national security. The meeting ended abruptly. The superintendent was furious. He'd call the director of the National Park Service, who was waiting to hear from him. The director could certainly reach the secretary. As soon as that happened, they'd reconvene. Gummer took off running, like he had to find a restroom. The elk biologist who first reported the oversized elk racks was waiting for Rachel beside her car. She skipped the pleasantries. "Are these elk contagious?"

"What do you mean?"

"I found one of my collared bulls near Madison Junction this morning, and he's moving south."

Rachel's muscles felt like wet rope, tightening in the hot sun; even her skin was tight. She needed Rainey, more than ever.

———

RAINEY WASN'T BESIDE HER when Jen woke up. Rachel had hiked out early. Soon after Rachel left, she and Rainey had made love. Their lovemaking was leisurely and caring—he was learning what she liked, and he doled it out sensitively and generously. She found it easy to reciprocate. Thinking about it made her happy.

Jen looked out the window and there he was pacing, sipping coffee and staring at the creek. She watched him for a long time. His slow, sure movements, his face knotted in that intricate, puzzled expression—everything he did, he did so thoroughly. Jen stretched. Agh. They had nothing in common. No, they shared a few important things: they were both sensitive and far too proud.

Since childhood, she'd used her keen sensitivity to manage men, particularly Cockeye and her father—who, she'd learned early on, had little or no idea what they were feeling most of the time. It seemed to her an adaptive skill, important for a girl growing up around cops. Excepting therapy, she'd never imagined this being reciprocated in a relationship with another adult, least of all a man.

Earl, at his best, had made her feel good. But he'd never actually understood her feelings. This was most painfully obvious when she was pregnant. And remembering Earl—since he'd died, it didn't always feel right to call him Cockeye—brought home that she and Rainey had something else in common: they'd both failed at relationships. The commonality stopped there, though. Her problem was getting out. His was staying in. Think about that, she reminded herself.

Jen watched Rainey, who was still pacing. She felt lively, kind of breezy. This man was, for her, stirring. "We got coffee?" she called out the window.

Rainey poured a cup and set it on a rock near the fire.

She came out, took a sip. Rainey was watching the creek again, pensive. His face was lined and sad. "What's wrong?" she asked.

"It's Rachel." Rainey hesitated, settling for, "As you said, she believes she's in love with me." His face hardened. "It's just—I dunno—out of nowhere. She came on strong. I backed her off."

"Why is she doing this now? Is it me?"

"Seeing us together has to be part of it. But you have to know her. Insight and understanding come to her in their own sweet time. Fully formed," he explained. "That's how it was when she wanted children."

"So when she gets it, it's a clear and certain understanding."

"Yes. Of her own feelings, anyway."

"Did you ever love her?" Jen asked.

"I thought I did—maybe I did—though now, I'm not sure what to make of our time together."

"And how do you feel about her now?"

Rainey put his arm around her, still watching the water moving over the stones. "When I think of Rachel—I feel affection, respect. That's all." He tossed a pebble into the creek. "It's over. She needs to move on."

"Did you tell her that?"

An osprey with a little trout in its claws flew above them. He pointed and then he watched her watching the bird. "Yes."

"Ouch," she almost said. Instead, Jen buried her face in the nape of his neck.

———

JESSE WAS ROCKING SLOWLY on his front porch swing. He was imagining Bodine, off in the woods somewhere stalking the devil bear, wearing a silver cross the size of a ping-pong paddle. He reminded himself to make sure that Gummer didn't see Bodine anytime soon. And damn—here was Gummer speeding up the gulch. Gummer left the Jeep and ran toward him.

Gummer stopped on the steps, below Jesse. "We got problems," he announced.

"Slow down, Gumbo. And take her from the top. Topic sentences, the whole works."

"Cut that shit out." Gummer had no idea where that came from. "What I mean, sir, is now that we're partners, I'd truly appreciate it if you treated me more respectfully."

Jesse's mouth hung open.

"I prefer to be called Gummer, sir. And I apologize for my choice of words. Anyway, you got to hear me out. Danny's on his way up here with some National Security cops, and they mean business."

"Go on." Was Gummer stoned?

"The work at the Sentry's been classified Top Secret. No one says word one about any of it or they get arrested and charged with all kinds of fancy federal law. If you go up there, they arrest you."

"I'd pay to see Bodine called up for violating the national security," Jesse said. "Maybe he'd burn down Congress." He stretched. Something else was wrong. Really wrong. "Gummer, you're upset. And it's not about this secrecy business. What happened?"

"The elk, sir. Rachel says if they ingest—I think that's eat or drink—"

"Yes," Jesse interrupted, making his hurry-up gesture with his fingers.

"Well, if they eat or drink the thermophiles, their babies have mutations and die."

Jesse looked skyward. God had stabbed him in the back, again. And here came Danny—in a fucking Lincoln Town Car—winding his way up toward Gopher Gulch.

Jesse said later that they were trespassers, that they didn't respect the sign on the gate. Whatever got hold of him, he hurried down the porch steps with his gopher gun. When the car turned up the gulch, he fired two shots, nailing two tires, front and rear left.

The Lincoln skidded off the road and came to a stop at the edge of a ten-foot drop to the meadow below. Jesse was laughing when three doors flew open. Danny and his lieutenants hit the ground firing.

It was Gummer who had the good sense to wave his white handkerchief in the air. It was too late, though, to save the picture windows. Gummer stood up. "It's a game," he shouted. "No one gets hurt. Just a game."

At Danny's signal, one enforcer held a T-shaped Cobray automatic weapon on Jesse and Gummer, while the other emptied several clips into the front of Jesse's Lodge. When it was over, the walls were shredded, and Jesse's cheek was twitching.

Danny waved his man over, then walked up to Jesse. As Gummer stepped forward to help his partner, the taller man hit him on the back of the head with his gun butt, then kicked his feet out from under him. As soon as Gummer hit the ground, the other man stepped on his hand, breaking his little finger.

As though they'd rehearsed it, the tall man forced the sheriff up the porch steps where he raised Jesse's left wrist and held it against a fir post. The short one held the sheriff's other arm behind his back. Danny jammed the muzzle of his pistol into the palm of Jesse's hand. Without a word, he fired. The bullet left a ragged hole about the size of a quarter.

Jesse's hand hurt, like it was on fire. He stared at the bloody hole.

"If you ever point a gun at me again—ever—I'll kill you," Danny said. "I call my IRS guy, you do ten years." His look was contemptuous. "You work for me now."

After ordering Jesse to get the Lincoln to the sheriff's office this afternoon *with two new tires*, Danny confiscated Gummer's Jeep. When the ranger protested angrily, Danny keyed the side of the Jeep.

Jesse watched the blood come out of the hole in his palm. He wrapped it with his neckerchief. He was thinking he could fix Danny. Only the hole would always be there. He couldn't fix that.

———

From her car Rachel could see Molly. She was sleeping soundly on a blanket spread out near the café's kitchen door. Rachel went inside, then she carefully lifted her daughter into her arms.

"You're a lifesaver," she told Ruth. "There's no one else I could ever leave her with. No one."

"Hon, it's a treat for me. Now fill me in."

Rachel told her about the Sentry, Phillipe's explanation, and the morning meeting. She knew she'd just said enough for Danny to put her in jail, but Ruth would sooner rob a bank than betray a friend. "Jen wants to see her boy. Can you set it up?"

"I'm supposed to meet Lloyd this afternoon." Ruth was quiet for a minute. "Have her behind the Conoco, the one near Big Sky, at two, and I'll bring her along."

Rachel nodded.

Ruth's tone changed. "Hon, I got bad news. There was a fire. Rainey's place burned down."

Rachel closed her eyes. The one and only thing that he had. "Jesse?" It was déjà vu.

"Jesse says it's Bodine. He's got him leaving Brad's pharmacy. The drugstore was set on fire, and Brad was shot up pretty bad."

"Oh. Jesus, no."

"Jesse says Bodine's on one of his burn sprees. Says he had it in for Rainey."

"Rainey accused him of poaching."

"I still think it was Jesse. One of Jesse's ex-bartenders says he saw Jesse drive by the tavern about a mile below the turnoff last night."

Molly stirred. Ruth went into the kitchen and came out with a bottle for her.

"I can't tell him," Rachel said.

"Lloyd'll tell him. There's no hurry. Nothing to be done now, anyway."

"Ruth, I don't know where this is going to come out. Everything's out of control. Christ, the animals in the Elk Creek drainage think it's the fall. And you just have to see one of these mutated newborns. It's like the world's gone crazy."

Ruth put an arm around Rachel. "Things like this have a way of shaking the dust out. Most people only make a change when they have to."

"Maybe. I told Rainey I was in love with him." And why am I telling her this?

Ruth clapped her hands together. "Does he get it?"

"Un-unh. When I try and talk to him about it, I just make him mad."

"Sometimes a man needs to get angry. It's like sex. For a little while after, they can think about complicated things."

Rachel squeezed Ruth's hand. "It doesn't help that he's infatuated, or in love, with another woman."

"That city gal?"

"Jen. Right. She's a good woman, too."

"There's lots of good women." Ruth scoffed. "This one's smart and exciting. Like him. Only she's fast and reckless-exciting and he's careful, intense-exciting. Rainey wants to put the parking brake on at a stoplight, so he won't lose control and run the light. Thinks about it anyway."

"Yeah, yeah." She smiled; Ruth was so smart.

"You ask me," Ruth went on, "Rainey's got about as much chance of making a life with that woman as I have of being playmate of the month."

Rachel giggled. "It's just they don't know that."

"Some men need a whack on the head with a two-by-four just to wake up in the morning. Make him mad, girl, that's my advice. Now get out of here. You got to keep these people from screwing things up any more." She took Molly, then gave Rachel a one-armed hug. "Between us, you're the only one of the lot got the God-given sense to fix this. Trust your instincts, hon. They're good ones."

———

AT FIRST BODINE WORRIED the helicopters were looking for him. But no, it wasn't that. They were doing something over by the Hell Hole. What it was, he figured, was like building some kind of evil empire, right here, in his home forest. About the third time one landed, he decided to check it out.

He saw the chopper sitting right at the Sentry Hot Spring, unloading supplies, military supplies. Right at the bad place. There at the pool. He remembered how just after the so-called science boys showed up, the Sentry started blowing. Spooked him that first time. He was crossing the meadow at night when it spewed behind him. Made him jump. When he looked back, that pool was smoking, bubbling and spouting in the moonlight. He should a known right there. Right then. The way it was hissing. Then the animals got strange. They looked weird. They did unnatural things. And then the fire. He should have known. He'd bet the science boys were back. Yeah, with his binoculars he could see the nasty one he damn near set on fire. But there were soldiers, too. Armed. And it looked like they were digging in—tents, a generator, portable phones. Shit, their tents were fancier than his house. And they were laughing. Damn-fool soldiers to guard Satan's hot, steamy hole.

He saw the fire, still burning on the hillside below. The wind was just starting to come up, and it was pushing the pissant fire slowly toward the Sentry. He snorted. The fire wasn't much. Without more wind, it would never get close. Unless he helped. He could juice it, make it breathe. He lobbed a spitball at a nearby fir. A good, long throw. He was getting his strength back, yeah. Coming up on a hill above the hot spring, he could see smoke, and then yes, the sucker was erupting. What were they doing to that hot spring? The idea came to him then about how the devil got out. Maybe he sprang from the red, hot center of the earth, sucked out by the geyser shooting its load.

He stopped, feeling a searing pain in his back. He ate two pills, a yellow one to kill the pain, then a red speedball to cut the fog. His mind drifted. Jesse, Gummer, the she-bitch, the blood, the geyser, the fire, the blood, Jesse again. Only this time Jesse was laughing. And his eyes were blood red. Bodine felt a little dizzy.

He spotted a soldier. He was at the edge of the meadow leaning against a big fir. Wearing some kind of camo outift. It would be easy to creep up behind him. Pound a stake through his red-hot heart. He could do it, too. He was born from the blood to take the devil down.

He could see where the soldiers had secured the meadow. Okay. Five of them on the perimeter. More guys in the big tent. He watched for a long time. Before he left, he crept up behind the big fir. The soldier was still there. Without a sound, Bodine snapped the man's neck, like one of Jesse's plastic toothpicks. Only the green olive stayed on. Bodine cut the soldier's leg. Checked his blood. Hot. Dark. Sticky. Like real blood. He was careful not to touch the blood when he took the man's camo jacket, his gear, even a field telephone. Bodine sat the man against the tree. With his hunting knife he sharpened a fat stick, then, using both hands, he thrust it into the soldier's red-hot heart. Bodine adjusted the body, just so. He had a vision then how later, he might use the head.

RAINEY DROPPED JEN BEHIND the Conoco at two, as scheduled. Ruth gave him the high sign and just like that, they were gone. It was the first time he and Jen had been apart since finding Cockeye, and he felt disoriented—off balance—as if her presence was his connection to the unlikely events of the past three days.

Ruth's old Dodge pickup wound south toward the park. Soon she'd turn off, disappear into the trees. Rainey wondered where. Then he thought about Rachel, what she'd said—the Top Secret classification, bombs, Danny Briley...how she felt about him. He didn't like what was happening, any of it.

Rainey looked east, toward the Gallatin Mountains. He could see the Northern Rim of Yellowstone Park in the distance. Stoney Ridge was just south of the peaks he could see. At the moment the ridge seemed further than the moon.

The Conoco was set back from the road between a roadside church and a souvenir shop. He went into the Conoco's convenience store. A ranger was there flirting with Suzy, the pretty, famously brassy New Yorker who worked the counter. He was telling her how they were checking cars as they drove into the park. He wasn't sure why but the whole northwest corner was closed tight as a drum. Rainey thought about the checkpoints as he poured his coffee.

He went to the counter. As Rainey paid for his coffee, the ranger asked her out. Suzy firmly said, "No, thank you."

"Why?" the ranger asked, piqued now.

She put her elbows on the counter. "Say I fall for you, what's the upside? Huh? I gotta start using leaves for toilet paper?"

Suzy never disappointed.

Rainey drove north along the Gallatin. He pulled off at a favorite fishing spot and sat on a fallen tree, watching a little section of the stream. It was quiet, no insects hatching, no fish working.

The Gallatin made a slow turn here, and two large boulders created a small pool at the far side of the stream. He didn't want to go back to the Bear Creek cabin. He needed time alone. He'd go home. Have a drink on his own front porch. He pulled the pickup back onto the highway.

Rainey tried not to think until, finally, he turned up his favorite road. Three miles in he could feel himself start to unwind. As he pulled into the stand of lodgepole pine, he could see that several cars had been at his house. Odd. Maybe Jesse had sent the building inspector back. He walked through the trees toward the meadow. When he stepped out of the trees he started to run. He ran because he didn't know what else to do.

———

HE SAT ON THE blackened hearth of his fireplace. Everything had burned: his house, his books, his letters, his fishing memorabilia, his box of old photos, everything. What was left of his home was just a black, smoky spot above the garden. Rainey's head was aching, and his skin was hot and sweaty, like steam was building up inside with nowhere to go. He had to do something.

Maybe he'd go to Jesse's ranch, burn it down. The idea of it seemed clear, clean. He was planning his approach when he heard a car. He hid behind what was left of his chimney. A few minutes later he saw someone making good time through the meadow. Long strides. Rachel.

He showed himself, then Rainey watched her run towards him.

When she reached him, Rachel took his hands. She held on to them, standing in the rubble, saying only, "I'm sorry."

Her hands were cool in his sweaty palms.

They stood like that for a long time. When he stepped back, Rainey felt tired, worn down.

She sat beside him on the hearth. "Ruth told me. I didn't think you'd come here. But when your truck was gone, I just had this feeling..."

"I'm thinking I should burn down Jesse's ranch."

"No. Please. You can't do that."

He didn't seem to hear her. "After, I'll go back East. Get away."

She took his arm. "Don't do that, either. Please?"

He didn't respond. Why was she here? He didn't want to think about her. His eyes stayed on his blackened river-rock chimney. He remembered the bookcases he'd made, lengths cut to fit the irregular width of the chimney. How he'd organized his books. The coal-black chimney stood alone now. His books were ashes.

He rose to watch traces of smoke rising from the charred shell of his burned-out kitchen. "This didn't have to happen." He waved a hand toward his fire-ravaged house. "Hell no it didn't."

"What choice did you have? What were you supposed to do? Kill Jesse?"

"Maybe. I'm always waiting. Holding back. Afraid I'll be the bull in life's fucking china shop. I'm forty-two. I have no wife, no children, no home...Rachel, what—just what am I waiting for?"

Rachel chose her words carefully. Plainly, she'd been thinking about this. "I love that you're cautious," she eventually said. "Even when it pisses me off." When Rainey looked back at the remains of his home, Rachel walked around to face him. "And dammit, you never just wait. You're careful, yeah, but you just keep peeling away layers. Like you're trying to take apart an onion."

Rainey waved her off. He didn't want to talk about this.

She held her ground. "Hear me out. I finally get this...I think you do things carefully because you're so intense. And because you have some sense that what's inside the onion is likely fragile and complicated." She stepped closer. "And because you want to get it right. For everyone. It's not your fault if it doesn't always work." He looked toward his ash-covered garden. Rachel went on, "When you've got something figured, sometimes you are like a bull—fierce, even dangerous. Only you're smart about it." She touched his shoulder. "Remember how we—"

"I don't want to think about us now." Rainey was sure of that. He turned away.

"Okay. Don't worry about us now. I mean that," she said to his back. And then, "Rainey, please, I need a favor. And I need it now." She waited until he looked at her. "You know I wouldn't ask for a favor now if I didn't absolutely have to. It's that important...I'm sorry—" She gestured toward his ruined home. "But please listen... the elk are migrating. We're about to have a national disaster on our hands. And I don't know what to do. We need to slow down the thermophiles. I have some ideas but they're vague and disorganized. And there's no time. If I could choose one person in the world to help me, it would be you. I need you now. Right now. Will you help me?"

Rainey flashed on Jesse, walking through his house. He stepped away, wanting to be alone.

Rachel watched him pull a melted fishing reel from the ashes, heave it into the meadow.

"You want payback. Fine," she said to his back. "You want to bring down some real assholes? I've got the best list, ever. And somewhere, somehow, I know Jesse's on it." She waited, again, until he turned. "Will you help me?"

What was she thinking? "Why are you doing this? Why? You're the one said I should have walked away."

"I was angry, and jealous—"

"I can't deal with something like this. Not now. Ask the chief of research, or—I dunno—there has to be someone else."

"This is outside the law—the real deal. Look, it's like you said in my office—*I need help, and I don't know who else to ask.* Rainey, I don't trust anyone else to do this. Hell, there is no one else."

He poked a toe at a burned beam. Rachel was relentless. Dogged. Hell, no one could frustrate him more. He had to do something, though, Rainey knew that much. And she was right, this mess was outside the law, like a nefarious tar baby, with all the real scum stuck to it. Jesse, he knew, was stuck fast. It was, as she put it, the real deal. And he was tired of pussyfooting around. Being careful. Taking Jesse's crap. Even so, what she was asking, it was much harder, and riskier even, than burning down Jesse's ranch. He could feel something stirring, though, feelings he'd kept down. His expression moved through despair to rage, and then slowly turned to something hard. "This Danny's gonna go crazy if I foul up his plans. And Jesse's not afraid of me anymore."

A little breeze made ashes swirl around their feet.

"We can keep Jen and Jimmy out of it," she said.

"I'm going to want you out of it, too."

Rachel watched his face. The familiar lines were set. "I'll do what you say."

"I mean it."

"Okay. Yeah."

Rainey lifted a worn hand. "One way or another, I'm going to get Jesse." There it was.

"Where do you want to start?" she asked, after a long moment.

"Slow down the thermophiles. Stop the mutations, right?"

"Yes."

"Phillipe." They said it at the same time.

One in a Million

"WHAT DO YOU MEAN he answers to the Joint Chiefs?" Jesse yelled at the portable phone. "Jesus, Nellie, Danny fucking Briley? What do you mean he's *wet*? Political assassinations? For christsake, this is Montana...sensitive domestic operations. Yeah, that's exactly what we've got here. How do you bag a guy like that, Nellie? A deer rifle? Three hundred yards? I see...I'll be careful."

He checked his bandage again. The doctor had met him at the office, cleaned and dressed the wound. "No big deal," the doc said. Doc was wrong, Jesse decided, looking at his hand.

He'd thought about killing Danny himself. Walking into his damn shack and killing him slow. But as much as he liked the idea, he knew he shouldn't do it. A person had to set some limits. Make some rules. He knew that for him it was like drinking. You just stopped or you never stopped. You couldn't just kill every now and then. Fine. Someone else could kill him.

In two hours he'd come up with only one good idea, and it was a tricky one. He'd called Gummer, who knew the location of Bodine's cache, then he'd sent his deputy to leave a message for Bodine at the cache. The message was simple, "I know a way at the devil bear. Tonight. Call me." Tim had taped the message to Bodine's duffle. He said the poacher had smeared animal guts, and blood, all over the damn bag. And there were snakeheads nailed to the tree. That fit. He'd found the old Ford pickup, too. Hidden near the cache. Jesse snorted. Figure that—the mad dog drove his ratty old truck up there. So now Jesse just had to wait.

Wait and worry. At the moment, he was worrying about mutations. About how—with the elk, the plant, and the processing secret—he was going to be in for half a million bucks, easy, and now he learns that elk calves in the Rocky Mountain West could be born with birth defects and die. Farmed elk included. Their processing plant numbers depended on a stable herd, and processing antlers from all over the West. Cut that by say a third, and they'd lose money, fast. Cut it by more than that and they could kiss their elk farm goodbye. So he had to stop the thermophiles from spreading. Mutations. Smiley damn Phillipe. The shifty little Frenchie had been blowing smoke up his ass, puffing like a chimney from the get-go.

Jesse was working numbers when the call came. "Just tell me where we can meet," Jesse said to Bodine.

"Cut-Across Trail, at the park boundary."

"I'll come up Blue Grouse Creek. Take me an hour and a half."

Bodine broke the connection.

———

THE JERRY-RIGGED SPLINT MADE Gummer's left hand look like a spatula, at least that's what Darcie thought. They were at Jack Creek, and Gummer was talking a mile a minute. It scared her, the way he'd come right into the Dairy Queen, told her she had to take a break. He'd driven her up here without saying one word. Not even explaining how he messed up his finger. And now he was talking like he was an auctioneer or something, telling her stuff he normally wouldn't tell. How Bodine had started him thinking about life. How he was at a crossroads.

It was interesting to her, this idea that he'd reached a crossroads. She'd seen it coming. She understood the part about the elk farm. Being a partner was smart business. And she understood the part about the Defense Department research. You didn't have to be a genius to see that itty-bitty bombs made out of invisible vegetables were more important to the army than Jesse's hunting plans, or the animals in the park. And she knew you had to be dumb as a dog bone to take baby G's jeep and—oh-my-god—*key it*. It was *his* jeep. He wouldn't even let her drive it. His security blanket was more like it.

The part she didn't get, the part that he was going on about, was the business about the animals mutating and dying. She had pretty good antennae when it came to Gummer, and she could tell this was awfully important to him. So she'd asked him to explain it to her again. Why it was, exactly, that this was so—well—significant to him, personally.

"Honey, I like animals. You know that."

"Uh-huh."

"You could say, animals are my life. Not counting money, and you."

She thought about that, then shyly offered, "Those three, put together just right—that could be a good life, G."

———

HE LOVED THE WAY her eyes didn't give an inch when she said something like that. And, he had to say, she hit the nail—bam—dead on the head. "You're one in a million," he said, meaning it. Gummer took her hand, thinking she should hear it all, step by step. "Okay. Check my thinking here, hon—I'll go over just my high points. When those fancy federal guys called this Sentry deal Top Secret, it really worried me. It meant that they were going to keep cooking that hot spring and shooting those killer thermophiles into Elk Creek. When they shot up Jesse's house, then put a hole in his hand, I could see they weren't scared of him. Not one bit." He paused. "That meant that they had real muscle, and I mean more than a few hard guys, to back them up. Then they took my Jeep, without a word. And I had to do something." He nodded, aware he had her full attention. "When they cuffed us to the post, it gave me time to think. And I had over an hour of thinking, cuffed to Jesse, who was hot—and I mean steaming on the inside and the outside—and humiliated as all get out. That's when Stacy rolls up. Which was a good thing because Jesse was about to eat that fir post. Anyway, what I came to, sweetie, is that I care about three things in the world. First is you." He looked at her, thinking she was cute as a button. But how did she get to be first? Things kept popping out of his mouth before he was ready. Well, maybe she should be first.

Darcie laid a hand on his chest, surprised. "That's sweet, Gummer."

"Second, of course, is making money. We share an interest in that...third is animals. And the reason it's animals is because that's what I know. It's what I can do. And when these big shots start thinking they can kill the animal babies I'm needing for my work, I've got to do something. I'm not sure what, but something."

"Why are you taking it so personal?"

"I don't know. I mean Jesse's gonna get Danny. You should a seen Jesse when they were shooting down his house. I thought he'd start spouting blood from his eyes. And then Danny shot a hole right through his hand. And I don't have to tell you how I feel about my Jeep. Danny thinks he's Darth Vader or something. Anyway, Jesse didn't say word one during the time we were cuffed together. At the office he said not to bother him until further notice. God only knows what he's cooking up for this Danny guy. Anyway, my point was that I think I'm turning into some kind of animal environmentalist, if there is such a thing."

"You get knocked over the head, baby?"

"Darce, I mean it. I like animals. I don't like the idea that some out-of-town guys who don't know an elk from an antelope can start killing off little elk calves, eaglets, fish fry, bear cubs, you name it."

"I'll tell you a secret." She relaxed a little. He noticed that her teenage edge was gone. "I think that's nice."

Gummer shrugged, uncharacteristically self-conscious. "I mean I can live with a normal elk farm," he explained. "With our processing secret, we'll make good money off of normal elk. What I can't have those D.C. guys doing, what I can't allow, is for them to keep pumping that stuff into the water and kill half the elk in the Rocky Mountain West. And I swear, they'd do that before you can say 'boo.' They wouldn't even notice."

"Half the elk in the Rockies?"

"More. It could happen. You let these city boys keep dicking around with nature—excuse me, but that's what they're doing—and if these elk start moving, breeding with other herds, before you know it, you'll have two-headed baby elk dying all over the West. It'll be like one a those late-night movies, only it'll be the elk got nuked instead of the people."

"I see what you mean, G. No, we can't have that." She put her arms around his neck. "And I like that you got a soft spot for something besides young girls." She took his hand. "So what're we going to do?"

"Good question."

She considered. "I think you need one more partner."

"You mean you?"

"No. I'm already your partner."

"I'm glad to hear you say that. Who are you thinking of?"

"Jesse's going to go to war with this Danny guy. That's fine. But it won't stop the elk from drinking the water. You need someone who wants to help those elk as much as you do."

"Well," he paused, thinking it over. "That'd be Rachel."

"Who's Rachel?" Darcie had that look in her eye that reminded Gummer she was still eighteen.

"She's a darn good bear biologist."

"She better be." Darcie kissed her ranger.

———

THEY FOUND PHILLIPE AT the lab, preparing petri dishes to move the thermophiles. He was measuring out different doses of a nitrogenous solution when Rainey and Rachel walked in. The metal case from the Sentry sat on the table behind him. "Stand back," he instructed. "I'm busy here."

With his forearm, Rainey sent all six petri dishes crashing to the floor. When Phillipe came at him, Rainey backhanded his face. The Frenchman fell, eyes tearing. Rainey picked him up by his hair and the back of his wide rodeo belt, then hung him by his belt from a hook on the wall. In one motion, Rainey released his belt and grabbed him by the throat. "Listen carefully," he said, almost a whisper.

He turned to Rachel. "Can I have a dish from the Sentry?"

She opened the case, checked the labels, then carefully took a petri dish from its thermos-like container.

Rachel set the dish in front of Phillipe on a lab table. "Superheated thermophiles from the Sentry." She checked the label—207 degrees—then Rachel lifted the vial of nitrogenous solution and dripped little drops of it into the dish. At three drops, Phillipe protested red-faced. At four, he started yelling, "Stop... imbecile."

"Help me out here," Rainey said squeezing his throat again, for emphasis. "I'm close. You see, I've been thinking about fires. And Phillipe, I'm saying to myself there are a lot of fires around these thermophiles. Too many. And then, I'm realizing how explosions can cause fires. So where I'm going is I'm seeing you packing these petri dishes—"

"Nitric acid." Rachel picked up the bottle he'd been using when they came in. "Highly volatile stuff."

"Phillipe, you and I both know what killed Dr. Moody."

"Her foucking bear is what," Phillipe hissed.

Rainey's eyes were hard now, watching Phillipe. "No, the bear didn't kill him. Did it? I'd guess it was a superheated thermophile explosion." He unhooked the Frenchman, then released Phillipe's throat, his point made. Phillipe gasped, sucking in air, as he steadied himself against the wall.

Rachel stared, wide-eyed. A year she'd been trying to figure this. She turned to Phillipe, putting it together. "You were the one who packed the petri dishes. His little helper. But you needed to keep the thermophiles at a higher temperature for your own experiments. And if there's too much of the nitrogenous solution in a dish... Jesus. It's like a time bomb. Why you miserable—"

"It was an accident." Phillipe looked ten years older. "He was not supposed to touch these dishes."

"Accident or not," Rainey said. "You killed him, and you covered it up. I sure as hell can publish that."

"It was an accident," Phillipe repeated softly.

"So what?" Rachel yelled. "So what?"

Phillipe lit a cigarette, silenced. "What do you need?" he finally asked.

"Do you have thermophiles from other hot springs here in the lab?"

"Mais oui. Of course."

"Thermophiles that reproduce faster and grow more quickly than the Sentry thermophiles?" she asked.

"Perhaps, yes."

"Even at high temperatures?"

"Agh," Phillipe blew smoke at the ceiling. "I do not like this."

"Suppose we introduce that strain of thermophiles into the Sentry pool?"

"It will drive out the Sentry thermophiles. Destroy my work. Impossible."

"I'd reconsider that," Rachel snapped, then explained to Rainey, "It's Darwinian selection, survival of the fittest. The resources in the pool—food, heat, and oxygen—are limited. You introduce an organism that's more fit and reproduces more quickly, it's going to push out the Sentry thermophiles. They won't be able to compete."

She turned back to Phillipe. "How long would it take?"

"At these temperatures, the thermophiles, they reproduce at astonishing rates. Even the small advantage would be decisive. In days the Sentry thermophiles, they are finished. Poof. Gone."

"And?" Rachel was glaring.

"I have what you want," Phillipe offered, grudgingly. "But please, you must move several thermophile mats out of the Sentry pool first." He raised his hands. "Please, I implore you. Otherwise, all of my work—Dr. Moody's work—it will be lost."

It was, Rachel decided, the only way they could count on him to provide the right strain. "If you help us," she said to Phillipe, "we'll move the mats."

"Okay. Yes."

"Get it ready, then. I'm leaving tonight," Rainey said.

"I was working with the superheated thermophiles, studying the viruses. Dr. Moody didn't know this. I packed the extra dose in the petri dishes before I left for supplies," Phillipe told Rachel. "I suppose he added more, without knowing. He may have taken it outside for packing, or to add more samples. I can't say. It was an accident."

"He's still dead. If you'd told me, they never would have gotten away with the bear management closure."

"It would have been something else. They do what they please."

For the second time in twenty-four hours, Rachel almost whacked him with the Bunsen burner. "Shut up," she said instead, then signaled Rainey.

He tossed her a roll of duct tape, then Rainey lifted the Frenchman by his hair and belt again and sat him in a lab chair. He held Phillipe's wrists while Rachel taped them to the arms of the chair. Rainey taped the leg of the chair to the stationary table, then took a vial of ENT from his pocket.

"This is how they heat the pool—" He showed the vial to Phillipe. "Exothermic nitrogenous compound. Far more powerful than any nitrogenous solution you or Dr. Moody ever dreamed of," Rainy said, then dripped little drops of it into the petri dish. Phillipe was sweating.

Rainey emptied the dropper into the steaming dish, then turned to leave.

"Please. What do you want?" Phillipe was red-faced and sucking air again.

"Let's talk about Sheriff Jesse Stinson."

"Yes...definitely."

———

JEN WAS LOST. THEY'D twisted and turned up and down old logging roads, doubling back every so often to make sure they weren't being followed. Finally, Ruth pulled in behind two willows.

After covering the car with branches, they hiked about a mile. It didn't surprise Jen that the trail followed a creek. It was just another one of those obvious things about nature (once you got the idea of it, that is). Like big cities growing at the intersection of great waterways. No, that wasn't really nature. She let it drop.

When Ruth turned off the trail, Jen followed her orange Hawaiian shift more closely. Less than fifteen minutes later they heard Lloyd's laugh. And then they were at a bend in the creek where Jimmy was telling Lloyd a story. Jimmy was sitting on the bank, his feet in the water. Lloyd was tying on a fly. Jen stopped in her tracks, listening to her son. "So, my dad," he said. "He helped me clean the fish and cook it."

"You're a damn fine cook, too." Lloyd said, roll casting just so, the little caddis landing half an inch from the far bank. "Sorry about the language, mom," he said to Jen.

Jimmy turned around. He ran up to her and hugged her hard.

"You and Lloyd are friends, I see," Jen said, wondering how this cafe cowboy had her son making conversation.

He nodded.

"What have you guys been doing?"

He took her hand, excited. "I caught so many fish. And we watched bears eating berries in a ravine. I saw three. Two were babies."

"Grizzly bears?"

"Uh-huh."

She took his hand. Jimmy frowned, pulled her down to one knee. "Everything okay with you?"

Jen sighed. "Not yet. But I think we're making progress."

"Are you going away again?"

She thought that over. "I'll stay with you tonight. After that, I'm not sure what to do."

Jimmy walked away. He sat on a rock with his back to her, his feet in the stream again.

He needed her, every night, for quite a while. She came over, put her hands on his shoulders. "I'm sorry. I have to finish what I started here."

"I want you to take me home."

"I'd like to tell you what's going on. Just hear me out. Then let's decide what you and I should do."

She told him everything—his dad and the petri dishes, the Sentry, the unseasonal animal behavior, the mutations, the secret experiments, the bombs, even about Rainey. It took almost fifteen minutes. He interrupted her twice. Once when she told him about the mutations, the second time when she told him about her interest in Rainey. Both times he said, "gross."

When she was finished, he said, "My dad sure knew how to get in trouble."

"I don't think this was his fault."

"Can you find out, for sure?"

"I think so."

"That would be good."

———

DANNY WAS STANDING ON his front porch. The whites of his eyes still showed a web of pink lines. Ramsey had just called, filled him in. Danny was apoplectic. Who would decapitate one of his men? And drive a stake through his heart? A goddamn crazy fuck is who.

205

Ramsey had said it was *off*. For the Ram, losing the Vietnam War was a *bump*, nuking Hiroshima was a *grace note*. So *off* was pretty damn scary.

Was this one of Jesse's schemes? It didn't feel like Jesse. And where was the wormy little sheriff, anyway? His men had checked the ranch, the secretary's house, the office, even the saloons. No one knew where he'd gone.

Danny lit a Kool Filter King. His fuzzy, friend-of-the-earth days were history. Thank God. And it was nice to have people around who understood what he could do.

The sound of the helicopter brought him back to the problem at hand. A headless soldier, a stake through his heart. If someone was killing his people, it was war.

The small black chopper set down just so. It was nice working with people who got it right the first time. The Ram was not a talker, but he got it right. Every time. Danny ran to the helicopter. Fifteen minutes later, as the sun just about touched the peaks of the Madison Range, they landed at the Sentry Hot Spring.

The decapitated soldier with a stake through his heart was spooky. Not a Jesse sort of thing.

Danny counted seven soldiers on the perimeter of the meadow and four more in camp. The Ram was running the show on two handheld radios.

They were approaching the lab tent when they saw smoke, pluming to the south. They jumped in the chopper to check it out. When they were several hundred feet above the hot spring, Danny cursed. The entire forest southeast of the Sentry was blazing! A fucking fifty-acre sea of flames, coming their way.

———

BODINE THOUGHT ABOUT SHOOTING down the helicopter. If he'd had his .30-06, he would have tried it. But he'd taken the army assault weapon, in case he had to clean house, and it was good for nothing at long range. Besides, it was like the soldier. You kill one, Satan sends six more.

He went back to watching his fire beast. Proud. The fire was a good beginning. He could tell—watching it put his mind in a calm groove. So far so good. His archenemy didn't know what he was up against yet. He ran over it, again. The fire would drive off the soldiers. First the soldiers, then the helpers, then the hoodoo bear.

He was in his forest, sitting on a big branch above the fire. Going over the past—just what he'd done, step by step—carving it deep in his mind. He'd been back to the cache. It seemed like a long time ago. He called Jesse. Yeah. When he took the phone off the soldier's belt, he knew there was a reason.

Jesse had said he could help him. He wasn't sure. How did Jesse know a way at the bear? He'd find out. Later. After. He almost told Jesse to change his tone. One thing at a time, he'd reminded himself. He'd stuffed extra pills in his shirt pocket and grabbed the gas can. Quiet as a shadow, he'd climbed straight up to scout out the little fire.

The fire was simmering in a stand of spruce and fir behind the patrol cabin. Four, maybe five acres. The wind was hardly blowing. This fire was going nowhere. Doing nothing. Huh. He'd climbed a big fir, feeling the power.

He'd taken his time, chosen his spot carefully. He'd decided on a stand of old beetle-kill lodgepole pine. It was northwest of the burned down cabin, on the slope. There was a lot of deadfall in this stand, and it went all the way over to Elk Creek. With a little help, it would burn real good.

Once he'd picked his spot, he worked his way into the stand of beetle-kill pine, skirting the meadow.

Some of his strength was back. He'd even been able to go for a while without the uppers. Thinking about fire helped, too. It was looking his enemy right in the eye. Talking his language. Backed the bastard off a little, he could feel that. And the so-called soldiers weren't fireproof. His blood was pumping hard now, hot in his veins. He'd cut his forearm with his hunting knife, then put some pressure above the cut to force the blood out. If any trace of evil was still there, this would take care of it. When he was satisfied, he'd stopped the bleeding with his shirtsleeve; then he stood up, went back to work. He'd found an area where there was lots of deadfall, and the wood was dry and corky from the bugs. He'd built up two piles of it. Laid old branches on top of them. Then he'd poured the gas on. Two piles. One match each. Then he felt the blood.

Pounding in his head. Racing through his veins. He'd even felt his heart pumping. Pumping strong, like an oil rig. Blood gushed. Fire raged. Everywhere.

And now he was back from the past—in his forest above the smoky, spewing hole, watching his fire beast come alive. There was lots of snaggly dead wood in there that would burn like bacon grease. High fuel load, that's what the firefighters called it. They hated it. Hah. It was his favorite. Bodine whispered to the forest. Fire. Blood. Power. Evil dies. Again. Good things were starting to happen. He could feel the wind picking up. His fire beast would be angry soon, raging mad. He tried to see into the future, after his meeting with Jesse. He saw himself back in his tree, watching Satan's soldiers sweat. Then he saw the hoodoo bear up on this mountain—the top of the world—rising on two legs, blocking out the sun, fire shooting out of his eyes.

The Hell Hole

RAINEY CHOSE THE BACK way, climbing up through the Tom Miner Basin. He planned to hike over the ridge, check out the meadow from above, then pick his way down to the Sentry. He drove along Tom Miner Creek until he found a dirt road that dead-ended at a remote campground. Rainey left his pickup at an out-of-the-way campsite. He felt better, even a little loose. The waiting was over.

The trail started at seven thousand feet, twisting and turning for almost six miles before reaching the ridge. With less than three hours before dark, Rainey hiked as fast as he was able. To the southwest he could see the cliffs and the ancient trees of the Gallatin Petrified Forest. Behind him the Yellowstone River roared through Yankee Jim Canyon, making its way from the park to the Paradise Valley.

He carried a daypack. He'd thrown in the essentials, then packed the tools he needed to move a thermophile mat, and two petri dishes holding the strain of thermophiles that would compete successfully with the explosive Sentry thermophiles. Several miles later he turned up the Rainbow Creek Trail. There were still steep cliffs to the southwest, but to the east the country had opened up into multicolored meadows.

The evening light all but disappeared when the trail wound up and into a wide forested draw. The trees made a heavy veil, offering only the briefest glimpses of the easier, open spaces beyond. His flashlight helped with the steep, increasingly claustrophobic climb.

An hour and a half later he came into the familiar parklands. He could see the night sky now—vast, clear, and dusted with stars. A three quarter moon threw fine, gentle light across the meadow.

Rainey crossed the parklands for his first look down into the Elk Creek drainage. He rubbed his eyes. The bottom half of the drainage was lit by a raging fire, perhaps a hundred blazing acres. And just above the flames, the Sentry was decked out like some surrealist's version of the Gates of Hell.

The wind was pushing the fire northwest toward the hot spring. The Elk Creek Trail was so choked with smoke, it was likely impassable. Flames were marching relentlessly toward the creek. This fire wasn't sleeping. Anything but. He could see little balls of flame shooting through the air, jumping ahead of the fire. He focused his night vision binoculars. Those were electric lights, flickering around the Sentry. Someone had set up an elaborate camp. The lights were strung from poles set among the tents. The entire meadow looked like it had been lit up for Christmas. And like little ants with a purpose, people were moving in and around the tents.

He heard a chopper. At first he thought it was the smoke jumpers, firefighters brought in to contain the fire. But when the helicopter passed overhead, he knew instantly that this was no firefighting aircraft. No. This camo-colored monster was U. S. Army. He watched it set down at the hot spring.

Gingerly, he picked his way down the slope. In the next half hour the army chopper came and went, then came back again. He guessed it was moving people and supplies out of the path of the fire. Now he heard a helicopter down below. With his binoculars, he could make it out by the firelight. This one was a firefighting unit. One of the big Chinooks, scoping out the fire. The park had a let-burn policy but only to a certain point. The wind had picked up, and the fire was gaining momentum. Unattended, it would soon be out of control.

Rainey circled southeast, climbing a wooded hillside until he was well above the blaze. The flames were ravenous, feeding on anything their trembling, tangerine-colored tentacles could reach. From his hiding place he had a clear view down to the meadow and the steamy, spewing hot spring. He counted five tents in the southern half of the meadow. Armed soldiers moved in and around them. He could see how the lights strung on the poles were wired to a good-sized generator. Beams from a passing chopper washed across the tents, then spread out into the meadow where they momentarily lit up the Sentry, light bouncing off the spray as if the hot spring was an extraordinary outdoor fountain.

A man stepped out of a black helicopter Rainey hadn't noticed before. The man fired up a cigarette. From his manner, and the way the commanding officer greeted him, Rainey guessed that this was Danny Briley. Two soldiers carried something out, setting it on a table for Danny to see. Rainey followed with the binoculars. Jesus. A dead man, headless, a stake through his heart.

Danny turned, pointing impatiently at the fire then at the lab tent. He grabbed a handheld radio—one angry sonofabitch—and disappeared into the chopper. Rainey wondered just how much muscle this so-called "federal liaison" had.

He had his answer shortly. Parachutes rained down on the meadow, smoke jumpers to turn the fire. Minutes after the first white spot hit the meadow, Danny's chopper was airborne.

———

RACHEL WAS YELLING AT Mitchell, trying to get the facts about the fire, when Gummer knocked on her door. It was just after 10:30 P.M. "It's open," she yelled, covering the phone. Then back to Mitchell, "I don't give a damn if it's classified. I want to know exactly where the fire is…I'll call Missoula…they report to you on this…you coordinate the interagency fire team? Mitchell, how can you do that? Don't you dare hang up on me—" She sighed, looking up at Gummer. "What an asshole."

Gummer couldn't help smiling.

"Well, come in, Gummer. Don't just stand there. Use the chair. That's what it's for. Why are you here?" This had to be good.

Gummer sat, crossing his legs. She watched him check out her house. It was simple, inviting, and, she had to admit, as cluttered as her office.

"Nice," he said. "You okay?" he asked, when she just stared at him, waiting.

"I'm awful. The fire's spread. The firefighters think it might be arson."

"Who'd you talk with?"

"One of the fire spotters. He says it's like a war zone up there. They took infrared photos. The fire started at a single point source. They think someone set it."

"Uh-huh."

Gummer wasn't at all surprised. "Why are you here?" she asked again, a hard little sparkle in her big brown eyes. He was nervous, she thought, which was rare for him.

"I'd like to work with you on this."

What? "Work with me? Excuse me, but is this about money?"

"In part. I've invested in an elk farm—"

"Are you with Jesse?"

"Yes, his partner."

"Well at least you're not hiding it. Do I need to tell you how I feel about Jesse?"

"Give me a chance here. Please. The thing is," he said, "I want to stop Danny. I think we can help each other." Gummer's expression changed. What it was, Rachel realized, he looked relieved.

Still, she was skeptical. "I don't get this. You and Mitchell, you're thick as thieves. And you and Jesse—" She sighed. "Hell, Gummer. I know you're making money off his deals."

"I'm not as smart as you think," he confessed. "I really am a little goofy. Always have been. But I think a lot about my future. About my finances. And I've always been good at that. There's a girl now, too. It's serious. So I'm going to have responsibilities."

"Go on," Rachel said, genuinely surprised.

"I want to make a go of elk farming, and antler processing. Legally." He hesitated. "We bought a processing secret. So I can't have those army guys killing off the elk."

"A processing secret? No—" Phillipe hadn't said anything about that. "That's...that's supposed to be impossible."

Gummer shrugged. "Jesse set a guy up. It's still going to cost a lot of money."

"You guys are lunatics." She paused, her lips turning up ever so slightly. "And Jesse must be going nuts."

"He's had a bad day," Gummer agreed. "On top of everything else, Danny shot up his house, then he shot a big hole in his hand. Afterwards he left us handcuffed to this post on the front porch."

She couldn't suppress a laugh. "No way. C'mon—"

"Yeah, it's true. I think you really ticked Danny off. Anyway, Jesse took off somewhere. No one knows where he is."

"I'll be." She looked at Gummer, thoughtful. If he was for real...she forced herself to slow down. "How can you help me?"

"Here's how I see that. If we're a team—share information, make a plan...you know. If we do that, and don't tell anyone about it, we'll end up knowing just about everything. I can get stuff from Mitchell and Jesse—"

"Like what?"

"I think I know who started the fire. And more."

Rachel waited. He was trying, she had to give him that.

"You know Darrell Bodine?" Gummer asked.

"The poacher?"

"Right. He went crazy. Tried to attack my girl." Rachel watched his face change. "Tried to rape her. She hurt him and got away. But he flipped. Set a fire up on Rattlesnake Ridge. Shot up Brad over at the drugstore. Set his place on fire, too. I'm sure he's up there. And here's the other thing...what Jesse told me. What he said, uh," Gummer sighed, long-faced. "Rachel, he told me Bodine thinks your bear is the devil. He could really think that..."

Nothing would surprise her today. Nothing. "Go on," she said, turning grim.

"Jesse called me earlier. Told me he needed the frequency of the collar on your bear. Something about Bodine. I told him I didn't have it. He hung up on me. He could a got it from Mitchell."

"What for?" That feeling of dread was back, like some weird churning pressure in the pit of her stomach.

"I'm not sure. But I know how Jesse's mind works. And I think he's trying to make some kind of deal with Bodine. Get him to do his dirty work. With the frequency. Trade him the bear for, say, Danny."

"No. Oh god, no."

"I'd bet Jesse's up there now. With that crazy man. Telling him where to set the fires, how to lure Danny in."

Rachel tried hard to focus. She couldn't let Bodine kill her bear. "I'm going up. Tonight." She hoped Rainey would understand.

"In the fire, in the dark?"

"You want to be my partner? Be at the Blue Grouse Creek trailhead in an hour."

"Okay. You bet." Gummer hurried for the door.

When she heard the door open, Rachel turned. "Gummer, how old is your girlfriend?"

"Twenty," he lied, then thinking better of it, "Almost twenty, anyway."

Rachel suppressed a smile. "I'm going to bet you wouldn't marry her if she wasn't smart and practical."

"Oh, she can do whatever she sets her mind to."

"Call her up and set her mind to babysitting."

"Okay. Sure." Gummer flashed a genuine smile. "You won't be sorry."

———

JESSE HATED HIKING. AND here he was, climbing at least two miles in the dark with a heavy pack, his hand hurting every time he moved his fingers.

He'd followed Blue Grouse Creek straight to the Cut-Across Trail, then taken it east to the park boundary. He was on time. At the right damn place. So where in hell was Bodine? Once or twice he thought he smelled smoke. The guy was probably swinging through the fucking trees, lighting fires as he went. Tarzan the Fireman.

———

BODINE WAS IN A tree, watching Jesse through night-vision binoculars. Wanting to be sure that his beady eyes weren't red. He'd been watching for a while, long enough to slide down a little from the pills. And so far Jesse's eyes had stayed okay. The thing of it was, he knew, that they could change in a heartbeat. Yeah, that fast, ice to fire. So it was important to wait and watch. See if Jesse had gone over.

So far, so good. Bodine climbed down and without a sound, he made his way to the meeting place. His face was blackened. He was wearing camo he'd covered with dirt and twigs. Bodine stepped quietly onto the trail, so Jesse could see him in the moonlight.

"Hey there, Bodine," Jesse said, coming on cool as a cuke. Bodine knew better. "You caused me some problems in town."

Bodine just looked at him. Feeling the power. Jesse the heathen couldn't hurt him anymore.

Jesse waited him out.

After a long silence, Bodine spit, a mixture of phlegm, chaw, and blood. "I want the devil bear."

"Uh-huh. You bet. And I got a sure way at him. I need some help, though."

Bodine grunted.

"I found the man who made your devil bear. And I know how he did it." Jesse drew it out. When Bodine took a step closer, he went on. "He's been in disguise. He's the master of evil. He came from far away to poison the Sentry Hot Spring. Mess up the animals. Kill their babies."

In the past few days Bodine had seen a dead fawn with no spots and no legs. And two dead moose calves, joined at the hip. Today, he'd caught the no-eared bear cub in his snare set.

"I want you to keep the scientists out of the Sentry—"

"You know what's up there?" Bodine broke in.

Jesse shook his head, no.

"Army. Satan's soldiers guarding his hot, smoky hole."

"Uh... okay."

In the moonlight Bodine saw Jesse's raisin eyes widen.

"So...how did they get there?" Jesse asked.

Bodine saw the red. "Chopper." He spit, more blood.

"You need a doctor?"

Bodine shook his head. "The son of Satan's sow."

"Right." Jesse reached into his pack, pulled out a Telonics receiver. "I got the bear's frequency," he explained. "Work with me here. Help me stop the evil genius, Satan's right-hand man, and I'll help you kill that devil bear."

The red was coming on more regular now. Bodine was sure of it.

"You're not afraid to fight the master of evil are you?"

Bodine shook his head.

"His name is Danny Briley. He makes them put his poison in the pool. Then he makes them keep that pool red-hot. So it shoots his poison into the creek. He comes in the helicopter. I have his picture." Jesse took a picture—a digital photo from Nellie—out of his knapsack and handed it to the wild-eyed forest creature.

Bodine studied the photo. "He's from the Hell Hole." A fact.

"Right. If you get him, all of this will stop."

The red was there now, all the time. His vision had been right. Bodine took a pill from under his camo outfit. He chewed it.

"I want you to burn 'em out," Jesse said. "If they stop cooking the pool, and you put the evil one back in the Hell Hole..." Jesse tapped his forefinger on Danny's photo. "It's over."

Bodine squinted. He was way ahead of that. "The hoodoo bear," he whispered, starting to feel dizzy.

"Hoodoo?..un-huh, that's just what he is...a hoodoo bear. And I got the frequency written down." Jesse handed Bodine the piece of paper.

Bodine grunted, satisfied. He had what he needed. And watching Jesse's beady red eyes, he felt the pill kick in. "Something to show you," he said, and he turned toward the trees.

They followed a game trail into the woods. Bodine knew Jesse had to work hard to keep up, even though he—Jesse's hired hand, the so-called misfit—was the one who was wounded and carrying the receiver. About half a mile in they turned off the game trail into a small, forested draw. Bodine could smell the rotting meat as they approached the clearing where he'd been putting out carcasses, trying to attract the bear. In the little clearing there was a culvert trap, a heavy metal cylinder. He'd suspended a lure from an overhanging branch. On top of the trap he'd set a cross—made from two silver candlesticks. Bodine pointed into the trap.

Jesse stepped closer, grimacing against the smell. Bodine turned on a flashlight. The trap was baited, part of a maggot-infested elk, and something else. Jesse held his breath, looked where the poacher was pointing his flashlight.

In the back of the trap there was a black bear cub with a rope around its neck. The cub lunged toward them, and his head snapped back. The rope holding the young bear was tied down somewhere in the trap. In the beam of light Jesse could see that the cub had no ears. He stared. There was just hair and skin where the ears should be. Bodine came up quietly behind red-eyed Jesse. He whispered his name. The sheriff turned into the rifle butt, cracking down on his head.

———

"Decapitated...headless, right...it's like Haiti, that Voodoo shit." Danny was trying to explain the situation to his liaison at the Defense Department. He sat at Mitchell's desk. "Your boss is never happy...tell him we'll be back in by noon tomorrow...I'll call him myself when we're set up...the firefighters are on it. I got fire lines— what do they call them? Breakers, that's it. Breakers. Just below the hot spring. If they can't slow it down, we're going to call in our own people...Ramsey, he's got planes on standby loaded with a chemical that'll zap this forest back to the ice age...it's like the opposite of napalm...I'd call it fire retardant, sir...I still want more troops...I left ten, backing up the firefighters...thanks. And not to worry. It's just one crazy. You can tell the general to relax. This job's a pussy." He hung up. Mitchell was in the reception area, waiting. Park service staff, coordinating with the interagency fire team, were in the conference room down the hall. Danny had commandeered Mitchell's office. It looked like a war zone. Marked up maps covered the walls. He opened the door and called Mitchell in.

"You have any theories on the freak doing the killing up there?" Rotating in Mitchell's swivel chair, Danny eyed the assistant superintendent.

Mitchell shook his head. Since Danny had taken charge he had to watch every word, be careful all the time.

"What about Jesse?" he asked. "His car was found near the Blue Grouse Creek Trailhead."

"He could have gone up there." Mitchell said. "But the man you're after, that's not Jesse."

"I hope not, for his sake. I want to meet with the head fire honcho. Right away. Set it up."

"Right. Incidentally, someone set a fire in town. Stole some drugs. Shot the pharmacist."

"Incidentally?" Danny's face was expressionless. "My men will run it down. Mitchell, you ride with me. Get the fire boss." He pointed at Mitchell. "Incidentally, you're hanging by a thread."

Mitchell cleaned his glasses, worried about the hanging-by-a-thread business. Every time he thought he was on Danny's good side, the guy would pull the rug out from under him. The Nixon guys had been like that. "I'll ring him now," he said, and Mitchell went into the conference room to track down the fire boss.

"Gentlemen," Danny addressed his pair of enforcers, sitting outside the door. "Check the fire at the pharmacy—get a name—then get back over to Jesse's car. Walk in—say a mile—from where he's parked. I want anyone coming through there. Anyone. I'll be in touch."

The helicopter lifted off just after 10:30 P.M. On the flight in, the chopper circled the fire. Smoke was billowing in tall white plumes. The wind had picked up, coming from the east, blowing the fire west and north. The fire covered almost a hundred fifty acres now. Flames danced over fifty feet into the air. They had to swing east, around the smoke, to reach the Sentry. Mitchell had set a meeting with the fire boss in the Sentry meadow. Mitchell thought it looked like the end of the world down there.

Fire Beast

RAINEY WATCHED A SMALL herd of deer on the northern edge of the meadow. They were moving east, away from the fire. The deer traveled purposefully, without panic. Unlike him, they seemed to know what to do. Earlier, he'd watched ravens and nutcrackers swooping down at the edge of the fire. He guessed they were picking off the insects as they fled the flames. Now, he was in the trees, well above the deer. Even where he was hiding, well back in the trees, the fire was oppressively hot. His skin felt like it was sunburned.

He'd been waiting now for over an hour, killing time, watching the smoke jumpers. A transport plane had brought in about forty. From his perch he'd watched the big white parachutes drop into the meadow, backlit by the fire. No sooner did they hit the meadow than he heard the grinding of chain saws, the clanking of hoedads. Firefighters were making breaks, knocking over trees, moving snags. They were clearing narrow strips south of the meadow, emptying the strips of any and all fuel, then digging up the soil and turning it over so the fire would have nothing to feed on but dirt. He saw another group working on the far side of the breaks, spraying retardant from packs on their backs. And always the helicopters, dumping fire-retardant chemicals.

Danny had clearly leaned on the fire boss, told him to turn this fire before it reached the Sentry. And the smoke jumpers were doing their damnedest. In case this psycho liked killing firemen, Danny had left ten men south of the meadow, covering their backs. Rainey watched them moving away from the chopper and into the forest, like they were at war. Pairs of two faded into the trees between the meadow and the firefighters.

At first, he'd stayed in the tree. But it was uncomfortable, and the waiting was making him edgy. So he'd crept down the hillside, working his way southwest into a stand of lodgepole pine. He was still there, on the northeastern edge of the meadow, looking for a way in. Maybe ten minutes ago one of the soldiers had fired a burst in the trees south of the meadow, bringing down a cow elk. The elk had staggered out into the meadow to die. And now the smaller black helicopter was landing in the northwest corner of the meadow, where the other chopper had parked. He watched a man get out, working a walkie-talkie. Danny, he guessed, ordering these smoke jumpers around.

He considered just making his way to the pool, going in slow and easy behind the soldiers, doing his business. No way. Even if he got to the spring unnoticed, he'd need time. Phillipe had explained how to move the thermophile mats. He'd have to use a special chisel to chip a chunk of the geyserite off the edge of the pool. Delicate work, especially in this blistering heat. Putting in the new strain was going to take time, too. He had a probing device in his pack. A thing that looked like a turkey baster. He had to use it to suck up what was in the petri dishes and then carefully implant it in an existing mat. And he'd attract attention once he was at the pool.

The firefighting chopper was circling into the smoke again, dumping fire retardant just below the firebreaks. They seemed to be succeeding in driving the fire toward the creek, away from the Sentry. Rainey worked his way toward the little cabin set among the trees at the northeastern edge of the meadow. He went slowly, tree to tree.

At the cabin the heat was barely tolerable. He settled behind a tree to watch the activity in and around the tents. They were pitched in the southern half of the meadow, southwest of the cabin, north of the soldiers and the firefighters. In the last hour several firefighters had gone into one of the tents, taken off their helmets, masks and jackets before using the Porta Potty outside. Ten minutes later, a firefighter went into the tent then came out without his gear. When the firefighter was in the Porta Potty, Rainey worked his way south, staying in the trees. Fighting a wave of heat, he cut briskly through the meadow to the tent.

Rainey took a yellow fire resistant Nomex jacket off the back of a chair then grabbed a helmet and a smoke mask. Dressed as a firefighter, Rainey walked confidently to the walled lab tent nearby. Inside, he took a small metal container to pack out the thermophile mats. He noticed that most of the petri dishes were gone. On a lab table he could see where several racks still held vials of ENT.

The short walk to the pool was unbearably long. Less than halfway there he broke into a trot, deciding that clear, urgent purpose was the best cover. The soldiers paid no attention. They were in the trees, holding their ground, watching for a killer that stalked the forest. Rainey was sweating when he reached the hot spring.

Although the fire raged nearby, the hot spring was a world unto itself: the colors, the smells, the textures, even the climate, were that different. The aqua-blue pool was almost half full. When he stepped on the white, calcified rock surrounding the pool, Rainey felt the humid heat of the steam rising from the cauldron. Little jets of water spurted several feet into the air on the far side of the pool. He knelt on a ledge just below the lip of the geyser, where he could do his work without being too conspicuous.

———

JEN WATCHED THE MOONLIGHT reflecting off a bend pool in the small stream near their camp. While Jimmy slept, she sat on the bank, dangling her feet in the water. The slightest movement of her foot sent little ripples across the stream, making the moonlight shimmer on the water. She thought about Rainey, about Jimmy. She was remembering Jimmy—as a baby, as a toddler, Jimmy with his dad. And then she was back on Cockeye. Wondering who killed him. And why? And just like that, she was off on this thing that kept eluding her. It kept buzzing around her head, teasing her, but she couldn't quite see it.

Lloyd sat down beside her. "You've got a fine boy."

"He is, isn't he? It surprises me sometimes, given—" she hesitated. "Given what he's been through."

Lloyd sat quietly, then he said, "The one I'm worried about, it's Rainey." Lloyd told her about Rainey's house, about the fire.

Oh, god. "I'm so sorry," was all she said.

"No one's fault, honey." Lloyd spit some chaw into the near willows. "The man lets a thing simmer 'til it bites him on the ass."

Jen didn't see it that way. She thought that Rainey was on his own quiet trajectory.

"Ruth told me about the bomb factory," Lloyd interrupted her thoughts. "Nasty business."

She saw it then—the thing that had been eluding her. Damn. Bombs. Little undetectable bombs. Just like that Jen had a picture in her mind, and it made sense. Okay. "Lloyd, could you walk us out of here, tonight?"

"Yeah. Sure. What you got in mind?"

"I think I know how Cockeye died."

"How's that?"

She took a moment, piecing this together. "Okay, here's what I'm thinking. I know Cockeye. I see him waiting in the Caddy, letting Jimmy sleep. And he's smoking, killing time. There were places for five petri dishes in the metal case we found, but there were only four petri dishes inside." Jen turned toward him; this was important. "What if Cockeye had one of those petri dishes? I'm guessing he took it out of its container and left it on the dash, in the hot sun, all morning. So being Cockeye, he's curious. It'd be just like him to check it out, shake it up near his ear, toss it in the air, whatever. The thing is, if he's left it cooking in the hot sun, and then he shakes it around..." She winced. "If he does that, and if it's full of their extra-strength nitrogenous compound and superheated thermophiles, couldn't it explode, like a bomb? You see that's what he didn't know: the superheated Sentry thermophiles became explosive at higher temperatures. They're working on bombs up there, and I think the sorry sonofabitch set one off by mistake." She tossed a stone into the stream. "If I'm right, it makes a lie of Jesse's murder charges and it gives the press a way in. You think Lester would tell Cockeye's story?"

"Ex-cop killed. Bomb factory in Yellowstone Park. A murder mystery." Lloyd grinned his toothy grin. "That ignorant Irish sonofabitch would do it, yeah. Even the tabloids would show up for that."

She looked at him. "I think Cockeye, and his son, would like it."

———

RAINEY WAS ON THE ledge, just below the lip of the geyser. He took off his pack, set it on the lip. Steam was rising around him. The air was heavy, humid, and he was awash in sweat. He could see ashes floating in the pool. Rainey tried to ignore the wet heat, the rotten-egg smell, as he laid out his equipment and hunkered down to work. He put on neoprene fishing gloves then applied the chisel to a chunk of geyserite near the lip. Phillipe had said that the thermophile mats he needed would be in the top layer. Still, it took him almost three minutes to chip a piece away. It felt like a week. In his firefighter's gear, the heat was stifling. He had to stop regularly— stand up, cool down, then wipe his mask so he could see to work properly. It took another five minutes to prepare the container and get the thermophile-rich geyserite properly installed.

Below the lip of the pool it was as if the fire didn't exist. The soldiers, several hundred yards away, were in another climate zone. Rainey's world was articulated by steam, the sulfur smell, the bubbling blue water, the intricate texture of the geyserite, and the moist, palpable heat—so different from the heat of the fire. Hot water was spurting near his boots now. He could see that bubbling water was entering the pool, and the water level was rising. This geyser would erupt before too long. First, he'd try and implant one dose of the new thermophiles in a nearby mat. He had the petri dishes out—and Rainey was concentrating on using his turkey baster to suck up the thermophiles—when someone called down, "Hey buddy, what the hell you doing?"

It was a firefighter, a short one, carrying a chain saw. Rainey lifted his mask just enough to uncover his mouth. "Got to get a sample for some park service guy."

"Okay." The short firefighter walked on. Rainey saw the boiling water lapping against the heel of his boot. The pool was filling up, rising faster than he would have guessed. A jet of scalding water shot up beside him. The ledge he'd have chosen would soon be underwater. He had to find another spot before he got burned. Carefully, he set one knee, then hoisted himself up onto the lip of the pool. Beside the pool Rainey gently repacked the petri dishes. The firefighter was coming back his way. Rainey turned toward the pool, ignoring him.

"Fire boss wants to talk with you," the firefighter yelled. "Now, buddy." He was about thirty feet away, waving him toward the chopper in the northwest corner of the meadow. He could make out another firefighter, without a jacket or helmet, talking with the fire boss.

"One minute," Rainey shouted back. While the firefighter waited, Rainey lowered himself down onto a ledge. The pool was churning now, really cooking. It had gone from clear blue-green to a murkier silvery blue.

When the firefighter turned to look at the chopper, Rainey popped back up, grabbed his pack, and went straight for the tents. The steam rising from the pool, and the traffic in the meadow, gave him cover. He ran the first fifty yards. Rainey was near the trees when the short firefighter looked down into the steaming pool and realized he'd been had.

Rainey didn't slow down until he was well hidden near Little Elk Creek, almost half a mile northeast of the Sentry. The most important thing, introducing the new strain of thermophiles, was still undone.

In the trees, the night air was cooler. The sounds of the firefighting machinery, the helicopters, and the roar of the fire itself, didn't jibe with the softer night sounds of the forest. He leaned against a tree, catching his breath—and felt a gun barrel dig into the back of his neck.

"Real slow," a man whispered.

Rainey took two steps away from the tree. One of the soldiers must have followed him. He tried to turn but the gun butt smashed against the side of his head. Blood ran from his ear. He put his hand against a tree for balance. His captor spit a wad of chaw. Rainey watched the dark murky liquid drip down the tree beneath his fingers. It came together then, a bone-chilling epiphany—the murder, the stake in the heart, the fire, the gun barrel pressed hard to his injured ear. Darrell Bodine.

———

BECAUSE OF THE FIRE, Rachel had chosen to hike up the Blue Grouse Creek Trail then follow the Cut-Across Trail to Elk Creek. She more or less jogged to the Cut-Across Trail. On the Cut-Across Trail Rachel maintained their pace. Gummer had to smile—as Rachel's partner, he got more exercise in one day than in a month tagging along with Jesse.

There is a view from the cut-across trail, before reaching Elk Creek, where the vista to the east sweeps across the entire drainage. Rachel stopped at this spot, struck dumb by what she saw. When he caught up with her, Gummer closed his eyes, opened them, then again, slowly, as he shook his head side to side.

To the southeast, little more than a mile away, the fire was raging toward them, a huge, multi-headed creature, incinerating everything in its path. Red-orange flames were shooting high into the sky—pulsating hundred foot pillars of fire—throwing off shimmering waves of heat. By now the fire temperature was almost a thousand degrees. As they watched, a tall conifer ignited, the entire tree bursting into flames from the heat. The smoke moved toward them, billowing into plumes as thick as custard.

"I'm scared of fires," Gummer softly said.

Rachel nodded, stared at the fire, then she told him how this view would come back to her in dreams.

When Rachel turned south into the woods, Gummer asked where they were going.

"Check my trap."

It made perfect sense to Gummer. The trap was in the path of this fire. Why, he wondered, did some people care so much about animals, while others didn't even notice them?

———

RACHEL HAD NO TROUBLE finding a game trail that would take them southwest toward her trap. As they wound through the trees, she slowed, shining her flashlight on the ground ahead of her. Gummer could see footprints on the trail.

They went ahead carefully, finding their way through the forest without the flashlight. Occasionally moonlight broke through the heavy canopy, but the irregular shafts of light only made them more aware of the blackness surrounding them. Rachel missed the familiar scent of pine, lost in the smell of smoke. They stopped when they heard a long, low wail. It was an unfamiliar, inhuman noise. The wailing was incessant and eerie. Rachel opened the bear-mace holster on her belt.

The wail came again, higher pitched this time. Rachel signaled a stop at a pair of old fir trees. They were close to the sound now, and she thought it was coming from her trap. But it wasn't a bear. It could be an animal sound, though. They found their separate ways to the clearing. On her signal they shined their flashlights on the culvert trap. The wailing was past desperation, a terrified droning.

Rachel gasped when she saw the silver cross set on top of her trap. She could see that the steel-barred trapdoor had sprung shut. The trap was a metal cylinder, five feet in diameter and ten or eleven feet deep. The only opening for air or light was between the bars of the guillotine gate. Gummer ran his light through the door, over the rotting elk. Rachel focused her light on something else. A bear cub was hanging by a rope around its neck. The rope had been pulled over the hook holding the elk carcass, lifting the little bear off its feet. The cub was dead. Rachel passed her light over the bear cub's body, stopping on a missing ear. It felt like a bad omen, and Rachel let out a slow breath. The wailing got louder still. It was coming from the darkness behind the elk carcass. And yes, between the old elk carcass and the dead bear cub, something had moved.

Playing their lights on the source of the noise, they saw a bloody human torso. Jesus. Wild black hair. Jesse.

Gummer gasped, as if his heart might stop.

Rachel opened the trapdoor. In no time at all she was inside. It was cold and dark, and the smell was unbearable. She followed her light toward the back where Jesse hid his head like a terrified child. She could see that he'd been clawed, long raking marks along his naked body. She shone the light on his face. It was pale and haunted by demons. His left eye was twitching uncontrollably. He grabbed her leg, clutching it with both powerful arms. She felt pity, then, for this awful man.

———

BODINE HAD WAITED JUST above the meadow. Knowing that his fire was good. His fire beast was angry now, raging mad. His fire beast would work loose the vile things, force them out into the open.

He flashed back to his gramma—how one time, she cast a fiery wall-of-protection spell. She used her own blood, roots, herbs, and fire to protect them from the evil eye. When the vile things came, he might need that.

He'd come down from the ledge, taking his time, easing up on the red-hot, spewing hole. Watching. Thinking maybe he should do Danny last. Stuff him back in his hole, just before he slammed it shut.

That's when he saw a firefighter dropping down into the hole. Right in it. And then the guy was out, setting his pack up top, beside the hole. He had him in the glasses now. A big guy. The firefighter lifted his mask, wiped the sweat off his face. Bodine grinned, a real twisted shit-eater. This was no firefighter. This was the bastard that damn near sent him to prison. It hit him then—sort of a revelation— how this pit bull bastard had to be a devil warrior, how his enemy must have pulled his warrior from the Hell Hole over a year back.

So he'd waited. With the pills, he never got too tired. The man came back out of the hole with a lot of new strength. When he ran into his forest, Bodine followed. Got the drop on him. He wanted to put a hole in his head right then, check his blood, but he didn't. He was having a hard time keeping in a groove though, beating back temptations. And now they were walking west toward the creek. Bodine kept the gun to the back of Rainey's head.

At a clearing Bodine tapped Rainey's neck with the gun, motioning for him to wait. He stuck his gun barrel in Rainey's ear, twisting sharply, opening the wound. He inspected the blood on the barrel. It looked like real blood. But it wasn't.

Bodine prodded him forward. He'd wait—stake out this warrior with red-eyed Jesse. Make them bleed. He knew the bear would come. Like he came for the elk. It was his nature. The hoodoo bear would eat his helpers to keep the evil from getting away. He watched the blood, oozing from Rainey's ear. The warrior's pack was hooked over his neck, and his hands were tied together in front of him. Bodine watched him carefully, talking to himself. He repeated his words, a precaution. Blood. Power. Fire. Evil dies. Again. He began chanting his words. He knew he had to be careful. He was ready to kill this warrior if the moonlight shone funny on a tree.

Bodine touched his gun to the bloody ear again, checked the blood, then he raised his voice, feeling the power, calling out his archenemy now, challenging him.

Rainey turned his head. Bodine was sure the warrior had understood his words, and he smashed the pistol across the back of Rainey's head, driving him to the ground. Rainey lay there. Bodine stood over him, chanting, feeling the power. When he looked to the sky, the top of the world, the warrior brought his hands up, hard, between his legs.

Bodine kneeled over, fighting for breath. He could feel his head spinning. Then he felt another blow, clenched hands driving hard into his face. There was no pain, but there was blood now, coming from his nose. His face was on the ground, and the warrior had his foot on his back, in the bad place, pushing at the blood hole. Pain now. Dull, throbbing pain. He couldn't move at all. The evil warrior knew his weak point. The blood running down his face helped him think. He hadn't come this far to be struck down in his own forest by a helper, even if he was a great warrior. But the warrior had his gun. And he kept that heavy foot on his blood hole, pushing so hard Bodine thought his head might pop open. He waited, still, while the tricky bastard took his hunting knife from its sheath.

Bodine could hear him cut his hands free with his own knife, the one he sharpened every day. Next, the warrior took the handheld off his belt, then he eased the .30-06 off his shoulder.

"Get up. Hands on your head," Rainey ordered.

Bodine did as he was told.

"Turn around, hands behind your back."

Bodine nodded.

The warrior held his pistol in his left hand, pointed right at him. In his right hand, he held the .30-06.

Bodine started to turn, slowly, carefully. He was chanting again, softly. Then he spun, the skinning knife slicing through Rainey's left forearm. Blood spurted. Devil blood. Bodine knew his enemy was a great warrior because he held onto the gun. Bodine ran, hoping a bullet wouldn't rip another hole in his back. The blood helped him run. The warrior didn't fire.

———

At first Jesse was silent. Gummer thought he looked even worse than when he was really low. He was clawed up pretty bad. Chewed on, too. Bloody wounds all over his body. That freak Bodine must have left him locked in the trap with the live bear cub, another mutation. Rachel showed him where the cub was missing toes on two paws. Gummer had noticed the ear right off, but he never would have thought to check the toes.

After they helped Jesse into his clothes, he started talking. Angry ranting about his father then something about a black bear. His left eye was still twitching like all get-out. Finally he asked Rachel for a martini. Dry, three olives. Gummer had never seen him like this. It was upsetting.

———

Once the sheriff was dressed, Rachel hurried him along. She wanted to be as far as possible from the trap. She'd seen bear sign, and she worried about the bear—or Bodine—coming back. She led them through the forest. The fire was spreading, moving west. Jesse was having trouble walking, and if the wind shifted, the smoke could reach the Blue Grouse Creek Trail. Rachel considered options. Okay, Gummer could take Jesse down the Silver Creek Trail, a little further west. It was an easier hike out, especially at night. When she came out of the forest at Blue Grouse Creek, she looked toward Silver Creek. In the moonlight she could see sage-covered hills rolling toward another forest. It seemed serene, tranquil, until you turned back to watch the raging fire. Like an incoming tide, it was creeping relentlessly their way. By dawn these tranquil hills could look like a burned-out moonscape.

Rachel took Gummer aside, told him what she had in mind. He'd walk Jesse to safety. And she'd go back up. She could see he didn't like it. He finally admitted they couldn't just leave Jesse, she was right about that. After he finally gave in, Gummer told her to be careful. Before he left, Gummer added that he knew how she got when her mind was set.

Rachel watched Gummer help Jesse toward the trail. They stopped to sit on a log. She liked that he was kind and patient with the traumatized sheriff. Rachel retraced her path through the forest. Though it was a familiar part of her subarea, now it was unwelcoming. The smoke was heavy enough that she feared the Elk Creek Trail might be impassable. She could see smoke coming her way.

When a big Chinook helicopter passed overhead, an idea pretty much grabbed her by the throat. The fire spotters would help. She had to get down, get hold of a radio.

She turned southwest and lengthened her stride, cutting through the trees until she reached the Blue Grouse Creek Trail. She hurried down the familiar trail. Tonight it was disquieting—the sounds, the smells, the smoke, the weird light from the fire. It was, she thought, primeval. Less than half a mile from the trailhead, she rounded a bend and went crashing to the ground. Her feet just flew out from under her, and she landed on her stomach, face planted in the dirt. She was gasping, trying to catch her breath, when a man stepped over a trip wire and set his heavy black boot on the nape of her neck.

Another man tied Rachel's hands behind her back. As they walked her down the trail, she heard a chopper, though she couldn't see it. At the trailhead they threw her up onto the chopper's metal floor.

A black wing-tipped shoe cracked against her jaw. "My turn," Danny said.

The Killing Shot

R AINEY WAS SITTING ON a fallen pine tree beside Little Elk Creek, a tributary of the larger stream. At this altitude, the creek was narrow. It made soothing, gurgling, sounds as the water poured over a large tree root then several big stones before turning to cascade over a two-foot drop, a little waterfall. He was cleaning and dressing his wounds. The cut in his left forearm was still bleeding, in spite of his crudely fashioned bandage. Bodine had sliced right through the fleshy underside of his arm. Where had he hidden his second knife? Side of his boot probably. He re-taped the gauze dressing so it covered the wound. In the dark, he dropped a twig into the creek. Watched it go over the falls.

Rainey could still see the crazed, unhinged look on Bodine's blackened face. The poacher's ranting still rang in his ears.

Rainey was pretty sure he'd understood what he'd heard. Bodine believed he was the hero in some kind of epic struggle against evil, right here in Yellowstone. Fires. Beheadings. And his chanting—Power. Blood. Fire. Evil dies. Rainey wondered if psychos like Bodine came out whenever the world went mad.

He turned on Bodine's handheld and recognized the voice of the fire boss. He was talking to a fire spotter in a chopper. Mitchell kept breaking in, giving orders. Mitchell told the fire boss that more soldiers were coming in to track down this killer. When the boss suggested his men move southwest to try and contain the fire, Mitchell said that the firefighters damn well better stay at the Sentry until Danny said they could leave. While the fire boss suggested that Mitchell was a bootlicking flunky, Rainey shouldered his pack and turned toward the Sentry, knowing what had to be done.

———

THE PUERTO RICAN FIRE boss was waiting when Danny stepped down from the chopper.

"I'm impressed," Danny said. "And that doesn't happen often."

"Hmm," he responded. He knew fires. His men would walk through flames for him. Often did. He didn't give a shit about much else. "Sir, can we jump southwest of here, see if we can contain this fire in the one drainage?"

Danny ignored him. "Stopped that sucker. On a dime." Danny pointed toward the smoke jumpers. "Very nice."

"Can we move out then?"

"No. Your objective is to protect this hot spring pool. You stay right here."

"Mister, I got a call from the superintendent himself. That's the only reason I'm in this meadow. Now I did what he asked."

"Whatever. Keep up the good work." Danny turned. His thin lips twisted up in his let's-drown-the-cat smile as his men led Rachel from the chopper. He turned back. "Aren't we finished?"

"Not yet. Mister, I've got a responsibility here. I'm taking my men west. This fire could turn. Make sure you got a way out of here."

Danny planted his forefinger on the fire boss's chest. "Your job is to keep this fire from turning. Your only job. You fail, and you'll be swallowing fireballs at some Mexican circus."

"Listen, asshole—"

Danny grabbed the fire boss's upper arm, squeezing two pressure points until he gasped. "You don't get it," Danny hissed. "You're a soldier in my command. If I tell you to piss the fire out, you start drinking water." Danny paused, applying more pressure, forcing the fire boss to his knees. "You stay until I say go. You turn smartass, I'll have you arrested."

———

MADE A FOOL OF me, Bodine thought. Played me like a dumb country peckerwood. The warrior was a temptation. One of Satan's tricks to keep him away from the bear. He'd have to be more careful, stop confusing the order of things. The warrior would go back to the hole. He'd kill him there. After. When the bear burned up, the warrior's power would be gone.

His back hurt, and his nose was bleeding again. He'd taken another pill, and for just a second, he went in and out of the here and now. He sat among the pines, making a new plan.

Okay. Up again. And now he was moving fast, north of the Cut-Across Trail, above the smoke, thinking red-eyed Jesse could smell it now. He cut down into the forest, walking blind through the trees. Off trail, in the dark, he went straight for the culvert trap. He'd find it. Since he was a boy he could always find things in the forest. Especially at night.

Near the trap he felt something bad. It was like an icy wind shooting down the back of his neck. Maybe it was the pills. No. There was bear sign, a pile of scat on the trail. At the clearing he knew for sure. The trap door was open. He could feel the blood now, pounding in his head. The hoodoo bear had come. Here. Ahead of him. Tempted him with his warrior so he could free his helper. Bodine screamed his rage.

Sometime later, Bodine began chanting. As he repeated his words, it came to him, what he had to do, and frantically, Bodine gathered deadfall. When he had a good pile, Bodine lit a fire. Right behind the trap. When it came alive, he felt better. He spun, a wary mongoose turning on a snake. Yes—his cross was still there. He climbed up on top of the trap. Carefully, he unfastened the silver cross, then Bodine ran through the forest straight for his cache.

At the cache he turned on the receiver, set the frequency. He waited, chanting until there was a signal. North, toward the rim. He yelled into his forest. Thankful. Breathing deep. Feeling the power.

Bodine inspected his shotgun then loaded it with carved twelve-gauge slugs. He took a second reading on the receiver before putting it in his pack. With a stick, he dug up the loose dirt at the base of a near pine tree. From the hole he extracted the blood-caked head that he'd carefully cut off the soldier. It had been in his vision, how he should keep the head, how he would need it later.

He stuffed the head into his pack. Using the skinning knife, he cut two blood lines across his chest, then he emptied the extra gas can on a brush pile near his cache. One match. Yeah.

———

"AN AMBULANCE WOULD BE good," Gummer said to Stacy from the pay phone at the Conoco. "No, he's not hurt that bad. Let's just say he's not his normal self. No, Stace, he's not his down self either—at least not in the usual way. Just come and see for yourself, honey. Okay?" Gummer hung up and turned to Jesse, who was reading the pet shop listings in the yellow pages. The sheriff's left cheek was still twitching to beat the band.

Gummer led him toward the convenience store bench and tried to talk with him. Jesse sat for half a minute, then he walked into the store. Suzy looked at the sheriff kind of funny when he asked her if she had any gin. "Sheriff, this is a convenience store in *your* county," she said. "What is this, some kind of bimbo test?" But Jesse was already in the back at the big refrigerator, sorting through the beer.

Gummer hoped that Jesse would get over this. The way Gummer saw it, Jesse just wasn't used to being on the receiving end of things. Give him some time. He'd get back to his old self. Maybe a bender would help.

Gummer sat, feeling low. Was he feeling this way just because Jesse was so bad off? That was part of it. He hated to see him like this. But the way he felt, there had to be something more. Well, he sure wasn't looking forward to telling Jesse how he was done with trophy hunts, and poachers, and looking the other way whenever Jesse told him to. Still, at the culvert trap, he'd made up his mind about those things, and that was that. So, no. Something else was making him sad. He had it then, plain as day—his partnership with Jesse was over.

After Jesse was packed into the ambulance, Gummer drove back into the park. On the way, he listened to the park band. One of the fire spotters reported in, then Mitchell was bitching about the new fires. The fire boss said he could find this firestarter. Gummer thought that mixing it up with Bodine wasn't such a good idea. Still, it got him thinking.

He called Mitchell, finding him where the interagency fire team had taken over an office in North. "Yo, Mitchell, buddy. Gummer here."

"Where in hell have you been?"

"I've been up there."

"Up where?"

"Just west of the fire."

"Doing what?"

"Well, I found Jesse. Yes sir. And on top of that, I think I can help you find this firestarter."

"How's that?"

"It's complicated. I'll be there in a minute to tell you the whole wild story. In the meantime I need some info on this fire. Can you patch me through to a fire spotter?"

"I'll see." Gummer could hear Mitchell puffing on his pipe. "Can't patch you through, but he has a radio in the chopper." Mitchell gave him the frequency.

"Thank you. I'm on my way to you," he lied. "As soon as I get there, I'll give you the gory details."

"Where's Jesse?"

"On the way to town. See you soon." Gummer broke the connection.

He got Will, the fire spotter, right away. Ten minutes later Gummer was climbing into the helicopter, telling him they had to find Rachel.

———

RAINEY PUT THE FIRE at two hundred acres, easy. Although the wind was not blowing hard, the fire was spreading. It was not yet big enough to create it's own wind. But left untended, it could get there. And, yes, a second fire was burning. No, two more! These fires were still small but distinctly separate from the first blaze. They were burning north of Blackstone Butte, just below the Cut-Across Trail. Bodine was on a tear.

Rainey made his way toward the hot spring. He heard a chopper coming up Elk Creek, but it turned away and he lost it behind the smoke. Ten minutes later he was above the Sentry, perched in the same tree he'd been cramping up in earlier this evening.

The landscape below him had the startling irrational reality of a dream. The fire was moving west, following the smoke toward Elk Creek. In the distance, smoke was rising in thick doughy piles, backlit by trembling tentacles of flame. It was after 2:00 A.M., but the fire lit up the night sky. In places, Rainey thought it looked like dawn. At the Sentry, lights were on everywhere. Hot white eyes in the drifting smoke. And the geyser was erupting, spewing boiling water into the eerie, oddly beautiful night sky. He counted three helicopters, two army choppers and a firefighting unit. Through his glasses he could see the firefighters making more breaks, protecting the southwest corner of the meadow. They weren't moving too fast. Odd. He saw a group of them clustered around their chopper.

Beyond the lab tent, near the tree line, he could make out another group: Danny, and there was Rachel. Her hands were tied behind her back. She was flanked by two men: one tall, the other short. Rainey started to sweat. He set down the binoculars and took a slow breath. When he looked again, Phillipe was in front of the lab tent—talking with Danny, pointing at the pool.

———

It was too hot in the lab tent, so Danny had ordered two firefighters to carry out a table, lanterns, and chairs. They walked toward the tent and just kept going, back to the fire line. So he called in two soldiers to do it. Before they went back to their posts, he thought about sending them after the two firemen. Make an example of them. Kneecap these willful smoke jumpers.

The firefighters who were not working had retreated to the far edge of the meadow. They'd set down their chopper as far as possible from Danny and the soldiers. The soldiers were still staked out in the trees along the southwestern perimeter. Danny sat at the table, listening to Phillipe. He knew guys like this. Parasites. They showed up in every backwater country whenever there was a shift in power, crawling out of the woodwork to suck the blood of the newly powerful. This guy had hitched a ride with the firefighting chopper to offer up Rachel, Jesse, and a new player—some hard-case local named Rainey. Selling them cheap. All he wanted was permission to take a thermophile mat out of the pool, move it somewhere.

"You're telling me that they're planning to put a new strain into my pool." Danny was in ice pick mode. "A strain that will kill my thermophiles?"

"Compete with them, sir. Outlive them."

"In English, dammit."

Phillipe winced. He'd actually bitten his own tongue. "Replace them, not kill them," he offered, carefully. "However, these new thermophiles, they will not be volatile."

"Not explosive?"

"Exactly."

Danny stood up, seething. "Can you tell if it's done?"

"I can analyze a sample, onsite."

"Do it. Right away," he ordered.

Phillipe went into the lab tent and came out with the gear he needed. Danny signaled and two soldiers stepped forward to escort Phillipe to the pool. Danny waited until he was at the pool, then he found Rachel, behind the tent. "Where's this Rainey?"

"Fuck you, Danny."

He hit her face with his fist. It sent her reeling to the ground.

The left side of Rachel's face was discolored and swollen. Blood flowed from her torn mouth. She rose to spit blood at him.

Danny hit her again, breaking her nose, then he picked up a handheld radio. "I want Ramsey...then wake him the fuck up!"

A few minutes later he heard, "Ramsey, sir."

"Get up here, now. Bring more men. At least ten." Danny broke the connection.

———

RAINEY COULD FEEL SWEAT on his back now, and it had nothing to do with the fire. Danny had called his men in from the perimeter, positioning them around the Sentry hot spring. He and Phillipe were circling the pool. Phillipe was explaining something. He wondered if Phillipe could somehow tell whether the new competitive strain had been introduced. If so, he had to be telling Danny that it had not.

Rainey came down from his perch and worked his way into the forest. He was at the edge of the trees now, watching as Danny's pair of thugs dragged Rachel behind the lab tent toward the pines.

She was hidden there, out of sight from the meadow. The short one held her head back by her hair. The tall one raised her hands above her head and tied them to a stout branch of a pine tree. When he was satisfied with his work, he hung a Coleman lantern on the next tree over. Through the glasses Rainey could see that her face was bleeding and swollen. And it was making him sweat.

Tree to tree, he made his way closer until he reached the cabin. The firefighters were grouped at the southwestern edge of the meadow, out of sight and out of earshot. And then there was no time to think because there was Danny, sending Phillipe away with one of the soldiers, then coming behind the tent. Rainey could see him clearly now, walking up to Rachel. Asking her something, then slapping her face. At Danny's signal the short guy gagged her with a handkerchief.

Danny took the bear mace out of the holster on her belt and pointed the can at her face. He sprayed her dead on—a long burst—and Rainey watched her head twist and turn in agony. He swallowed down hard on the rage welling up from his stomach. Danny pursed his lips, watching Rachel's body contort, then he sprayed her again. Timing the swings of her head, he grabbed her swollen jaw, loosened the gag, and whispered something in her ear. She was twisting, writhing piteously. When she didn't respond, he called the two men back. They tightened the gag, then held her steady while Danny slowly bent back the index finger of her left hand. When her finger broke, Rachel threw her head back, and Rainey thought his heart would explode. She was retching violently. When she tried to catch her breath, Danny grabbed her by the hair. He was aiming the can of mace at her face when suddenly his body twisted. He stepped back. Danny looked to the woods, confused. His mouth opened and closed, but no sound came out. He glared at Rachel, then he fell to the ground, blood pumping from a gaping hole in his chest. It took Rainey a moment to realize that he was holding the .30-06 that had fired the killing shot.

Top of the World

D ANNY'S TWO MEN RAN for the helicopter as soon as Danny
went down. They knew he was dead. And they knew better
than to stay in the open with a sniper working.

Rainey ran full out for Rachel.

The darkness helped. Rainey came through the trees as fast as
he'd ever moved. He reached Rachel, cut her down. She fell into his
arms, burying her face in his shirt. "You're okay now," he whispered.
"Just hang on." Rainey carried her back into the forest. They went
north, above the fire. Rainey ran as fast as he could with Rachel
over his shoulder. At Little Elk Creek he stopped so she could put
her face in the water. Her eyes were swollen shut—blood-red and
tearing nonstop. Her index finger hung at an odd angle. Her nose
was bleeding, and she had to slave for every breath. "Where can we
hide?" he asked her softly.

Using two fingers to hold one eye barely open, Rachel managed
to turn north toward the rim. With her damaged hand, she held
onto his arm. She moved as fast as she was able through the dark
forest.

He was right beside her—steadying her, admiring her stride.

———

THE FIRE BOSS WAS fuming. No one treated him this way. No-fuckin'-
body. He was remembering how the superintendent had asked
him, politely, to please listen to this guy. "Work with him," he said.
"He's the boss on this deal." Well, he might be your boss, but that

don't make him *my* fuckin' boss, he thought. Getting worked up about it. And what about the firestarter? Hell, he knew what he had to do. So he marched past the soldiers guarding the Sentry back to the lab tent. He was taking his men out. Now. Dealing with this fire and this firestarter. He was going to tell Danny where to get off first. And this time he'd be ready.

No one was in or near the tent. He turned, surprised, as the black chopper took off. Maybe Danny had changed his mind. It didn't make sense. He walked south toward the other tents.

At the tree line he saw the body lit by the Coleman lantern. Danny was flat on his back. The fire boss wondered if he'd been coldcocked. He came closer, saw the open wound. It was a hole as big as a half dollar right where Danny's left nipple should be. Blood spilled into an oval-shaped, dark red puddle spreading across Danny's chest and stomach. The puddle leaked down over his groin and into the grass. The asshole didn't look so damn full of himself, not at the moment.

He turned around and walked back to the remaining army chopper. "Your boss is dead," he told the pilot. "Behind the tent. Get on it." Then he started moving his men out.

When Major Ramsey arrived in another chopper with twelve more men, the firefighters were gone.

RAMSEY SENT HIS MEN north, fanning out through the woods. Then he sat on the table near the lab tent to do some headwork. Okay. It was one thing to kill privates, foot soldiers. Killing Danny Briley was something else entirely. Danny had clearances generals never got. The guy could pull strings, get things done faster than most of the big-shot politicians. Ramsey would be on the line for this one—personally—until he found this killer.

Find this killer, he repeated to himself, because the Ram hadn't put in thirty-odd years to have his retirement fouled by some psycho. Too many years of "Do you think so sir?" to the water walkers. Eight months left. And a condo, and a bank account in Costa Rica. Okay. Get 'er done. Yes, sir.

He looked over at Danny, lying there in the grass. A full-bird colonel, a dead one.

JEN SAT IN LESTER'S homey living room, listening to him putter around the kitchen. She'd been talking pretty much nonstop—about Cockeye and the Sentry thermophiles, then about Rainey and Jesse—since she'd woken Lester up, hours ago. He'd agreed to write up her version of the story, then give her twelve hours to confirm certain facts and confront Jesse. Now he was making coffee; he had a story to write. And she was thinking, again, about Rainey.

Lester had explained that Rainey was so careful because he wasn't afraid of the usual things. The things that held most people back—a friend's disapproval, conflict, likely failure, even pain—didn't slow him down. Rainey was the one-and-only thing that stood between other people and his uncommon, at times frightening, intensity.

Jen understood, then, how Rachel must have hurt such a man. He would have given himself wholly—fearlessly—to her. How hard to bear her rejection must have been. And now he could barely remember their time together.

GUMMER HATED FLYING IN helicopters, so he kept his eyes closed while Will, the firespotter, flew his helicopter around the smoke. Will took it up over Stoney Ridge then swung back around and down to the Sentry. He landed just after one of the huge army choppers took off. When Gummer opened his eyes, he thought he was dreaming. It was like being in a war movie.

As he got out of the helicopter, Gummer worried that his new partnership might already be over. He'd called around. No one had heard word one from Rachel. She might be locked in Bodine's damn bear shrine, or worse. He approached a wiry little major standing beside the lab tent.

"EXCUSE ME, SIR, I'M Gummer Mosk, an enforcement ranger responsible for this district."

"Nice work," Ramsey said.

"I beg your pardon."

"If I were responsible for this district, I'd shoot myself."

"But you're not," Gummer replied. "Un-unh."

"There's that," Ramsey admitted, and who was this guy, anyway? There was something about the ranger—the cut of his jib—that piqued the Ram's interest.

"I'm responsible and, to tell you the truth, I'm feeling better all the time," Gummer said. "Now what the hell is going on?"

"Classified."

Gummer stepped forward, his hand on his gun. "I'm sick and tired of this classified mumbo jumbo. I want to know everything that's happened. I especially want to know about Danny Briley and a woman named Rachel Stanley."

The secret to Ramsey's success was twofold: he kept his mouth shut; and he got results, usually with little or no respect for private property, propriety, or the conventional wisdom. Should he kill this ranger? To what end? The guy wasn't going to hurt him. And on this weird deal, a local could be useful. "Ranger, we'll talk."

"Danny Briley, Rachel Stanley."

"Quid pro quo."

"You mean—say—one hand washes the other?"

Ramsey just looked at him. "Someone's killing my men. Who?"

"I can take you to his hidey-hole."

Hidey-hole? This guy never let you down.

When Ramsey took a call, Gummer walked behind the tent where Danny was being bagged. When the ranger saw the bullet hole, Ramsey was sure the guy said, "Holy cow." Ramsey took him aside. "For the record, Danny Briley was never up here."

Gummer nodded. "We can work with that."

————

BODINE CLIMBED NORTH TOWARD Stoney Ridge. Since setting the fires he was back in a groove. Resisting temptation. Pumping up for the one trophy money couldn't buy. He came over a hill and saw the black outlines of the ridgetop in the moonlight. He recognized this place from his vision. It loomed on the far side of a meadow.

A small forest spread down from the hilltop, thinning at the valley floor, then breaking up into little patches of trees that made spots in the meadow. It was quiet, only the wind in the trees, the distant bubbling of the creek below, and the night sounds, the ones he heard that other people never noticed. Since Satan's sow marked him, he could hear the forest whispering at night. The words were hard to understand, but he'd learned how. You had to be alone, and you had to have a certain feel for it. Once he had the power, it came easy. Tonight, it sounded like: "Red eyes. Evil dies." Over and over.

He'd have to cross this meadow to reach the ridge. It didn't seem far. Something about it, though. Something unnatural. It was like evil things were jabbing at his mind, trying to work their way inside. But he was ready this time. Locked down. Nothing was going to get in, or out. He knew there would be devil tricks in this nice looking meadow. But he didn't see any smoke holes.

He took a reading on his receiver. The signal was hot, clear. It was coming from the top of the ridge. Top of the world. His mind started to spin out. But he caught it, nailed it back down. He came out of the trees where a streambed wound down from a snowfield. Bodine stopped to check the receiver again. The hoodoo bear wasn't going anywhere. The trees gave way to grass here, and the meadow stretched across the valley, climbing the slope until it became rock and scree. At night the meadow could tempt him. He flexed his chest, making it bleed, then he moved on, chanting his words. He held his hands over his ears and closed his eyes, fighting the meadow spell. He could feel it trying to suck out his mind.

At the far edge of the meadow he opened his eyes. It was dark, hard to see. But it was safe here. His mind was in a groove.

He could see the steep scree slope now, the one he had to climb to reach the ridgetop. This would be a hard climb, and he'd need his strength when he got to the top. He went over his plan. When he got to the top of the world, he'd set the bloody bait on a pole. That would bring the bear. Then he'd use the twelve gauge and the fire.

First he had to get there. In the moonlight he could see a stringer of fir, snaking up into an old avalanche chute. The chute disappeared in a patch of snow. The snow glittered in the moonlight. He wanted to shoot the snow patch with his twelve gauge. But he fought back the temptation. No, he'd rest in a little clump of whitebark pine, here in the safe place. Wait for the dawn. Daylight would help. Give him an edge. Light was his helper. He'd rest until the sun rose, and then he'd face the archenemy. He had a vision...blood dripping off the sun. Blinding blood-red sunlight. Then darkness.

————

THE HIDING PLACE WAS in the cliffs above the junction of Elk Creek and Little Elk Creek. Rachel directed them. She held one eye open, just a slit. Still, it was enough to get Rainey to the trail. Rainey led Rachel down the hard-to-find bighorn sheep trail to a fair-sized cave, a natural den. From below it seemed little more than a depression in the cliff face. Inside, it was six feet high, almost ten feet across, and eleven or twelve feet deep. She'd discovered it years ago when it had been used by mountain lions. The cave was inaccessible from below. It was set near the top of the cliff wall, just before it angled back toward the crest of the ridge. As the crow flies, it was less than a mile from where she'd seen Woolly Bugger's den, days that seemed light years ago.

Inside the cave, Rachel folded into his arms. She was sweating, feverish. Rainey held her. They'd stopped to rig a splint for her finger. A shard of bone stuck through the skin, so rigging the splint had been difficult and painful. He'd also washed out her eyes. She'd taken so much mace, though, she was still practically blind.

In the cave, he bandaged her finger properly. Her breathing was still labored. She had to work desperately hard, wheezing and gasping to draw in air. He told her about Bodine, about the soldiers. He said that finding Bodine, before the soldiers found him, was essential. But first, he insisted, she had to rest, turn off her mind. Maybe half an hour. And he wanted time to get his bearings. When her finger was re-bandaged, he took a cloth and a water bottle from his pack. Rainey wiped her brow, then he carefully rinsed her eyes again. Gently, he massaged her neck then her temples. He only stopped when her breathing was slower.

When she turned her swollen face, he kissed her brow.

They both slept. It was the last thing they had intended. Rachel woke up first, startled. She untangled herself from Rainey and moved to the mouth of the cave. The cool air felt good against her battered face. It was dawn. The fire was still burning ravenously, though it was less frightening in the early morning light. She could see again, but she had to work to keep her good eye even half open. She took binoculars out of his pack and found the Sentry. Her movements were slow, careful. The fire was burning south and west of the hot spring. She supposed the smoke jumpers were trying to contain it at Elk Creek. The wind had died down. If the wind shifted, though, the Sentry could be in the path of the fire again. An army chopper was just a speck, flying up from the Gallatin River. She watched it circle the fire then set down at the hot spring. She could just make out the soldiers as they climbed down.

Her face ached. Her throat still burned. Breathing was painful, and her nose would never look right. Still, she felt better, stronger. Rachel raised the binoculars. She focused on the northern edge of the fire—it looked like there might be new, smaller fires to the west—then she saw a blaze-orange dot moving northeast, coming above the Cut-Across Trail toward the Sentry. The man was hard to miss in those damn blaze-orange overalls. Blaze orange? Oh no. He was following hounds. They weren't allowed in the park under anything but the most unusual circumstances. Right. They seemed to be turning north toward the rim. But why? Had they missed Rainey's scent altogether?

It took her a minute to put it together. They weren't on their scent at all. No, they were tracking Bodine. Of course. Bodine had gone back to the culvert trap for Jesse. That's why they were coming from the west. And when Jesse wasn't there, he must have turned north toward Woolly Bugger. She cried out. Bodine had a receiver, and he had the bear's frequency. Somehow—mistakenly—Rachel had thought she'd have more time. Thought that Bodine would have other, easier, atrocities on his agenda before taking on a grizzly bear.

Later, she would say she never really stopped to think. She shook Rainey awake. "We have to hurry. He means to kill my bear."

THE SUN GLISTENED OFF the snow patch. Bodine thought it was a sign. He'd slept, and now he was rechecking his weapons. Sleeping was good. His strength was back. He didn't even need the uppers. He'd have help today. He could feel it. He thought of David, going to waste Goliath. Then the Terminator, sent back in time to kill for the future. Maybe he was from the future. He'd find out soon. He stared at the red-hot sun. He did not look away until his eyes burned.

When he turned on the receiver, the signal was strong. The hoodoo bear was lurking somewhere on the ridgetop. Hiding from the sunlight. On edge. Still, he'd be cocky up there.

He tested his skinning knife, cutting a line in his arm, feeling the power. It was time. He checked the bait and set the shotgun on top of his pack, so he could get to it, fast. He'd leave the receiver here. He wouldn't need it anymore.

Bodine studied the steep scree slope. The avalanche chute was the best way up. He'd keep to the stringer of fir, where there would be footing in the downhill grassy side. He chanted his words while he adjusted his pack, then Bodine started up toward the ridge. He kept chanting, fighting the temptation all around him. The climb was not too bad. He had to stop twice: once to adjust the cross which hung out of his pack at an odd angle; again, to take a pain pill, because he didn't want to feel the blood hole when he reached the top of the world. Both times he locked his mind in a steel box. Nailed it shut.

In the overgrown chute it was easy to find footing. He came out of the trees. The patch of snow was still several hundred yards above him. This was the hard part. In the clump of whitebark pine, beside the snow, it would not be so steep. Bodine worked himself up the scree toward the pine tree, chanting as he climbed.

He carefully made his way toward a pine root that snaked down the scree slope. It took almost five minutes to reach it. Hand over hand, he used the root to scramble up. As he got higher the entire root structure of the near pine was exposed. It offered good handholds, and he pulled himself up toward a clump of cover. He reached the edge of the pines and stopped to rest. He felt the blood. Really felt it. He found another handhold and pulled himself up onto a mound of dirt. He had another kind of feeling then, and he wanted to be ready. Bodine's dirty lips turned up as he reached back into his pack for the twelve gauge. He held it in front of him, a carved slug in each barrel, safety off. When he raised his head over the dirt, Bodine looked for red embers. Devil eyes. He mounted his twelve gauge. Then he heard a deep grunting noise, and the ground seemed to move. He thought it was a trick until he smelled the devil's fetid breath.

———

RACHEL WAS MOVING FAST, pulling on some reserve of adrenalin. Rainey was right behind her. He could hear her drawing difficult, raspy breaths. Her throat, eyes and nasal passages had to itch and burn horribly, and he was sure the inside of her head was buzzing like a hornet's nest. Still, they ran west along Stoney Ridge, retracing the route Rachel had taken the night she'd gone to find Woolly Bugger. He pulled ahead, asked her if she wanted to rest. She shook her head.

They ran on in silence. Rainey could see down into the Tom Miner Basin. The Paradise Valley was changing colors—grays and browns turning lighter, showing more yellow, even gold—and the greens were coming on, sharp and clean. The Yellowstone River was little more than a pencil-thin line, twisting along the valley floor. He wondered if Jesse had found his pickup. Where was Jesse, anyway? He'd almost forgotten about him.

Rachel was watching the Gallatin side for any sign of Bodine. So far she'd seen nothing. She slowed when they were just above the clump of whitebark pine. The den was below them now, south and west. Using Rainey's binoculars, she could see the detail of the pine trees and fresh tracks—footprints—in the patch of snow. Lower still, in the meadow below the scree, she saw sunlight glistening off metal. A receiver.

"Bodine's nearby," she said.

Rainey followed the tracks up the chute. He shifted the .30-06 from his pack to his right hand. "How much time do we have before the dogs get here?"

"An hour, tops. Even if they were thrown off, they'll pick up his scent again above Elk Creek."

"And if the dogs pick up our scent?"

"We'll have to figure something, I guess."

Rainey didn't respond.

She looked down toward the clump of pine, wondering if she should tell him just how close they were to the den. Or what it would be like if they got caught between the bear and the dogs.

She focused on a pile of dirt in the avalanche chute, just below the clump of trees. It looked like a new mound. It sat at the base of a tree, covered with downfall. At the far side of the mound she saw something catch the sunlight. A marker. Jesus. Bodine's silver cross.

She backtracked to where the slope was gentler and she could get down to the meadow. Rainey followed. He didn't know what else to do.

She ran to the receiver, crossing the meadow without stopping, ignoring the burning in her throat, her lungs. Before Rainey had caught his breath, she had the receiver working. Her face was pale, anxious.

"The bear's close, but his collar's in mortality mode," she said. "He's not moving. There's no activity pattern."

"Dead?"

"I'm scared, Rainey." She trained the glasses on the new mound. "Stay here," she said. And she was off.

Rainey ignored her request and followed her up the steep slope. She turned and looked at him, a question.

Rainey kept climbing.

"Keep very quiet," she whispered, "and cover me."

It was hard to find reliable footing in the scree, so the climb was slow and difficult. The mound was near the top of the avalanche chute. As they got closer she could see that the mound was recently covered with branches, downfall, and duff from the chute. She stopped and checked the receiver again. The pulse was still in mortality mode, low and short. The bear wasn't moving at all. "Stay low. Bodine may be on the ridge."

Rachel waited anxiously, at least five endless minutes. Several times she glassed the clump of whitebark pine, checking every possible hiding place. Rainey kept the rifle mounted. She inspected the mound yet again. Inch by inch.

In a crouch, she walked toward the mound. Rainey followed, a bullet in the chamber. At the mound she pulled off an old branch then brushed back some dirt. A rock tumbled down from the ridge. Rainey and Rachel dropped behind the mound. After several minutes Rachel went back to her digging. Rainey was scanning the ridge when she took his hand in both of hers. He followed her eyes to the mound, to a ravaged limb, an arm.

Rainey took the arm and pulled Bodine out of the cache. There were puncture holes in his skull, his face, and in the shoulder area. His neck was broken. Long raking marks covered his torso and thigh. Rachel pictured Woolly Bugger taking Bodine's head in his powerful jaws then lifting him high in the air, like an elk calf, shaking until his neck was broken. One good jerk of his massive head would do it. She cried, relieved. Rainey held her as she dried her eyes, then he picked up the silver cross. It lay against the mound, apparently of no interest whatsoever to Woolly Bugger.

On the far side of the mound Rachel found Bodine's shotgun, then she pulled at the strap of Bodine's pack. It was a large pack, heavy. She pulled again. A bloody head rolled out, severed at the neck. "Agh!" she gasped.

Rainey studied the head. "One of the soldiers," he explained. He put it back in the pack, unloaded the shotgun, then tied it to the pack. "And the bear?"

"Sleeping." She sounded queasy. "In his den."

"Where's that?"

Rachel pointed up the slope at the clump of whitebark pine.

"A hundred yards? Jesus, Rachel."

"That kind of day."

Rainey slung Bodine's shattered body over his shoulder and made his way east, away from the den. Rachel followed, carrying the pack at arm's length. He stopped just above the fir tree that Woolly Bugger had snapped in two. The remains of the trunk sat above the cliff that dropped down to the meadow. He looked at her, a question. She nodded her agreement. Without a wasted motion, Rainey rolled Bodine's body down the slope. It went over the cliff, bouncing down into the meadow far below. The body rolled until it hit a pine tree, one of a cluster well out in the meadow. Rainey took the .30-06 off his shoulder, wiped it clean of prints and flung it after the body. It landed about thirty yards from Bodine's corpse. The pack was next. Then the cross.

They heard dogs. They were in the forest below, coming toward the meadow.

"We gotta go," Rachel said. "Far and fast."

He took out the handheld. "Call your firespotter friend. Tell him to meet us on the Tom Miner side."

She nodded, not surprised that he'd worked it out. She pointed toward the ridgetop, then she was gone.

The dogs were coming down the hillside toward the meadow. Rainey and Rachel ran up the slope, fighting exhaustion until they reached the ridge. From the ridgetop they watched the dogs change their course: They came out of the forest below the den, but then they turned, crossing the meadow straight for Darrell Bodine.

———

GUMMER GRABBED THE RADIO from Will, who was flying the helicopter toward Blue Grouse Creek. "Rachel, this is your partner Gummer here. You alright?"

"I been better."

"We have every firefighter in the drainage looking for you."

Rainey stepped closer to hear what Gummer was saying. "Who's listening in on this band?" Rachel asked.

"The fire team. The fire boss. Mitchell, who's gone nuts since Danny bought the farm. Did you know Bodine nailed the sonofagun? Took out the big boss. I'm not kidding. Shot him."

"I was there."

"No! You saw it?"

"I did."

Rainey touched the brim of an imaginary hat, a "well-done" gesture.

"Right in the dang heart," the ranger added.

"Calm down, Gummer."

"Right. Anyway, the army's probably listening in, too."

"Well, if they're not listening, you can tell 'em Darrell Bodine went after my bear, thought he was the devil, or something. The bear killed him. The dogs are on Bodine now. The bear's close. Call the damn dogs off." She paused, took a difficult breath. "And I need a ride out of here. Will, you know the spot where we saw that pair of bighorn sheep last spring?"

"Roger."

"Fifteen minutes." Rachel clicked off the radio when she heard Gummer ask for Major Ramsey, whoever that was.

She took Rainey's arm, leaned against his shoulder. They saw a hawk swoop down, its talons extended toward the meadow below them. It rose, carrying a vole. Eventually her breathing was more regular, and she raised her head. "Is it over?" she asked.

"No. Not yet."

"Meaning?"

"We have to deal with the Sentry."

"Rainey—" Her bruised face lost its color. "No. You didn't—you didn't put in the new strain?"

"No time." He frowned. "I have an idea, though."

"An idea?"

"Yeah."

"What?"

"Rache, it's primitive."

"Oh fuck," she said, quietly. "It's primitive."

She cried while he explained his idea. When he was finished, she dried her eyes. "Oh fuck," she said again.

Rough Justice

THERE IS AN ODD, albeit imperfect, balance to life, Mitchell thought, when he learned that Darrell Bodine had killed Danny. "Rough justice," if you will. The unfortunate part was that he'd been Danny's man. And it had left him dangling, perfectly positioned to be drawn and quartered. Still, he knew there was an opportunity here—this was where the true political artist turned his liability into an asset.

The question, of course, was who would be in charge, and Mitchell thought he saw an answer that worked for everyone. So he'd gone straight to his temporary office in North, organized his ideas on note cards, then called the assistant undersecretary at the Department of the Interior to cut a deal. The assistant undersecretary, after consulting with his contact at the Defense Department, suggested that Mitchell could be promoted, even brought back to D.C., if—and only if—Mitchell could keep the research at the Sentry going until they achieved the desired results. When Mitchell asked what resources were available to him, the guy said, "What do you need?"

With that—he thought of it as his mandate—Mitchell called Major Ramsey, the Ram, in from the field for a strategy session. The Major was to be the field officer in charge until the higher-ups sent someone to replace Danny. Mitchell hoped he could work with a guy who was nicknamed after a sheep, or a goat.

He reached the Ram in the meadow below Stoney Ridge, where the Major's men were loading Bodine's body into a helicopter. Even the Ram had to admit it was grim.

The houndsman had been at a fever pitch when they found the body. He wanted permission to hunt and kill the bear. The dogs were so pumped up they had to be tied to a tree. The bear that did this was in the area, the houndsman was explaining, when Ramsey interrupted him. "Did what?" he asked.

"Eat this psycho guy's head is what."

"What guy?"

"Are you crazy?"

"Are you crazy?" Ramsey asked back, as the body was loaded into the helicopter. "I don't see any guy."

The houndsman looked at him, getting it. "It never happened, huh?"

"What never happened?"

After the body was loaded, Ramsey flew directly to Mitchell's office in North.

Mitchell made Ramsey wait in the hall for seven minutes. "How is it looking at the scene?" he asked, after he showed him in.

"A-okay," Ramsey said.

"Given the circumstances, what exactly does that mean, Major?"

"Means the fire's under control, and we got the killer." He was supposed to humor this guy. It was gonna be hard.

"And the press?"

"They get zip, sir."

"Zip? Yes, yes, of course. Can we proceed without Mr. Briley?"

"Yes, sir. Scientists can be back up in a day."

"I presume any information about Mr. Briley's unfortunate death is classified."

"Eyes only. He was never up there, so far as I know."

"So all's well that ends well, eh?"

"Yes, sir." Ramsey couldn't muster a smile. He blamed guys like Mitchell for losing the Vietnam War.

"Where are the firefighters now?"

"Elk Creek."

"And the soldiers?"

"I left six at the spring. Sent the others for some shut-eye."

"Very good. Major, was anyone else at the Sentry?"

"One of your rangers. Tall—"

"Gummer?"

"Yes, sir." Ramsey had decided to play it straight. He wanted the ranger in it, now. "Came up in that firefighter chopper. Wanted to know all about Danny and that woman, Rachel."

"What about Rachel?"

"I never saw her, but your man Gummer seemed to think she was in the area."

"Gummer and Rachel. Then something's going on up there."

"Do you think so, sir?" Ramsey asked, straight-faced.

———

JEN AND JIMMY WERE eating ice cream cones on the porch swing at the *Chronicle*. Both of them were lost in their own thoughts.

Jen was thinking how weird it was to know something and not to know it at the same time. Rainey was sure he knew how he felt about Rachel. But he didn't know how he felt at all. She suspected how he felt, but she wouldn't let herself know it. The only one who knew how she felt was Rachel, and she woke up one morning just knowing it, nineteen months after the fact.

That's when Jimmy leaned against her and asked her to tell him, again, just what she thought had happened to his dad, how he died. He was especially interested in the experiments at the Sentry. Jen kept it simple, though she held nothing back.

"So no one killed him?" Jimmy asked, tentative, when she'd finished.

"No."

"Then why did he die?"

Jen understood that it wasn't a technical question. She thought it over. "I think he was out of luck. I think he died of bad luck."

"Do I have that?"

"No. Not anymore. You have the opposite of that."

"Can we go home now?"

"We'll be home soon." And yes, finally, she knew what she knew.

———

WHILE THEY WAITED ON the Tom Miner side for the chopper, Rainey and Rachel worked out the details of his plan. When they were finished, she looked him in the eye. "I think it's pretty crazy."

"You got a better idea?"

"Un-unh." They watched Will ease the chopper over the ridge, then set it down gently in the meadow.

In the chopper Gummer looked at Rachel, horrified. "Who did this to you?"

"Danny."

"Fucking animal," Gummer muttered. "Bodine picked him off like a turkey, I'd bet."

"Yeah, he shot him from behind the cabin. Bodine was pretty far gone. He walked out of the trees yelling something about the devil."

"Darrell Bodine was the devil." Gummer took a deep, satisfied breath. "Well, your bear took care a Bodine, didn't he? Tell me this. Was it slow?"

"Slow?" She frowned. "Gummer, the bear had Bodine's head in its mouth. There were puncture holes in his skull, his face. From Bodine's point of view, it was pretty damn slow."

"Great."

"We've got to stop at the hot spring," Rainey said as they lifted off.

"What's up?" Gummer asked.

"Nothing much, just a look-see," Rachel said. "Will, are the smoke jumpers out of there?"

"Yeah, they're southwest of the Sentry, trying to contain the fire at Elk Creek."

Rachel asked Will to swing down toward Woolly Bugger's den. She wondered where this hugely resourceful animal had gone to wait out the ruckus. She thought about the dogs, the soldiers, the drone of the choppers.

They hovered over the meadow while Rachel pointed at the clump of whitebark pine that hid the grizzly's den. It was Rainey who first saw the bear. He found him with his binoculars, just above the patch of snow. The grizzly was looking out over the meadow, not far from where Rachel had first spotted him days that seemed ages ago. Woolly Bugger stood on his hind legs, then he turned, lumbered off toward the pines, and disappeared.

The helicopter climbed above the hill where Darrell Bodine had heard the forest whispering, then turned toward the Sentry. Below them Elk Creek wound all the way down to the Gallatin.

They could see where the fire had burned from the patrol cabin north toward the Sentry and west to Elk Creek. The fire had altered the landscape of the entire drainage. The flames had cut stark, blackened swaths through verdant green forests and meadows. From the air, you could see just how the smoke jumpers had manipulated the path of the blaze, and now, it looked like the fire was very nearly contained.

Will set his chopper down in the Sentry meadow between the lab tent and the pool. The meadow was covered with ash that had turned light gray where the hot water from the geyser had washed over it. Six soldiers guarded the spring, forming a large, loose circle with the Sentry pool as its midpoint. To the north and east, three soldiers faced the forest. To the south and west, two soldiers protected the pool from the dangers lurking in the firebreaks. A sixth soldier stood beside the pool.

As soon as the chopper set down, Rachel flashed her ID and called out to a sentry on the perimeter. "Park business. Who do I talk to?"

He pointed out the young man standing near the steaming pool.

Perfect. While Rainey slipped into the lab tent, Rachel marched toward the young soldier. "You in charge?"

The young soldier stepped forward. "Yes, ma'am."

She offered her good hand.

The soldier ignored it, looking at her swollen, bruised face, her broken nose.

She touched her cheek with her broken finger. "I took a bad fall tracking a bear."

"What's your business?"

"Rachel Stanley, wildlife biologist." She showed him her ID. "I'm trying to locate a grizzly bear. He could be dangerous." Rainey appeared beside her to help Rachel take a receiver out of her pack. He set his own pack on the ground near the pool. "I'm getting a signal that he's in this area. Can I take a couple of readings?"

It was as simple as that. Anticlimactic, in fact. While five soldiers faced the trees, guarding the pool against God-only-knows-what, and the young man in charge explained to Rachel that she'd have to speak with Major Ramsey, Rainey backhanded ten large vials of the most highly concentrated exothermic nitrogenous compound, ENT, from his pack into the Sentry pool. Minutes later the color of the pool changed from deep blue to metallic slate.

Rachel asked the soldier to keep an eye out for bears, then she and Rainey packed up their gear and turned toward the helicopter. When they were airborne, Gummer got on the radio and called Mitchell. He caught up with him in Ramsey's chopper, on his way up to the Sentry. "Mitchell, I've been at the pool. It looks weird. You better warn these soldiers and get right up here."

Mitchell almost lost his composure. "What do you mean it looks weird?"

"I dunno. We were up there, checking things out, and golly, it was making these crazy sounds, huffing and steaming and roiling to beat the band. Weird steely color too. Looked like it was gonna blow, or something." Rachel gave Gummer a thumbs-up.

———

THE HELICOPTER SET DOWN in a meadow behind the *Chronicle* offices in North. Jen came out the back door. Rainey stepped down. Rachel and Gummer were going on to Mammoth to see the superintendent. The chopper blades began churning. Rainey turned back. "Rachel, can I talk with you for a minute?"

He watched her say a few words to Gummer, then she came down.

"I want to tell you something. It won't take long."

"Okay."

"At the Sentry, when Danny was hurting you...when Danny fell—I'm sorry—I don't know how to put this—"

She pressed a finger to her lips, shushing him. "When Danny fell, I was sure it was you. I kept hoping that you were out there. When he was hurting me, it was the one thing I could keep in my mind."

"Rache?"

She wrapped her arms around his neck.

He held her close. "Jesus, I'm glad I killed him."

"I love you, Rainey, I do," she whispered. "I always will." Then softer still, "Think about it. Take your time, you've got the right."

"It won't be long," he said, and then she was back in the helicopter. Rainey watched the chopper rise up, then he turned to Jen.

"She woke you up, huh?" Jen's tone was jovial, but her eyes gave her away.

"No, you did that." He took her hands. "You knew, didn't you?"

"Sort of. I didn't finally put it together until late last night."

"I didn't get it. I had no idea. That's not an excuse." Rainey looked into her pale green eyes. They were misty and, for the first time, tentative, even skittish. "I'm sorry."

Jen stepped back, started to cry. "I thought about hitting you."

"Would it help?"

"No."

The Fire-Breathing Dragon

J ESSE WAS AT THE bar of the Gold Nugget, sipping a Bombay gin martini, extra dry. He'd had a few pills at the hospital, then at dawn he'd ordered the ambulance driver to take him to his saloon, where he fell asleep behind the bar. At 10:30 A.M. the sheriff woke up and picked up the phone, summoning the bartender. There was an eight-foot-five-inch grizzly bear, Jesse told him, standing on its hind legs against the sidewall.

When the bartender arrived, Jesse was sitting at the bar looking at the mounted grizzly bear. A pitcher of martinis sat on the bar, half empty. There was a manila file folder on the bar, unopened. Jesse's left eye was twitching, regular spasms that sent a ripple through his cheek muscles. Every so often Jesse would nod at the bear. The bartender had never seen the sheriff like this, so he'd slipped off to call Stacy. She'd been watching Jesse now for about an hour. When she tried to talk with him about antlers, he asked her the price on grizzly cubs. When she said she didn't know, he turned back to the mounted grizzly.

A half hour later the bar phone rang. Stacy turned to Jesse. "Rainey and that Chicago policewoman are at the office."

"Tell 'em I've been waiting," Jesse snarled. "You bet."

———

"IT LOOKS LIKE A fucking fire-breathing dragon is what it looks like, Rachel." Mitchell was standing in the Sentry meadow, yelling into the chopper phone. "It's shooting out steam and spray hundreds of feet in the air. It's making these loud whooshing sounds, like giant waves. And there are regular explosions. They seem to be getting bigger, more frequent."

At the superintendent's office, the superintendent, Rachel, and Gummer were gathered around the speakerphone. "Mitchell, those are thermophile explosions you're seeing," Rachel explained. "It sounds like the pool's overheated. Listen carefully. There can be ten billion bacteria in one quart of water. Just imagine the billions upon billions of organisms in the Sentry pool." She paused. "You with me?"

"What's your point?" Mitchell snapped.

"Do the math. As many as five percent of these thermophiles are potentially explosive." She let that hang. "I think if it gets hot enough fast enough, then stays hot long enough, the thermophile explosions could feed on each other until there's a chain reaction. That kind of heat will turn the Sentry into one big pressure cooker. You better get everyone out of there. Right now. Be careful, it could go anytime."

"Dammit, we have to do something. Isn't there something that will stop it?"

"Political pressure?" Rachel couldn't help asking.

"I'll remember that." Mitchell hesitated. She imagined his patronizing look. "I'm calling the undersecretary's office. I know you're responsible for this."

"For what?" she asked.

"I'll figure it out."

"We just got off the phone with the undersecretary. He said that you're responsible now," Rachel offered.

Mitchell broke the connection. "What can we do?" he asked Ramsey. The major was standing beside the helicopter, which had set down at the northwest corner of the meadow. The soldiers were already loaded in the chopper.

"I'm done here," Ramsey said. "You could try the circus, sir," he offered.

———

WHEN RAINEY AND JEN walked in, Stacy thought Jesse got back some of his old self. Some of the meanness, anyway. Rainey sat beside him. "My house...I'm here to settle that."

Jesse chuckled.

Jen set Lester's story about Cockeye in front of the sheriff. "Read this before you crack another smile, smartass."

The sheriff read it then threw it on the bar. "So?" he said. "So? So?" The third "So?" was pretty loud.

"Cockeye is dead because of you. But sheriff, he wasn't murdered. He died in a thermophile explosion." Jen was right in his face. "I'm your worst nightmare. I know all about corrupt cops. And I know how to bring them down. We can prove you framed Rainey, and we have a witness that saw you leaving his house the night of the fire."

"It gets worse for you, Jesse," Rainey said softly. "This morning Gummer Mosk told us about the trophy hunts, the poaching, *how* you framed me, about Bodine working for you, and more. The DA is interested in that story."

Jen added, "I brought in an IRS agent who's standing by to audit—the bars, the saloon, the real estate, everything."

"You just resigned, sheriff," Rainey said. "The only question is how bad is it going to be for you."

The left side of Jesse's face twitched. His scar was flame red, twisting up like a snake. "I got something to show you." He opened the file folder on the bar, took out Mary's deposition. "You lied."

"You know better. But we're past that." Rainey closed the file. "It's me or you now, Jesse—all or nothing." Rainey locked on to Jesse's furtive raisin eyes, something fierce in his own glare. "We're at war. No deals. Do your worst, Jesse. But I promise you this—I won't live in a county where you're sheriff. And I'm going to rebuild my house where it stands."

Jesse lay a hand on Mary's deposition, his face twitching violently now. "You lied, you're nothing. You're gone—*sport*—one way or another."

"Jesse, I know what Bodine did to you up there, and I'm sorry for that. But it doesn't change anything. I'll explain this one last time." Rainey got close enough to smell Jesse's martini breath. "Your life, as you know it, is over. Either you resign, now, or I'm coming after you. Cockeye's just the lead-in. Lester will print my entire story. The DA will subpoena Gummer, and under oath, he'll corroborate. An IRS audit will pound the nails in your coffin, and you'll go to prison. You're not going to be sheriff, you're not going to push people around, and you're never—ever—going to threaten me again." Rainey stood, finished.

With unexpected quickness, Jesse drew back his palm and brought it hard toward Rainey's face. He was too late. Rainey had his throat, pinching tightly with two fingers. The slap melted. Jesse gagged. The sheriff's face was red. Both cheeks were twitching and spittle ran down his lips. "Did you think you could just burn down my home?" Rainey asked, then he let Jesse collapse on the floor. He watched the sheriff curl up into a fetal ball, whimpering softly now.

Stacy found a blanket behind the bar. Rainey lay it over the broken sheriff, then turned to Stacy. "He should resign today. Please handle that. And if you care for him, get him some good psychiatric help."

Stacy looked at the sheriff, who's whimpers had become low wails, then back at Rainey. "I'll get the paperwork to Lester."

Rainey and Jen left.

Sometime later Jesse stood and tentatively stepped around the bar. Carefully, he raised the bartender's twelve gauge, aimed, then fired at the stuffed grizzly bear standing beside the bar. The pellets tore open the bear's chest. Afterwards he turned to his bartender. "Are you dead from the neck up? You got a dying bear to take care of." Jesse sat beside the fallen bear, took off his bandage and stared at the bloody hole in his hand.

———

Soon after the helicopter took off, Phillipe came scurrying out of the cabin where he'd been hiding. He still had to get his samples, but now the spring was too hot to get close to. The metal-colored water was spewing continuously from a series of small explosions. He guessed the geyser was shooting boiling water over two hundred feet into the air.

With each explosion there was a whooshing thud followed by a distant echo, then a shower of boiling water. Phillipe knew what was happening. The pool was boiling, as hot as it could be, so hot that countless thermophilic organisms were exploding. If the high temperatures were sustained, these explosions would build to a chain reaction.

Heat creates pressure. Never in the history of the geyser had so much pressure been applied in so short a time. And the explosions were further exacerbating the pressure on the vents. Every few minutes a larger explosion would send bits of geyserite spinning off into the meadow. He guessed that somehow Rachel had dropped large quantities of their super-concentrated nitrogenous compound, ENT, into the pool. An explosion tore another chunk of geyserite off the lip and flung it into the air.

It solved his problem. Phillipe ran to the spot where the geyserite had landed and began chipping away with his chisel. The thermophile mats he needed would be in the geyserite. He ignored the escalating blasts that rocked the pool. He didn't even see the thunderous explosion that broke both of his eardrums and knocked him unconscious.

The explosion that slowed down Phillipe's quest for fame also caved-in the vent of the geyser. The ground around the pool gave way when the brittle rock underneath was thrown heavenward by the enormous volume of water the dying geyser spit into the sky. The pool hissed and sizzled, blowing steam, rock, and boiling water all over the heavens. Huge chunks of geyserite rained down on the meadow. Then it crumbled in on itself, sucking in air, taking a last desperate breath. It was as if the Sentry blew itself up then swallowed what was left. The geyser had caved-in and domed over. It was extinct.

Cowboy Country

J IMMY WAS UP TO his waist in the Gallatin, not ten yards from the back eddy where Rainey had landed the suitcase. It was a crisp, clear day. The sky was wonderfully blue, salted with little wispy clouds, white as baby powder. The wildflowers waited for a day like this to flaunt their best colors, and those colors were somehow perfected, floating in and among the soft greens of the meadow. A warm breeze sent waves rippling through the meadow until they disappeared into the forested foothills of the Gallatin Mountains. A small group of bison grazed lazily at the tree line. It was the kind of day that discouraged brooding.

Jen lay on the grass. Rainey sat next to her, feet stretched out beside the blanket that held the remains of their picnic. The river broke over a long riffle not forty yards below his feet. "He's got another one," Rainey said, watching Jimmy land a ten-inch rainbow.

"Is he good?"

"Really good."

"Funny. He's not good at sports. You know—football, or baseball."

"I was good at football...I wish I'd been able to fish like Jimmy."

Jen watched the little clouds float over Stoney Ridge. They hovered at the ridgeline, slowly rising, like smoke coming off the mountains. She pulled her hair back out of her face. "We're leaving tomorrow," Jen said. "Jimmy wants to go home. I think it's time, too."

Rainey watched Jimmy miss a fish. This was sooner than he'd expected. As usual, she was ahead of him. He laid a hand on her back. "You helped me. More than you know."

She sat up and held him, burying her face against his neck. "That goes two ways. Jimmy's even a little proud of his mom." Jen sat back, watching him closely. "I've never known a man like you. You seem to be going so painfully slowly when in fact you're on task, relying on some inner compass. And mister, you stayed the course."

"Whoa...I didn't even get what Rachel was saying."

"In the end, you did," she softly said.

They held each other in the stillness of the meadow, a time for what they knew to sink in, then settle. Rainey wanted to say more, but he couldn't find the words. "What are you going to do?" she eventually asked.

"Fill out insurance forms. Build a house. Work. Fish...I don't know."

"And Rachel?" she asked.

"I'd like a second chance with her."

Jen leaned over and picked a red Indian paintbrush out of the meadow, then she waved at Jimmy who was looking her way, checking in—which he'd been doing a lot of lately. "Have you told her how you feel?"

"I think she knows."

"Do me this favor. Tell her. Move in with her. Just do it. Right away." She lay back in the grass. "I'll learn to love you both," she muttered, mostly to herself. "Who would have thought?" And she took his hand.

"You have plans?" he asked.

"Not really. One step at a time I guess."

"It's been less than a week."

She pointed at the river. "The suitcase, right there."

Why was it that he couldn't find the words to thank her? He thought about it. Eventually, he settled for, "The lives you touch are made better. This past week, that goes for every single one. Especially mine." He could see the pleasure in her eyes. He hesitated a moment. "Please forgive me if I misled you."

Jen sat up to face him. "What you did—what we did—it was good for me and it was good for you. For what it's worth, you changed the way I think about men...let's leave it there."

Rainey ran gnarly fingers through his hair, aware that his luck had changed.

"Are you okay about Danny?" she eventually asked.

He set his elbow in the grass, propped his head on his hand. "Yeah. I think so."

"He would have killed her."

"Probably, yeah."

"And?"

"Some things you do right without thinking. It's good to know that about yourself."

———

"I THINK AN IRISH wake would be good," Jen said.

"What's an Irish wake?" Jimmy asked. They were waiting for their connection at the Salt Lake City airport. Jimmy was eating frozen yogurt. Earl "Cockeye" Donahue had been cremated, and Jen was carrying his ashes in an urn at the bottom of her tote bag.

"After the funeral people get together and have a sort of party. Talk about the person, eat, drink. Celebrate his life."

"Talk about the things he did?"

"Well, yeah."

"That could get gross."

"So?"

Jen knew that for many reasons—a visit from Major Ramsey, a restraining order, and the elliptical but emphatic arguments that she and Rachel had made to him after she learned just what Rainey had done at the Sentry—Lester never ran a single story about Cockeye, the Sentry, or the Sentry thermophiles. He did, however, call a friend at the *Chicago Tribune* to write Cockeye's obituary. The obituary had made the Chicago paper, and when Jen and Jimmy arrived at their Northside apartment, there were twelve messages from people who had known Earl Donahue. The story was more flattering than Jen had expected. Earl came off as an able forensic investigator, which, she had to admit, he probably was at one time. There were a lot of people who wanted to remember Earl as he'd been when he was a fine police officer. So Jen and Jimmy decided to have a private memorial service, then throw a wake for anyone who wanted to come.

Sixty people crowded into her two-bedroom apartment to eat, drink and celebrate Earl "Cockeye" Donahue's up-and-down life.

Many of them were police officers and their families. There was a judge or two. Mostly, they were the crowd Earl and Jen had hung out with when they were younger. The toasts were colorful.

The apartment had a large living room with a twelve-foot ceiling. The off-white walls were accented by carefully-crafted dark wood trim and an old mahogany mantle above the fireplace. Jimmy sat in the window seat, listening to his mom talk about his dad.

"It was my birthday. Twenty-six, I think. He takes me to this downtown hotel room. It was the Drake. In the room there's over a thousand roses. I swear to God. Roses everywhere. Turns out it's payback from Saulie, the funeral guy. I didn't even care."

"Saulie was a pistol," Sergeant "Red" Duncan confirmed. "Cockeye used to call him whenever we had a John Doe."

That's when Rainey and Rachel walked in. Rainey wore a gray herringbone jacket, blue shirt and dark gray slacks. Rachel, a simple black dress.

Jimmy saw them first. "Hey mom!"

Jen thought she might melt. Then she was hugging them, one at a time, trying to stay calm. "How did you even know?"

"Jimmy called Lloyd," Rainey said, "who would have come, only Ruth told him to stop bothering people."

Jen took Rachel's arm. "Thank you for coming," Jen said.

"We wanted to be here."

Jen looked at all the people in her living room. The people who made her son proud of his father. "This is only possible because of what you did."

"You're the one helped the living," Rachel said. "That's a fact."

"Let's drink to the living," Jen said and led them toward the bar.

Eventually they brought her to a quiet corner where Rainey explained how two Federal guys had come to investigate. Rachel broke in, "Gummer, well, he stepped right up. He hated Bodine. He told these guys how Jesse had conned Bodine into believing Danny was doing the devil's dirty work. Step by step."

"At first the Federal guys were skeptical," Rainey added. "But Gummer was at his best telling these guys just how crazy Bodine was. And how easy it was for Jesse to punch his ticket, get him worked up. What with Bodine's history, especially the murder, they had to admit that it fit. What they couldn't see was a sheriff working with a creature like Bodine. So Gummer went over some of Jesse's 'accomplishments' before he resigned. And then they visited Jesse at the place in California—"

"The psychiatric facility?"

"Yeah. Well that helped them see it."

"Did Gummer know?"

"You can't ever tell with him. He sure acted like Bodine had killed Danny."

"And the explosion. Are you in the clear?"

"The official version is that Dr. Moody did something to make the pool volatile. The park service discovered how dangerous it was and called in some experts. Before the east coast guys could sort it out, nature—how did they put it?"

"Self-corrected," Rachel volunteered.

"Self-corrected, yeah." Rainey grunted. "The northwest corner's open to the public again. The rest is classified."

"So no one's ever going to know just what went down in cowboy country?" Jen let it hang there.

Rachel took her arm. "Just us cowgirls, babe."

Jen held her close, then stepped back. "One last question." Jen tilted her head, looking at Rainey. "You see Jesse again?"

"Un-unh."

"You going to?"

"To what?"

"See Jesse."

"Unlikely." And that was that.

Epilogue

T HEY STOPPED AT LLOYD'S, where he was adding on to his kitchen. Why he wanted more room, no one knew. Rainey had heard him talking about this big machine that cleaned saltwater fish, like tuna. He was afraid to ask.

It was late June—a year since the Sentry had domed over—and Rainey and Rachel were going to fish the Gallatin. By now most of the animals in the Elk Creek drainage were back to their normal, seasonal patterns. Rachel had seen many tragic mutations among the young this past spring, and a significant number of out-of-sync animals didn't survive the winter. Her friend Jenny Ann, the elk biologist, had reported that several of the elk with oversized racks had died prematurely. No one was sure why. So they'd mix fishing outings with her field observation. Ruth enjoyed watching Molly, who was already twenty months old and certain that anything she could get her hands on belonged in her mouth. Often, Rainey, Rachel, and Molly would end up staying the night in the big cabin.

It was almost 5:00 P.M. when Rainey poked his head out back where Lloyd was sawing lengths of pine. He set a little fly box in front of Lloyd, who looked up, then took the fly box without acknowledging him.

"Try the salmon fly." Rainey shrugged. "A hunch."

"Looks like a moldy pastrami sandwich."

"Oh," Rainey had yet to receive a compliment from Lloyd on one of his ties, though Lloyd had been selling his own modified versions of them for almost a year. "Thanks for taking Molly."

Lloyd grunted.

Rainey went out to the pickup, where Rachel was waiting.

They passed through North, where Gummer was the new sheriff. He'd squeaked by Jesse's deputy, Tim Hansen, and people gave his child bride, Darcie, the credit. She'd given coffees, printed posters, and called in more markers than a nineteen-year-old ought to have. Rachel had campaigned for him, too. Surprisingly, sensible management of the Greater Yellowstone Ecosystem had become one of his goals. What Rainey especially liked was that Jesse's sign was gone.

As they drove south, Rachel slept. With her head resting against the window, she reminded him of Jen. That got him thinking about Jen, and about how his life had changed.

They decided to fish the gentler water above the Taylor's Fork. Rainey had a fish on by 6:05. To the southeast he could see Blackstone Butte, just beyond the park boundary. Rainey and Rachel fished together, moving slowly upstream, catching and releasing midsized trout.

They talked about Phillipe. Rachel had recently received another letter from him, asking her if his thermophiles were thriving in the new pool. Wanting to know when he could come back, finish up his research.

"Tell him Gummer's reopened the Moody investigation."

"I already did." She took his arm as they waded upstream.

By 9:00 Rachel was looking for elk. She'd left Rainey just below Blue Grouse Creek and was walking above the highway, climbing toward Blackstone Butte. On a hilltop, just below the butte, she saw a bull. He was in velvet.

Not three hundred yards from the highway there's a high, sage-covered shelf, and often, just before dark, she'd see elk coming out of the trees onto the flat area. This evening there was a group of six cows, a nursing group. She crept to within two hundred yards, watching the cows, then scanning the sagebrush, trying to find their calves. These calves would be newborns, less than a month old. She spotted them in a patch of sagebrush, off to the right of the cows.

The cow elk began lifting their heads. It was almost dark, and she lay down behind a clump of sage, focusing her binoculars. One of the cows started high-stepping towards the timber. The rest were milling around, barking, when a bear came out of the trees. He was a big grizzly, larger than any bear she'd seen this year. The cows' barking intensified, a high chirping bark. As a group they moved toward the bear. The bolder cows feinted in his direction. Getting pretty close. The bear didn't move. Rachel was sure that this grizzly was old enough to know that the cows were trying to draw his attention away from their young.

The grizzly put his nose to the ground and began ferreting around like a giant bird dog. The milling and barking grew more frantic. A calf bolted, looking for its mother.

Even now, when Rachel saw a grizzly run, it made the hackles rise on the back of her neck. This bear was up to full speed in no time at all. He was too fast for the little elk calf, and he had it in his mouth before it reached the cows. The grizzly shook the calf, breaking its neck, then turned toward the timber, holding the dead calf in its jaws. A lone mother elk followed at a distance. It seemed to Rachel that the bear was strutting.

The bear was favoring his right front paw. Rachel could see he had a slight limp.

She waited until the grizzly had disappeared into the timber, and the elk had dispersed. It was almost dark when she crept toward the spot where the bear had seized the calf. She studied the prints. There it was, the missing toe, the scar.

She turned. Rainey was watching her.

"Did you see it?" she asked.

"No."

"Woolly Bugger," she said.

Two Outstanding Consultants

Matt Reid—a wildlife biologist with thirty years experience research-ing, managing, and advocating for grizzly bears and their habitat, Matt regularly advised me about grizzly bear behavior, wildlife is-sues and working in Yellowstone Park. He tirelessly responded to all of my detailed questions and shepherded me through the park. Through his remarkable example, he taught me what it meant to "think like a bear."

Andrew Mehle—while getting his PhD in virology at Harvard, Andy helped me connect thermophile, hormonal abnormalities, and viruses. He convincingly walked me through how the unsea-sonal animal behavior and the mutations in the young that occur in *In Velvet* might have happened, and made plausible the science in this book.

Acknowledgements

Paul Bertelli, Bill Bryan, Tyson Cornell, Dorothy Escribano, David Field, Brendan Kiley, Patricia Kingsley, Peter Lewis, Richard Marek, Marianne Moloney, Sarah Osebold, Avery Rimer, John Sargent, Leslie Stoltz, Andrew Ward, Ben Weissbourd, Emily Weissbourd, Jenny Weissbourd, Kathy Weissbourd, Richard Weissbourd, Robert Weissbourd.

Special Acknowledgement

The author and publisher would like to extend a special acknowledgement to photographer Tom Murphy for the extraordinary cover and interior photos that capture beautifully the Yellowstone depicted in this book and help this story come to life.

In addition, a portion of the proceeds from *In Velvet* will be donated to The Yellowstone Park Foundation, specifically to preserve the population of grizzly bears in Yellowstone Park.